Nissitissit Witch

by
Rose Mary Chaulk

authorHOUSE®

AuthorHouse™
1663 Liberty Drive, Suite 200
Bloomington, IN 47403
www.authorhouse.com
Phone: 1-800-839-8640

© *2008 Rosemary Chaulk. All rights reserved.*

No part of this book may be reproduced, stored in a retrieval system, or transmitted by any means without the written permission of the author.

First published by AuthorHouse 9/10/2008

ISBN: 978-1-4389-1713-9 (sc)
ISBN: 978-1-4389-1714-6 (hc)

Library of Congress Control Number: 2008908418

Printed in the United States of America
Bloomington, Indiana

This book is printed on acid-free paper.

Second Printing
Illustrations: Joseph Marsella of Pepperell, MA
Edited by: Donna Erickson of Abington, MA

This book is dedicated to Susan Smith for her valuable contribution of old newspaper clippings about North Village.

I want to give special thanks to Donna Erickson for her patience in editing my story. To my high school English and Typing instructors, I would like to say, "You were right. I should have paid more attention."

Also, I wish to express my gratitude to Kathleen Fitzpatrick and Anastasia for their help with all the last minute details in completing this book.

So, in closing ladies, thank you all for **your** contributions, and the book has benefited from the help I got from each and every one of you.

This story is a composite of fact and fiction, written and presented as a tall tale. It blends together what really happened, what might have happened, and what still could happen. Some historic names and incidents have been used from my research of the area. However, the names of the characters in my book are strictly fictional. They are not intended to resemble any actual family names or depict any residents who lived in North Village at the time of the story.

Many of the chapters were based on events that occurred in North Village, and information was derived from published articles in *The Times Free Press*. Other Internet research was used for authenticity, such as the crossing of Baltimore by the Union troops from Lowell. Additional research pertained to the various chemicals and heavy metals to which the villagers were exposed and the resultant health effects of such exposures.

With numerous newspaper and magazine articles written about the unusual events that allegedly occurred, North Village is steeped in myth to this day. Some homeowners continue to report that their houses are haunted. My saga deviates from the microcosm of North Village and examines why some of these bizarre incidents may have happened. Finally, my story makes us wonder about the Indian souls who inhabited the valley for thousands of years. Most importantly, it illustrates the power they had with the land, long before any settlers had invaded their valley.

Nissitissit Witch
CHAPTER ONE

"By the banks of the Nissitisset River at the north end of town, are the ruins of a village that has slowly fallen down." (1)

Dwelling in the mist of the Nissitissit River are the spirits of a tribe who had lived on its bank. They existed for more years than there are stars in the sky. Although the tribe had been slaughtered one hundred and sixty years ago, their spirits and their ancestors' spirits are still active, as they are nearly as old as the valley itself. The tribe had survived on this land for five thousand years and had lived in harmony with nature; they had learned to respect the spirits of the mist.

Ebb knew that this was the day. He rose from bed early and put on his best clothes. His dreams of the mist during the night signaled that today would be his last. The tumor lodged in his stomach had just about drawn the life out of him. He knew what he had to do and where he had to go. As the sun was rising, Ebb set off down the road, fueled by the last bit of his strength. As he walked, he turned and took one final look at his house. He left his house behind for anyone who might need it. He had no descendants, having never married because of the dreams. How he hated those never-ending dreams! They had tortured him since the war. At first, the dreams were only about the war. After the war, the dreams were about the mist. In fact, every waking thought was about the mist. Although Ebb had been instilled with a fear of the mist before leaving North Village, he now found himself longing to be immersed in the mist. He turned from his modest, but well constructed house, which had been built with his own hands, upon returning from the Civil War. He faced the road again, but even the power of the mist could not keep Ebb's mind from drifting back to the time when he left for war. How could a war so far away be responsible for so much death and suffering right here in New England? How did North Pepperell become a casualty of such a war?

During the Civil War, Ebb had been a lieutenant with the Massachusetts Sixth Regiment Infantry, which was comprised of tough farm boys from the area and rugged Irishmen from Lowell. Ebb's mind suddenly flashed back to the day that he left for the war.

Ebb entered the house at about 9 p.m. on a cold January night. "Need more wood on the fire, Abel?"

"I would be grateful to ya, if you did. My knees are hurting from the cold."

Ebb stocked the fire high, went out, and brought in more wood.

"I have something to say."

"I have something to say." They had both spoken at once.

"Okay, Ebb, you go first."

"Abel, you have been like a father to me for these last forty-four years. I know you are aging and need help, but right now there is something I must do. A war between the states is inevitable. I feel that I must enlist. They are forming a militia in Lowell, and I'm gonna join. You have managed well with my labor in the fields, and I know there are men in the village willing to work for you while I am away."

"Well, you seem to have my needs figured out, but what about you? God has spoken to me, and I decided to sell the property. I had this deed prepared - forty-four acres on the east slope. It's good land and should provide good water. That's one acre for every year you worked my fields."

Abel continued, "My knees are bad, and I can't make the stairs here anymore. The widow Baldwin, in the center of town, has two rooms on the first floor for rent. With the money from the farm, I can live out my last years in comfort. But now, based on what you said, I am going to make a change in the deed."

Ebb looked confused. "But you just… are you against the…?"

"Easy, Ebb. All I am going to do is change the deed to both of our names with Rights of Survivorship. That way if you go off to war and perish, the land will not be lost. You are free to go. All you need do is to return home, but I warn you, this upcoming conflict could be bloody. The southern landowners will not be willing to give up their slaves and their way of life without a fight."

"Well, God did move both our hands today," said Ebb. "It's a sign that it's the right thing to do."

Abel thought for a moment and spoke. "I was gonna have the village handyman build you a rudimentary house, but I promise, if you come home from this war, I will have it built then. I made arrangements to move in with the widow Baldwin at the end of the month."

"Then the deed is done. I leave for Lowell in two days time. There are six of us going. There are four from Hollis Village and two from NNN.. North Village."

Ebb stumbled with the name, as he recalled his mother. She died only a few years after she had brought Ebb to live with Uncle Abel. Ebb still did not understand her actions. What he saw as a cowardly act, was, in fact, a desperate move fueled by his mother's love.

Two days later, Ebb was packed and ready to go. "God speed Ebb, God speed." They embraced for the very first time and parted, never to see each other again.

The next three months were a blur in Ebb's mind. They were referred to as *The Three Month Militia* (8), rather than a regular militia. The soldiers were drilled daily and trained with broomsticks for rifles. Finally, in March, uniforms were issued, along with Springfield rifles. The scuttlebutt in the barracks was that they would be leaving soon. (2)

It was early morning, on April 14, 1861, when Amos, one of the other men from Hollis, came bursting into the barracks. "Ebb…Ebb, listen to this. Last Friday at four-thirty in the morning, General Pierre G. T. Beauregard and the South Carolina militia, opened fire on Fort Sumter. They bombarded the fort for thirty-four hours until Major Anderson surrendered, after the fort had used its store of powder and ball." (4)

They did not have to wait long. On the next day, Monday, April 15th, 1861, President Lincoln called for seventy thousand volunteers, in a fiery speech. The President said that the soldiers would be needed for three months. According to the Act of 1795, the militia could legally be called up, only until thirty days following the next meeting of Congress (7). Therefore, the soldiers going off to war expected to be home in three months' time. The President knew they would be gone more than three months. However, under the law, he had to tell the soldiers that they would serve for the next ninety days. The next day, the seven-hundred uniformed and armed members of the infantry took the train to Boston. On the following day, under the command of Colonel Edward F. Jones, seven hundred armed and uniformed members of the Massachusetts Sixth prepared to leave Boston, following special orders.

Out of the seven hundred there, Ebb knew only five. He had become close friends with Amos Adams, who stood next to him. Near them were Aaron Hosley and John Nutting. Further off, in the sea of blue uniforms, were Jacob and Simon, the twins from North Village. All six of them had joined at the same time.

Amos leaned towards Ebb and shouted, "Have you ever seen so many people?"

"No, I ain't never seen nothin' like this. It's crowded enough here with just the Sixth, but those thousands of cheering supporters who have shown up are oppressive. I ain't never been 'mongst more people than I have fingers; to be 'mongst so many makes me unsettled. They cheer like we won the war, and we ain't even fought yet."

"I know what ya mean," said Amos. "I feel a bit squirrelly myself. I got a bad feeling 'bout all this. To be so joyous beforehand is bound to be bad luck."

Suddenly, a cheer went up from one section of the crowd. The Irish from the Sixth had formed a cluster in the ranks, off to one side. The Irish, who were in the crowd, joined them.

"Hurrah!" shouted the Irish soldiers.

"HURRAH!" the crowd screamed back.

"Hurrah!" the Irish soldiers shouted back.

"HURRAH!" the crowd screamed, even louder, waving their tams in the air.

Amos poked Ebb. "Some of them Irish are somethin', ain't they?"

"Some of them are built like brick latrines."

Some of the Irish had come out of the factories from the loading docks. They were well built, due to the heavy loads they moved from the factories onto the trains. They had spent time in the bars of Lowell and were tough fighters. Some had begun brawling as teenagers and were quite experienced with fisticuffs. The beer, whiskey and pub food had made many of them gigantic. When they were signing up,

Captain Follansbee had a hard time finding regulation shirts to fit their enormous chests. In shirtsleeves, during heavy drilling in March, the Irish were impressive. Their huge, freckled biceps and forearms covered in carrot red hair, matched their carrot-topped heads.

Other Irish in the group had worked inside the mills. They were much more slender and somewhat sickly, not having had the fresh air from the loading dock or yard work. Farmers were also present. The crop farmers, such as Ebb, were thin, yet strong, having had to winter over, but the dairymen were as big and strong as some of the more impressive Irish. They didn't have to winter over, since their cows produced milk year-round. Along with plenty of milk, they never ran short of cream, butter or cheese.

As they huddled together, the Irish soldiers changed the cheer. "Company D!" they shouted.

"Company D!" the crowd screamed back, nearing frenzy.

Colonel Edward F. Jones decided that the men had been sufficiently aroused and started loading the soldiers onto the trains. Company D was the furthest away, and they were directed to the last few cars. The crowds swelled around the cars, as they were loaded. As they cleared out of the station, the Irish were screaming from the windows, "Company D."

The whole crowd responded with a thundering "COMPANY D!"

They could hear the crowd still chanting, as their train chugged away, out of sight. Every station they reached was filled with a crowd full of jubilation, even in the middle of the night. Late in the afternoon, on Friday, April 19, 1861, they were on their way to Washington, DC to defend the Capitol, in case the southern states had decided to attack. As they traveled north of Baltimore, after re-boarding from the last rest stop, Captain Follansbee entered the car. One of the enlisted men called out "Ten hut." The men jumped to attention.

"At ease, men."

Captain Follansbee continued. "Men, we are about to enter Baltimore, and it has been brought to my attention that earlier today The Pennsylvania 25th had some difficulty crossing the city. It seems that steam locomotives are not permitted within city limits. This means our cars will be disconnected from the locomotive and our cars will be drawn across the city by teams of horses. We may be forced to march in formation through the city, and I have a few things to tell you about the protocol. If we are forced to march in formation, every man will keep his eyes straight forward, and you are commanded to not engage in promiscuous conversations with the ruffians. You are commanded not to speak and not to respond with indiscriminate violence, to any insults. You will keep your face forward at all times. Your weapons will be fully loaded, and your munitions belts will be fully charged. You will only fire if needed and only upon my command. Keep your bayonets in their sheaths to prevent unwanted accidents. I expect you to be the soldiers that I trained you to be. If the order is given to fire, do not fire into promiscuous crowds, but shoot only the men who are shooting at you, and shoot to kill." (3)

Baltimore, a large, deep-water port on the east coast, without the ice of the northern harbors, had year-round access. Although it was the terminus of five railroads, local ordinances prohibited the steam locomotives from passing through the city. (4) (9) This policy was most likely enforced because of the fear of fire and the noise from the locomotives.

In order to cross Baltimore, passengers had to leave their train and travel by coach or horse-drawn wagon to the departing station. If you were wealthy or prominent enough to have your own rail car, it was detached from the locomotive when you reached the city. A team of horses would then haul away the car. Making its way through the city on connecting rails proved to be a slow and arduous process.

The Massachusetts Sixth arrived in Baltimore, late Friday afternoon on April the 19th. Within thirty minutes of their arrival, a mob of onlookers had gathered at the train station. The crowd had just returned, having raced back from manhandling the Pennsylvania 25th on the other side of town. They had received word that the Massachusetts Sixth had arrived.

"Look out!" Ebb screamed. He pulled Amos out of the way, as a brick sailed through the window

"Dang. Thanks."

"I think we need to stay close and watch each other's back," Ebb said.

Suddenly, the crowd surged to the front of the train, as each of the first nine cars had been hooked to a team of horses. The driver began drawing the first seven companies of the Massachusetts Sixth out of the station. They no longer felt the pressure of the crowd. The remaining soldiers, near Ebb, watched the cars and the crowd leave the station. A few bricks were thrown, but the cars passed with hardly any problems. However, threats and curses abounded. The crowd chanted, "White niggers. White niggers," among other curses. (7)

As horses were hitched to the remaining cars, Amos cried, "Ebb, we're moving."

"Okay, steady. Stay close," Ebb said, as he moved next to Amos.

They made it a few hundred yards, when suddenly, the crowd turned vicious. A thick surge of paving stones and debris began pelting the cars. The drivers of the teams were afraid of the threats from the crowd. They decided to unhitch the teams. Then they hitched them to the rear of the cars and dragged them back into the station. (4) They arrived back at the station just as the police came to their aid, but by now, the crowd had torn up the tracks.

"Out of the cars and form up!" Colonel Jones shouted from the platform.

The Massachusetts soldiers poured off the train. The decision was to leave the unarmed band with their instruments behind.

"Form up columns of two's," Jones commanded.

The group hustled into rows of two and, with the help of the police, tried to leave the station. However, a group of eight hundred men with a Confederate flag made a bold move. A socialite, named Hettie Carie, had created the first Saint Andrews Cross Flag with its twelve stars. (4) This flag later became the battle flag of the Confederate Army. A hail of paving stones drove back the police and the Massachusetts Sixth. Following the order of "Bout face," the column turned around and headed to the opposite end of the station. The Irish, who were the last ones off the train, were now first in line.

"Head them off!" someone screamed, and the crowd ran to the southern exit. As the Massachusetts Sixth departed from the station, the rebels, with the newly constructed flag, dashed to the area outside of the station and confronted the Massachusetts Sixth. The men with the rebel flag darted in front of the troops and led the procession for about a mile, mocking and making jest of the soldiers who followed behind. (4) Missiles from the crowd had hurt many of the Irish, causing them to become peeved. With the help of the police, the tough Lowell street fighters started clubbing, punching and shoving people as the column moved out of the station. These rugged street fighters, who had been beating each other up a year ago while being chased by the Lowell police, were now forming into a band of brothers. Flanked by the police, they fought against the angry mob. With the shower of missiles soaring at them, they began bashing their way south through Baltimore.

"Here we go, Ebb."

"God speed, Amos."

As they were moving forward, every missile that could be thrown was assailing them. No one escaped injury. Suddenly, the column stopped. The crowd grew silent as a well-dressed man appeared at the front.

He raised his hands to silence the crowd. "Citizens of Baltimore, you must let these soldiers through."

"Boo!" the crowd hissed back. "Some mayor *you* are."

"You must do your civic duty and…" Just then, a brick grazed the mayor's head, causing him to stop speaking. The mayor was disoriented for a moment but then grabbed one of the soldier's guns. (4) With careful aim, he shot the man who had thrown the brick. As another man in the crowd pulled out a revolver to shoot the mayor, a police officer shot the unidentified man. A paving brick struck Amos, and he fell into the crowd. Ebb tried to grab Amos, but he was gone in an instant. The crowd had dragged him away to be beaten. A small squadron of police ran to get Amos back from the crowd before they killed him.

"Open fire!" screamed Colonel Jones.

The Springfield rifles exploded as gunfire spewed into the face of the crowd. The stunned crowd fell back, in shock. Several died instantly. Jones seized the moment to condense his troops.

"Form up columns of four. Fix bayonets," ordered Jones. The startled crowd remained silent.

Ebb had no idea where the crowd had dragged Amos. He fell in line, sick with grief, not knowing if his friend was dead or alive.

"Double time!" shouted Jones as he pointed his sword and led the column.

With the police flanking them, the men of the Sixth bolted towards the new station. The Irish loading dockworkers stabbed, bashed and butted those who were unfortunate enough to be in their way. The troops attacked the crowd in front of them, showing mercy to no one. They bayoneted those who refused to yield. The troops were moving too fast for the crowd to regroup, and that helped reduce the violence. If the police had not been there in such numbers, the crowds would have killed the remaining four companies of the Sixth.

Ebb thought, "We're almost there. We're almost th...."

In an instant, Ebb was back in his neighborhood in 1905. Once again, he was an old man making his way along the road towards North Village. "Won't you dreams leave me alone?" Ebb mumbled to himself. "You have clouded my every waking moment. I have no peace. Be gone; you have ruined my life these last forty years."

The war had damaged Ebb, but the war had hurt North Village even more. Ebb would soon discover just how much. As Ebb continued walking, he had one last thought about his house. "Dang, I'll miss that well."

Ebb's house was constructed out of stone and mortar with a slate roof. He built it to keep the world out and, also, to contain his loud cries from the dreams. The walls were thick, so that no one could hear his suffering. Ebb never let anyone know about the mental anguish from the war. The Civil War had poisoned Ebb's mind. Constant dreams of the war tortured him, as he would lie in bed. Ebb had seen death and suffering on a huge scale. By the end of the war, he was numb to it. He had reached the point where he did not care whether he lived or died. At that stage, he fought for spite. He killed, not out of fear but for revenge. He learned to kill; he learned it well and he learned to like it. Ebb never showed mercy to any rebel. If you were in front of Ebb's gun, then you were about to become a dead man.

Ebb was no longer needed when the war ended. He had become

a killing machine, which now had no prey. For a while, he was despondent. He had learned to love killing, and it was hard for him to come back to the world of farming. It took time to relearn the patience required to run a farm. He had to learn, once again, that problems had solutions, other than a lead slug.

Ebb returned to Brookline Village and was devastated to find that Uncle Abel had died of a stroke. Luckily, Abel had kept his promise about the land and had even put money aside to build a new house. Ebb tried to put the war behind him and concentrate on construction.

Ebb loved the new house; he realized the dreams were not the fault of the house. The home would last for generations to come but would not be for his generations. Near the house was a well with the coldest, sweetest water in the whole town. Ebb had learned how to divine water, while away at war, and had picked the site for his house because of the heavy twitch and dip of the willow switch. When he built his own stone well, the quality of the water was superb. The old man gave credit to the water for providing him with good health and a long life; this year, he would have turned ninety-three. Even with the tumor in his stomach, he was still able to keep up a good pace as he walked. In a few hours, he had managed to climb out of Hollis Village and stood at the crest of the hill where the orchards were located.

He loved the orchards and would walk to them in the spring, when the apple trees resembled large cotton balls covering the hills in orderly rows. The apple crop was concentrated in the hilly area, southwest of town, on the backside of the hills that ran down to the Nissitissit. Ebb had made it a point to avoid walking near the orchards on the days they were spraying the trees. (6) One morning, Ebb landed in the midst of the spray, as he was walking out to see Amos. The spray settled in his lungs for a few days. Ebb mistrusted the spray. "If it kills insects," he thought, "it must somehow be bad for people." Amos was exposed to it regularly. Secretly, Ebb blamed the spray for the death of his friend, Amos.

It was midsummer as Ebb walked through the apple orchards, and he could see the small apples beginning to grow. Ebb loved the fall when the apples would be ready for picking. Years ago, he would visit Amos, who owned the orchard. Amos and his three sons were quite adept at making hard cider. As Ebb walked by his old friend's place, he waved at the two, remaining sons. The curse of North Village had claimed one of the brothers.

"Hey, Ebb. Glad to see you doing so well," shouted one of the brothers.

"Just out for a constitutional," Ebb answered back as he continued walking. He missed his friend, Amos, who had owned the farm. Amos had never seen the great battles. He had come back wounded from the conflict in Baltimore. He ended up slightly brain-damaged, after being hit with the paving brick. Amos became one of the first casualties, after President Lincoln had declared war. Ironically, Nickolas Biddle, a black servant of Captain James Wren was the first death, after Lincoln declared war to free the slaves. Nickolas was killed in Baltimore on April 18th, when the Pennsylvania 25th crossed through the city. (9)

Amos had been happiest when spraying the orchards. His sons let him, so that Amos could feel he was helping out. Insects were troublesome on the trees, which were near the bottom of the hills, leading to the river. Amos had always given the trees a good, long spray to keep away the bugs. He never thought of the fact that lead arsenate was leaching into the river.

Amos became ill about fifteen years after the war. He died a horrible death, but his sons would only say he died in an unusual way. The residents of North Village were dying in the same, unusual way. Although the rest of the world thought the deaths were unusual, such a vast number of people in North Village had died that way, that it had become the usual way of death. The deaths were so horrible that no one in town ever spoke about it. Sadly, all who had lived in North Village felt doomed to the same fate.

As Ebb crested the hill, he came upon the lower part of the orchard while heading down the road towards North Village. The part of the orchard, which Amos had always sprayed twice, was before him. Ebb's nose twitched as he noticed the trees had been recently sprayed. He walked a little further, until he could no longer smell the spray and found a familiar, comfortable rock to sit on. Ebb rested for a spell, drinking more water he had brought from his well. The water was pure and sweet as it flowed over his tongue and down his throat. Then he rested for quite a while longer, to regain his strength. He knew he would make it, as it was all downhill the rest of the way. He was headed south and, then, west. Ebb was being drawn back to his birthplace in the remains of North Village, just like the salmon had returned to their place of birth in the Nissitissit, so long ago. He was the last one related to the original bloodlines. He had managed to outlive them all, and the mist craved his ancient soul.

Ebb noticed he was sitting on the exact rock he had sat on eighty-seven years ago, when his mother had removed him from North Village. Ebb had never been this deep within the valley, since that mournful day. At first, Ebb had been resentful, even hateful toward his mother, who had taken him over the giant hill to the village of Hollis. He was only five-years-old when she brought him to his uncle's house. He still remembered that day. That morning, while living in North Village, his mother came in to his bed. They had lived in one of the mill houses-the term *house* being used loosely. They were twelve-by sixteen-foot shacks constructed of green wood from the mill in the village. When the green wood dried, it shrank, leaving drafts everywhere. The outside walls had vertical boards and battens tacked with nails and glued with pine pitch. Young Ebb liked the houses, as they all were painted with a bright, happy shade of green. (5)

"Ebb, Ebb, wake up. It's time for our trip."

Young Ebb stirred and woke up instantly. She had talked for days about going to see Uncle Abel, who lived in a different watershed on the other side of the big hill in Hollis Village. "We need to pack your stuff 'cause we'll be there for a while."

Mother packed Ebb's few clothes and a couple of crude toys into a carrying bag and opened the door to peek outside. The mist was still heavy, and she quickly closed the door. They had their breakfast of oatmeal and water. Mother drew the water from a spring, a short distance away, at the side of a hill. Ebb had never drunk anything other than the spring water that Mother brought home.

Ebb was born in 1812, on a day when a mysterious, old woman came into North Village. The village accepted the woman and invited her to stay. When she was asked to see the baby, she went willingly. She sat with Ebb's mother and helped tend to her needs. For a while, the old woman and Ebb's mother were alone. The old woman leaned down close to the mother and baby.

"Do not let him drink from the river or its wellsss."

"What?" asked Ebb's mother.

"Do not let him drink from the river or its wellsss."

Something in the old woman's voice seemed strange. Ebb's mother, Prudence, could have sworn that she heard many voices speaking at once. "We don't drink from the wells here. I don't like the taste of the water."

The old woman leaned close to Prudence and began to talk softly in her ear. The other woman from the village had returned, but before the old woman rose from talking with Prudence, she whispered one last thing. "Take care of him, for he is destined to be lasssttt."

She had sounded like a snake hissing out a message. "What scary, strange words," thought Prudence as the old woman left. "What did she mean?"

The years went by quickly, and Ebb was about to turn five. Prudence, who was unclear about the meaning of the words that had been whispered to her, nonetheless gave Ebb water only from a nearby spring. When Ebb was five, the old woman, who was now known as the Quaker Witch, was walking past the mill house. Ebb and his mother were playing near the road during one of the few days she had off. She looked at Prudence. "If you love the boy, you will get him out of here. If you get him out of here, he will still be the lasssttt."

Ebb's mother felt a chill run through her as she remembered the words of warning from the day of Ebb's birth. Those were the very words that led to her decision to move Ebb. Prudence thought something did not seem right. Sensing something was wrong with the valley, she knew she had to save her son. In addition, the old woman who had come to the village the day of Ebb's birth had become known as a witch, mainly because of her uncanny ability to foresee the outcome of certain events. Rather than listening to her warnings, the people in the village dismissed her - that is, until her warnings became a reality. Then the half-witted locals saw each of her warnings as a curse, rather than the words of a wise, well-educated woman who was trying to help them.

The mist was clearing, and Ebb's mother grasped his hand and opened the door. With a small amount of mist still lingering in the air, Ebb's mother left anyway. The mist swirling was around them as they walked. Near the end of the mist, Ebb's mother stopped short, and Ebb looked up, impatiently, at his mother. It appeared as though she was listening to something. Then she nodded and smiled before continuing.

"What is it, Mother?"

"Nothing, Ebb. Someday you will understand."

Young Ebb went back to bouncing and skipping down the road with his mother. As they stood atop the big hill and were heading towards Hollis Village, his mother began to explain. "My brother has three daughters and no sons. He needs help with the farm, and he could really use your extra set of hands at harvest time. He has a fine piece of land and, with your help, a handsome living could be made."

"What are you saying? You want me to stay with Uncle Abel? Don't you want me to stay with you? Don't you love me? Why are you doing this to me?" Ebb's bottom lip was beginning to tremble.

Prudence continued. "My job at the velvet shop provides only a meager wage, and we are always so poor. My brother Abel can take better care of you than I ever could. By working the farm with my brother, you will, in a way, be helping me. It's been two years since the death of your father in the sawmill, and life has been arduous. Come on, Ebb, don't you want to help Mother?"

Poor Ebb's young heart was breaking. "Mother, I want to stay with you. I'll be good. I will come in early when the mist comes. I love you. Please don't let go of me. I'll behave."

Uncle Abel saw them arriving and met them halfway down the walkway that led to the house. Even after all these years, the old family issues still kept him from welcoming his sister into his home. They had told her she was dishonoring the family, but she married him anyway. The couple had moved to North Village, and now, six years later, their predictions had come true with a vengeance. Unlike the others, Abel took pity on the boy, as he felt that too many innocent sons in North Village had paid for the sins of their fathers.

Abel's strong hands held Ebb back as his mother walked away. "Ebb, this is best for everyone. Things are not right in North Village.

You'll be safe now. You are well above the mist here."

Ebb felt terribly hurt, and tears streamed down his young face. How could his mother not want him? What could be so bad that would make her leave him behind? "Mother, Mother!" he cried repeatedly. "Mother, Mother, come back. I love you."

"You have to stay because it is the only way you can help your mother," explained Uncle Abel. As she walked away, Abel could see that his sister had aged from working in the mill. Although still young, she was beginning to walk like an old woman, and Abel also noticed that her voice was weak when she talked.

Her heart was breaking as she walked away, hearing her only son cry out for her, but she continued on her way. She had to be back by dark, before the mist would appear. As she walked, the words of the Quaker replayed in her mind. Prudence hurried along because she had to be at her new job at the velvet shop early in the morning. She would be in charge of the steam closet, where the velvet clothes were hung to remove the wrinkles before packing and shipping.

Ebb reluctantly stayed on the farm and worked for Uncle Abel, but he resented the fact that his mother had abandoned him. Now, eighty-seven years later, he thought of her while he rested, before continuing his migration back to North Village. By removing him from the growing madness, she had made the right choice. He realized that now. He had lived a long life because of her loving deed.

Sadly, Ebb remembered how his mother had visited him a few times after that day, but his bitterness had grown. He would ignore her, and eventually, she quit coming.

As Ebb sat and rested, he recalled how a few years after being left at his uncle's farm, his mother had died. When it happened, Uncle Abel had come out to the field where Ebb was working. Abel had been brushing back tears as he walked. "Ebb, your mother died last night. I had her body brought to the funeral parlor. We'll have a service tonight, and first thing tomorrow, we'll bury her."

Ebb stood firmly upright and did not move. Then, slowly and deliberately, he responded. "I'll be back when I finish turning this windrow of hay."

"Ebb, you can leave that until morning! Come in and get cleaned up. Put your Sunday go-to-meeting clothes on."

Ebb whirled around with fire in his eyes. Even though he was only nine, he was an intense child, full of emotion. "She brought me here because there was so much work to do, so I'm going to finish this work first." His tone was harsh.

Abel staggered back a step or two as if Ebb's words had hit him in the chest. He went to speak but then stopped, turned, and walked away. When Abel was out of Ebb's sight, he sat on a stump at the edge of the field. He broke down and wept uncontrollably.

He looked upward. "Oh God, forgive me. I had the room; she could have come here, and now, because of foolish family pride, she's gone. She suffered so much at the end. I could have taken them both when she was widowed. I could have lifted them above the madness. And now I've helped turn her son against her. "

After sitting for a long time crying, Abel got up and went back to the farmhouse. He hooked up the team to the wagon. Then he went inside and put on his Sundays' best. After a while, Ebb came back, walking slowly, with a hay rake slung over his shoulder.

"Let's get a goin'. You got to get dressed," Abel shouted.

"I'm going just like this."

"Oh, Ebb...Show some respect."

"Why should I? She didn't want me in her life. She left me here to be a farm hand, so I'll go in my farm hand clothes."

"What she did, she did for you, not for her. She gained nothing and lost the last thing she cared about when she left you here."

Abel said nothing else as they silently rode to town together and entered the funeral parlor.

"Why is the coffin closed?"

"Your mother died in an unusual way, and it would be disrespectful to show her like that."

Once again, Ebb snapped back to the present. Over the years, he had come to know, what that "unusual way" was, and a shudder ran down his spine as he thought about his mother's death. His aging frame arose, and he headed down the road to North Village again. As he walked, his heart was heavy. His mother had saved him, and he never thanked her. He had heard about all of them dying. He heard how they all had suffered terribly at the end. They died a horrible death and he did, in fact, live to be the last one.

The road to the village was quiet. Everything was gone- all of the buildings, except the school. The school had survived because one lesson still needed to be learned in North Village, and it was about to happen. Ebb walked by the school, and all was quiet. During its time, the school had been packed with children. Now it was empty, waiting to give that last lesson and, ultimately, collapse.

Prudence had saved Ebb from an early, painful death. He had lived long, but he knew that, had he stayed, she could not have saved him from the mist. He had to return; he longed to return. Destiny had plotted his course, and now Ebb was completing his duty. The circle of his life was closing.

Ebb had to pay the price for his mother's decision. She had married a descendant of the original settlers, and now, Ebb, an innocent son, had to succumb to the sins of his forefathers. The final soul needed to be added to the tally, in order for the curse to end. Ebb was the last living descendant of the original settlers, the ones who had killed the

Chief. The mist controlled him; the mist needed him, and he longed to be in the mist once again. Ebb knew he needed the mist.

Ebb found the cellar hole of the mill house, which he and his mother had occupied. There he sat on the ground. He rested his back against a tree and looked at the Nissitissit. The water flowed by slowly as his weary eyes watched the swirls of the current. Then, he could see it. It was starting in the usual place; he knew it would be there. It had been calling to him all his life.

When the guns of battle were blasting and his mind had filled with horror, it would come to him. The mist would slip into his dreams and calm his soul. Later on, as an old man, the mist would calm him again whenever evil nightmares about the war would return. Ebb had come to accept the mist. In the end, he knew the mist would be with him.

The mist had become heavy and drifted towards Ebb. He eased back further against the tree. He could see it coming, and he was ready. He relaxed as the mist enveloped his body. His tumor no longer hurt, and the old war wounds stopped aching. Ebb was at peace and he let go. He was the last, and he had made it to a ripe, old age.

CHAPTER TWO

Ebb lay there, and all was quiet. With his eyes closed, he was enjoying the fact that nothing hurt anymore. He could feel the presence of the mist. Then, out of the mist, came a voice.

"Ebb, you are, in fact, the last." The voice was clear with a hint of sadness.

Ebb felt afraid. "Who is that?"

"You signify the last bloodline of the settlers!"

"Who are you? Are you God? I can't seem to be able to see."

"No, I am not God. The reason you cannot see is that your soul is still inside your dead body. Your eyes will never see again. You now have to learn to see with your soul."

"Oh, my God, my dead body?? Where am I?"

"You are by the bank of the Nissitissit, right where you laid down to die and right where you were born. Your circle of life has closed upon itself."

"But, if I am dead, how can I hear you? Are my ears not quite dead yet? Who are you?"

"Stand up and free your soul, and I will show you who I am."

All Ebb had to do was think about getting up, and his spirit rose from his body. He looked down and saw that his feet remained in his old body. Instinctively, he removed one foot and then the other. The second foot appeared to be stuck. He pulled with force. Finally, his foot popped out, and his body shook in one last death spasm.

Ebb looked up, in the direction of the voice, and saw the great Chief standing there, beside a magnificent, white horse. Could this be the same Chief they whispered about in the taverns?

"Are we in hell?"

"No, we are not in hell. There is no hell!"

"No hell? Where are we then?"

"We are on the cusp. We are between worlds."

Ebb was astonished. "Between worlds? I was taught that when someone dies they either go to Heaven or they go to hell."

"Not exactly. There is a Heaven, but there is no hell."

Ebb thought for a moment. "Hey, what kind of treachery is this? How do we come to be able to speak?"

"We speak in the language of the souls."

Ebb sounded doubtful. "The language of the souls?"

"Yes, we speak in basic needs and emotions. Deep down, all souls are the same. So, at a certain level we are all equal, and, at that level, we can exchange thoughts and ideas and are able to converse. In this place of pure happiness, there can be no communication problems. So, by communicating in thoughts, we can all talk to each other."

Ebb was curious. "What is this cusp, and why are we in it?"

"The cusp is the world between. It is where troubled souls remain, who have left their bodies before their bodies were dead."

"How does that happen?" Ebb replied.

"It is caused by many things-insanity, madness, grief, loneliness, a curse, or even love."

"Love?"

"Yes, or more exactly, loss of love. You have a way to go before you will understand."

"Why am I here?"

"Because you are the last one. You are here because of me. You are my charge, and I am responsible for you. You are here to learn."

"How are you responsible for me? You died long before I was born."

"In our tribe, we believe if you save a person's life, you are responsible for that person and the actions of that person, whether right or wrong. I saved Sarah's life, and later, Sarah saved you. So, I am responsible for you."

"Sarah?"

"Yes. Sarah was the Quaker woman who came to North Village on the day you were born. Think back. You remember her; she stopped and talked to your mother a few weeks before you left North Village."

Way back in Ebb's memory, he did remember her. "Mother had talked about her arriving on the day I was born. She said it was because of her that we would not drink water from the river. She told my mother to get me out of North Village when I was five. I remember."

"Yes, and in doing so, she saved your life. Had she not done that, you would have died right after your mother. You would have died in the same, unusual way."

"What would have killed me?"

"You will see."

"How did the Quaker woman know?"

"You will see."

Ebb was anxious. "When will I know?"

"People see what they believe; first you need to learn to believe. In time, you will know, but first we need to go back to the beginning of my tribe. You need to understand this valley. Only after you understand this valley, will you know. Come, take the reins of the stallion, and the three of us will travel."

"Where are we going?"

"We are going back. We are going back six thousand years, before I uttered that dreadful curse. We are going back to the dawn of my tribe. We are going back to the first inhabitants of the valley. When your ancestors massacred my tribe, they killed a tribe who had lived in harmony with the valley for over six thousand years."

Suddenly, the ruins of North Village were gone, and they were looking at a small Indian tribe who had set up their camp quite a distance from the river. Smoke was drifting up from the campfire as the invisible spirits of Ebb and the Chief floated away into the clearing.

"Look at all the fish!" Ebb exclaimed. "It's like I can smell them. What are they? Are they from the river? I never saw fish so big in the Nissitissit."

"They are salmon. By your lifetime, they were gone. The dams on the Nashua and the mighty Merrimack blocked them from returning home. Having no descendants, the race of the salmon died and is no more, just like my people. It is because of your ways that the fish are gone. It is because of your ways that my people are gone. It is because of your ways that this valley was lost. It is the way of your people that all is lost. It is 'The White Way' which doomed us all." (10)

"The White Way?"

"Yes. The White Way has doomed our world."

Ebb was confused. "How is it that I can smell the fire and the fish?"

"Because we are in the cusp. You can still experience the world of the living, but you cannot affect most people."

"What do you mean, 'most people'?"

"There are those who live amongst you who are in tune with the rhythm of life. Those people have great wisdom and see all. They can sense our presence in the cusp. In our world, the ones who were like them were known as wise men. They spoke with the great spirits of the river, and we lived by the rules of the mist, as laid down to us by the wise men."

The Chief paused, as if to take a breath. Old habits died hard. "The wise men told us that we were to worship the Mist of the Nissitissit. It was told that the ground where this mist went, at night, was sacred. Within that mist, the spirits of the Nissitissit must be allowed to roam, unhindered by campsites. It was also told that this land had to be pure, and no animal or human waste, no animal carcasses, no gore from fish or any type of poison should ever be placed in the area of the mist. The wise men warned that any animal found dead, within this sacred zone, was to be dragged uphill, away from the sacred ground of the mist. This ground was to be worshipped and preserved. We were told that we could use this zone, when in the light, but we were to leave it unchanged, especially at night."

"How does this camp know where that zone is?"

"Come with me, toward the river." The Chief and Ebb released the reins of the horse and left the animal behind, as they walked downhill. The Chief pointed to a tree. "See that hawk feather stuck in the trunk of that tree?"

"Yes."

"That is the edge of the mist. When a tribe moved into a new area, they occupied land, well above the mist. While they lived there, they observed the mist at night from the high ground and marked the furthest edge of the mist with a hawk feather. They were taught to honor the ground within the area of mist. By honoring this area, they were able to live in harmony with the river, and then, the river and the fish remained pure and healthy."

"What about the nights when mist covers all of the ground, both high and low, like in the spring, when the mist eats the snow?"

"That is the mist of the land. In the spring, the spirits of the land come out and eat the snow, so that spring growth may start. When the spirits of the land eat the snow, it puts the water from the snow back into the ground and into the river. This makes the spirits of the river happy and protects the land. If there is a spring when there is no snow on the ground for the mist of the land to eat, then we know the great spirits are unhappy. We know terrible things will happen during the upcoming summer. That is when we would all migrate up to Lake Potanopa. The lake is near the headwaters of the valley. We knew there we would be safe when the storms of summer would strike the land with great bolts of light. This would cause the land to burst into flames, consuming all in its way. The lake was deep and provided water and fish, even in the driest weather. If the land burst into flames and threatened the tribe, the wise men would take all of the tribe to a spot on the lake where they could wade way out. By staying in the water, they would avoid the wrath of the fire gods. It is in this way that we lived here for six thousand years. Ebb, let's go back to the stallion. I want to show you the entire river at this time, so you can understand. You are the last, and you need to understand. Your heart was pure when you were young. The spirits knew you would be the last, and you were given a long life, by letting your mother take you from the valley. It was not the fault of the spirits that you went to war and saw such tragedies; that was of your own doing. But even there, in the midst of those terrible battles, the spirits of the Nissitissit were with you; you have never been alone. The spirits traveled down the river, to the great salt pond, and then followed the rivers and the brooks to where you were."

"Honest?"

"Yes, I cannot lie to you. Remember that battle in the swamp? The night you called to the Death Angel?"

"Oh, my God. Yes, I remember. I had reached my wit's end. I had seen such misery that I no longer wanted to live. I called to the Angel of Death to take me in the next conflict. I did not have to wait long for the battle. That evening, as the mist of the swamp enveloped the camp, the Rebs attacked. They snuck up within the mist, and a great conflict broke out. I wanted to die but was determined to take a few of them Rebs with me. So I slung several munitions belts over my shoulder and took after them Rebs. I stood there, firing into the Rebel troops, as their bullets whizzed by. The mist of the swamp and the smoke of the guns had caused a great fog. It was hard to see. Yet, I advanced forward and, with the help of Providence, my hand was steady and my aim was true."

"That was not the hand of your God. It was the spirits of the mist, for long ago, it was decided that you would be the one. It was not your destiny to die in that swamp. The spirits deflected the death bullets and allowed you to have those numerous flesh wounds, hoping that you would lie down and be quiet. There were those amongst the Rebs who had the power and could see, so the spirits of the mist flew in their faces, terrifying them. The other Rebels were frightened by the fact that every man amongst them was firing at you. Even the marksmen were missing their mark. Upon seeing the look of terror and insanity on the faces of their companions, the whole Rebel Company turned and fled. They left you standing there, wounded and firing at the Rebs. Every bullet you fired was a kill shot, causing the Rebels to flee with great haste and fear."

"I remember that night. They made me a lieutenant because of that night."

"Did you think that the outcome was all because of you?"

"I didn't know. All I know is that I did not care to live any longer.

During the war, I saw that if someone reached that point, they had great power. Because they did not fear death, they acted in a bold way, and because of the sheer boldness of their actions, they survived. If they feared death, they would have died. I thought I survived because of that. I thought that the boldness of my actions saved my life."

"No, Ebb. There were two hundred men, all firing at you. No amount of attitude would have carried you through that conflict. The spirits of the mist deflected all deadly bullets. Remember when you lay in the hospital tent after that healing from your wounds?"

"I'm not sure. My head was very addled from the conflict. I wanted to die in that battle, and when I survived, I thought I might go completely insane."

"Do you remember the dreams about the mist which would come to you during the long nights?" asked the Chief.

"Yes. I remember the dreams of the Mist of the Nissitissit coming and calming my soul."

"The spirits of the mist massaged your soul back into your body," said the Chief. "Your soul was about to leave, even though your body was alive. It was determined long ago that you would be here with me at this time. You were not allowed to be a troubled soul, wandering around the cusp."

"Well, tell me, how it is that I wander the cusp with you?"

"We are the last. I am the last of my people, and you are the last descendent of the settlers who killed my people. We are here to see if we can be at peace with one another in the Place of Happiness. We have but one chance, and that is with you. Take the reins of the horse with me. I want to show you the land during those early times." Suddenly, they were looking upon the Atlantic Ocean. "We will start here, at the edge of the great salt pond where land and life begins."

Ebb was dumbfounded as they stood on the northern end of Plum

Island, looking at the mighty Merrimack. Everything was gone. Gone were the fishing and whaling villages. Gone were the docks and boats. Gone were the great ships, resting at anchor, after returning from the sea. To the west, a small tribe of Indians worked the Joppa Flats area for clams and oysters. They lived on the bounty of the river and caught fish year round. In the winter, the tribe would trade dried and salted fish, along with trinkets made from shells, for fresh game and dried corn from the Indians who lived inland. They lived in harmony with the land and with their neighbors. The river, the fish, and the tribes were all interdependent on one another.

"You see how they live in harmony with the land and the sea? They knew nothing of 'The White Way,' which led to the eventual demise of us all."

"You have mentioned this 'White Way' before. What is it?"

"All in time, but first we need to stop at all the Indian camps along the river, up to where the Nissitissit starts as a small spring in the side of a mountain. There is no need for haste as we have all the time in the world. There is no such thing as time, when in the cusp. I will show you the camps and the seasons when it was used. Most camps were not permanent, year-round places to live, but each camp supplied our needs during its season. We would migrate from camp to camp, letting the land rest when not in season. We spread the footprint of our life around the valley, so that we never left too much of a mark on the land." The Chief paused, looking sad and then continued. "We never ripped poisons out of the earth. We never blocked the flow of the river. We never killed the forest for houses. We worshipped the land until you white settlers defiled it. You killed the land, and as a result, you killed us all."

"I did not kill the land; it was done by others before me," replied Ebb.

"The sons of the fathers reap what has been sown for them, and your forefathers planted death wherever they went. You left such deep footprints that the land died. But, let us not fight each other. Come with me and I will show you."

As promised, Ebb and the Chief went from camp to camp, and the Chief showed him how they lived. Ebb was amazed at how orderly the Indian nation was and that he never saw anyone preparing for battle.

"Why is there never war amongst the savages?"

The Chief was angry and snapped back. "We were not the savages! You were! You and your white ways killed us all. We did not kill the land; we did not kill whole tribes and slaughter their children, ending the tribe's existence forever. We did not defile the river. We did not kill the fish."

The Chief stopped and checked his anger. "But let us not argue for now. We must teach each other one final lesson. Let us continue our journey. If we learn to accept each other, after all that has happened, our spirits will be able to leave the cusp and wander as friends in the Place of Happiness."

Ebb looked confused. "I don't understand. We walked the earth as enemies, yet we will reside in eternity as friends?"

"Yes. Do not put too much thought into it right now. Take the reins."

"Where are we now?" asked Ebb.

"In the village by the rapids. Later, these rapids were overcome with factories, and you came to know it as Lowell. See how the tribes come and harvest the salmon and the shad. They all live in unison with the land. The great tribe commands it."

"The great tribe?"

"Yes. One great tribe, far to the north of here, controls all of the smaller tribes. In winter, when the tribes have idle time, they send their representatives to the councils of the great tribe. The great wise men listen to the stories of the representatives and advise them on what to do in the approaching year. The wise men were also in charge of justice."

"Justice? You mean to tell me that you Indians had a government and corporal punishment?"

"You call it government. To us, it was a council of tribes and the great tribe combined all of the best of our little tribes. Unlike your politicians, our wise men had the interest of all tribes in mind. They were brave hunters with strong squaws who produced magnificent sons to be sent off to manage important areas. The Indian camps, at the time, all had braves who were good runners. A message of symbols was prepared on a hide with animal's blood and placed in a round holder made of birch bark. Then it was wrapped in more animal hide and sealed with pitch. The brave would run to the next village, calling for the next runner. The message was given to the new runner, and that runner would head for the next village. With a brave constantly running north with the message, it would reach the council of tribes in three days."

"Then what?"

"Then the council would decide action, either by sending a message back or dispatching 'Silent Death' upon them. Silent Death was a band of the most ferocious and strongest of all of the tribes. In seven days, they could reach even the remotest camp, and woe to the camp that caused them to be called. They came quickly and silently. With the power of the spirits, they slew the offenders and rarely got hurt in the process. No camp wanted Silent Death to come, so uprisings of young rebellious braves seldom happened, and we all lived in harmony."

"What happened to all that?"

"What happened was The White Way. Your way is to take more

than you need…to take so much that you make the land cry. It is time for you to see." All of a sudden, they were back in North Village. "That camp is my camp. I had been sent down many moons ago from the council to live at this spot. My mother produced two great Chiefs, Paugus and myself. I looked after this important spot for my whole life. Many villages upstream depended on the salmon, which swam through this spot. Forty thousand acres, as you call them, drain down through this narrow slot. This spot is sacred, as it was the line between the mighty rivers and the land where the mist is sacred. The tribe who lived here had to take only enough fish needed to live, and my task was to keep this enforced. I had taken in a local squaw, and she bore me two, fine sons. They are all lost. Watch, as your White Way comes into my valley."

Ebb and the Chief were near the terminus of the Nissitissit above the Nashua River. They were in the spot that would become North Village. Ebb could see the Chief and a few braves communicating with three white men. The white men wanted to enter the valley and build a dam on the Nissitissit.

During his life on earth, the Chief's English was poor. "No white men. River sacred. Spirits say no."

Ebb turned to the Chief. "How is it that you are there with your spirit intact, yet your spirit is here with me?"

"Just be silent and watch."

As Ebb and the Chief watched the scene from the past, one of the white men turned to the Chief and his braves. "I'll show you what I think of your spirits," he said with disgust as he walked to the bank of the river and prepared to urinate.

The spirit of the Chief watched himself in a scene from the past as he spun his spear around and knocked the white man out. The two, remaining white men dragged their friend away.

"Ebb, I am sorry. You saw enough death when you went to war. Your soul is still heavy from it, and you know how horrific battles can be. But it has been deemed that you now witness this slaughter."

As the Chief finished speaking, Ebb could hear the sounds of a great battle, over in the area of Bloody Hollow. He never knew why it was called that, but now he understood. He heard shots and screams. He listened to the sounds of braves fighting and dying, the sounds of woman screaming, children crying, and then silence - dead silence. A storm was gathering in the west, but the calm before the storm was underway as all sounds of the battle had ended.

Then Ebb saw them. The Great White Horse appeared with the Chief sitting on top. Ebb went to speak, and the spirit of the Chief motioned him to be quiet. "Watch. Be still. This is very important."

The Chief was fatally wounded and lacked the strength to fall from the horse. The horse was bleeding profusely, and the Chief, nearly dead, slumped forward upon the neck of the great stallion. Some of the earlier settlers had presented the stallion as a gift for trading. Those same settlers were quietly waiting for the Chief to die, so that they could celebrate. (18) They saw that he was dying, so, to be cruel, they followed along, letting the suffering continue. The Great White Horse was almost entirely red from the blood of the Chief and from its own wounds as it stumbled forward. The western sky had dark clouds building, but all remained quiet when the mist started rising from the river and moving towards the dying Chief and his injured horse. Then suddenly, ghostly hands of many ancestors protruded from the mist, helping the Chief and the horse towards the river. The settlers watched, in horror. They had never witnessed anything like this.

They saw the spirits that dwelled within the mist of the Nissitissit carry the horse to the edge of the river. Right before the horse fell forward, the Chief faced the settlers. With his last breath, he proclaimed,

"My spirit will not rest until I get revenge on you and the sons of your sons. All will perish in the end. The land will have its revenge."

The great horse staggered forward and fell into the river. The wind from the coming storm swiftly hit, screaming in the settlers' ears. They pushed forward to the spot where the horse fell. The river was broiling with blood. Although the river was only a few feet deep, the settlers could not see the bodies. Lightning was striking all around them as they ran back, fleeing into the woods. They raced back home, telling no one what had happened, other than saying the Chief was dead. Later, they swore to tell no one what had really happened, as their greed for the land was more powerful than their fear of the spirits. The Nissitissit ran red for days as the blood of six thousand years leached from the spot where the Chief had died. Already, The White Way was beginning to poison the land.

CHAPTER THREE

The spirits of Ebb and the Chief watched the scene for some time. The Chief was moved by what he saw and needed a few moments to regain composure. Witnessing his own death left the Chief infused with sadness for a while. Ebb quietly stood nearby. Slowly, he was beginning to understand. He was beginning to see the flaws of his race; he was beginning to see that eventually The White Way would kill everyone and everything.

"That was the curse that killed the valley and doomed you," said the Chief. "After the massacre, my spirit wandered the river valley. The spirits of the river decided that my punishment for the curse would be to be present whenever any of the doomed expired. My horse and I were to be the skeleton in the closet whenever anyone died. The only time the curse was discussed was over ale at the pub, late at night and only in hushed tones, for fear that the spirits would hear the talk about them. It is time for you to meet Sarah. We save her, and then she saves you; then, you save me. It will be a circle of life that links us together for eternity. Right now, Sarah is just an infant, wrapped in a blanket. Her parents, being Quakers, where driven from one of your villages and were wandering the wilderness. They were looking for a place to settle, away from the small-minded Puritans who hated anyone who was different. Take the reins, Ebb, and we will go there next."

When they came upon the scene, two bears were brutally attacking Sarah's parents and ripping apart their flesh. Sarah was lying on the ground, wailing in tears. She had the attention of one of the bears because of her loud crying. The Chief had pity on her, and his spirit entered her body. Her heart was pure, so the Chief calmed her voice. The bears had enough of the slaughter. They overlooked the quiet child and licked their front paws clean, before wandering off.

"I knew of a wise, old woman who lived near a spring, not too far away. Take the reins, and we will go there."

"Who is there? I can see your forms, out in the mist," cried the old Indian woman.

"Smiling Water, it is the Chief. I have come for your help."

"You were killed a while ago."

"Yes, Smiling Water, I was. Now I am one of the spirits of the mist. I am trapped here in the cusp because of the curse I made."

"I know, Chief. Strange things are happening. I fear that our way of life is lost."

"Smiling Waters, I need you to send your two daughters out to collect an infant. She is the one I chose to help try and break the curse."

"This is Ebb. He is, and will be, the last."

The old woman motioned to her two daughters; they were both over sixty years old.

"The infant is at the head of your path, near the spring where the bears drink. The bears are gorged and will be sleeping. I have entered the child's heart to quiet her and now, because of that, she is part of me; she is now part of us, just as Ebb is now part of us - part of the struggle to get to the Place of Happiness. Bring us the child!" the Chief commanded.

The two, old daughters made their way silently through the woods and disappeared out of sight. As they walked, Ebb could see a patch of mist that encircled them. Within the mist, Ebb could begin to see other figures.

Ebb turned to speak to the Chief, but before he could speak, the Chief looked at Ebb and smiled. "I can see from your expression that you are beginning to see. Soon you will be able to understand."

Up until now, Ebb had not questioned the Chief or his actions, but now, Ebb was thoroughly confused. "How does all this work? We save her… she saves me… and, then, I save you?" Ebb continued. "How can someone like me, born in the future, come back in time and save someone who will save me in the future? So the future is affecting the past?"

The Chief started slowly as he was at the limits of his knowledge. "Time is a thing of the living. Here in the cusp, where you and I are, there is no time. We just are; we live in the past, the present and sometimes, even the future, all at the same time. I am at the limit of what the spirits of the mist have told me. I can explain it no further than to tell you that it just is. Be quiet and sit by the fire. There we will wait for the child."

The three of them sat quietly as the old woman smoked some nasty concoction. The smoke wafted out, in all directions. Being in the cusp, Ebb could still sense the smoke as the light breeze blew it gently around him. The daughters returned with the child - the child who would become, Sarah the Wise. Her parents' blood covered the swaddling around her. The daughters cleaned off the child, wrapped her in a fur, and placed her beside Ebb's feet.

Even though Ebb was in spirit, the smoke had somehow addled his thoughts. "What is this?"

The Chief had a stern tone to his voice. "These next years, I am busy collecting many souls in North Village. They were souls that are stained and need to be returned to the ground. If you had not been chosen as the last, your soul would have been returned to the ground to await another try."

Ebb was astounded. "Stained souls don't go to hell? They get another chance to get it right?" That went against everything he had been taught. "How many chances does a soul get?"

"The spirits know not of what you call hell. Any stained souls are returned to the earth and given another chance, in a different life, to get it right. There is no limit; you keep returning to the earth until you get it right. It is not important *when* you get it right; it is only important *that* you get it right. It is deemed that you experience the Nissitissit Valley from its beginning, up to the point that you lay down to die. The spirits command that you see it all, and I will be busy and can't be with you. Sarah the Wise will be your vessel. Through her eyes, you will witness what happened that caused her to save you. She will carry you within her heart. By my entering her body, I instilled the power of the mist within her. She has the strength and the purity to carry you. She will be wise and strong and will witness many horrors, but she will continue on. She is now part of the circle of your life as you and her are part of mine. As you are now part of hers, your paths have been spun together for all time. The spirits weave a tapestry of life that the fumbling hands of man cannot undo."

Ebb was now afraid and tried to rise, but the smoke, somehow, held him in place "What is going on?"

"Easy, your soul will be made pure by your journey with Sarah the Wise."

"But… I am here because my soul was pure at birth or because my soul was pure at death?"

"Your soul will be pure because of the journey you are about to take with Sarah. At the moment of your death, your soul was not pure. Remember, the spirits live the past, the present, and the future, all at once. They are very wise. That is how they know the outcome of actions taken now. And, what I do is right."

The spirit of the Chief leaned down, taking the hand of the infant. The infant took a deep breath and inhaled the smoke, which contained the spirit of Ebb. When the infant exhaled, only the smoke exited, and her heart would hold the spirit of Ebb. His spirit would remain part of her, until his birth in 1812. Whatever Sarah experienced, Ebb would feel. Somehow Sarah would also know that Ebb existed within her, for even as an infant she had become Sarah the Wise. The spirits of the mist saw her as a vessel of hope.

Sarah's first memories were of the mist. The wise, old woman and her daughters would bring Sarah down to the mist when it formed. The mist never frightened Sarah. In time, she was able to see the spirits that were around her. She learned to communicate in the language of the souls and they experienced each other. Sarah was the young princess of the mist. The mist would pass over Sarah, leaving her body cleansed and damp. At the same time, the spirits of the mist would pass their hands over the heart of Sarah, purifying it even more. In the process, the spirits helped to purify Ebb's soul within her heart. Years passed, and finally, the day came when it was time for Sarah to leave.

"Sarah," the old woman said calmly. "It is time for you to return to your people. It is time for you to experience the evil of The White Way. We have prepared you as best we can. You will bring with you some of the spirits of the mist who will help protect you from the evils. The fact that you now contain the soul of the last shows you completed your task. When you leave the valley, the mist cannot help you, but the spirits you carry will help you in many ways which will ensure the completion of the journey."

A small patch of mist came out of the Nissitissit and floated toward Sarah. Sarah took a deep breath, and when she exhaled, nothing came out. The spirits were within her for the remainder of her life. The wise, old Indian woman and her daughters prepared Sarah for the journey. Inside a leather pouch, they placed a broken pendant and a man's ring they had found on the ground near the carnage of her parents. Then, they hung it around Sarah's neck.

"Sarah, you are thirteen, and you must return to your people while you are young, so you can learn their language and their ways. The spirits you contain will carry you through the difficult times." The old woman watched Sarah walk down the path towards the village of North Brookline. Sarah walked as if she were of noble blood and carried herself proudly. She would present herself to the world that way, but the world would never understand.

CHAPTER FOUR

"Look. Who is that? See that young girl coming out of the woods? Is that a white Indian?" cried one of the villagers.

They turned from their work to look at her.

"She has white skin and blond hair but is dressed in Indian garb. She looks so wild," the Foreman exclaimed as he shut down the mill.

"Ring the bell," he ordered to one of the men. "Get all the townspeople up here."

The bell rang out from the mill. The townspeople stopped what they were doing. The ringing of the bell usually meant there was an accident and for the doctor to come at once. The mill worker would ring the bell for a minute and stop if the doctor was needed, but the bell had been ringing for several minutes.

A group of townspeople were running towards the mill to see why the bell was ringing. A crowd of people began to cluster around the child. Sarah was not frightened by the mob and calmly took the pouch off her neck and held it out. She could not understand a word of the gibberish being spoken around her. Something inside warned her not to speak in the Indian language. The spirits had already begun to take care of her by giving her wisdom in thought.

Someone grabbed the pouch and revealed the contents– the ring and pendant. The unidentified villager opened the pendant to expose two names carved inside a heart, "Anna & Daniel." The date was fifteen years earlier. As someone in the crowd read the inscription, a woman cried out. "Oh, my God, it is Sarah, the daughter of Anna and Daniel who left here over a dozen years ago. She is my sister's daughter, returned from the dead."

Sarah recognized her name and was surprised that they knew it. Upon hearing her name, Sarah turned gracefully towards the woman. "See, I told ya," said the woman. "She turned when I called her name! She is my sister's child. I'm as sure of it as the next breath that I take." The woman opened her arms in the direction of the child.

Sarah walked towards the woman. She was thinking this must be the start of the journey that the wise, old woman at the edge of the mist kept telling her about. Sarah purposely did not speak the Indian language and, instead, communicated in gestures and graceful movements.

"Look. She acts as if she were some kind of princess," laughed someone in the crowd.

"Well, let's all thank Providence that my niece, Sarah, has returned from the wilderness!"

Aunt Mary was wearing her work clothes. She had donned a simple, un-dyed cotton dress and a natural wool sweater. In time, Aunt Mary would find out how important clothes were to Sarah, among other things. Sarah accompanied Aunt Mary to her house, and the problems began immediately. The steps to the porch were granite, and the floors were oiled hardwood. The flooring – simple, but durable - was not an issue, but Sarah shied away from entering the door. It was painted a bright white with paint containing lead. Sarah felt scared. Instinctively, she was afraid of the paint. She had never seen any paint in her life. Up until now, Sarah had only come in contact with natural materials, and any fabric dyes had been extracted from berries.

Aunt Mary was loving, yet firm. She kept gesturing for Sarah to come inside, thinking that Sarah was afraid to enter a house. Sarah knew that she must face the dangers of The White Way. She knew that she would eventually have to enter, so as quickly as possible, she passed through door. Aunt Mary clasped Sarah's hand, and she led her through the house. The whole inside of the house was wood. Mary and her husband, Joe, were Quakers and lived a simple life. Paint was deemed to be a luxury of the rich, so the whole wood interior of the house was oiled in linseed and polished with beeswax. Sarah felt comfortable. To her, it felt as if she were inside a tree. She was relaxed, as Aunt Mary led her into a room with a huge pot on the floor - a pot big enough to stand in.

"What is this?" thought Sarah.

Aunt Mary made a gesture for Sarah to stay and returned in a few moments with two buckets of water from the well. The buckets were oak with metal bands. Sarah knew what metal was. The wise, old woman had two metal cook pots, and Sarah had used them for preparing food at the camp by the mist. Aunt Mary poured the water into the big pot on the floor and gestured for Sarah to move towards it. She kept forming a word with her mouth and saying it over and over.

"Tub," Sarah said, imitating her.

Aunt Mary smiled and nodded affirmatively. "Yes"

Sarah thought for a moment and pointed to the metal pot. "Tub. Yes." Then Sarah shook her head up and down. Aunt Mary was astounded at how bright Sarah was and decided to try another word. She shook her from side to side while she wagged her finger at Sarah and said, "No." Sarah recognized the wagging of the finger, as the wise, old woman used it with her. Sarah nodded. "Yes." Then, as she waved her head from side to side, she said, "No."

Aunt Mary, with the greatest of patience, was making a gesture to Sarah to take her clothes off and kept repeating, "Yes" as she made the gesture. Sarah got the message and took off all her clothes. She was raised by women and was not the least bit shy to be naked in the presence of another woman. Sarah stood proudly as if she were royalty.

Inside Sarah, Ebb's soul was experiencing everything at the same time. He knew the meaning of the words, but he could not tell Sarah. He existed inside her, but he could not do anything to affect her. The spirits also could not talk directly with Sarah, but they could affect her in other ways. Ebb was not embarrassed to be part of Sarah, and he found her body and how it functioned to be natural. Ebb had been given the ultimate gift. Having been a male, and now, being part of a woman, Ebb had an insight for life that few people ever experience.

Ebb knew he existed; he just could not communicate with Sarah, but she could feel his existence as well as the other spirits. The wise, old woman had told Sarah about Ebb and the spirits - and how important it was for her to carry them within her.

Aunt Mary stepped into the tub, pointed to Sara, and said, "Yes."

Sarah wagged her finger and shook her head. "No."

Aunt Mary tried several more times and then attempted something different. She made the motion of washing herself and said, "Wash."

Sarah's face showed recognition as she said, "Wash. Yes." While she spoke, she shook her head affirmatively.

Aunt Mary was joyful and pointed to the tub. Then, she pointed to Sarah. "You. Tub. Wash."

Sarah understood instantly and pointed to herself. "You. Wash. Yes." Then she smiled innocently.

Aunt Mary figured that was close enough and said, "Yes."

Sarah stepped into the tub and let Aunt Mary pour the pure well water over her. Sarah looked for the sand to wash with as in the river. Clean, wet sand would remove all the other dirt. Sarah motioned as if she wanted to wash and held out her hand, hoping for sand.

"Oh, my. Yes. You want soap." Aunt Mary hadn't realized that Sarah had never seen soap.

She held the soap towards Sarah. Sarah shook her head and wagged her finger. "No."

Sarah did not know what to say. She did not know the word for sand. Aunt Mary plunged the soap into the water and rubbed some on Sarah. The soap seemed caustic but not poisonous, so Sarah allowed Aunt Mary to "soap 'you' up in the tub" and "yes, rinse 'you' off" with buckets of clean water from the well. Sarah was now learning the language, for she had already learned half a dozen words within a few minutes.

Sarah smiled sweetly. She was beginning to learn the ways of these people, just as the wise, old woman and the spirits of the mist had told her. Sarah had great dignity for her young age. She regally positioned herself as if she were royalty and allowed Aunt Mary to bathe her. When Sarah was clean, Aunt Mary took her to another room. This room had a smaller room full of clothes. Sarah was amazed. Why would one woman have so many clothes?

Aunt Mary pointed to the clothes for Sarah to choose from. Sarah knew what Aunt Mary meant and pointed to an un-dyed, cotton dress. Aunt Mary smiled as she thought the girl was already trying to emulate her. As a reward, Aunt Mary added a green sweater she had made from wool that had been cleaned and dyed by the woolen mill in the village. She then threw it upon Sarah's shoulders, whereupon Sarah screamed as if her skin were on fire. The spirits within Sarah cried out; the poisons in the color had caused Sarah and the spirits to feel great pain. Sarah shook, and the sweater fell to the floor. Her aunt reached out, touching her shoulder to comfort her, and was shocked at how hot Sarah's skin was.

"Lord, Almighty!" gasped her aunt. "You're on fire." Aunt Mary had heard Sarah's voice when she cried out. Curiously, she felt a moment of fear when she thought she heard many voices instead of only one.

Sarah pointed to the sweater of color and to the few other garments that had been dyed. She pointed to herself and said, "You." Then she wagged her finger, shook her head, and said, "No!"

"Oh, I see," said her aunt. "You are not used to colored clothes." She then handed Sarah a natural, wool sweater.

Sarah nodded. "Yes," she said and smiled as she took the sweater.

Joe returned from his work in the hayfields. Neighbors had been running out to him, on his way home, telling him of the miracle - how Providence had saved young Sarah. He came bustling into the house. "Mary! Mary, where are you? Where is the girl?"

"We are here, Joseph, in our bedroom."

Joe knew that Mary liked to use the name Joseph, but he hated it. They had always been greeted at the church, with a smile, when they had been introduced as Mary and Joseph, so Joseph learned to go by the name, Joe. He headed for the bedroom and stopped upon entering the room.

"Mary, call me Joe, so the child will get it right."

"She's gifted, Joe. She has already learned some English." They both looked at Sarah.

Sarah smiled and pointed to herself. "You, Sarah." Then she pointed to Joe.

"Me, Joe" he said, pointing to himself.

Then Sarah looked at Mary. "Me, Mary," she said, pointing to herself. Sarah looked a little confused but smiled. She pointed to herself and said, "You, Sarah." Next she pointed to Joe and said "Me, Joe" and then to Mary saying, "Me, Mary."

Joe laughed and remarked, "She needs a little work, but I suppose that is a start."

They all laughed, and Sarah's aunt and uncle welcomed her into the family and into their hearts. They had no children, and a child at any age was welcome, even one that seemed slightly odd. Sarah now understood that Mary was the sister of her real mother and that the wise, old mother by the mist was her surrogate.

Over the next few weeks, Joe and Mary were astounded at how bright Sarah was. During that time, she learned to speak English quite well. She only had to be told the meaning of a word, just once, and she would remember it. Sarah did stumble with some words, such as the word *give*. She learned how to say, "Please give that to me," but then was confused when she was asked to give something back.

"Give means to come to me, right Aunt Mary?"

"Not really, Sarah. Give means to give up possession of something. *Get* is when it comes to you. You can tell someone to give, to give to you, and then you are the one who gets."

"Let me show you, Sarah. Pretend there is a woman next to me. Now, tell me to give the sweater on this bed to her."

Sarah thought and then spoke. "Please give the sweater to her."

"Now she gets the sweater," Aunt Mary said as she pretended to present the sweater to someone beside her.

Sarah was smart and understood, but the spirits of the mist were still puzzled and caused her to ask a question. "Why not just use the word *get*? Why can I not point to what you have and say '*get*,' and then she gets it?" she asked as she pointed to the imaginary woman. Why do you have to say, 'Please give that to her'? Why do you have to use so many words (Sarah asked this as she held up five fingers.) instead of just using *get*?" And she held up one finger.

"Because you have to ask the person who possesses something to give it up first, before someone gets it."

"Possesses?"

"Yes, give up something you own."

"Own?"

"Yes, just as Joe and I own this land."

"You and Uncle Joe possess this land?" asked Sarah. "Do you possess the land when your bones are dust?"

"No. Then someone else will own it."

"But, if the land is the constant through the ages, how can someone own it? Do not the spirits of the land own the land?"

"Sakes alive, girl! What did those wicked savages fill your head with?"

"Are you savages?" Sarah asked.

"No, we are civilized. We have laws," replied Mary.

Sarah responded, "They are unlike you, but they are not savages; they have laws. You are savages for what you do to the land, and they are civilized because they lived with the land."

Aunt Mary did not have an answer, and at times like this, she always searched the scriptures of the Bible for one. Then Aunt Mary realized the girl would not know what the Bible was anyway. "I have an idea. I will teach you to read."

"Read?" Sarah asked.

"Yes. That is when the spoken word is put on paper so others can hear it."

Sarah and the spirits were confused. "If they just heard it, why do you have to write it?" Ebb's spirit was amused, which caused Sarah to smile.

"It is for someone to read, or shall we say, hear - to hear your words at a future date and listen to what they say."

Sarah was incredulous. "Someone in the future can hear what I say now, if I write it?"

"Yes."

"Do they write back?"

"No, Sarah. They can not write back."

"Can they speak back?"

"No, child; don't be silly."

"But the spirits of the mist can talk to the spirits of past, present and the future, all at the same time."

A chill came over Aunt Mary. "It is best not to think of such things, child–let alone speak them, lest people will think you are possessed."

"If I was possessed, who would own me?" asked Sarah

"The Devil would own you, dear child."

"What is this Devil?"

"Why, child, the Devil is the prince of darkness who makes the wicked suffer."

"Oh, I see. White people."

"Sakes alive, child. Why, do you think Joe and I and the settlers are the Devil?"

"The white people who entered this valley are a dark cloud on the landscape. Many have suffered and died. You called my people wicked, yet they have suffered greatly."

Aunt Mary was flustered. "Yes, your people are wicked savages. No…uh… those are not your people; you are one of us. And we are not the Devil!" exclaimed Aunt Mary.

Sarah was proud and indignant. "I am not one of you!"

"Well, you are not one of them."

"Then I am one of me," Sarah stated, as she flung her hair back and leaned slightly forward. I am destined to be Sarah the Wise. I am their vessel of hope."

"Hope for what?"

Sarah paused. The spirits were trying to keep her silent, but she was still an impetuous child. "Hope to release the spirits."

"What spirits, child?"

"The spirits of the Nissitissit."

Aunt Mary gasped. "Who told you that?"

"The spirits of the Nissitissit taught me that. The spirits of past, present and future told me. Like reading, only different."

"Stop that! I will hear no such thing. Don't ever talk like that in this house again!"

Sarah knew she had said too much. "I'm sorry, Aunt Mary. With everything going on I think I was confused."

"That's better, child. Do not speak of spirits again!"

"Yes, Aunt Mary."

The following day, Aunt Mary took out a chalkboard and some chalk. She started teaching Sarah her letters and the sounds each letter made. She showed her how to write the letter, call it by its name, and then, how to phonetically say the letter. Afterwards, she showed her how to form the words with the letters. Sarah and the spirits, as well as Ebb, learned how to read and write with fantastic speed. Ebb was beginning to become very wise.

While out shopping, one of the women at the store in town inquired, "How is the young savage doing?"

"She is not a savage. She is like you and I and is becoming quite a lady. I am teaching her to read and write."

"You must have seen too much sun, Mary. Don't you mean you are teaching her how to speak?"

"NO. She speaks quite well. I am teaching her how to read and write!"

The woman laughed as she left the store. "That is something that I would like to see," she said, over her shoulder, as she walked out.

Mary borrowed a few more primers from the small library in the store and brought them home for Sarah to read. Mary was angered by what the woman had said. She wanted Sarah well read before she went to town to meet all the people.

A few weeks later, Sarah had learned to read all of the primers, and Aunt Mary brought them back. Sarah was a sight to watch when she read. She always wore cotton gloves, and she kept the book downwind. Sarah found that the books were made with something that burned her hands, and even the smell of the books made her nauseous. However, the words contained in the books were too important to not read.

Aunt Mary thought that Sarah was ready for a trip to town. She cleaned one of Sarah's best, un-dyed dresses and had an unbleached cotton ruffle for her head. Then they set off.

A woman they met on the road inquired, "Is this Sarah? My, my… She looks so grown up and sophisticated. Can she speak to me?"

Sarah turned to the woman. "Good morning, Madam. It is a fine, fall day and the sound of those geese, leaving in the distance, is music to my soul."

The woman's jaw dropped. Aunt Mary was so proud of Sarah that she did not see the reaction of the woman. She bounded down the road with Sarah. Sarah had seen the reaction and thought that she must have said something wrong. She noticed that the people she talked to would act shocked, but unabashed Aunt Mary did not notice and dragged Sarah towards town. Sarah kept thinking about what she said. She knew she had said everything properly.

When they were at the store, Aunt Mary wanted to show the storekeeper just how much Sarah had learned from his books. "Hi, Joshua. This is Sarah."

Rose Mary Chaulk

Joshua was high up on a ladder, having just finished hanging his new sign. He winked at Mary and looked down at Sarah. "Hi, Sarah. How do like my new sign?"

Sarah looked up and saw that she could help. "Mr. Joshua," she said in clear, plain English, "mercantile is spelled with only one *L*."

Joshua was shocked that the girl could even *speak* English, let alone that she could spell too. This surprise caused Joshua to lose his balance and fall onto the porch, breaking his arm. As he lay there in pain, he screamed at Mary. "It is not natural that she learns things that fast. Something is not quite right here. Get her out of here."

Mary and Sarah ran back home. Mary was confused. Sarah had not done anything wrong. Sarah was bemused; she was confused by their actions but was amused at how stupid they were. Mary had been so close to Sarah that she had not noticed how quickly the child had been learning. She began to realize Sarah's ability to learn was unusual. Later that night when Sarah went to bed, Mary talked with Joe.

"Joseph, we have to talk. You have seen how smart Sarah is and how fast she has learned. I took her to town, and I fear that she is too much for these backwards people. I have set her this day on reading the Bible, which will keep her busy over the winter. But that is the last book left to read. She needs to be where she can learn more. Why don't you write your brother in Boston and see if he can help?"

That same night, Joshua was in the pub, nursing his broken arm with large measures of rum. Most of the men had heard from their wives about the strange girl and about Joshua breaking his arm. Many had come to console the storekeeper. As the rum affected Joshua, he stood up amongst his friends and, with slurred speech uttered, "There is ssssomething wrong with SSSSarah!" and passed out drunk.

Some of Joshua's friends carefully carried him home. They placed him gently in bed, making sure his arm was still set and left two bottles of rum on the nightstand. They repeated his words to their wives back at home, slurs and all.

The next day, Mary and Joe worded a carefully written letter to Joe's brother who was a doctor in Boston. They explained how gifted Sarah was, but also how she would not touch colored fabric or paint. Joe's brother, Samuel, received the letter about a week later. When Samuel finished reading the letter, he thought, "Maybe she is intelligent." Since volunteering his time to help the sick factory workers, Samuel had learned that fabric dyes and paints were killing the men who made them. In addition, hatters had been going mad, turning into raving lunatics and dying with unusual pain and hysteria. (12)

He thought out loud. "I will send for her, and, in the mean time, I will prepare a pure place for her at the rear of my house." Based on what he had seen in the paint factories, he wanted to have a toxin-free area in his house anyway. He had even begun wearing un-dyed clothes during the past couple of years for the same reason.

"This could be the hand of Providence!" he exclaimed. He spoke aloud, as he penned a quick letter in haste. "Send her in a few months. I need time to prepare a place for her," he wrote and set off for the post office.

A week later, Mary and Joe received the letter and were relieved. They put the letter away. The fireplace kept Sarah warm while she sat at a partially opened window, so that she would not smell the book. She was turning the pages of the Bible back and forth with her gloved hands as she attempted to figure out what someone from the past was trying to tell her. The spirits of the mist and Ebb studied also. Sarah was beginning to be able to communicate with the spirits of the mist within her. The spirits kept pointing out, to Sarah and Ebb, the flaws contained in the Bible and how some things could never have happened as described. Time after time, the same conclusion was always the result: The White Way was flawed and, at some point in the future, would end in disaster.

A new pamphlet about plowing arrived at the store when Mary happened to be there. The Department of Agriculture had sent it. Mary thought, "How can she get in trouble with this?" and brought it home.

Sarah read it and understood. Farmers were advised to plow their rows around a hill to keep the soil from eroding away, instead of plowing the rows up and down the hill. She knew what it meant, and it made sense to her. Mary returned the booklet to the shelf in the store, and there it sat all winter as none of the farmers could read.

Spring arrived, and Sarah wanted to walk outdoors. Mary could not see any harm in it, as it had been a long winter. She called to Sarah, "Stay on the farm."

"I will."

Sarah wandered around the perimeter of the farm. On the side nearest town, she watched a farmer plow his field. The soil was mucky, and the footing was soft for the horse, so the farmer had the horse plow downhill. Then the farmer would pull the plow out of the soil and turn it sideways. He would then have the horse drag it freely to the top, and he would plow downhill again. Sarah could see the soil-laden water leach from the land and run downhill. The farmer noticed her leaning on the fence and stopped plowing. He knew it was Sarah, the one they talked about at the pub. The farmer was mentally slow and nothing scared him, so he approached Sarah.

Sarah spoke first. "If you plow your fields like that and we get a nor'easter, your soil is going to wash away."

"What was that, young Sarah? You are going to call up a nor'easter and wash my fields away?"

He came right up to her and put his face up to hers. "I was with

Chamberlain when we were in Maine and killed the great Chief Paugus at Lake Lovell. He was the last, and we put an end to your Indian bullshit spirits. You run along, young Sarah. I need to finish plowing my field."

It seemed as if the spirits had listened to Sarah. The very next day, a great nor'easter rolled in with three days of driving rain. After the rain, the farmer went to check his fields and found most of them had washed away. He ran to town and found some men at the tavern.

He stuttered and stammered, "The wwwitch Ssssarah cursed my la…land and told me she wwould wa…wash it away and nnow it is g…gone. Come look."

They rushed out to his farm and, sure enough, the topsoil was gone. Gravel and some exposed ledge were all that was left. The sight was grim.

Joe saw the activity next door and came to the fence. "Hey, fellas. What's happened?"

"That witch! That Sarah caused this. My farm is ruined."

The men restrained the farmer, and Joe ran back to the farmhouse to find out what had happened. Sarah was sitting outside reading, unaware of what was happening.

"Sarah, did you talk with the farmer on the side closest to town?"

"Yes, Uncle Joe, That was four days ago. After reading that pamphlet on plowing, I told him he was plowing wrong."

"What did he say?"

"He got all mad and told me to leave."

Joe remembered Mary reading the pamphlet to him and realized that the farmer had plowed his field the wrong way. He knew Sarah was right about what she had told the farmer; he also knew if he were to explain that Sarah was correct, the stupid locals would never believe him.

I came to tell you something, Sarah."

"What is it, Uncle?"

"Remember my brother, the doctor in Boston?"

"Yes."

"You are going to visit him for a while. Go pack your bags now. We leave tonight."

Sarah was not surprised by the news. The spirits had told her that she would have to leave the valley to learn. They told her that she had to go to a great city to become Sarah the Wise. Sarah put her few, simple clothes, made of un-dyed cotton and natural wools, into a cotton bag. Joe hooked the horses to the covered coach he had in the barn. The sun was setting as he brought them to the door.

"I cannot touch that," Sarah stated.

"I have thought of that," said Aunt Mary. I will wrap you in these old, cotton sheets that I was going to give to the Shoddy Mill. When we stop at the liveries for horses, we will tell them you are a burn victim, and we are taking you to Uncle Joe's brother, the doctor in Boston."

Under the cover of darkness, Uncle Joe, Aunt Mary and Sarah quietly left town. They had a long journey ahead.

CHAPTER FIVE

Before long, Uncle Joe found the hospital where his brother worked. He quickly lifted Sarah out of the coach, all bundled up, and onto the dirt street. Joe left the coach at the edge of the park across the street from the hospital. He and Mary hastily removed the gauze around Sarah's face and the sheets that had surrounded her body.

They saw no one in view and thought they were safe. They noticed a gentleman, off to the side on a bench, who was leaving on the train in a few hours. He was a mill owner from the village and had taken a coach to the well-known hospital in Boston to seek treatment. The mill owner had not been well lately. For the past two years, he had been mixing the dyes since his helper got afflicted and died.

Once released back into the light of day, Sarah rejoiced and danced in the sun. She was frolicking with the dragonflies that darted about. The gentleman had recognized Joe's coach when they arrived. He also noticed the frenzy of the child. He got up and walked off towards the livery. He would be back at Potanopa the next day, and he would make sure the village heard about this.

Joe went into the hospital and quickly found his brother. They hadn't seen each other for years, and they embraced strongly, slapping each other on the back.

"Let's go to my office, Joe."

"I'd be glad to," said Joe. They made their way to the office, which was on the second floor with a magnificent view of the park.

Samuel looked out the window. "Is that Mary and the child?"

"Yes."

"Why, she looks quite lovely," remarked Samuel.

"She is very bright. She learned to read and write in a few months, and she read the entire Bible over the winter. She was only returned to us last summer." Joe paused. "Although she is amazingly bright, she is quite odd."

"I have dealt with very gifted people, and sometimes we misinterpret them and think they are odd," said Samuel.

Samuel reflected on how his own colleagues thought him odd for donating so much time at the free clinic for the poor factory workers. Over the years, the doctors had begun to let their Hippocratic oaths slide. The poor factory workers never had any money, and the only treatment they could find was at Samuel's clinic. The doctors were beginning to believe what the mill owners were saying was right. The mill workers were always sick and dying, and they felt that the sick should be left to die as quickly as possible. The doctors spoke as if they were trying to save the workers from such horrible pain. In reality, they wanted the sickly to die, so that they could receive their money for treating the next victims.

"Providence has brought you to me this day, Joe, for I have no rounds today. Let us go to the park, so I can meet this girl. My house is just a short walk away from the park. We can sit for a while and chat while she plays and then walk her to the house."

Joe replied, "That's a might better way for the last of her journey than how she got here."

"How was that?"

"Well, she cannot touch paint or tanned leather, of which my coach has both," replied Joe. "The only solution was to wrap her in sheets and gauze and bring her to you. At the livery stops, we had her lean against Mary and moan. We told them she had bad burns, and we were bringing her to this hospital. They were happy to hurry us along."

Samuel said, "No wonder the child dances with such frenzy after being wrapped up so long." Samuel was already learning and understanding Sarah.

The two brothers left the office and went to the park. Samuel, Mary and Joe sat on a bench for a long time talking while Sarah danced around. The time had come to take Sarah to Samuel's house. Joe called to her. "Sarah! Samuel's house is across the park, and we can walk to it."

Sarah was delighted. "Oh, Uncle Joe, that would be much nicer than those stifling, old wraps."

Sarah reverted back to her quiet, almost regal, way. She had expelled her childhood energy. In a stately manner, Sarah quietly accompanied the adults through the park while they made pleasant conversation for her benefit. As they approached the house, Sarah stopped and would not go any further. She was looking at a house completely painted - the stairs, the floors, and the walls; she could not go there.

Joe was upset. He could not take Sarah back the way she came. "I thought you told us you were going to prepare your house," said Joe.

"Yes. Relax, Joe. I wanted to make a special place just for her. My house is filled with books and chemicals, as well as medicines and excess hospital equipment. It's no place for the child," said Samuel. "Sarah, child, I have had an ell added to the rear of the house and a garden area for you. Come down this stone walk, and I will show it to you."

They walked around the corner, and Sarah was breathless. Samuel had a reflection pond built with stones in the water, which led to a stone table and chair on a platform in the middle of the pool. The stonemasons had been quite creative, and it was all quite beautiful. An oasis was right there in the city. Lilies were growing in the water with buds that would bloom later in the season.

"Sarah, come with me," said Samuel, and they turned to face a beautiful, little addition. Various kinds of wood were used, which had been treated with linseed oil. The siding was untreated, natural cedar, which was still fragrant. They entered her exquisite quarters. Natural woods, stones, or tiles had been used for all the components - nothing with toxins. An earthy feel had been created.

"OH. Thank you, Samuel. It is wonderful. How can I ever thank you?" Sarah cooed, obviously pleased.

"Well, I intend to teach you mathematics, and you can do my books."

"Do your books?"

"I will teach you. I will teach you many things. I have arranged for tutors to periodically come by and help you in your studies. You will become Sarah the Wise."

Mary shuddered, for she had heard the girl utter those same words not long ago but said nothing. "How could it be that Samuel came by those words?" she thought. "What can she get done? She will just become another woman who no one will listen to, but then again, she is quite different."

Joe had walked back to get the carriage and Sarah's few, simple things, which he brought to Sarah at her new place. Mary and Joe kissed Sarah goodbye and left to make the long trip back to the village by the lake. The journey home took a little longer. Joe and Mary were tired after the scurry to Boston. Although Joe had spring chores and seeds to plant, it took them several days to retrace their journey.

The trip had been expensive. Every livery stop charged to feed the horses, charged for the horses rented, and charged a deposit for the return of the horses. Joe finally quit complaining about the horses when he got his team back from the first livery stop they had made when they left. They had gone through most of the seed money. Joe was too proud to ask his brother for money, but Mary knew their Quaker friends would somehow find extra seeds, and they would get their crops in.

When Mary and Joe got to town late Sunday afternoon, there was a ruckus going on. The owner of the woolen mill was arguing with a farmer. The mill owner was upset and was having trouble arguing, as he seemed to be in the middle of a coughing spell.

The farmer was screaming, "You killed my cows!" He held out the bells of his two, prized milk cows.

The mill owner knew that he had dumped a bad batch of chemicals the previous night. He had added too much arsenic to the copper solution. The color was useless, so he dumped the whole batch.

The mill owner denied the accusations. "I did nothing," he said, coughing. He glanced at Mary and Joe. "It was the witch, that Sarah. She did it, just like she cursed those fields."

Joe hated to lie, especially on the Sabbath, but he spoke firmly. "The girl is not a witch but merely disturbed. We have delivered her to bedlam at a hospital faraway where she will stay."

The people in the crowd felt relieved. Many believed that was where Sarah belonged. The crowd no longer addressed Mary and Joe, and they scurried home while the others turned back to the argument. The mill owner was coughing violently, and specks of blood hit the ground.

The farmer was disgusted. "I would beat you and burn your mill, but I can see that your treachery is about to consume you." After that utterance, the farmer left.

During the next few weeks, the mill owner began acting stranger and stranger. He started sleeping in the woolen mill, breathing even more of the vapors. Before long, the man was totally insane. One night in his crazed state, he felt he was going to get even with the farmer. He took all of the chemicals he had and started dumping them out the back door and into the river. The last barrel was full to the top. It tipped over prematurely, and the contents began running over the floor. The fallen barrel hit the lantern that the mill owner had placed on the floor near the door. The whole scene erupted into flames, consuming the owner and the mill. The poisons were extremely potent and killed farm animals all the way downstream. The chemicals passed through North Village, killing the cows that grazed downstream. The farmer below North Village thought it was from the mill in North Village, unaware that it was a mill at Potanopa. That night, in a state of frenzy, he snuck up to North Village and burned the mill.

The backward locals in North Village were stunned. They did not know about poisons and potions but did remember talk of the Chief's curse. They heard of the fire at the lake and the path of death down the river, ending with animal loss and the burning of the mill in North Village. The backwards village folk saw this as the wrath of the spirits from the river, directed at them.

The villagers remembered that a few days before this had happened, an Indian had come to North Village and drank at the tavern. The Indian was tall and strong and had a long rifle. Fortunately, the brave could not read. For some reason, the post office in North Village was named Paugus, the name of the brave's father. Had the brave known this, he would have burned down the building. The brave caused quite a stir in the tavern. Many of the patrons tried to talk with the brave, but he remained silent. The brave was so large and burly that none of the intoxicated men in the tavern wanted to raise their fists to him. As the brave rose to leave, he turned at the door and said, "You will soon begin to fear the spirits of the mist."

One of the men in the tavern had a strange feeling. He had been with Chamberlain when his men had killed Chief Paugus at Lovell Lake in Maine. Something was familiar about the lines spoken by the Indian, and his profile was somewhat recognizable. The next morning, the man traveled to Chamberlain's house in Groton. "There was an Indian brave at the tavern last night. He had a strange resemblance to Chief Paugus, and he made a threat to North Village."

"Thank you," Chamberlain said after listening to the story. "Here are a few coins for your trouble. Buy a round of drinks at the tavern tonight at sunset."

Chamberlain saw this as no idle threat and took his long rifle off the wall. The rifle had always fired accurately - the rifle that killed Paugus. With the rifle cleaned, the aged Chamberlain hid himself in the shadows of the brush near the trail to his house. In front of him, the setting sun illuminated the trail. Chamberlain's body might have been old, but his mind was sharp and he had set the perfect trap. (14)

As they clinked their glasses in the tavern at sunset to toast Chamberlain and his victory in Maine, while the last of the light faded in the west, the brave appeared in the trail. The brave looked like Paugus, himself. Chamberlain gasped but steadied his old hand and fired a shot. The bullet passed through the heart of the brave and killed him instantly. Chamberlain was a hero once more - this time for killing the son of Paugus. The following night, at the tavern in North Village, they toasted Chamberlain once again.

A few days later, when the fires and animal deaths had occurred, the people of North Village believed it was an act of revenge from the brave. They began to fear the mist even more. Although few ever spoke about it, they all knew about the Chief's curse.

Sarah's visit to Boston was turning out well. Samuel said, "Sarah, you must be very tired from your long journey and having to be wrapped up like that. There is bread and jam in the cupboard, as well as salted fish from the sea and dried beef from the farms way out in the country where the water is pure. I will see what you like, and I will take care of your needs. Your bedroom is in that room, and I have taken care that no fabric has any dyes or toxins."

Samuel had begun to believe that the workers were sick from the chemicals they handled and not because they were a sickly bunch to begin with. Sarah entered the room and adored it. The room had a selection of beautifully crafted clothes made of natural un-dyed materials. "What are these?" asked Sarah, running her hand over some wonderful, light and flowing garments.

"That is made from silk, which is made by silkworms."

"Silkworms? It's from worms?" asked Sarah.

"Yes, Sarah. Silk is a natural fabric, which comes from the Orient.

Sarah was inquisitive. "Orient?"

"Be patient, young lady. You will learn *that* and *more* in your lessons," Samuel explained.

"May I clean up and go sit in the middle of the pool?"

"Yes, Sarah. This ell and the backyard are yours to use whenever and however you wish. I am tired and am going to retire for the evening. The sun will set soon, and I have to be at the hospital early in the morning to help the sick."

Samuel left, and Sarah cleansed herself using a white, cotton towel and water from the well. Then she gave in to temptation, and she put on the flowing, white, silk nightgown and the silk top, which was hanging with it. The silk felt wonderful on her skin, and the fabric flowed when she walked. Sarah was pleased when she walked; the flowing fabric gave her the feeling of being back in the mist, as it swirled around her. Silently, she slipped out the door and approached the reflection pond. Samuel happened to be looking out of his bedroom window as he prepared for bed. He saw Sarah wearing the silk with the fabric flowing behind her. As she stepped across the rocks to the table in the center, he seemed to notice a mist coming up out of the water and gathering around her.

"Damn, tired, old eyes," Samuel said as he rubbed his eyes and went to bed.

Sarah sat in the center of the reflecting pool. The mist gathered around her, rising from the water, but it was not like the mist of the Nissitissit, filled with great spirits. The water was from the well. However, even the water from wells contains the essence of life. The mist settled on Sarah, cleansing her skin. The spirits within her were restful. Quietly, Sarah sat there like a queen on her thrown as the mist caressed her. After a while, Sarah got up and started to leave. As she left the pool, the mist began to dissipate. Some of the mist was captured between the folds of the silk. The fine mist drifted outward as she walked, lingering for a moment in the still, night air and then disappeared.

The following day, Sarah's lessons began. In her living quarters, she had a chalkboard and plenty of chalk. True to his word, Samuel had arranged for a tutor to come by. He was going to teach her basic mathematics. Sarah found it engrossing and put a lot of time into studying. The summer went by quickly. Between studying and her soirees with the mist, Sarah had a pleasant and relaxing time.

Winter came, and Sarah would bundle up in furs to go out during the day and read at the table in the frozen pool. She spent a couple of years being matriculated; before long, she was managing, not only the doctor's personal books, but also, the clinic's record-keeping for the sick and dying workers.

One evening, Samuel approached Sarah. "Tomorrow, your studies will be in chemistry."

"Chemistry?"

"Yes, the mixing of chemicals and elements to form compounds."

During the next year, chemists and scientists were stopping by, explaining the details of compounding and chemical bonding. Samuel was pleased with Sarah's progress. He was determined to put her to work at the clinic somehow, even if it were for research only. Sarah had a good connection with the library. Samuel had found a local boy who ran books back and forth from the Boston Public Library. Samuel rewarded him handsomely, so the boy was always highly motivated.

"Sarah. You are now going to help me with a paper I will someday present to the medical community. I feel the chemicals the workers handle are killing them. With your knowledge of chemistry, you will help me identify these compounds and I will relate them to the symptoms."

For the next few years, Sarah used her knowledge to help Samuel. The spirits inside her began to understand the "White Way Poisons." The spirits and Sarah had been sent, in one last attempt, to study The White Ways and to see if there was a way to stop them. It seemed more white people were in existence than the amount of poisons to kill them. Men were dying in the mills at an extraordinary rate, and there were always others waiting to replace them.

A new color of green paint (Scheele's green) (5), which had become quite popular because of its bright hue, was killing factory workers who made it. Additionally, the men in the wallpaper factories were becoming deathly ill as the popular, brightly flowered wallpaper originated from arsenic compounds, vermilion, and other heavy metals. The chemicals in the factories smelled of dusty mice as the poisons in the air filtered throughout the structure and into the lungs of the workers. On damp nights, which were common in North Village, the humidity would cause any newly hung wallpaper (especially the green wallpaper) to release a poisonous gas into the home. Worldwide, hundreds and hundreds of children died in their bedrooms by breathing the toxic fumes from the gas. (21)

The spirit of Ebb felt sad. He recognized the green paint as the color used on all of the mill houses. The superstitious mill owners felt that the shiny green helped repulse the spirits of the mist. The houses of the mill owners were not in the mist and were painted bright colors. However, because of the superstitions, nearly all the mill owners were covering the walls of their nurseries with this new, shiny, green paper to repel any errant spirits. They were a stupid and superstitious lot, and too many children died in their nurseries in North Village. Ebb's spirit was learning along with Sarah as she took her lessons. Ebb was beginning to comprehend what the Chief had meant about how "he would understand." With what he had learned so far, Ebb could see how all the toxins had engulfed North Village along with the symptoms of some of the poisons. The symptoms seemed eerily close to those of the people in North Village who had died in the so-called, "unusual way."

Sarah studied intently and the years passed. During the last ten years Samuel had noticed that her skin was extremely susceptible to aging. Unknown to Samuel, the spirits of the Nissitissit, which Sarah carried with her, had caused this abnormality. Even the smallest of airborne pollutants caused a reaction to her skin. Though she had been there only ten years, she looked as though she had aged twenty. During this time, Sarah was also gaining the wisdom of the centuries. Nevertheless, with all she had learned, she still saw no way to combat The White Way.

Before long, Samuels's project was complete. The mill owners would be devastated, since the results of the study proved that the mills were killing the workers. The document was quite impressive with all the chemicals and symptoms contained in it. One morning, he presented it to a member of the Medical Board to be considered for their next meeting. The doctor on the Board read it, but instead of submitting it, he took the document to his brother who owned a large mill. He knew this paper would destroy his brother and the whole family, including him, if it were published.

"Don't worry. I will take care of this," said the mill owner to his brother, the doctor.

Later on, just after dark, Samuel was crossing the park to have dinner with Sarah. He loved having dinner with Sarah in her cozy, little ell. Sarah would buy eggs, meat, and vegetables from farmers who did not use the new chemical development called pesticides. Samuel's mind was on dinner when three thugs unexpectedly came out from the bushes. One of them quickly hovered over Samuel. The ruthless assassin instantaneously plunged a thin knife into the doctor's heart. Samuel was dead before he hit the ground.

"Grab the money from his wallet," whispered one of the criminals. "Make it look like a robbery."

In her little ell, Sarah had jumped in pain when the knife entered Samuel. A few moments later, a ruckus began in the park when the body was found. Even before the police came to the door, Sarah knew that Samuel was dead. That night, Sarah packed her canvas bags and left. Lately, she had felt the Nissitissit calling to her. Like the salmon, she was being drawn back to the place of her birth. She headed north during the night and when she reached the ocean she followed the shore for another day and night to the Merrimack River. She got to the river just before dawn. The Merrimack mist was still lingering, awaiting the rising of the sun.

CHAPTER SIX

Sarah was filled with confusion and despair. Her life had never been darker. Her heart belonged to her Indian roots. She had been their last hope and she had failed. Sarah would have killed herself if she had not had the sprit of Ebb within her. If just her life was at stake, the situation would be different, but she could not take another's life even if it was the spirit of a dead man. Sarah had helped Ebb by carrying him, educating him, and helping him understand. Ebb was now able to return the favor. By forcing Sarah to carry on and stay alive, she would then be able to understand. The spirits of the mist had foreseen this, and Ebb and the spirits were there to protect Sarah. Her mission had been a waste of time; she could not find a way to stop the advance of the white men. The spirits knew this, but they had to try. An unlimited amount of white men were seen everywhere. They were like rats spilling out of the cities and ravishing the countryside. They brought diseases from the congested cities with them, spreading death as they came.

The gods of the land reeled at their advance; they had never seen anything like it before. The human horde swarmed the land near the cities, cutting down everything in sight. A large, wooden ship with three masts used the wood from two thousand, mature trees. All over New England, the woods had been cleared. The creatures of the woods retreated as the white man advanced. With the white men came the rats - the scavengers and the pestilence of The White Way.

Sarah sat by the end of the Merrimack at the northern tip of Plum Island where it met the ocean. She was mumbling and beginning to cry. "I failed everyone. The spirits and the wise, old woman taught me the old ways. I had learned the secrets of the ages and how water was the cradle of life and how all life depended on water to live. Now look…" Sarah broke down in tears. She looked out at the sad river. "They poison the water they need to live. They poison the very cradle of life…they will kill us all. I have studied their ways and there is no stopping them. Their appetite is insatiable."

Sarah sat crying for a while, and the disappearing mist of the Merrimack drew away from her. The spirits of the mist shared Sarah's sadness. The white men had ruined the river. The cradle of life had been turned into a dumping ground.

The morning sun rose. Ebb's spirit wailed at what he saw through Sarah's tear-swollen eyes. He had been to this exact spot with the spirit of the Chief. Gone were the peaceful Indians who had worked the Joppa Flats. The harbor was full of ships. Ebb was learning to see beyond what lay in front of him. What Ebb had seen was not a fleet but the remains of one hundred thousand trees. He thought to himself only one tree in three was good enough for shipboards. Carpenters would use the other two out of three trees as lumber for houses, and the leftover wood would be turned into charcoal for the cities. Ebb realized he was looking at the end result from clearing away one third of a million trees. His spirit reeled at the magnitude of the number.

Through Sarah's senses, Ebb could smell the Joppa Flats. When he had been there with the Chief, the flats had produced a rich, marine smell. However, at this point in time, the flats stunk of excrement and chemicals. The smell was acrid and burned the senses. The foul smell was the smell of death.

As Sarah sat, the sun began to fill the flats with light. Sarah mumbled through her tears. "The river runs red with blood."

In reality, Sarah knew she could quote the chemicals, poisons, and toxins in the red dye that flowed past her. The night before, a mill upstream had released a cauldron of spent dye after getting a new batch of red flannel ready for the drying room. Dead fish were floating by as a result of the batch of poisons that had been released. Sarah rose to begin the long journey up river against the current of The White Way. A trail of many tears lay ahead of her and the spirits within.

While making her way along a road by the river, Sarah heard a wagon behind her and moved out of the way.

"Whoa, there. Whoa." The wagon drew next to her and stopped. "Hey, old woman, can I help you along with a ride?"

Sarah was startled. "Are you talking to me?" Then she remembered that the toxins of the city had greatly aged her outward appearance.

"You're the only one around, and besides, you look like a Quaker."

Sarah turned to look at him and recognized the simple garments worn by Quakers. At the same time, she noticed the wagon had never been painted. She was about to get in, but she cautiously spotted the cargo. Oilcloth was wrapped around it and bound it tight. Another piece of oilcloth was fashioned in a tent above the cargo.

"What is your cargo, kind sir?"

"Ahh. Well, Ma'am, it's kegs of black powder."

"And how does a Quaker come to have a load of black powder on his wagon? Are you not afraid of the danger and the exposure to chemicals?"

"The exposure is minimal. The kegs and the bungs have been coated with molten beeswax to keep the powder dry. The kegs are quite safe."

Sarah was inquisitive. "If it is safe, why are they paying you instead of shipping on the usual freight wagons?"

"I am hauling it because the usual freight companies are very busy. Also, the fee the companies wanted to charge was quite substantial. They hired me for half that amount to take it there with my team."

Sarah looked at the Quaker. "Well, that is why *they* are doing it. What is the reason *you* are doing this deed?"

"Well, Ma'am, my youngest is sick, and we rightly need money. The pay to deliver this will supply us with money for medicine for my youngest and still leave us with enough to live on for the rest of the year. To do so is a sin, but I am stuck between what is right for my family and what is right for my beliefs. My family has always come first, and I love my son," the driver said mournfully. "I am making camp tonight just north of Lowell, and tomorrow I head cross country to North Village."

Sarah asked, "North Village, on the Nissitissit?"

"Yes, do you know the place?" he asked.

"I know that it gates the valley of the Nissitissit. I know that all the water from forty thousand acres of land runs through this sacred spot," she said with a sigh. "But what of this ride you offer? You are like Satan, himself, offering me a ride to the river valley I seek. In order to get my ride, I have to ride atop a batch of poisonous explosives. It is a double-edged sword that you offer me."

"Ride with me, sister. The black powder will get there whether we deliver it or not. Save your tired body the strain, and take a ride with me. The powder is sealed and cannot escape. I have taken great pains at keeping my wagon pure."

Sarah was feeling desperate. The rain in the cities was toxic to her skin. The dust in the roads contained the residuals of spilled chemicals and burned her feet. Her outward appearance matched the gloom of her depression. Although she was still of childbearing age, she looked as if she were seventy. She made a concession and took the ride but was sick inside. She had yielded to sin. Her depression deepened as her sense of failure increased.

The driver got down and helped her into the wagon. "Thank you. I am Sarah."

"Glad to meet you, Ma'am. I'm Caleb. Where are you going?"

"Lake Potanopa and then up one of the tributaries," Sarah responded flatly.

Caleb looked puzzled. "Why there?"

"I am returning home," Sarah replied slowly as she watched the road while they traveled along.

Caleb could sense her anguish and silently drove the team. Only his occasional commands to the team broke the silence. Soon they were traveling through Lowell. The squalor of the mill workers' homes made Sarah even sadder. The houses were jammed between the mills. The dark, nasty smoke from the stacks was being blown around the mill houses. Children were playing amidst the toxic gasses.

"How do they survive?" asked Sarah.

"What do you mean?"

"They live in their own swill," responded Sarah. "They killed all the Indians. They killed the water and the air. They killed the fish. They killed the wild animals. They killed all the trees. They kill… kill…kill… They torture the earth with plows and pour chemicals into it to make it do what they want. What was once proud, natural and beautiful is now gone, yet they survive; they survive against all odds. Why don't they just die?" Sarah began to cry.

"I'm sorry, Ma'am. I can see you are very moved by what used to be and that you are very troubled by what is."

"It's much more than that," said Sarah. "I don't have the time or strength to try and explain. Just let me sit quietly atop this load of poison while we make our way along."

"Poison, Ma'am?"

"Yes. The nitrates in the black powder poison the body and mind."

"We have a wagonload of poison?"

"In a way," replied Sarah. "It is made with substances which poison the earth and water."

Caleb became as depressed as Sarah, and they rode a few more miles north without speaking. They made a silent camp for the night, before heading west. In the morning, they broke camp, in silence once again, and headed west towards North Village."

"I'm sorry, Ma'am. I'm sorry for both of us. Life has boxed us in and forced us to choose against our ways."

"It's not your fault. You let your morals slide, in taking the load, and I let my morals slide by taking the ride. We are both guilty, so let us not beat each other or ourselves with our sins. Let us complete our tasks and try to do better in the future. There is no way out of this for either of us."

The morning passed, and before long they were heading down the hill to North Village, past the new school with its brand new bell. At the time, North Village was the busiest and richest part of Pepperell. North Village was the only hamlet for many miles that could afford not only a bell, but also a new brick building with a bell tower. The people of North Village were eager to show the world that they were as good as anyone.

As she rode along, Sarah observed that all of the mill workers' cottages had been painted the new, popular color of green. Known as Scheele's green, the vivid color was produced from oxidizing copper with arsenic sulfide. The same color was killing the factory workers who had made it. Sarah wondered why they had painted all the buildings that color.

Caleb placed the wagon in one of the buildings near the end of the mill, and Sarah thanked him for the ride. The shed was past the end of the mill. Every mill had a chemical shed. Sarah could sense the evil in it. The shed was situated away from the mill, beyond the dam and Paugus Pond, and downstream from everyone, so that if it leaked, they would be safe.

"Caleb, see that shed?"

"Yes. What about it?"

"It contains chemicals and poisons"

"That's why it is downstream," stated Caleb.

"Well, is not one village's tail water the headwater for the next village? There are five villages upstream from here, and we are in their tail water," stated Sarah.

"What are you getting at?"

"What I am trying to tell you is not to drink the water from the river or any well near it."

North Village was humming; the mill was cutting lumber, and the bustle of industry was in the air. Sarah could see the millwheel from the road - the waterwheel, wet and gleaming in the sun. The mill was the last building furthest away from Prescott Street and was nestled into the side of a hill, just before the river valley became steep and narrow. The picture was classic New England - the river and the mill; the look was pretty and pristine.

Sarah drifted back a couple of years in her mind, when she had been completing her studies. The engineering project in front of her had momentarily broken Sarah's depression. Lately, Sarah had begun talking to herself. Actually, she had begun talking to Ebb and the spirits as if they were right there next to her.

"That type of waterwheel is a breast wheel." Sarah continued. "It's used in mills where the average drop is about five feet. The water hits the wheel at about the height of the axle, falls into the troughs on the wheel, and travels for one-quarter revolution. If they had more drop in the river, they could have used an overshot waterwheel, where the water hits the top of the wheel and travels for one-half rotation. The overshot is twice as efficient as a breast wheel and also gets one hundred percent of the kinetic of the falling water."

The foreman of the mill was watching her talk to herself as Caleb, who was a short distance away, called out. "Did you say something, Sarah?"

Sarah noticed the mill worker looking at her and called back. "No, I was just thanking you for the ride." After that, Sarah walked on.

She found the local store and stood in front of it until the owner came outside. "May I help you, Madam?" the owner asked.

"Yes, sir. You may help. The day is so nice that I did not want to go inside but hoped you might go inside for me and gather together my needs and put them into this sack." Sarah handed him a canvas bag.

"Why, sure Madam. Tell me what you need, and I will go inside. It is such a nice day that I can understand why you want to be outside."

"Thank you, sir. I need several dozen fish hooks, a small hand saw, a small hatchet, two flint and steel kits, one-hundred feet of white, braided fishing line, fifty feet of every size cotton twine you have, fifty feet of one-quarter-inch hemp rope, a dozen assorted needles, two spools of white thread, three yards of white, cotton fabric, two yards of white canvas, two pounds of tea, a pound of salt, and one last thing."

"What is that, Madam?"

"Do you sell Quaker goods on consignment?"

He knew he did not like the looks of her. Now he knew why. "Yes, we sell some Quakers' goods on consignment. What do you seek?"

"I wish oats, grown by a Quaker."

"The oats from the farm down below are much plumper and sweeter. Are you sure you don't want them instead?"

"No thank you, sir. I will have five pounds of Quaker Oats."

The Quakers had managed to live long lives by drinking pure water and eating only naturally grown foods. When they traveled, they bought only food grown and prepared by Quakers, even if they had to identify themselves and risk persecution. Most people in the Nissitissit Valley were Puritans and hated the Quakers. The simple-minded, backwoods people thought that Quaker women could foretell the future. They thought all Quaker women were witches.

The storeowner went inside, and a few moments later, he was at the door with her canvas bag packed with goods. "That will be three-fifty, Ma'am."

Sarah handed him a five-dollar gold piece, which she had taken from the things she packed in Boston, and put in her purse. As she took the coin out, she made sure the storeowner saw the purse was empty.

"My uncle's brother gave me this as a gift when I left last week. Sure could have used another," Sarah said disarmingly.

"Yeah, well, we all could use a little more," replied the owner flatly.

"Sir, please bring me only coins for change, no paper."

"Yes, Ma'am." He came back with her change, and she made sure he saw her put it back into the empty purse. "Your bags are heavy and many. How do you intend to travel?"

"I am traveling up the river valley. I have supplies and plenty of time before fall," Sarah said, trying to be friendly. "I am going to carry half of the load north for three hours, walk back to get the other half, and then bring that forward. That will make for a good day's work."

The storeowner, never wanting to miss a sale, made Sarah an offer. "I can get you a boy and a horse for fifty cents to take you one day's journey north."

"No thank you, sir. I wish to travel the river on foot. May I leave the package I just bought from you on your front porch and return for it in six hours?"

"Sure, Ma'am, but I need to ask a question. How does a Quaker woman come to be riding into North Village atop a load of black powder?" asked the storekeeper in a mocking tone, beginning to show his dislike of Quakers.

"I was desperate for a ride and would not be near that poison otherwise, sir."

He looked quizzical. "Poison? That's not poison. It is an explosive!"

"Sir, it is made with nitrates and, if you use it near the river, it will poison the water."

The storekeeper was becoming more annoyed "What kind of madness do you talk about, woman? How could you, a woman, know about such things? I will not hear of such talk. Take your baggage and go. Your parcel will be here when you return."

Now Sarah was back to feeling depressed. "Why will no one listen to me?"

As she left the store, the owner quietly answered the question. "Because you are a witch. All Quaker women are witches." (16)

Sarah shouldered the bags that she had been traveling with and went down Prescott Street; she then turned left onto North Street. After walking about a mile, she saw a cart path on the left leading back towards the river. She headed down the narrow lane to the meadows upstream from North Village. The dam in North Village had added water to lush lowlands, making it a rich and fertile dale. Sarah found a spot with plentiful grass and hid her bags in the middle of the grassy area. She was on the top of a small knoll amidst the meadows. Hurriedly, Sarah turned and headed back into town for her other package. She was able to walk faster and arrived back in town before long. Just before she came into town, William, the foreman from the mill had gone into the store.

"Hey, there is a package on your porch."

"I know. That Quaker Witch left it there earlier today and will be back for it."

"What is this talk of witches?" asked William. "You know I don't believe in that stuff. You people are queer to worry about such things. There are many Quakers beginning to live in the area. They can't all be witches. She is just some confused, old woman. I saw her standing and talking to herself by the mill this morning."

"Be careful what you say. There she is, coming down Prescott Street as we speak. Step back in the shadow here, so she can not see us."

They both watched her through the window from a dark corner of the store as she picked up her package and walked off, out of sight. William said, "I don't believe in witches or any of that nonsense. All of you should be ashamed of yourselves, painting everything green to repel the evil spirits of the mist. How ridiculous!" He accentuated it by spitting on the floor.

William went back to the mill for the last few hours of the workday. His job, every Friday after the men went home, was to adjust and grease the bearings on the mill shafts. This required leaving the sluice open and the waterwheel turning. William was working while nipping from a bottle in his back pocket, thinking about the fun ahead when he would be playing darts in the tavern. For the time being, he was enjoying his work and the bottle. When the drive shafts were done, so was his bottle. Therefore, he went out to the sluice to close it. The mist was building on Paugus Pond and the boards were wet. As William leaned forward to close the sluice, he lost his balance, falling into the mist-shrouded water. He came up once for air but could not swim and drowned.

An old timer, terrified of the mist, was on his way home from the tavern and was crossing the bridge. He could see the mist and the mill. He saw William lean forward and disappear into the mist. The old timer burst through the door of the tavern. "A misty hand reached up from the river and grabbed William, the mill foreman, and dragged him down into the water and mist. Then, when he came up for air, the mist pressed him below the water and drowned him."

The tavern went silent. Then, one of the younger men spoke. "Ah, you old lush. The rum is in your eyes."

The old man looked serious. "May I never have another drink in this place if I am lying."

The tavern was silent again, until the storeowner spoke with a shaky voice. "There was a Quaker witch at the mill this morning, and William overheard her uttering a curse. He came to my store laughing about it. I told him to take it seriously, but he laughed. The witch also told me about poisoning the water of the river with night rights or something. I think she meant that death would come at night."

The men grabbed torches and headed down to the mill. The oil lamps remained lit, and the mill shafts were still turning, but William was nowhere to be seen. "Close that sluice, so his body can't float downstream. Take the torches, and look for him," ordered the tavern owner.

The men went up and down both sides of Paugus Pond with torches but found no body. The mist was building up heavily, and the men were panicking from the condensation on their faces. Terror was building amongst them. Then, they all heard it. An ear-splitting scream broke the silence of the night. It sounded like a woman, but, at the same time, it sounded like many voices. In fact, it seemed as if it were thousands of voices. One's body, as well as one's ears, felt the volume. The men abruptly stopped with mouths and eyes wide open. Their bodies shook in terror. The doors to the mill houses flew open with women and children clustered in the doorways, their faces full of fear. Small children began to cry. The mist suddenly thickened and swirled around them, as if a breeze had blown, but the leaves of the trees remained motionless.

Richard, one of the men in the group, was terrified. "I see shapes in the mist. Oh, dear God, Almighty, save me. Get me out of here."

One of the other men shouted out. "All right, m… m… men, we can look for him in the morning. The sluice is closed, and his body can't go anywhere. We will find him in the m… m… morning, during the light of day."

All of a sudden, the mist was the thickest they had ever seen. The women in the doorways saw their men disappear into the thick mist. The men were petrified. They were running and falling as they thrashed their way through the mist. Branches and brush were cutting their legs and faces as they ran in terror. Many of them dropped or lost their torches while in flight. The mist felt toxic and burned the exposed parts of their bodies. When they breathed the mist, it seemed to burn their lungs, making them scream even louder.

The married men fled to their homes, slamming the doors behind them. The wives were glad to see their men, but they could not remain calm. They were not versed at dealing with the fear they saw on the faces of their rugged husbands, many of whom were bleeding. They stripped their husbands of their reeking clothes and threw them in the wash pile. The smell of the clothes permeated the house as the doors and windows were closed tightly against the onset of the mist. The entire valley had a strange smell. Large doses of medicinal rum had been dispersed throughout the village that night.

The single men returned to the tavern with great haste and numbed their wounds with copious amounts of liquor. They talked in worried tones about the visit of the witch and what it had meant. Some also spoke in hushed voices about their fathers' tales. The older generation had told them about the curse on the original settlers for slaughtering the tribe. They had explained how the original settlers had already died under strange circumstances. The men drank and talked for hours. Since the following day was Saturday, the men chose to sleep on the tables and the benches, finding strength in numbers, rather than walk home in the mist that night.

Sarah had been gone for twenty years, and upon her return, she was in the same predicament - being thought of as a witch. Sarah was learning that life is a series of complex circles. You chase after something better, but in the end you are always back where you had started. For Sarah, the circle of events that involved her leaving, going to the city, studying under the best, and being treated like a gifted soul, was over. She was back in the valley and back to being a witch. She just did not know it yet.

CHAPTER SEVEN

Sarah did not see the men in the shadows of the store talking about her as she picked up her last package. She was heading back up North Street, down the path she had taken before, and out to the knoll in the meadows. Sarah was glad that she had taken the time to hide her baggage because when she returned, she could hear voices drifting across the meadow. It sounded as if three men were heatedly arguing back and forth. She could not quite hear the words, but she could see smoke filtering through the trees from the direction of the voices. Sarah sat for a while and listened to the men argue. They went on and on without stopping. While sitting, she ate some dried fish, a bit of cheese, and some crackers and listened to the men argue with each other.

After a while, Sarah wondered what they could be arguing about, since they had been screaming frantically for more than an hour. The wise, old woman had taught her how to move silently over the land. Because the sun was nearing the western horizon, Sarah thought that she would see what was causing the commotion. She glided towards the voices and was heading toward the river as dusk approached. As she got near the river, the mist began to rise. The air was tense as the men continued to scream at one another. To Sarah, two of the men looked insane, and the third looked terrified as he carried out their orders.

They were starting to break down camp and were packing heavy chests upon two, rugged wagons. In the morning, they would walk to the next farm and get the horses that they boarded a few months ago.

The men had set up camp at the mouth of Sucker Brook, which flowed from Pepperell Center. They had a sluice made out of lumber from the mill in North Village and a rough, low shanty. One end was open with a huge fire pit in front. Sarah was positioned directly across from them with the mist swirling around her and concealing her presence.

Daniel shouted to the third man. He appeared as if he were a servant following orders from Daniel and the other man. "Take that quicksilver and put it in the root cellar in the side of the hill, in case we ever come back here to look for gold. And make haste, for tomorrow we leave, and your indentured servitude will be over."

"Yes, sir," the servant replied as he made several trips to the crude root cellar.

He was carrying clay jars with ninety-eight pounds of quicksilver in each. The jars weighed two pounds, so each two-handled jug weighed one hundred pounds. Six were left, out of the original eight with which they had started out. When Calvin and Daniel had begun in the spring, the two brothers had used two jugs. The contents of two jugs were poured into the sluice they made. A developing theory in crude gold mining speculated that the mercury would settle into the troughs in the sluice. It was theorized that smaller gold particles, which might have been washed out by the action of the water, would be attracted to the mercury. The gold particles were assumed to have settled to the bottom of the pool of mercury. They would remain in the trough.

The brothers had done some mining for metals when they had first arrived. They had mined a pile of crushed stone to run through the sluice. After running the sluice for many hours, much of the mercury was gone and had been replaced by stone. The brothers had scraped the paste out and put it in the smelter. The paste released an evil smoke, when heated, which had filtered out to the river. When all the mercury had evaporated, the brothers spooned out what was left. Instead of gold, they found worthless pieces of stone. The servant remembered how he hated the smell and had stayed upwind from the whole operation.

"Hey, quit daydreaming and give me a hand," Daniel ordered.

"Yes, sir." The servant helped load heavy chests into the back of the wagons.

"Move it along. Tomorrow you are free, and Calvin and I will be headed back to England with our metals."

They packed everything except the sleep rolls. Calvin and Daniel were arguing once more. Being brothers, they were used to quarreling, but lately they argued all the time at an ever-increasing volume and intensity.

"Light the campfire," ordered Calvin. "We must have it burning bright before the mist comes." On the nights when the mist appeared, the three of them would sleep in the shanty with a roaring fire on the open side.

The servant stooped down to push around the ashes from the previous night. He found some active coals and brought the fire back to life. He thought about how much he hated this place and felt as if he were living in hell.

"What about the sluice and the chemicals?" asked Daniel.

"That was your stupid idea. We spent all that time building a sluice and hauling all that mercury here, all for nothing. If it were not for that rare, crystalline arsenic that I found, we would have nothing. The chests containing those ultra-pure crystals will be worth a small fortune when we return to England!" screamed Calvin, nearly in the face of Daniel. They were both full of anger and riddled with insanity.

With a sudden shift in mood, Daniel smiled. "Hey, I have an idea."

"*Now* what?"

"Let's sell the metals in Boston. We know the process. We can go to some paint and paper factories to show them how brilliant the greens are when they're produced using this rare form of arsenic. We can say we are selling to them exclusively to get the highest price, but we will sell a chest to each and then sail to London, unencumbered by the chests." (11)

Calvin was ready for an argument, but even in his madness, he could see the logic. "Hey, that's a good idea."

Daniel looked at the sluice. The sections were piled together, and jugs of chemicals, which were going to be used for gold, sat on top, unused. "What about this?"

"I'll show you what to do." Calvin screamed, looking crazed as he hit a jug of flammable chemicals with the camp axe and threw a burning log from the fire onto the sluice, which erupted into flames.

Watching them, Sarah became horrified and screamed out, "NO!" The spirits amplified her voice to a profound volume. Her voice sounded as if many voices had spoken.

The three men stopped and looked. In an instant, they could see Sarah.

"You are poisoning the river," Sarah said angrily.

"What is that, a witch?" screamed Daniel as he reached for his gun.

The mist gathered around Sarah, and the poisonous smoke from the sluice forced the men to retreat up the dirt road to higher ground. The smoke was heavy from the vaporized mercury and chemicals as it followed the downhill gradient of the river towards North Village. When the smoke hit Paugus Pond, it settled in and spread out over the men who were looking for the body of William.

Sarah arrived back for her goods. The mist kept a slight breeze blowing the toxins away from her. Her heart was heavy from the massive pollution she had witnessed. She felt sick from the experience. She mumbled aloud, "Death might not be fast in coming, but anyone who breathed that mist is now condemned. What a tragedy it is, the horror of The White Way."

Early the next morning, Sarah started out with half her load. Once again, she headed north. She made it as far as the outskirts of West Hollis, before halting the daily advance and returning to retrieve the other half of her gear. As she was shouldering the second half of her load, she could hear the sound of black powder explosions echoing through the valley.

Squire Heald's son had ordered the black powder. The squire had started a mine on the side of a hill, just north of Heald Pond in the headwaters of Gulf Brook. He had started the mine some years before but had found no gold or silver. From the start, the mine seemed to be cursed. One of the mineworkers' sons had gone to bring his father a forgotten lunch and had run down the steep part of the road, before the pond. The child tripped and fell, breaking his neck. From then on, that hill was called Breakneck Hill. (16)

The Squire persisted in his search for gold and silver. Squire Heald had not told anyone that they were following a vein of arsenic crystals, in anticipation of finding gold. Arsenic was often found in conjunction with gold, and many thought that certain kinds of arsenic crystal would act as a precursor for finding gold. The Squire had been following a vein of such crystals when the toxic mine air had ruined his good health. In later years, his son became caught up in "gold fever" after listening to his father. Against the protest of his sick father, he reopened the mine. However, he promised his father he would close it again, if he were to find no gold after the wagonload of black powder was all gone. Hence, the Squire's son started blowing the original mine deeper into the side of the hill, still following the vein of crystals that had poisoned his father. Between the chemical poisoning from handling black powder nitrates and breathing the nasty air, the Squire's son decided his father had been right. After the first load of black powder was used, he abandoned the mine, along with their family's dream of wealth flowing from the ground.

Sarah could hear the explosions as she carried the last half of her load towards West Hollis. Her heart grew heavier, knowing that the black powder had come from the wagon she had ridden in the day before. She continued on her journey and by late afternoon returned to her first load from the morning. Sarah sat for a moment near the edge of a road. She could see a Quaker coming along on his wagon. Sarah walked to the road as the wagon approached.

"Excuse me, sir. Tomorrow is the Sabbath. Do you know of anywhere a Quaker woman might find some clean water and a hot meal and a place to worship in the morning?"

"Whoa. Whoa there, horse. Well, madam, I can tell you are also a Quaker. You are invited to my house. I have a fine well on the side of the hill away from the river. My farm has its own clean brook from the watershed I own upstream. Please, old woman, put your baggage in the wagon and come home for supper."

"Thank you, sir. Could you grab the heavy bag in the tall grass?"

The young man jumped down and threw all of her baggage into the back of the wagon. He observed protocol with the old woman and only made polite conversation about what they passed on their way. He had learned from his religion to help people without invading their privacy or dignity.

Sarah accepted the ride and was quiet. She was troubled by what had happened the previous night and wondered what kind of a day North Village was having. As it turned out, that day in the village was bizarre and frightful. After milling around uphill from the poisonous smoke, the two Englishmen and the servant had decided that they would head to the neighboring farm for their horses. They arrived well before dawn and rousted the farmer and his family. The farmer was annoyed at being woken up so early but was glad to be rid of the two teams. They had consumed large amounts of water and feed, and he had spent a lot of time caring for them when he had his own animals to tend.

Calvin handed the farmer a twenty-dollar gold piece, which was a small fortune for a few months of grain, hay and water. "Here. This is for your time and trouble."

"Thank you, sir." Even though he was not happy about being awakened, the farmer was grinning from ear to ear.

"Excuse me, sirs," said the servant. "While you have your purse out, might I ask you, in the presence of these two witnesses, to end my servitude and also give me the three gold coins, as promised when we set off for this land?" Thereupon, he pulled out a piece of oilcloth from beneath his shirt and unwrapped it to reveal a copy of the servitude document signed by the brothers and him.

Daniel was not totally insane and could see that they were not going to be able to convince the man to go back with them, no matter what they said. Therefore, he and Calvin signed the agreement and had the farmer witness it. "Here are your three gold coins," Calvin said as he threw the coins into the servant's hand.

"Thank you, sirs!" cried the ex-servant as he caught the coins and ran off. He rewrapped the agreement in the oilcloth and put it back beneath his shirt as he ran.

"What's wrong with *him*?" asked the farmer.

Calvin replied, "He's had enough. That's all."

The farmer noticed that the two Englishmen looked older and rowdier than a few months earlier when they had arrived. Their eyes were wild with insanity. He looked briefly at the two men by the rising sun, and feeling the presence of evil, he ended the conversation. "Well, thank you for your business. We must prepare for our upcoming day."

The farmer shuffled his wife and children back inside and went to the barn with the men to help hook up the teams. Moments later, while the two men led the teams down the road and back to their camp, he breathed a sigh of relief. By this time, the fire was out. Luckily, the two loaded wagons had been out of the direction of the wind from the blaze. Neither one was damaged nor contaminated by the smoke. Daniel could see that the vegetation along the river was dying, and dead fish were floating along its edge. He suspected the chemicals were the cause and hoped the smoke did not reach North Village. The men hooked up the teams and began heading back, knowing they had to pass through the village on their way out of the area.

Many of the people in North Village woke up with hangovers, which made it even harder for them to deal with what was outside. As they looked around, they saw a frightening path of death coming down both sides of Paugus Pond. Singed leaves hung from the trees, and hundreds of dead fish were floating in the pond. A stench of death was in the air as the sun began to hit the decaying fish.

Richard had gained his composure from the night before and was gathering together the men to look for William's body. Once again, they searched Paugus Pond, but this time they had hooks on the end of long poles. The hooks were used to snag logs out of the pond. They worked the two banks slowly and carefully but could not find the body of William, the unfortunate foreman.

Around midday, the two wagons of the Englishmen approached

town. Daniel and Calvin were driving the teams along while arguing loudly. As they neared town, Daniel motioned for Calvin to be quiet. At the last bend in the road, the river was nearby. They could see the path of death had, in fact, proceeded down to the village.

"Quiet, Calvin. They can't know we did this. Not yet. Let's just get through town without an issue."

As they crossed the bridge heading towards the school, Daniel and Calvin watched the villagers fishing the banks of Paugus Pond with their long hooks from the mill. Daniel was puzzled and pulled back on the reins. "Whoa, team. Whoa. What are you looking for?" he shouted to one of the Englishmen.

Richard yelled back. "We are looking for the body of poor William who fell in the mill pond and drowned last night after a witch passed through the village. Then, she must have sent this cursed fog which choked our lungs and burned the vegetation."

Daniel quickly realized he had a convenient alibi to use for his innocence. "Yeah, we saw her last night. Was she an old woman dressed in white with wild, white hair?"

Richard put down his hook and walked over to the wagons. "Yes, that was she. What did she do to you?"

Sarah had done nothing. Whatever happened, they had done to themselves, but once again, she was accused of being a witch. Repeatedly, she had become the object of ridicule. Luck had always been against her, or maybe the spirits had arranged the situation as part of their plan. Making sure she would never become a part of them was one way to keep her from being tainted by society and The White Way.

Daniel continued. "She said that poison, poison, that uh... she was going to poison the river, whereupon she let this nasty vapor rise from the river. We fled the valley in fear and went and got our teams and packed this morning and left. Our gear and our wagons were away from the river and we were so afraid that we did not go back to the camp before leaving. Right, Calvin?"

"Uh, yeah, poison vapors. It was terrifying." Calvin would say no more and looked back at the pond, knowing that he and his brother had caused all the death and destruction. 'The hell with them,' he thought. 'They are just backwards locals, not worth a damn.'

"Well, we got to go," Daniel said abruptly. "We still have all our original equipment, and the wagons are heavy. We wish to make Hollis Village before sunset and be away from all of this. We will try our mining elsewhere. That spot was a bust. There was no gold or silver."

Richard asked one, last question. "What happened to that servant fellow you arrived with, the one who came to town occasionally for supplies?"

"His debt was paid, and we released him at the farm on Brookline Road where our horses were boarded," Daniel replied. "We had the farmer witness it. We paid the fellow, and he took off towards Pepperell Center at a run. He was petrified of the witch he saw last night. Unless you have something else to inquire about, Calvin and I must leave immediately. We have had enough of this cursed valley. Giddy up."

Richard watched as the heavily laden wagons clambered up the hill and out of town. "They look pretty heavy to me, but I don't see much gear," he mumbled out loud. Turning back to the river, Richard shouted upstream. "Jeremiah, have you found poor William's body?"

"No. He must be caught on the bottom or he went through the sluice."

'The flow below the dam is slow, and he could not have floated downstream. The only place he could be is in Paugus Pond,' thought Richard. He shouted back to Jeremiah. "I'm going to get the mill owner. We need to drain the pond. These fish and poor William are turning the pond rancid."

Richard left and returned a while later with the mill owner. "Sir, I want to drain Paugus Pond and try and find poor William. Also, the fish kill is really starting to smell," said Richard.

Aaron, the owner of the mill, thought for a moment. "Well, you were William's assistant, so I am making you mill Foreman. I will pay you the same as what William got. Take all the boards out of the sluice, and put the winter grate in. Tomorrow is Sunday, and we will have a service, here at the mill, for William. Meanwhile, keep the men looking for the body. Keep them busy, and don't let them dwell on this witch nonsense."

"Yes, Aaron."

"Then, on Monday we will remove the breast wheel and do some maintenance on the wheel and the mill. Paugus Pond should be empty by then. We should have William's body by that time, and things can return to normal. Pick up all those stinking dead fish, and throw them downstream from the dam."

"Yes, sir."

"One last thing."

"Yes, sir. What is it?"

"Go to William's house and tell his father!"

"But, Aaron…"

"Do you want to be foreman or not?"

"Yes."

"Then gather your resolve together and go tell him."

"He is mad as a hatter. I'm afraid he is possessed."

Aaron was getting angry. "I will not tell you again. He was there with my father when they seized the land from the savages. He helped slay the savage beasts and helped establish our claim of the watershed. NOW, GO!"

"Yes, sir."

"And, Richard…"

"Yes?"

"Bring him supplies every week. We owe him that much for this fine watershed."

"Yes, sir." Richard's voice was full of fear and resentment.

The whole village had grown afraid of John for the past few years. The poor, old man had lost his mind. William had brought him food and saw to his needs, but William was gone. Aaron turned and walked back up the hill towards his house. As he climbed up the hill, Aaron could see his fine looking home. He was lucky to be so young and have such a charming house. North Village was quite profitable, and his father had built it with profits from the mill. As he walked, Aaron remembered his father mentioning how hard he had worked with John to establish the mill. At one point, the mill even supplied coffins to all of Pepperell and the surrounding communities. Anytime the death of an indigent with no money occurred, the Selectmen would pay Aaron's father and John for their services. They would pick up the body and embalm it, and then transport the remains to the cemetery on Heald Street. The body would be buried out back in the furthest section. It was situated next to the wetlands of Sucker Brook, which flowed into the Nissitissit and back to North Village.

Aaron felt a slight shiver as he thought about his father, a raving lunatic in an asylum in the city. Five years earlier, he had died there. They told no one about it because they did not want the town to know. When people inquired where he was, Aaron would simply state his father was sick and had taken to his bed. After he died, Aaron smuggled his body back to the house and put the corpse into his bed to appear as if he had died at home. Aaron remembered how foggy that night had been. The mist of the land had combined with the mist of the

Nissitissit. The haze of the combination, which contained the spirits of the river mist, had spun around him that evening. The spirits were there to verify the death. They were there to confirm that Aaron was the only son. They were there to witness the bloodline in their family tree was dwindling. Aaron, alone, would carry the name of the family bloodline.

Five years had passed since John had slipped into insanity. Aaron knew what had driven him insane but told no one. Twenty years earlier, John and Aaron's father owned a business together. They made felt for the winter lining of boots. The shoemaker in the village used the felt for the winter boots that he sold. He would travel to the farms, measuring the feet of his customers, and would then make a fine pair of felt-lined winter boots for each of them. Some of the farmers and their wives treasured the boots and would often order a second pair, so they would always have a dry pair to wear outside. During the winter season, John and Aaron's father had produced the felt inside the shack, at the rear of the mill, for a number of years. When the winter ice caused the mill to close, they labored away making felt.

Aaron remembered bringing a lunch down to his father and John when he was seven. He recalled how the shed had stunk of chemicals and that he would not go inside. The following spring, he was glad when his father and John had decided not to make felt anymore. They poured the chemicals into the river during the spring flood. That summer, they transformed the place into a shoddy shack, where they shredded old rags into a material called shoddy, and shipped it to the newly developed mills in Lowell. Aaron recounted the time, during his first year at the University in Lowell, when he was called home because of his father's insanity. A week before receiving the letter about his father, Aaron had been in school walking across a hall when he detected a familiar smell. The odor was coming from a lab with the door and windows open for ventilation.

He poked his head into the room. "What's that smell?"

"Put on one of those masks on the wall," a professor replied with a muffled voice.

Aaron complied and put on a mask. "I know that smell."

"How so?" the professor asked from behind his mask.

"It smells like what my father used for making felt," answered Aaron.

"You are smelling mercury vapors. We are doing tests on lab rats by exposing them to concentrated vapors of the chemicals used to make hats and uh… I'm sorry, son, used in felt-making." The professor's expression looked sad. He took Aaron's elbow. "Come with me, son, and look at these lab rats. These are the ones we did today, and they show no symptoms. Here are the ones we did last week, and they still seem to appear all right. The cages on the wall are one week apart."

He shuffled Aaron along the wall to the last few cages. As they approached the last one, Aaron noted the rats looked as if they were insane, snarling and slashing at each other. In the last cage, the rats were deceased, posed in horrible positions of death.

"Did you breathe any of the vapors?" asked the professor.

"No, but my father breathed them for a few years."

"I'm sorry, son," the professor said with sorrowful eyes.

Richard watched Aaron walk up the hill until he was out of sight. He hoped Aaron would never find out about the secret of that night. Richard had been in town for about fifteen years and was not sure if he liked the village. The late-night talk always had an undertone about the slaughter of the Indians and the curse of the Chief. Being an outsider, he mostly overheard small bits of conversation when the old timers would begin to get loud in the tavern.

Richard pulled all of the boards from the mill sluice and put the winter iron grate in place. Immediately, he noticed a dead fish stuck in the grate. He grabbed a hook and flung the fish over the dam. He would spend all afternoon and most of the evening throwing limp fish downstream until the level of Paugus Pond dropped and the flow of lifeless fish had slowed.

"I am beginning to hate this place," Richard muttered as he wearily stumbled home. He planned to visit William's father in the morning and hoped they would have a body to show the crazy old man. Talking with him would be hard enough as it was.

CHAPTER EIGHT

The next morning, the men nearly drained Paugus Pond and tried to locate William's body, but the search was in vain; they did not find him. Richard felt dread as he walked towards John's cabin. Other than the buildings along Prescott Street, the area contained the only camp built on the east side of the river. The camp was set on a point of land where Mine Brook reached the river. The place was nice, situated next to Paugus Pond. When John was younger, the road was well traveled with many of the old timers who would come and spend time with him.

Legend has it that the camp was built at the spot where the Indian Chief and his horse had perished. William had often spoken of the old timers and how they would sit and drink while reminiscing about that day - the day they had claimed the land from the savages. William's mother had died giving birth to him, and his father, John, had raised him. He believed most of those stories were the exaggerations of old men and would scoff at the talk about curses.

The village feared that John had gone quite insane. At night when the mist came, John would stand in the doorway and call the names of the original settlers. John was the last of the first settlers and among the men, who were present when the Chief was killed. All had all died young, and of horrible maladies or tragic accidents.

During the nights when the mist appeared, the villagers would hear John calling out the settlers' names. "David, Nathaniel, I see you out there in the mist. I see you all. Why won't you come in? I have missed you all. I see you. I see you."

He would develop a singsong rhythm and continue all night long. "I see you." When the mist was heavy, he would call out again and again. Throughout the village, people were affected by his cries. Many felt sick when they heard him. They knew that something was, in fact, within the mist.

Richard wondered out loud. "Where was John the last two nights when the fog was heavy? I didn't hear him calling." He quickened his pace, wondering if something had happened. He had a bucket of water and some food. He knew the shallow well next to the river would be dry. The once wide and well-used road had been turning into a narrow, brush-infested lane.

Richard reached the cabin and knocked on the door. "John...John are you there?" He opened the door and saw John cowering in the corner. "John, get up out of there," Richard said as he pulled him up, out of the corner. He noticed that John had soiled himself.

"Richard, Richard, Richard…." John mumbled. "They took my William. Last night, I saw him in the fog. I saw him in the fog with the Chief and the death horse. The Chief told me I was next. The Chief said he had been waiting a long time for this moment and would wreak terrible vengeance upon me for killing his family. Richard, I didn't know that it was the Chief's family I killed. We just killed them all. They were savages, and we killed them all, showing no mercy for their savage ways."

John seemed fairly lucid, so Richard removed a washbowl and cloth from the shelf. He spotted some pants and a shirt on his chest of drawers.

He placed the clean clothes on the bed and filled the washbowl.

"John, you need to leave now. Go wash up and come down to the mill. We are having a service for your son."

"Leave? You want me to leave? If I leave, they will get me." John had descended into a state of insanity. As Richard left, he could see John fleeing to his corner. He closed the door and went back to the mill.

At eleven o'clock, the school bell rang to assemble the village people for William's service. The men had quit looking for him and arrived at the bridge over Paugus Pond, covered in mud and smelling of fish. They held a small service at the bridge, amidst the smell of rotting fish. Flowers were thrown into what remained of Paugus Pond. Even though the water was clear and only a couple of feet deep, the flowers immediately sank and disappeared from sight.

The small group let out a collective gasp, and a poignant moment of silence was held. Aaron was the first to speak. He had come with Aaron Junior and Rebecca, his wife. Richard had watched the three of them come down the hill, just moments before.

"Go home, folks and rest. Tomorrow we will service the waterwheel and start filling Paugus Pond, and the mill will be up and running on Tuesday."

The tattered, dirty and scared village people went back to their homes and settled in for the night. Even though the pond had been drained, a heavy mist was expected, and nobody wanted to be out in it.

Richard watched Rebecca walk up the hill. He thought to himself, "Thank God the boy looks like her." He missed their summer trysts in the Nissitissit hills. The year before, Rebecca had put an end to the trysts, feeling that it was too dangerous and fearing that they would be caught. Richard still longed for her and ached for her touch. He remembered the first time, seven years earlier, when Rebecca had wandered down the hill looking for William to fix a broken board in the kitchen floor. William had been tending to his sick father and was not around.

"Let me get some boards, a saw, hammer and nails and I will go fix it for you," Richard had said with a smile. She was the most beautiful creature in the village and Richard was immediately smitten. He knew she had been a Lexington socialite and was a couple of years older than Aaron. At eighteen, when Aaron's father had died, Aaron found himself a wife, determined to carry on the family name. Two years later, they were still childless.

"Thank you, sir. What is your name?" she asked, smiling demurely. She was attracted to him. He was a full-grown man and she longed to touch him.

"Richard," he said as he walked. "Where is your husband, Aaron?"

"He is off hunting with some of his friends."

"When will he be home?"

"Tomorrow," she stated.

"Oh." Suddenly, Richard found himself "carrying more wood" than a moment earlier. Rebecca saw the "wood" Richard was "carrying" and blushed. She was ready to leave Aaron. He had become abusive to her because they did not have children. He blamed her for the problems he was having. She had been with Richard only ten minutes and he seemed to have no trouble in that area.

They walked to the house and Rebecca showed Richard the broken floorboard. Richard took off his Sunday shirt, exposing his undershirt and hairy arms. He turned and began fixing the floor, feeling her eyes upon his back. Rebecca made tea and watched Richard repair the floor. She longed to be with a man - a real man - and Richard, indeed, looked real to her.

When he finished the floor, Richard stood up. He turned to face Rebecca. She held two cups of tea. Richard took one cup, looked at it and put it on the table. Rebecca, sensing what he intended, put her cup down also and took Richard's hand.

Richard was back in the present as he watched Rebecca walk up the hill. He pressed close to the bridge railing. He did not want anyone to see the "wood he was carrying" for Rebecca at that moment. Rebecca walked up the hill, away from the ceremony for William, knowing that Richard's eyes were on her. She recalled how she had taken Richard's hand that night in the kitchen and led him up to her room and how they had ravished each other for hours. He was the hardest man she had ever known. Her body trembled slightly as she remembered his muscular body lying on top of her, and her face turned bright red with the memory. She thought back to the following day, that Monday, when Aaron had returned home. She had gone to his room, wearing her most revealing nightgown, and danced the *Dance of a Thousand Virgins*. She remembered that Aaron was stimulated enough that night to be a man. She recollected how Aaron strutted around the house for weeks, acting as if he was, indeed, *the man.*

Months later, when he found out that Rebecca was pregnant, he was bursting with pride. Rebecca knew that ravishing Aaron after his hunting trip had been the one of the hardest, yet smartest, actions she had ever taken. While she made love to him she had thought about Richard. She did not know who the father was, but in their hearts, Rebecca and Richard knew the child was theirs. The year after the birth of their child, Aaron could no longer "carry wood." Aaron Junior would be their only child.

Rebecca could only think about the eyes she knew had been following her. Richard watched the three of them walk up the hill and disappear. "I have to find a way to be with her forever," he muttered.

Richard walked to the tavern and looked surprised. Most of the villagers were inside drinking. A race was taking place - to see how many drinks could be downed before sunset. Even women and children were among those in the tavern, huddled together in one corner of the room. When the sun began to set, the married men and their families left. The single men stayed and drank. Many of them had lived in the tavern since that Friday.

As dusk came, the onset of the mist appeared once again, sudden and thick. The night grew quiet as the mist filled the air. All of the villagers all went to bed, closing the windows and locking the doors. Then they could hear him from across the pond.

"I see you. I see you." They all knew it was John. "I see you. I see you." John stood in his doorway looking out into the mist. "I see you." As John started chanting, the mist from the river flowed out and wrapped around his feet as arms within the mist reached out. "I see you. I..... Ugh... No. No. NO!" John screamed, breaking the still night air. A swarm of misty arms picked up John and stuck him in the mud of the drained pond, so that he could not walk.

No, no!" John screamed.

The Chief and his horse appeared out of the mist. John screamed, "It's him! It's the Chief and the death horse. IT'S THE DEATH HORSE!!" John's screams reverberated throughout the silent valley.

The Chief looked down at John. He remained full of rage and sought revenge for the murder of his family, which had occurred so many years ago. "John, you are the last of the original settlers. I have been with each of them when they died, to torment them and punish them. Now it is your turn. I have waited long for this retaliation... for revenge for your killing of my family."

The Chief reared the horse back. Although spirits in the cusp seldom touch the living, the misty hooves of the horse trampled onto John's head, leaving him motionless in the mud. Everyone in the village had heard him. A couple of men feigned braveness and gave the impression they were going to get out of bed. However, their wives pulled them back, and they offered no resistance. No man in that village would have walked down the narrow lane by the river that night.

Monday morning came, and the mist disappeared. Across the river, people could see the body stuck in the mud and slumping forward. One of the workers ran up the hill to tell Aaron. Aaron went running back with the worker and met Richard on the bridge.

"What is going on?" demanded Aaron.

"I don't know. Last night, John was shouting like he usually does, when he suddenly screamed something about a death horse. That looks like him over there stuck in the mud."

Richard and Aaron walked down the narrow path to John's house. John was trapped in the mud of the exposed riverbank. The top of his head was caved in. There was not a single footprint of man or beast in the mud. They stopped and stared for a moment, dumbfounded.

"How can that be?" asked Richard.

"I don't know, but give me a hand. We need to pull him out and put him in the house, before others see him."

They struggled to pull the old man out of the mud he was lodged in. Finally, they freed him and brought him into the cabin while sending one of the men to get the undertaker. "Do not tell the men about this! This is too bizarre for them to deal with," Aaron said to Richard.

The two stood outside of John's cabin and waited until the undertaker came and took John's body away, up the hill to Pepperell Center. Aaron looked at his watch. "Let's round up the men and get them busy. I don't have time to wait for replacements from Lowell."

Aaron and Richard first went to the tavern. The men inside were asleep on the benches and tables. The place stunk of sour ale and unwashed feet.

"God," Aaron said. "You need a drink just to be able to stomach this place."

At twenty-seven, Aaron had begun to fill out and look like a man. "All right, men, get up. Any man who is not at the mill in an hour will be out of a job."

Aaron was met with a round of groans. "I mean it, men. You have one hour." Aaron turned and walked out. It was lucky the men had not known about John, or they probably would not have gotten up.

As Richard and Aaron walked back, Aaron pounded on the doors of the mill houses. "Work in one hour. Work in one hour."

The mill was too lucrative to let production slide. Carpenters continued building houses as fast as the mill workers could cut and dry the wood. Stacks of lumber, which had already been sold, were drying. The mill was profitable and fueled the economy of the valley.

They met two families on the road who were packed and ready to leave the cursed valley. "Don't try and stop us, Aaron. We have had enough. Any mill, in any other place, will be better than this place."

Aaron smiled and waved as they past. They had only been in town for a couple of years and meant nothing to him. "Let them try and find work somewhere. There are more people than jobs."

Upon hearing the story of John, two of the single men snuck off during the morning and never came back. At the end of the day, the mill was without four workers. Aaron sat at the desk in the office of the mill. He penned a letter for the outgoing mail in the morning to an address in Lowell. A few days later, another family and two single mill workers came to the village seeking employment. The new family moved into one of the empty houses left by the two families who had fled.

The following morning, a new face appeared at the mill. Winslow was the grandson of one of the original settlers. He lived with his mother and grandmother and was the only child in their extended family. His grandmother was one of the widows from the original, ten settlers who had part ownership in the mill. Nine widows were left because one family line had come to an end with no heirs.

Aaron's father had been one of the original settlers and wanted the fine watershed. It consisted of many tributaries beginning in the brooks, way above Potanopa Pond. The watershed of this river was enormous. Before white men had settled in the Nissitissit Valley, the flow in the river had been strong all year round.

Aaron's father had lots of money for investment and informed the townspeople of Groton that he was looking for ten able men. Groton was located on the east side of the Nashua River. The land to the west of the river was still savage land. He had a site for a dam and needed ten strong workers. The site was on the Nissitissit River, west of the Nashua River. When he made his selection of the ten ablest settlers, Aaron's father offered a deal.

"Men, I will hire you to build me a dam and mill site. I will pay you a fair wage for building all of this, and when it is done you will all have jobs at the mill. To ensure your loyalty and the quality of your product, you will all be given five percent in the profits of the mill. That way you will build the dam and the mill, fine and proud." The agreement was made and the mill was built. It was the beginning of the village of North Pepperell.

Every month, Aaron would send five percent of the profits from the mill to the nine, surviving widows of the original, ten men as per the original agreement. He banked the other fifty-five percent. The agreement called for forfeiture of ownership, if there were no direct, surviving heirs." Therefore, as time went on, Aaron would eventually receive one hundred percent of the profits.

Winslow was young and did not believe in the curses. He had been spending a lot of time out of the village and, on Sundays, would walk over to Hollis Village and attend church services. Winslow was sweet on Prudence. He had met her in church and he fell for her. They made eye contact during the service. Her brother, Abel, was raising Prudence. Their parents had been killed a few years earlier, when something had spooked the team of their wagon, causing it to overturn on the way home from Hollis Village. Abel was the oldest and assumed the responsibility of raising his brothers and sisters. Abel would get upset when he saw Winslow and Prudence eyeing each other. He would lecture her unmercifully about Winslow's lower social status.

Prudence was young and resented her brother telling her what she should do with her life. She knew she was falling in love with Winslow, and she would go to any church function where she thought she could see him. Winslow was smitten with her and did the same, making sure to attend every church service. The minister thought they were two of the nicest, pious young people he had ever met.

Following the death of John, North Village was quiet for a couple of years. Winslow kept going to church and finally asked Prudence to marry him. She accepted his proposal, and the local justice of the peace married the couple. Upon hearing the news, Abel had become furious with Prudence and threw her belongings out of the house, forbidding her from ever returning. The young couple spent the night at the inn in Hollis Village and headed down to North Village in the morning. When the people of the village heard the good news, they took the day off and had a holiday. The valley had needed some good news. The fathers and the sons gave the empty mill house a fresh coat of green paint while the women outfitted the interior. By evening, the mill house had become a cute, little "love nest." However, a slight odor of fresh paint was in the air.

Richard had been helping Aaron expand the mill. They had added on to the Shoddy Shack, extending the mill shaft to accommodate two new mill-driven sewing machines. A woman who set up a velvet shop leased the machines. The new machines enabled her to sell high-quality products because they were made well. She began supplying more expensive, stylish dresses to women throughout the area and was even mailing items to Boston. She had established herself as a prominent name, and her work was becoming renowned.

The shoddy operation continued along, and Richard devised a clever way to shred the rags using the mill shaft from the sewing machines. Shoddy production tripled. The butcher rented a smokehouse for bacon and hams. The smokehouse used the scraps of hardwood from the mill. The meat in the smokehouse came from pigs that were rounded up from the mud holes next to the river and tributaries. The muddy ground, where the pigs had rutted and defiled the area, was the same area that the Indians had seen as sacred.

A new cobbler arrived who made shoes and leased saw time to shape the leather soles. The store was thriving, and the school was full of children. The curse seemed to be fading, and the valley was thriving with industry. The money was flowing strongly, and Aaron was becoming rich. He had to share profits only from the original mill and not from the new ventures. The valley became prosperous, once again. Everybody was happy except for Richard. He despised the valley and pined for Rebecca. Aaron had been noticing how Rebecca would blush in Richard's presence and how she would never look in Richard's direction. Deep inside, he felt something was not right but could not pinpoint what was wrong. Rebecca never went down to the mill. She spent all her time with the boy, and Richard stayed away from the house. As far as Aaron knew, no contact had ever been made. He did not know why he felt resentment towards Richard, especially when

Rebecca was around. His working relationship with Richard was being affected by his feelings. As a result, he had started treating Richard in a demeaning manner, even though Richard's expert work had meant lots of money for Aaron.

One morning, Aaron arrived at the mill with Aaron Junior. Richard had not seen the youngster since the service for William had been held on the bridge. Aaron Junior had grown a lot, and Richard studied him. Aaron began barking out orders to Richard and, once again, his attitude was degrading. While explaining the work for the upcoming week, Aaron was insulting Richard and had been treating him as if he were a child.

"Please, Aaron, not in front of the boy?" Richard asked.

"I will say what I like in front of my own son. Someday this mill will be his. He needs to know how to handle mill workers! Now tend to your job."

Richard was furious and wanted to kill Aaron but held his tongue. He wouldn't say anymore in front of the boy. He devised a plan, but he would have to wait. Richard silently went to work, and the father and son walked away.

A few weeks later, the conditions were right. A heavy mist was forming on Paugus Pond. The time had come. Richard scrawled a note and headed to the mill. Earlier that day, he had told the men to disengage the millwheel because he planned to do some shaft maintenance. He lit the lamps at the mill and greased the shafts. He opened the sluice and powered up the shafts, including the saw, which was his usual practice. The people of the village heard the noise and were quite used to it since Richard had made it his weekly routine for the last few years.

Then he powered down the equipment, extinguished the lights, and placed a lantern by the sluice. He positioned his hat on the walk. It looked exactly as it did when William had disappeared. The mist was heavy, and no one saw Richard slip back into the mill. He darted up the hill to Aaron's house and tapped on the servant's door.

A maid answered. Richard politely said, "A woman in the village has sent this to Rebecca. Could you please give it to her?" The maid did not know Richard. On occasion, notes would come from the village, so she delivered it to Rebecca's room.

Rebecca read the note. "I have left. Signed, the woodworker" When the maid left, Rebecca wept. Her only true love had left the valley.

Richard walked through the dark, knowing that his actions at the mill would revive the fear of the mist. Meanwhile, back in North Village, Prudence and Winslow cuddled in their millhouse.

"Winslow?"

"Yes?"

"Let's have a family. I want a boy. I want to call him Ebb, after the currents in the river."

"Sure. Come to bed."

CHAPTER NINE

When Prudence awoke the next day she felt wonderful. She did not know about any of the curses and, for the moment, she thought North Village was the most wonderful place on earth. Winslow rolled over and watched his bride get out of bed.

"God," Winslow thought. "She is so beautiful. I will do anything to make her happy."

"Winslow?"

"Yes?"

"Should I get a job in one of the shops here in the village?"

"No. I have a small amount of money put aside. You will not have to worry about work. All I want you to do is be the happiest woman in the village."

"Oh, Winslow. I love you so much. I hope I can make you happy."

"You already have. You have made me the happiest man in the valley." Winslow grabbed the edge of her nightgown and pulled her toward the bed.

"Oh, in the daylight? It is so sinful."

"There are no sins when true love is involved."

They embraced and kissed as only newlyweds can. Their emotions ran red hot and their kisses were passionate. They made love several more times before lying back in bed, exhausted. The sun was high and it was almost noon.

"Maybe we should get up and tour the village," said Prudence. It is almost noon, and I want you to show me every nook and cranny of this lovely, little hamlet."

"All right, after we make love one last time. I just cannot get enough of you."

"We are acting like rabbits," Prudence said as if she were about to resist. "Oh, all right. Let's act like rabbits one last time before getting out of bed."

"Okay. Rub my lucky rabbit's foot."

"Oh, Winslow."

It was just past noon when Winslow and Prudence finally came out of the millhouse. Everywhere they walked, people greeted them with smiles and a cheery hello. Prudence waved to the other women and exchanged a friendly greeting. She could not keep from blushing. She knew the whole community had a good idea why they were finally leaving the house after noontime on a lovely day.

Winslow took Prudence to the sawmill where he worked. "Here is where I work. My responsibility is running this big saw. It is also my job to keep it sharp. Every board that comes out by the mill is cut by me." As he spoke, Winslow puffed up with pride. Prudence walked over to the saw and could see the teeth gleaming in the light. The saw had a roof but was open on the sides, so that the breeze could blow the sawdust outside. Prudence reached toward the blade and barely touched it.

"Ouch!" she exclaimed as she cut her finger. "The blade is razor sharp. Winslow, I am afraid of this blade. Please be careful when you work."

Prudence did not know why, but that saw scared her to death. The small cut on her finger stopped bleeding.

"I provide for the saw, and, in turn, the saw will provide us with a decent living. The saw may be dangerous, but the pay is high because of the danger. While I have this job, you will never have to work."

"I'm scared. Please be careful when running the saw. It looks so stern."

"Don't worry. I will be even more careful now that I have you. I don't ever want to do anything that will cause you consternation."

"Just be careful. Be very careful. I don't ever want to lose you. Without you, life is not worth living."

"Let me show you the rest of North Village. Come look at our wonderful school. It was built years ago, by some of the first settlers using local brick. The clay pit and brick kiln are located on Boynton Street, right here in Pepperell. About one-half mile down Boynton Street, on the left hand side of the road, on the opposite side of the meadow, there is a fine clay pit. That clay made the excellent brick we used for the school. The school will last for hundreds of years; it is built so well, it will outlast us all."

"What is the tower on the school?"

Winslow beamed with pride. "That is the bell tower; we have the only school in all of Pepperell and the surrounding villages that has a bell. We are truly lucky to be part of North Village. It was the site of the first mill in Pepperell, and we are the busiest and richest part of town. A man and his family could profit by staying and being a part of this thriving village." They continued walking along. "This is our post office."

"Why is it called Paugus? That name seems familiar."

"Well, Paugus was the great Indian Chief killed in Lovell, Maine by John Chamberlain."

"Why is this post office called that?"

"Someday I will tell you, but, for now, there are a few stupid, old superstitions that you are better off not hearing. They are just the prattling of old busybodies and mean nothing. Let's just keep going. There is a lot to show you."

Winslow was obviously proud of North Village. "This is the house and shop of John Danvers. He makes the finest winter boots in all the area. He makes the felt for his boot liners, right here in the mill, during the winter when the river is frozen. Aaron's father knew the process of making the felt, and he and one of the men made the felt in the winter. Everyone in the valley wears John Danvers' boots, and the fine felt we make has kept everyone's feet warm on cold, winter days. They make the felt from rabbit fur."

Even though Aaron had learned that his father died because of the felt-making process, he still kept the shop open, and Danvers made the felt. Aaron would never visit John Danvers' shop in the winter when the felt was being made. Hundreds of lives had already been lost, so that North Village could be built. Aaron thought, "They all needed the felt, so what would one or two more lives lost mean?" Not many of the backwards locals had any idea about how many toxins were around them and just how poisonous they were.

"Let me show you the store and the smokehouse," said Winslow to Prudence. We have the finest smokehouse in all of the area. In fact, everything that we have here is the best and the finest in all of New England. Outside the village, on the surrounding hills, are some of the best farms in the entire world. The view from these hills is superb. The sunsets are said to be even better than the legendary, Italian sunsets. They were described in writings from people who had traveled to this faraway place. Each porch on these farms in the hills is a wonderful spot to sit on a summer's afternoon and watch the clouds build up from the frequent, summer thunderstorms. North Village is built on a fine watershed. Aaron's father had purchased the water rights of the river and four tributaries, up to and including, rights across the border into New Hampshire, where Gulf Brook dumps into the Nissitissit. That way, we always have water here at the mill. In summer, when the water in the river starts running low, Aaron has the legal right to go to the other mills upstream and force them to let water out of their millponds."

"But, would that not hurt those smaller mills by losing their head waters?"

"Yes, it sometimes is a problem, but Aaron and his family have only allowed mills to be built that do not impede the flow of water. There is an overshot waterwheel downstream from Heald Pond, but it runs only on the unimpeded flow from the pond. The only mill that is allowed a dam is the newly built knife factory in Berkinshaw Village on Sucker Brook. But even that is just a small millpond and does not impede the flow of Sucker Brook."

"That seems like a lot of power for one family to have - control over the entire river basin. What a benefit to North Village."

"Yes, but it comes at a cost. Many families have fought with Aaron and his family to get better water rights. Some have even died over it." Winslow looked around and lowered his voice. "It is rumored that some died suspiciously by fires which consumed them and their houses while they slept. Many suspected Aaron's father, but no one could prove it."

"So, North Village has some skeletons in the closet?"

"It is something that happened all over New England. Here is no different than anywhere else, but I caution you never to repeat what I tell you or it will cost me my job. The benefits we have here far outweigh any of those stupid, old wives' tales. Winslow paused. "Prudence?"

"Yes?

"Promise me that, as we grow old, you will not become one of those gossip mongers."

"I promise. I also promise you that as long as I have you, I need nothing else and will never complain. You are all I will ever need."

The next few weeks went by quickly for Prudence. She was making friends with some of the other ladies but was busy seeing to the needs of Winslow. She was learning how to cook what he liked and caring to his wishes. Near the end of September, the leaves on the trees and the vegetation in the meadows began changing. Soon after, the trees in the woods and along the bank of the river began turning. The beech trees turned bright yellow. The maples turned brilliant shades of red. The last leaves to change were from the oaks, which turned a golden brown color. The oaks would hold their leaves until the first snow. Then, they would come fluttering down from the trees as the first snow clung to the leaves, weighing them down and bringing them to the ground.

Prudence loved that first snow in North Village. She happened to be outside in the small yard when the first snowflakes had begun to fall. The day was gray, and the whole village was silent. That magical moment occurred, just before the first snowflake, when neither man nor beast makes a sound. Prudence was still outside when Winslow came home from the mill. The wind had been blowing the snow under the roof of the mill and onto the floor near the saw. The floor had become slippery, making it dangerous to work. At almost four o'clock on Friday afternoon, Aaron let everyone go home early. He even paid them for that last hour they did not work. Aaron did not usually do anything like that, but that year at the mill had been profitable, and he was feeling generous. Aaron Junior was in school and doing well. He was excelling in arithmetic, which made Aaron proud. He thought it would be helpful to have a son who could help with the bookkeeping. As Aaron Junior grew, his features luckily still resembled Rebecca.

"What are you still doing outside? It is cold and snowing. Get inside before you catch your death," said Winslow.

"Isn't it beautiful outside? The snow is so clean and white that it makes the whole village look so wondrous and enchanted. I was outside when the first snowflake fell. It was so quiet it seemed like the whole world was holding its breath until that first flake fell. When that first snowflake hit the dry leaves, it seemed to make a loud noise when it hit, but it only seemed that way because of the dead silence. Then, the snow started falling, sounding like small drops of water hitting a hot stove. Winslow, it was so magical and now that the snow has built up a little, the ground has become quiet, but I can still hear the snow hitting the leaves on the oak trees. The village looks so pretty with the bright green of the millhouses accenting the white snow. It all looks so safe and cozy. How could anything bad ever happen here?"

"Bad things can happen anywhere, even right here in North Village." Winslow had dragged home a sled full of firewood from the mill. "Give me a hand, bringing in this load of firewood. These are the ends we cut off today from some nice, dry oak boards we were trimming. It will burn hot, and we will be warm and toasty all weekend."

Prudence helped bring the wood inside and went about fixing dinner. She had some tasty ham from the smokehouse and some winter squash she had bought earlier in the day at the store in North Village.

After Winslow finished eating, Prudence was washing the dishes in the wash pan when she stopped and spoke softly. "Winslow, I have some good news. I have waited two months to make sure. We are going to have a baby."

"That's wonderful! We will have a child in the spring when the land is green and lush. God has smiled on us by giving you a fertile womb."

"I will be the best mother this village has ever seen. Our child is going to grow up and be someone special. I just know it. With a wonderful father like you, the child will be special."

"And, Prudence, with your strong bloodlines, our child will live a long and productive life."

The young couple was infatuated with one another. In January, when the river froze solid with a severe, cold snap, Prudence thought it was wonderful that Winslow had all of January and February to be with his expectant bride.

"I have carved these toys out of some scrap wood from the mill for our baby."

"Oh, Winslow, they are wonderful. You have carved some beautiful horses and animals out of those small pieces of wood."

"I have another surprise. It is at the mill. I will go get it and be right back. I made it for us over the last few weeks. I had a feeling that we might need it"

"Put your heavy coat on. It is fearsome cold out."

Winslow put on his coat and went out the door. Prudence could hear his footsteps on the cold, squeaky snow. She watched the mist, created from every breath he took while he walked out of sight. Moments later, Winslow returned with something large, covered by an oilcloth. Prudence opened the door for him. Winslow stepped through the doorway, back into the warmth of their tiny house. With the flurry of a prestidigitator, Winslow removed the oilcloth.

"Oh, Winslow, that is the nicest cradle I have ever seen. I can't wait to rock our baby in it."

Prudence was skillful with a sewing needle and spent most of the winter in pure bliss. She sewed clothes for the arrival of the baby while Winslow spent most of his time carving and whittling and made a set of blocks he had cut from scrap wood at the mill. Over the long winter, he had spent a great deal of time carefully carving the letters into the sides of the blocks. The preparations were complete for the birth of the child.

CHAPTER TEN

While the couple awaited the birth of their child in North Village, upstream in West Hollis, Sarah could sense something was going to happen. She knew that she would have to leave before long. She had been allowed a few wonderful years of happiness on the Quaker farm. During that time, the spirits of the mist, as well as the spirit of Ebb, had remained calm.

Moses remembered that fateful day when he had met Sarah by the side of the road and brought her home to his wife, Anna. He smiled as he recalled the conversation.

"Anna, this is Sarah. I found her by the side of the road, on the way to West Hollis. She is a Quaker without a home. I invited her to come home with me, so she could bathe, and then, tomorrow, she will celebrate the Sabbath with us."

Anna was perplexed but did not let it show. They had sold most of their crops to buy schoolbooks for their children and barely had enough food for themselves. "Welcome to our home, Sarah. I am glad to meet you. I am blessed that we have enough food to be able to share it with you."

Sarah peeked into the house and was relieved. The interior was simple with untreated wood beams and boards on the walls painted with milk paint. Moses had made the paint on his farm. All of the ingredients were natural. More importantly, nearly all of the quilts and other materials had been made from natural, un-dyed fabrics.

"Thank you, Anna," Sarah responded with a warm smile. She could tell at a glance that they were simple, hardworking people without a great deal of money. She knew that offering her food and shelter, even for one evening, would cut into the limited resources they had on the farm. Sarah continued. "I have a whole sack of provisions. Let me help out with dinner. We will use some of my supplies. This way, I can contribute to the household and not be a burden. All I need is some potatoes and onions, and I will prepare you a wonderful meal from a faraway place."

Anna was instantly relieved. "That would be wonderful; potatoes and onions we have in abundance. What we are short of is grains. Amos has sold most of the grains to buy books for the children. School is in a week, and they need their primers. Their education is the most important thing to us."

Sarah smiled as she reached into her parcel. "I have this sack of Quaker Oats that I bought in North Village."

Moses chuckled and Anne laughed. She knew that the hand of Providence was at work. "Those are the very same oats that Moses and I sold and traded to get primers for the children. How odd that these oats have come back to us. I think there is a power stronger than us at work here. It seems that it is no accident that God has brought you to our door."

Moses brought Sarah's canvas sack of food into the kitchen, and Anne went to the root cellar for potatoes and onions. She also picked the last of the green beans that were still on the vine. The potatoes were an early crop, and the weather was still somewhat warm. Therefore, the potatoes needed to be eaten anyway. Later on, when the weather would turn colder, they would harvest the rest of the potatoes and onions, as well as the winter squash and pumpkins that were growing on the farm.

"I will make a dish which I learned while in Boston. A retired sea captain taught it to me. He was from Newfoundland. It is called "Fish and Brewis." The original recipe calls for only salted fish and hardtack, but I have made it healthier by adding fresh vegetables."

By then, the children were in the kitchen. Abigail, their daughter, inquired, "What is hard tack?"

Sarah smiled. She had been there less than an hour, and already she was educating the children. "Hardtack is a very dry and compact biscuit, which starts out as hard as rocks. It comes from Newfoundland and is a staple for fisherman on the North Atlantic. If the hardtack is kept dry, it will last forever. When the fishermen are catching and cleaning the fish, the cook will take a hammer, put the hardtack in a cloth bag, and smash it into smaller pieces. Then, the cook soaks the hardtack in water while he prepares the fish by filleting and removing the bones."

Abigail looked up at Sarah. "What is done next?"

"Then, the hardtack is drained and added to some cooked fish, which is then simmered on the stove. The hardtack, once wet, swells to nearly twice its size. When mixed with the fish, it provides a filling and frugal meal for the crew." Sarah reached into the sack. "Here is some nice dried and salted cod, which we will use."

"I could catch us some fish in the river," chimed Jacob, their son.

"No, we will use the dried cod. I want to tell you all not to eat the fish in the river. If you want fresh fish, go to some of the smaller ponds where there is no industry."

"Why is that?" Anna asked.

"Because the river is sick."

Anna turned towards Sarah. "Sick in what way?"

"The river is sick with potions and poisons of industry."

Moses was now interested in what Sarah had to say. "What kind of poisons?"

Sarah took a breath and began. "The worst is the mercurous nitrate that the hatters and felt makers use (12). Have you ever heard the term "mad as a hatter?"

"Well, yes I have," answered Moses.

Sarah continued. "Once the beavers were mostly eliminated by the trappers, the hatters began using rabbits from the local farms. Unlike rabbit fur, beaver fur has naturally serrated edges and can easily be shaved off and turned into felt. With rabbit fur, a solution of mercurous nitrate is brushed on the fur to roughen the fibers and make them mat more easily. This process is called carroting because it turns the fur a bright orange. The fibers are then shaved off the pelt and immersed in a boiling acid solution to thicken and harden it. This process will decompose the mercurous nitrate and turn it into elemental mercury. Then, the felt is pressed and steamed into hats, which releases mercury vapors. What is worse is the hatters do not know what they are dealing with and usually work in poorly ventilated shops. When the acid solution becomes weak and saturated with mercury, the whole batch of toxins gets dumped. Where do you think the hatters have dumped their spent batches of acid and mercury?"

"I know," chirped Jacob. "Most of it was probably dumped in the river?"

Sarah looked sad as she spoke. "Yes. Into the river."

Moses was dumbfounded and looked at Sarah. "I have not even heard of these potions, let alone what they do. Tell me, Sarah, why is mercury so dangerous?"

"Well, the mercury, at first, attacks the nerves, causing uncontrollable muscular tremors with twitching arms and legs called hatter's shakes. After that, comes distorted vision and confused speech. With prolonged exposure, the person suffers hallucinations and psychotic symptoms."

Moses looked confused "What does all that mean?"

"It means the mercury causes death," said Sarah, "and when the afflicted die they die in an unusual way. The person is doomed to die a complete, raving lunatic. Death cannot come soon enough to those suffering in the final stages. That's not all. Do you know what is in the white paint everybody uses in the villages?"

"No" was Moses' simple reply.

"White lead. Lead is another severe toxin that kills with prolonged exposure. Lead has some of the same symptoms as mercury, and lead also causes children to be born dead or abnormal." Sarah turned to Jacob. "And where do you think the bad batches of lead paint are dumped?"

Jacob looked distressed. "In the river?"

"Yes," Sarah said as she nodded solemnly. "But that is not all of the toxins in the river."

Moses was panic-stricken. "Good God, is there more?"

"There is a lot more." Sarah was grim but continued. "The black powder everybody uses to blow out the stumps in their fields contains nitrates and leaches out into the river. This also causes nerve damage to the handlers or anyone who drinks the water contaminated with nitrates. Once again, death is very painful. Also, the dyes used at the woolen mills are made from arsenic. Any of the blues and greens is extremely poisonous. The same holds true for the green wallpaper and the wallpaper with large, floral prints. Not only is it high in arsenic, but also, it contains heavy metals like vermilion. The chemicals that are used in tanning hides and making shoe leather are also toxic. The green paint everybody seems to like in North Village is called Scheele's green, named after the inventor. Not only is copper arsenate a component, but it also acts as the actual dye, itself. Scheele's green is also used to tint green candles, and many people have been killed while using them in a closed room. Also, the undertakers, up and down the river, use toxic chemicals to preserve the bodies. Now, Jacob, can you tell me where all of these things end up?"

Jacob felt almost sick while he thought of all the time he spent in the river during the hot summers. "In the river," he said, rather timidly.

"Yes. Now do you see why I don't want you or your family to eat the fish from the river?"

"Yes."

Up until now, Anna had been quiet. "Sarah, how is it that you come to know this?"

"I lived with my Uncle Samuel in Boston. He learned all of this by helping dying factory workers. He would find out where they worked and what chemicals were used in the processes, and he started compiling symptoms and relating them to the various compounds. Samuel taught me how to do mathematical calculations, and he hired chemists, historians and many other wise men to come and tutor me."

Moses spoke up. "And with all of that knowledge, what have you learned?"

"I learned that there is no stopping The White Way."

"What do you mean? You act as if you hate white men," stated Moses.

"I do."

Moses looked confused. "But, Sarah, you are white."

"I am white only on the outside."

Moses was starting to get annoyed. "Then what are you on the inside?"

"I am Indian."

Anna was also feeling irritated. "How preposterous!" she exclaimed.

Sarah saw that the situation was becoming uneasy. She reached into her sack and pulled out two pieces of hardtack. She dropped them onto the table, and they made a resounding bang when they hit. The intensity of the moment was broken, and Jacob and Abigail instantly concentrated on picking up and dropping the hardtack biscuits. Jacob tried to bite one of the biscuits but found it to be too hard.

"We are going to eat this?" exclaimed Jacob, making a funny face.

They all laughed, and the tension of the moment was over. Sarah said, "Abigail, get me an old pillow case or a piece of cotton cloth. Now, Jacob, you run to the well and get a bucket of water to soak the salt cod and hardtack."

After Jacob and Abigail left, Sarah spoke softly, so that the children would not hear. "I am sorry. I did not mean to upset the children with the talk of chemicals, but once I got started I could not stop. My uncle and I paid a dear price for that information."

"How dear?" asked Moses.

"My uncle ended up giving up his life. He and I had prepared a paper for the medical journal. He went to the editor of the journal and presented his work. The next day, he was killed in the park, and it was made to look like an accident. I fled Boston that night." Sarah was holding back tears. "That was two weeks ago today."

Anna put her arms around Sarah. "How awful, Sarah. You are safe here. Don't fret."

Sarah composed herself, just in time, before the children came back. "We will talk later when the children are in bed." She turned to Jacob. "Pour some of that water over the salt fish, and go get a hammer or a hatchet."

"Yes, Ma'am."

"Now, Abigail, put the hardtack biscuits into the old pillow case, and you children can crack them up while I prepare the potatoes and onions."

Sarah never had children and had little exposure to them throughout her life. She found the two children to be receptive and easy to talk with. They paid attention to her every word and command. Moses and Anna were surprised at how well Sarah and the children communicated.

"Let us boil the potatoes and onions while the fish and hardtack soak in the water," Sarah told the children.

When the potatoes were tender, they combined all the ingredients into one pan and put it back onto the stove. The bubbling concoction was starting to smell good and was soon ready. The table was set, and they all sat down to eat. Sarah dished out a bowl for everyone, and Moses said grace. They all sampled the dish Sarah had prepared. The flavor was superb, and the room was silent as they ate. About halfway through the meal, the speed at which everyone ate was slowing down. Moses said, "Sarah, this meal is incredibly filling. I have never felt so full on half a bowl of food."

Sarah smiled. "Now you see why the North Atlantic fishermen bring it with them. It has saved many lives aboard ship."

Jacob was inquisitive. "How does it save lives? It is just food."

"It saves lives by keeping the men well nourished, and when they are well nourished they are better able to cope with the bone-chilling cold of the Atlantic. The cold saltwater can suck every bit of strength out of a man and leave him weak and helpless. The Fish and Brewis is warm and filling. It fills the bellies of the men and adds warmth, helping them to fight the cold. Without this hot meal, the elements would eventually overpower them."

"Can you tell us more about these fishermen?" asked Abigail.

"Let us finish our meal. When the dishes are clean and put away, we will sit at the table, and I will give you a lesson about the sea."

The children were thrilled. Even though they were getting full, they finished the rest of the food in their bowls and hurriedly set about cleaning their dishes and putting the kitchen in order.

Anna was amazed. "Moses, have you ever seen anything like this? We have not even finished our bowls, and the children have the kitchen almost cleaned. They never move this fast after a meal."

The dishes were almost done, and the children waited patiently. Moses had just scooped up the last of his food when Jacob whisked the bowl away before Moses got the food into his mouth. "Lord Almighty, Jacob, give a man the chance to breathe."

"Sarah, are you a teacher?" asked Jacob.

"Yes, I am a teacher who cannot teach."

Moses was curious. "How is that so?"

"Because what I know, people do not want to learn. It is too inconvenient for them. If they truly learned what I have to say, they would have to change their ways. Too much money is made of the evilness that they control. I am afraid that too much has happened, and that things are already out of control."

Moses looked confused. "In what way?"

"Remember what I said about the toxins in the river?"

"Yes," responded Moses.

"Those metals and toxins are in the river forever."

Moses was now a little suspicious. "How can they be there forever?"

"The heavy metals are not soluble in water; they sink to the bottom of the deeper pools in the river. Then, these poisonous metals start to permeate into the gravel aquifer along the river. Those who drink directly from the river will die first. Next will be the people with wells closest to the river. Any well that directly or indirectly draws water through those aquifers will kill anyone who uses them."

The children were beginning to look worried and confused. Sarah changed the subject. "Let us not dwell on these subjects right now. The table is cleared, and we should talk about the fishermen. It will be much more entertaining to you children. Jacob, go and get my other parcel which I brought with me."

Jacob ran off and returned, dragging Sarah's heavy satchel. "Here it is, Sarah."

"Thank you, Jacob." Sarah reached into the bag and produced several quills and a bottle of special ink. One of Samuel's chemist friends had prepared it. The ink was all-natural and did not contain any toxins. Then she reached into the bag and took out a small roll of paper. The paper was made from rice, and Samuel had made certain that is was pure. The children were amazed at how thin and transparent the paper was and watched as Sarah tore off a few small squares.

"Children, let me start off by showing you where this recipe comes from." Sarah then drew a map. "This is Massachusetts Bay, and this point of land, which sticks out, is Cape Cod. This area to the north is known as The Gulf of Maine. Now, further north and east is Newfoundland. That is where the sea captain came from who taught me to prepare the food you just ate. Newfoundland is a journey of many months by land but only takes several days to get there by boat."

Sarah drew a line along the shoreline to Newfoundland and then drew a line from Boston to Newfoundland. "Children, can you see how much longer the line on land is as compared to the short line across the Gulf of Maine?"

The children were totally involved with what Sarah was teaching. Abigail spoke first. "Yes, Sarah, it is easy to see that the journey by land is much longer than the journey by sea."

Not only were the children captivated, but also, for the first time, Sarah felt the joy of sharing her knowledge with young and open minds. She felt their thirst for knowledge. Sarah had never been exposed to children. She had always been isolated from them. Her world had consisted of books and tutors. Teaching was a new and wonderful experience, and she was as thrilled as the children.

Next, Sarah drew the profile of a fishing schooner, complete with masts, sails, and rigging. "This part is called the hull. These are the masts that hold the canvas sails, and all these ropes are called the rigging. Every rope has a specific job."

The children were engrossed by the drawings, and Sarah was thrilled to have children to teach. She had the knowledge of the world, but having been kept away from society, never had the chance to share it with anyone - except Samuel, and now he was gone.

"While you children study the drawing of the exterior of the schooner, I will draw a picture of the interior of the boat."

As the children studied her first drawing, Sarah penned a sketch of the inside of the fishing boat. She made it in blueprint form, showing the central walkway, which led from the back of the boat where the captain and his mate stayed, to the crew's quarters in the front. The drawing showed the bins on either side, which were loaded with salt on the way out.

Sarah was almost done and started another lesson. "The salt cod you had earlier came back to port in one of these fish holds. When the crew catches fish, the fish are filleted, covered with salt, and placed in these holds. Then, when the ship is full, it returns to port. The cod fillets are washed in seawater to remove the crusted salt, and they are hung on racks in the sun to dry. That is how they caught and prepared the fish we ate this evening. What I have told you is enough for you to think about for tonight. Keep my sketches. I drew them for you to have."

Moses and Anna had been watching Sarah at the kitchen table, drawing for their children. They were both stunned. Abigail and Jacob had learned more in one hour than they would have learned in a month at the little, one-room schoolhouse in West Hollis.

Sarah left the kitchen and joined Moses and Anna in the living room. Moses said, "We have a small bedroom at the back of the house. I will show you where it is and carry your bags in there for you."

Moses picked up the bags and put them in Sarah's room. "I forgot, for an instant, how heavy these are." Moses tried to add a little humor to the moment. "What's in here, lead?"

"No, but it is very close to that."

Sarah loved the room. It had a small, comfortable bed with a feather mattress, goose down pillows, and a natural, wool comforter. Best of all, it had a small secretary's desk. Sarah sat down, lowered the lid of the desk, and composed a quick letter to a firm in Boston. Before she continued her journey, she would leave it with Moses the following day, after their Sunday service. Feeling exhausted from her travels, Sarah fell into a deep sleep.

Moses and Anna retired to bed shortly after that. "Moses?"

"Yes."

"Did you see how much the children learned in such a short time?"

"Yes. I was very impressed, but she is only staying for the Sabbath."

"Moses, can I ask you something?"

"Yes."

"Where did you find her?"

"By the side of the road. She was just standing by the side of the road."

"Why was she there?"

"I don't know."

"How strange. What was God's purpose in putting her there?" Anna thought as she drifted off to sleep.

Anna was up early and in the kitchen. Sarah heard her, got up and went to join her. "Good morning, Anna."

"Good morning, Sarah. I hope you slept well."

"I did. Thank you for asking."

"Sarah, what are you doing in this area?"

"I was originally from the Lake Potanopa area, before I moved to Boston. When my uncle was murdered, I ran for my life. Other than Boston, the Nissitissit River Valley was my home. It is where the spirits of the mist live."

Anna did not understand but did not question Sarah about that. "What are your plans?"

"I don't have any."

"Where are you going?"

Sarah looked out the window. "I do not have anywhere to go, for now. Right now, I am just passing time, waiting."

"Waiting for what?" asked Anna.

"Waiting for when the time is right. For now, I cannot tell you anymore."

"Sarah, will you stay one more night and give the children another lesson?"

"Of course. It would be my pleasure."

After breakfast, they had a simple service. The few Quakers in the area did not have a meeting house and worshipped at home. The

Puritans hated the Quakers and did not consider them to be Christians. Rumors claimed that Quaker women could foretell the future. Because of this belief, the Puritans saw the Quaker women as witches.

Sarah felt comfortable with these new friends. After the service, when the children were outside playing, she approached Moses and Anna. "Do you think I might be able to rent that back bedroom for a while? I have the resources to pay for it."

Sarah took a twenty-dollar gold piece out of the pocket of her dress. "Here is the first payment, should you choose to allow it."

Moses and Anna looked at each other. Anna remarked, "That is a great deal of money. We never see that much money at one time. Let Moses and I talk about it. We were not expecting anything like this."

Sarah went outside to enjoy the wonderful, late summer day. The nights were getting cold, but the sun still managed to warm the land up nicely during the day. Sarah went and sat down by the river, watching the currents in the water. The spirits could sense she was there, but the day was too warm and dry, so the spirits had to stay within the water.

Back in the house, Moses and Anna had a short discussion. At first, Moses was negative to the idea, but Anna persisted. "Moses, I feel that Providence has a hand in this. We really could use the money, and the children could use the help also. Why would God have her just standing there when you went by?"

"What do you mean, the children could use help?"

"Well, the children are falling behind in their lessons at school. The Puritan children torment them, and Jacob often comes home with a stomachache as a result of the taunting. Neither of the children can concentrate on their work while in school. Maybe Sarah could help them catch up."

Moses replied, "It is done then. Call her in and we will tell her."

Sarah looked up, just as Anna had opened the door. "Sarah, please come back in."

Sarah went back into the house, and went up to Moses. "Anna and I have decided to let you rent your room, but twenty dollars is a lot of money. We would not wish to take advantage of you, for we wish to barter for some of your services. We will take the twenty dollars and draw from that from time to time. But, more important is the fact that we want you to help the children with their lessons after school. The children at school are cruel to Abigail and Jacob, and they have difficulties concentrating on their schoolwork. Anna and I spent most of our money on books to try and help them. We feel that the education of our children is most important to us. The Puritans can take what they want from the Quakers, but the one thing we have they cannot take away is our knowledge - for once learned, it can never be removed."

Sarah was delighted. "I would love to have the responsibility of educating the children. Please bring me their readers, and I will inspect them."

Moses went outside to tend to the animals. The animals had daily needs, and Sabbath or not, chores needed to be done. Moses spoke to the children. "Come with me, and help feed the animals. There is something you need to be told."

Anna retrieved the primers and handed them to Sarah. "We just bought these, and they cost us dearly."

Sarah opened the books and thumbed through them. "Return these while they are new, and get your money back."

"Why?"

"Because they will not be needed. Go to any page and ask me a question."

Anna opened the book to a random page and asked Sarah a question. Sarah was able to answer any questions Anna had about the contents of the book. "Return the books and get your money. I will teach them, and, if you wish, I could school them at home, which will save them the persecution of the Puritans. I promise you that they will learn at a more accelerated rate than they ever could in that simple school."

Anna's respect grew enormously as there was no better way for Sarah to gain her love than for her to help her children.

In the barn, Moses spoke to the children. "Jacob, Abigail, I want to tell you that Sarah will be staying with us for a while." The children jumped up and down and shouted with joy. Moses looked annoyed. "This is no way to act on the Sabbath. Hush."

Jacob and Abigail became silent. "Sorry, father," they said in unison.

Later that day, after the children had gone to bed, Sarah approached Moses and Anna. "Before we consummate this contract, I need to speak with you both. I am a child of the mist. Years ago, when I was not yet a year old, bears killed my parents. They were missionaries trying to teach and understand the Indians in the valley. They were killed on the very same day that the early settlers brutally killed the tribe of Indians who lived in the area now known as North Village. They slaughtered the women and children, killing the Chief last so that he could witness the horror of it all."

Sarah looked at the two of them. Seeing that they were mesmerized by her words, she continued. "When the great Chief died, his spirit left his body and roamed the valley. The first sight he came across was that of the two bears, consuming the remains of my parents."

Anna cried out, "How terrible! How awful! How did you ever survive?"

"I survived because of knowledge," Sarah responded.

"How is that so?" asked Moses.

"I will tell you, but first, let us sit and meditate. I need you to clear your thoughts. We will sit and be quiet. When all is still with your daily thoughts put behind you, we will continue."

CHAPTER ELEVEN

After a short time of being still, Sarah went on. "I have been saved from death by knowledge. My parents were trying to gain some knowledge in understanding the Indians. They were traveling to an Indian camp to learn some of their ways, in hopes of living together in harmony with the red man in the valley. That is when the bears set upon my parents for slaughter. The spirit of the Chief came upon the horrific scene and realized he had knowledge of my parents. My parents were special to the Chief. They were the only white people to be allowed to visit the valley. The Chief respected my parents for trying to gain the knowledge of the Indian ways. He took pity on me and entered my soul, quieting my spirit, so that the bears would not be attracted. His actions saved my life."

Anna was nervous. "I am frightened by your talk of spirits."

"Please calm yourself, and I will continue," said Sarah. We, the white race, have only one God whom we worship. The Indians have many gods. They have a god for everything that affects them."

Anna replied, "Yes. That is why they are savages."

Sarah said, "It is our belief in a spirit greater than ours that sets us apart from the beasts. The Indians worship many spirits, but that does not make them savages."

"Civilized people have only one God," stated Moses. "To worship more than one God is heresy."

"Calm yourself, Moses, so I can continue," said Sarah. "Well then, by your own words, you all are savages as you worship more than one spirit. You worship God Almighty, but you also worship the spirit of Jesus, the spirits of Mary and Joseph, as well as the Devil."

"We do not worship the Devil." Again, Moses was getting upset.

"I agree. You and I do not worship the Devil, but there are those who do. I am just trying to show you that, as a civilized people, you worship many spirits," said Sarah. "So, the Indians are no worse than you. If they are savages, then so are you."

Anna was confused. "But Jesus was the Son of God. He was sent to earth by God."

"Jesus was the *Son* of God, an individual with a spirit of his own. He had many decisions that he had to make while on earth. Do you not worship the Holy Ghost in your religion? Is that not a separate spirit?"

"But Jesus served God. Jesus was part of God," stated Moses. "We are taught that Jesus served God, that Jesus was part of God's plan, that there is only one great and controlling spirit, and that is God. He is an all-knowing and all-powerful God."

Anna added, "Everything we have is a part of God."

Sarah said, "Then, if I use *that* logic, the Devil is part of God. If everything is part of God, then the Prince of Darkness has to be one of the faces of God."

Moses was shocked. "What heresy is this? Everyone knows that the Devil was a demon cast out of Heaven."

Sarah retorted. "Is not a demon just another name for a spirit? If God knows all, then He knows what the Devil does. If He knows the actions of the Devil and does not intervene, is he not guilty of some kind of sin? If you came upon a man raping a woman and walked away without helping, would you not be guilty of a sin for not helping?"

"That is different," stated Moses. "As humans, we are allowed to decide between good and evil. Those are the ways the righteous earn their place in Heaven. The Devil is the way of tempting the weak."

"If we are all born innocent, then why would a loving God let us be contaminated by evil, so that our souls could rot in hell? Moses, do you not feed your cows what is good for them?"

"Yes."

"Would you allow your cows to eat anything? Would you allow your cows to eat something you know might make them sick and die?"

"No."

"Why does God allow some souls to be consumed by evil?"

"I told you why," stated Moses. "So only the worthy are allowed in Heaven."

"But are we not all innocent at birth?" asked Sarah. "At birth, are we all not worthy of Heaven? If a child died during birth, would God punish that innocent child? If, on this day, three milk cows were born on your farm, would you raise them all the same with the same grain and care or would you set a test for them and only allow the best cow to survive?"

"Sarah, I would treat all the cows the same as they would all be important to me. Even the cow which produced the least milk would have some worth to it."

"Well then, if our God was all-loving, would not every soul be important to Him? If one soul were lost to evil, it would be a sin. Just as if you let one of your cows die of neglect, you would be guilty of a sin. If God saw the Devil as being evil, would God not want to limit how many souls the Devil gets and, therefore, limit his powers?"

"But, we are guilty of the original sin when Adam bit the apple," stated Moses. "We study the ways of our God in order to gain the knowledge to be allowed into Heaven."

"Then if knowledge of our God is the only way to Heaven, why was it a sin for Adam to have taken a bite from the Fruit of Knowledge?"

Moses was baffled. "Sarah, are you the Devil, trying to confuse and tempt us?"

"No. The Devil deals in lies and deceptions. Is there a single thing I have said to you which is a lie?"

Moses looked at her sheepishly. "No."

Sarah said, "What I have said here is not for the children to hear. I will not tell any of this to the children. What I have said here was an attempt to show you that just because the Indians seem to worship a different God or Gods, they are not savages and are just as worthy of Heaven as the white people. Whites are actually not as worthy as the Indians because they poison the world around them and kill for profit. They allow the factories to kill workers for the monetary gain of the owners. The Indians learned to survive in harmony with the land, while the whites greatly despoil what is around them. By having many spirits, the Indians are better able to understand life."

"How so?" asked Moses.

"Having many spirits gives the Indians a better ability to survive and be spiritually healthy. I have known many white people to cry out, 'My God, why have you forsaken me?' when they had only one thing go wrong in their lives. Even though it might be just one thing that went wrong, they felt their God had totally abandoned them. By having many spirits, the Indians are better able to understand and cope with life. If one aspect of their lives goes wrong, such as a poor salmon harvest, they might feel the spirits of the river were angry. But they would then turn to some of the other spirits, such as the spirits of the land, for help. That way, they always feel there is an option for help, rather than believing one, all-powerful God is condemning them for something they might not understand."

"You certainly have given us something to think about," remarked Moses. "At first, I was beginning to think you were a heretic, but I now see that you are so wise, you see life in many ways which escape the less educated." He nodded. "But, I agree with you that the children are too young and innocent for such theories. Keep these thoughts between the three of us, and we will let you stay."

"Thank you," said Sarah. "I wanted to be honest with you about my beliefs. I wanted you to know this, so when I eventually speak about my beliefs, you would not feel betrayed. I would not want you to think I would lie to you to gain your confidence. If I spoke to you now about my philosophy of life, you could either try to understand and accept it or you would ask me to leave. Either way, it would be less troublesome on you and the family."

"Thank you for your honesty," said Moses. Anna and I are going to bed and will discuss what you have said. I have a feeling it will not be just the children who will learn from you and your vast knowledge."

"Here is one last thought for you both," said Sarah. "Life evolves because people question what is around them. Without this constant thirst for knowledge, the human race would rot from within and fall from the Tree of Life. The world would never change if it lived on an unending diet of the same unchanging dogma. A stagnant society has never brought about any positive changes in man's existence."

Sarah retired to her room, feeling as if she may have done something to affect their lives in a positive way. She waited until she could no longer hear Moses and Anna talking and got out the silk garments she had enjoyed wearing in Boston when she had visited the pool. Quietly, she opened the door and slipped out. She went to a part of the river that could not be seen from the house.

As she walked, the silk garments flowed around her. The spirits of the mist could sense Sarah's approach, and the mist reached out to her. During the first night she spent on the river, the mist had saved her, once again, but the actions of the Englishmen and the poisonous cloud of mercury had kept Sarah and the spirits from communing with each other.

The night was still, and all of mankind was quiet. The mist wrapped around Sarah as she walked, and soon she was indistinguishable from the mist. The hands from thousands of spirits within the mist caressed her body. Sarah had learned much from her sabbatical to the city and was a lot wiser than when she had left. She was even wiser than the old Indian and her daughters who had raised her.

Sarah spoke sadly to the mist. "I am sorry I have failed you. My life has been a waste. There is no way to stop The White Way. I am disgraced and unworthy of your love. If it were not for the spirit of Ebb, whom you made my charge, I would have ended my existence."

The voice of the old, Indian woman came from the mist and resonated for Sarah to hear. "Sarah, we knew the mission was impossible, but we had to try. We love you even more for having tried, knowing that you would probably fail. The nobility lies in the earnestness of the quest and not the result. Anyone can set out to do something he or she knows is possible. The true hero is one who knows he will fail but will still try. You are such a hero to us, and when your life has run its course, you will have a place of honor with us forever."

Sarah's spirit had finally received a respite from her sense of failure. She sat quietly in the mist, feeling the loving and caring hands of the mist embracing her soul. Just before sunrise, Sarah crept into the house, quickly removed her garments and put on a cotton nightgown. About an hour later, she heard Anna moving about the house and got up. Although she had not slept, she was not the least bit tired. The spirits had refreshed her body and soul.

"Good morning, Sarah."

"Good morning, Anna. It looks to be the start of a fine day."

"I need a favor from you," said Anna."

"Anything."

"Will you watch the children while I go to town and return the schoolbooks?"

"Of course. I know school begins next week, but I could start the home schooling today," said Sarah. "Four hours in the morning will give them enough to think about for the rest of the day. That way, Abigail can help us around the house in the afternoon, while Jacob gives Moses more help with the chores of the farm. It should work out well for all of us."

While Anna walked into town, Sarah set up school. Her pens and the rice paper were all she needed. The rest was in her head. Time passed quickly. Sarah was absorbed with teaching in the morning and helping Anna in the afternoon. They all contributed to the harvest, storing vegetables and fruits in the root cellar.

As the women worked in the kitchen, Sarah began to educate Anna about the spirits. "Did you know that the Indians who once lived here held the spirits of the river more sacred than all the other spirits combined?"

"Why is that?"

"They saw the river as the cradle of life. Everything comes from or is associated with water. Life would not be possible without water. The Indians preserved the purity of the water by worshipping the area of the mist from the river. If they did not defile that area around the river, the river would stay pure and healthy for eternity. That is why I am so upset with The White Way. They spoil the very cradle of life." There was great sadness in Sarah's voice. "If it doesn't change, The White Way is doomed. The question is, when? Unfortunately, it will not be in our lifetime."

"I would like to know more about these Indians and the spirits of the mist. It is very intriguing and does not sound savage at all. It sounds like the Indians know how to live in harmony with the land," said Anna.

"It is more than that. Their society has both matriarchal and patriarchal aspects in balance and harmony. Men and women are both loved and held in high esteem. A woman is more than just a vessel to carry man's seed. Women are seen as givers of life and, as a result, have a place of honor in their world. The Indians treat everyone in the tribe with respect. When the hunters come back with game, everyone in the tribe eats. No one goes hungry. There were many religions that were matriarchal."

"What happened to them?" asked Anna.

"The patriarchal religions wiped them out. The male religions wiped out any gentle religion. It is the male aggression that has caused the world the most harm."

"Why do you call them male religions?"

"Well, let's talk about a religion which is almost two thousand years old," Sarah answered. "And, in almost two thousand years, there has never been a woman at the head of that church. Do you really think that in two thousand years there has never been a woman capable of being the leader of that church? Do you think that God really talks through men or even that God is a man? There were many religions based on women. They were gentle, earth-loving religions. They were all wiped out by the aggression of the patriarchal religions. The Christian religion, as a whole, is a religion of persecution and death. The very symbol of their church is a weapon of torture. If women controlled the Christian religions, there would be a drastic difference. Do you really think a woman would organize a group of knights to conduct a holy war? Do you think a woman would invade countries to search for something as stupid as a Holy Grail? The church is nothing more than a place with mass control of the people."

"How can you say that, Sarah?"

"Do you really think that if God talks to people, it would only be to some old man in Rome? Why would God entrust his needs to one fallible human or even one religion? How can one religion believe that it is the only, true religion and that all other religions are wrong? If the Popes really believed in their own religion, why would they live in such opulence? Why would such grand churches be built while some of their members starve for food? If you ask me, God would be made sick by the religions of today."

"Those are strong words."

"Well, I have my opinions. Where do you think you have a better chance of finding God? Do you think God is in the huge, opulent cathedrals built on the backs of poor people and funded by the tainted money of industry or do you think God resides in the church she built? God resides in the earth that the white men ruin. God does not exist in those opulent buildings called cathedrals."

"She? The church that *she* built?" asked Anna.

"Yes. God has to be a woman. Have you never heard the term, "Mother Nature?" Her church is all around us. To worship her is to worship life. To worship anything else is to worship death. Why would God even enter a cathedral? Do you think a loving God would enter a building full of treasures that were plundered at the expense of human lives? Jesus walked the earth free of possessions, so his judgment would be unencumbered by the false God of money. If the Pope and the priests believed their own religions, they would be as Jesus. They would walk amongst us with nothing more than the clothes on their backs, and they would even give those to others, whose needs were greater. If you ask me, God has been made sick by all of the current religions. The churches have tried to raise their own leaders to the level of God."

"Why do you say that?" asked Anna.

"Let me use just one example. Let us talk about confession. Do you actually think if you committed a sin that you can be absolved of it by confessing your sin to a mortal man? Can a mortal really give you absolution? How can a man be so self-inflated that he thinks God talks through him? This self-proclaimed power can even corrupt the religious leaders, clouding their judgment. Confession to anyone except God just encourages the evil of the world."

"But, Sarah, confession cleanses the soul."

"Only confessions to God can cleanse the soul. Confessions to a mortal are nothing more than idle conversations that help perpetuate sins. There is a reason why the most pious in churches are also the richest. Have you ever wondered why the people who donate the most money to a church are the ones who are given the seats closest to the front? Are their souls more important than the poor who sit at the back of the church? The owners of the mills, who poison their workers and contaminate the true church of God, are the first in line to confess. They try to take the stain off their souls with bribes. The larger the sin, the larger their bribe is to the church. The leaders of these churches are heretics for accepting this soiled money and lavishly furnishing their cathedrals. The churches of today worship money. A mill owner can slowly kill his workers with toxins and poisons, yet the owner can confess his sins to a mortal who is tempted by the very money that causes this corruption. That is why there are confessions; they allow the perpetuation of sins. A mill owner can kill and contaminate all week long and go cleanse his soul on the Sabbath, so he can begin the whole process again on Monday with a clean conscience."

Sarah's voice was full of emotion. "The Puritans are just as bad as all the rest of the religions. They fled England because of religious persecution. Once they arrived on these shores, they organized a religion just as close-minded and oppressive as the religion they were fleeing from. All of these patriarchal religions are doomed. They are built on deceit that is fueled by corrupted money. The only true religion is a religion based on Mother Nature. Women create the life that men take away. Only someone who creates life can truly appreciate the value of her creation."

Anna had many questions but wanted to hear more. "This is all so much to think about. I never looked at our religions in this light before. I think I am beginning to understand. I am starting to see the lives of the Indians in a different way."

Sarah continued. "When the white men invaded this valley, the Nissitissit was as pure as it was the day that the first Indians migrated here. That tribe of Indians lived here for more than five thousand years, and the valley remained pure. You have been here less than one hundred years and have killed the river and the land. You cut down the forests and killed the game. Since you have been here, some types of animals, who are also God's creation, no longer walk the earth. The White Way is the way of death, and death begets more death. It is a self-perpetuating evil."

"How do you know this?"

Sarah drew a breath and was almost afraid to explain. "I learned this from the spirits of the mist."

"This is not the first time I have heard you talk about the spirits of the river. Are they real? Can you show them to me?"

Sarah was quick to reply. "You can see them, but they will not talk to you. Your spirit is not yet pure enough. But anything is possible - maybe in time. Let us leave this subject alone for a while."

Anna stopped doing her housework "May I ask one more

question?"

"Certainly."

"When do you visit these spirits?"

"At night when you and Moses are asleep." Then, the two of them continued with the rest of their chores in silence.

Anna could not stop thinking about what Sarah had said. Several nights later, she lay awake, listening to see if she could hear Sarah sneaking out. She heard the door quietly close. She put on a robe and slipped out after Sarah. Anna watched as Sarah walked towards the river, her silk garments swaying around her. Anna was breathless as she observed thousands of misty hands reach out and stroke Sarah. Anna was totally amazed. At the same time, she felt ashamed because she believed she was violating something sacred while she focused on Sarah. Anna slithered away without a sound and never again followed Sarah out to the river at night.

Several years passed. Sarah knew that soon she would have to leave. Abigail and Jacob were fast learners; their knowledge had far surpassed the lessons taught in the one-room schools. When the family gathered at the dinner table, Sarah said, "I have received a message from a firm in Boston that handled Samuel's affairs. I have arranged tuition for the children at the finest universities in Boston. The firm has maintained Samuel's house, where the children, or you and the children, can live while at school. All expenses have been taken care of, including transportation home for weekends and holidays."

The family was stunned. Sarah added, "There is also money to help around the farm while the children are away. After the children graduate, I have instructed the firm to have the deed to the house put in your name. You are free to live there, live here, or sell whichever property you prefer, but you cannot sell the house in Boston until the children are out of school. I would suggest you sell the farm, here, before the chemicals in your environment can enter your bodies. Move to Boston and buy deep-sea fish and food from farms in the country that do not use pesticides and have water from deep wells. You can ask at the market, and they well tell you which farms to buy from. End your oppressive existence here in the country. There is enough money left in my uncle's estate to take care of your needs for the rest of your life."

"Why would you do this?" asked Moses.

"You and yours are the closest that I have for family. The welfare of you and your family has become important to me. My mission will take a few more years to complete. I do not need all of these worldly goods. Once my task is done, I am going to join the spirits of the mist and, once again, be among the Indians who raised me."

CHAPTER TWELVE

April had arrived and Sarah was packed. She had replenished the supplies in her parcels and was about to leave. The spirits had told Sarah she needed to be in North Village by the first day of May. The village was only a day's journey by foot, but Sarah had to make one last pilgrimage upstream.

The family gathered together to see her off. Anna said, "Sarah, we will miss you. You have been a welcome addition to this family. The children are the smartest in the valley because of your knowledge. It is truly a gift, and no one can take away what you have given them."

Sarah smiled as Anna continued. "You have also changed Moses and me forever. You have given us the insight to look above the toil of our daily existence. We have learned to see the world as one complete circle of life, where even the most insignificant person has some worth to the world. You have also showed us the true side of many religions and how their actions seem to go against what they preach. If God is all-powerful, then there can be no Devil, so the religions that reinforce themselves with threats of the Devil, actually have no God."

Moses added, "Not only have you enriched our lives spiritually, but you have left us Samuel's estate, so that the needs of our family will forever be taken care of. All that the children will ever thirst for is more knowledge. There is no way I can ever repay you for what you have done."

Sarah replied, "You and your family have given me more than you will ever know. I was a teacher who had never taught until you shared your children with me. I had no home to go to when you took me in as if I had been one of your own. I have no use for Samuel's estate, so I have given you something that I do not need. I do not see that as a gift. A true gift would be to give away something that I *do* need."

Anna's eyes brightened. "You gave us something you have sought for and needed all your life. It truly was a benefit to us, yet it cost you nothing and you lost nothing in giving it to us. But, to us, it is a gift. For this, we will forever be in your debt."

"Is this a riddle for me to cipher? If it is, I have the answer," replied Sarah.

"Well, then, what is it? I am also curious," said Moses.

Sarah smiled. "You have learned well, Anna. I gave you the gift of knowledge. The fact that you recognize that shows me it was worth the effort."

"Of course," chimed Moses. "I should have thought of that myself."

"Where will you go?" asked Anna.

"I am going up river, past Potanopa into the hills beyond. I wish to see the place where I lived as a young child, where the Chief brought me after saving my life. I wish to visit the place of the wise old Indian woman. I know she is not there anymore and that her spirit now resides within the mist. However, the circle of my life will not end where the old woman and I had once lived. The spirits have decided that I am needed in North Village for a few more years. The spirit of the great Chief is trapped in North Village. The White Way is unstoppable; the spirits must gather together for the journey to the Land of Happiness.

The spirits know that the time of the Indian is over. The river is no longer in their possession. All of the spirits are important. Every one of them will make the final journey, including the Chief and each and every sprit that has dwelled within the mist. I am supposed to help free the spirit of the Chief from the hell that he perceives himself to be in. Mankind creates hell, so only a man can save the Chief from the hell he has created. The one to finalize the process is not yet born. It is my duty to assure his birth, so that he can be the last. He is needed to complete the circle. He will be the only one who can save the spirit of the Chief. I am not exactly certain what I need to do, but the spirits will let me know."

Sarah had not told anyone that she already carried the spirit of "the last" within her. To explain it would be too complex. The living could not understand the workings of the spirits. The human brain has always seen life as a continuous line and can only react to something in the present. The brain would not have the ability to react to something in the future. Sarah knew the spirits lived in the past, present and future, all at once. She also knew if the white race were to survive, people needed to start living in the present and for the future, instead of living in the past.

Jacob and Abigail were crying as Sarah walked off. She had forever changed their lives. The universities they would attend would build upon the knowledge she gave them. As Sarah was walking away, she turned and waved. "Moses, take care of your family. There are dark clouds of ignorance starting to gather over the valley. Many will suffer and many will die. Sell your farm, and move from this cursed valley. Samuel's house will serve you well. Remember what I have said. Watch what you eat when in the city. Only consume fresh fish from the ocean or unpreserved meats from pure farms. Eat only fresh vegetables bought from those farms, and prepare the food with your own hands. Drink only from the well at Samuel's place, and when you sit at the table in the pool, think of me."

Sarah could see the rays of the setting sun reflecting from the tears in their eyes as she turned and walked away. From this day on, Sarah would only travel at night and only in the company of the mist.

After several nights of walking, Sarah finally arrived at the camp of the wise old Indian woman. She got there just before dawn. The camp was in ruins, and two walls of the shelter had fallen down. She made a simple bed and slept during the day, awakening right before sunset. She lit a fire in the open pit and waited. She knew the mist would be heavy that evening, so she began to prepare. She changed into her elegant silk gown and robe and awaited the mist. As the sun was setting, she could see the mist starting to build. She walked towards the brook and wetlands, her delicate robe flowing as she walked. She appeared as a queen amongst her subjects. The mist swirled around her, welcoming her back. Sarah sat on the same rock she had sat upon so many years ago. However, the innocence of her youth was gone and had been replaced by her determination to complete her assigned task.

Once more, thousands of hands from the mist caressed her body, cleansing and refreshing her. The spirits knew she had not succeeded in finding a way to stop The White Way and their way of life was dying. They knew many years ago when they had sent her off that she would return on that day. As a dying creature would try to take one last gasp, the spirits had one last hope - to deliver Sarah to the white people. She had done her best, but what she tried to do was too much for anyone to accomplish. The White Way could not be stopped. With the downfall of the Indians, the spirits knew the land would cry for hundreds of years. Most of all, they knew The White Way would have to end someday.

Sarah spoke softly as she sat in the mist. "The ways of the Indians are lost forever. There is no way to stop the white people. They have lived so long in their world of hate and bigotry that their force is relentless. That which is evil has overtaken the good, but what is worse is the white man has begun worshipping his possessions. The white people believe if they have a large amount of worldly goods, then their God is smiling on them. They accumulate these goods at the expense of other men and Mother Nature. Even their churches worship the false god of money. The members of the church are expected to donate money, which is more important than good deeds. When a minister takes on a new parish, the decision to take the job is based on how much money he will be paid and is not related to the needs of the parishioners. On Sunday, they do not gather at the house of someone who needs help to make someone's life better. Instead, they gather at a parish house where the pews are assigned in a monetary pecking order. Money and goods have become their gods, and forgiveness for their sins is bought with the blood money they make from poisoning the health of those who work for them. If anyone dares to question the motives behind the church, the minister will accuse that person of being possessed by the Devil. Any opposing view to what the minister professes is considered the work of the Devil."

A voice came from the mist. "What is this thing? This Devil? If they have a loving God, then how can they have a Devil? If their God is all-powerful, then where does the Devil get the power to exist?"

Sarah responded. "Their Devil is an anti-God, an evil spirit that they conveniently manufactured to use for an excuse. It is a way to try and cover up the dark side of their beliefs. It is something they use to hide the error of their views. When the short-sightedness of their ministers causes trouble, rather than admit to being human and making an error in judgment, they simply blame it on the Devil."

Even the spirits were confused. "There is such a thing as an evil spirit?"

Sarah was searching for the right answer. "In their minds, there is. They need to be able to blame their own ignorance and bad actions on anything other than themselves. We know there are no evil spirits in nature. If there were no longer men, then their false gods and devils would cease to exist. Mother Nature exists whether there is man or not, and she needs nothing more than respect. Mother Nature has no use for money or commercial goods."

A soft voice came from the mist. "If their Gods are false and their ways corrupt, why do they not die of their own poisons?"

"They *do* die of their own poisons; they die by the tens of thousands in the cities, working to feed their families. They die in their own fields by the poisons that they spread. Eventually it will overcome them and their days will end, but it won't be in our lifetime."

Sarah spent most of that month sleeping during the day and communing with the spirits at night. The time had come for her to fulfill her destiny. With only five days left in the month, she packed her bags for the last time. She prepared to head towards North Village. She was about to leave when she suddenly remembered something. She stepped away, facing one of the walls, and reached into a crack. A clay pipe was inside, along with a small clay container with a lid. The container had held the potion the old lady smoked years ago, when Ebb's spirit became trapped and was inhaled by Sarah as an infant. Before Sarah had left camp, the wise old Indian had told her about that night. Sarah and Ebb had both made a long journey. They had both learned a lot since that time. Ebb was able to see a lot more than he had during his mortal life. Sarah had experienced a difficult journey. She had become wise and was grateful to Ebb. Without him as her charge, she would not have had the strength to continue. With less than a week left, she started back downstream to the Nissitissit and followed the river down towards North Village. The vileness of The White Way was starting to impact North Village. The curse of the Chief and his judgment of the settlers appeared to be coming true, although the settlers were actually causing their own demise.

CHAPTER THIRTEEN

"Winslow, the women in the village say that I might have my baby on May Day. Wouldn't it be nice if our child was born on such a joyous day?" Prudence was getting large, and the baby was beginning to shift lower. She instinctively knew the day would soon arrive.

"Whatever day the baby is born will be a holiday to me. Just stay resting until then. I don't want you to do anything strenuous. Have you thought about any names for the baby if it is a girl?" Winslow asked.

"I thought I liked the name Florence. We could call her Flo for short. What do you think?"

"I suppose that is all right. Do you still want to call the baby Ebenezer if it is a boy?"

"I never said that I wanted to call the baby Ebenezer."

"Sure you did. Remember back when you said that you wanted a family?" asked Winslow.

"No. I said if we had a boy, I wanted to call him Ebb."

"Well, was that not short for Ebenezer?" asked Winslow.

"If the baby is a boy I want to call him Ebb, not Ebenezer," said Prudence. I wanted to call him that because of the currents in the river, remember?"

"Oh Prudence, I think that you are a little carried away with all of this infatuation about the river."

"That river is why North Village is here. It is the very thing that drives all of our industry. Without that river, we would not be living in this community," said Prudence.

"I do not want to worry you at such a critical time, but I feel that something is wrong in North Village. Lately, there have been more and more strange and tragic happenings. Remember what happened, just a few months ago, on that very misty night?" Winslow inquired.

"That was terrifying. That poor woman and the loss of the boy was more than the family could stand. (16) I remember that day. The ice on Paugus Pond had been there only a few days when the weather turned warm. The butcher's son had come down to play with a couple of boys here in the village. They were over by the widow Adams' house, and were playing. I saw the widow come out and tell the boys not to play on Paugus Pond. I heard her distinctly tell them the ice was not safe. The day was unusually warm, and I had the window open. The stove was hot from baking bread, and I was trying to cool off. I heard the insolent, young boys shout out 'Mind your own business, you miserable old witch.' They were quite disrespectful to the poor, old woman."

"You never told me this," said Winslow.

"I was too upset to talk about it. Then, the boys from the village went home for lunch. The butcher's son was left alone, and I think he went to cross the river to go home. He must have fallen through the ice. The widow Adams saw him drown but did not tell anyone. The poor old woman was demented before that, but, when she saw the butcher's son drown, she must have totally lost her mind. I could see her all afternoon, sitting in her chair by the window. I remember feeling sorry for her, as she looked even more crazy than usual. When the butcher's son did not return for lunch, his mother became worried and sent word to the father that the boy was missing. The whole family came out to look for him. First, they went to the house of the boys he had been playing with. The boys said the last time they saw him, he was at the widow Adams' place."

"What happened next?" asked Winslow.

"The family went to the widow Adams. She was sitting, looking out the window. I remember them pounding on her door, and she just sat there, looking out at the river. They let themselves in through the door and went up to her. When they asked her if she knew where the boy was, she just sat there, not moving. I fear that the whole episode finally drove the poor woman insane. She just kept sitting there, looking at the river. When she finally spoke, all she could say was 'Try looking for him downstream.' So, the family glanced over to the area where the widow's gaze seemed to be transfixed. To their horror, there was a hole in the ice," said Prudence.

"I know what happened next. They found the boy at the mill's sluice. I was busy running the saw when I saw all the commotion. By then, even the two boys playing with the butcher's son had joined in the search."

"Tell me, what did they say?" asked Prudence.

"They…uh…said that…um." Winslow stopped speaking.

"Tell me, Winslow, what did they say?"

"Well, the boys accused the old Adams widow of putting a spell on the boy."

"A spell?"

"Yes. They accused her of being a witch," Winslow said.

"Well, that explains what happened next," said Prudence. "The butcher and a few men from the village carried the boy's limp body up to the widow's porch. I can still remember the poor boy's arms swinging as the father carried him. It was evident, from the color of the boy, that he had been dead for a few hours. The family was full of grief. The boy had been named after the grandfather, and it was expected that he would proudly carry the name forward. I can still see them screaming at her. 'You did this! You did this!' All she did was sit there in her chair, looking at the hole in the ice. It was as if her life had gone down that hole along with the boy. I never saw her move after that. One of the women in the village took pity on her and lit a lamp and put it on the table beside her before they all left."

"Yes, that lamp was there when I saw her," said Winslow. "When I came home from work, she was just sitting there looking out the window. The lamp was flickering beside her. It looked spooky, the way the shadows played across her old face."

"Later that night, I could not sleep, so I was sitting by the window, looking out. I could barely see her through the mist, but she was still sitting there with the lamp flickering. Did she have a cat, Winslow?"

"No, the woman was too infirm to have any pets. Why do you ask?"

"I swear I saw a cat walking around the table near the lamp. I saw the cat knock the lamp over and then…" Prudence was visibly upset but she continued. "Then the house erupted into flames. The fire was everywhere, yet the woman just sat there looking out at the river. I could see her just sitting there. When the flames began to surround her, she never moved or screamed. Then I saw something, Winslow, just before the flames consumed her. I saw a shape in the fog."

"What did you see?" Winslow asked.

"A shape in the mist. It came from that creepy, old place across the river. I saw the misty form of a horse. It looked white against the gray of the mist. On top of the horse, I saw a great Indian Chief. The mist flowed out of the river, carrying the horse and the Chief up to the porch of the old widow," said Prudence.

Winslow was shaking a bit. "God, Prudence! Why did you not tell me this? Then what happened?"

"The Chief leaned forward and held out his hand as if he was gesturing to the old woman to come out, but she wouldn't budge. The Chief was still holding out his hand when the fire grew in intensity, and the flames consumed the woman. Then, the mist began to roll, and the Chief and the horse disappeared into the hole in the ice." Both remained silent for a moment. "Winslow, what is that creepy looking place across the river - the place where it looked like the figure came from?" Winslow looked panic-stricken and would not speak. Prudence could see the fear in his eyes. "Winslow, tell me whose place that is!"

"That place was the home of John and his son, William."

"Why is everyone afraid of that place? What happened there? What happened to John and his son?" asked Prudence.

"A few years ago, it was reported that William, the mill foreman, might have drowned in Paugus Pond," said Winslow.

"What do you mean?" asked Prudence. "Did he drown or not?"

"No one can say for sure. The body was never found. An old sot at the tavern claims he saw an evil misty hand reach up out of the water and pull poor William down. We tried to search the pond, but something happened the night William drowned. An evil mist filled the valley, burning the eyes of the men and choking their lungs while they searched. It caused the men to flee in horror. The next morning, there was a path of death that ran from the mill, upstream to Sucker Brook, where two men reported that they saw a witch who cast a spell on the river. We drained the pond to look for his body, but we never found it. That night, when the pond was drained, William's father, John, was killed in some kind of strange accident."

"What happened?" Prudence asked.

"He was found in the mud with his head kicked in by a horse. But the strange thing is there was no footprint of man or beast seen in the mud. Some of the superstitious old-timers say it was the revenge of the Chief. They claim the death horse killed him. The place where you saw the Chief and the death horse was the very same spot where the settlers killed the Chief and his horse. Before he died, the Chief uttered this curse: 'My spirit will not rest until I get revenge on you and the sons of your sons. All will perish in the end. The land will have its revenge.' Then the horse and the Chief fell into the water at that spot, never to be seen again," said Winslow.

"When did the strange deaths start to occur?" asked Prudence.

"Some say, shortly after that, when the valley was plagued by what is called The Pepperell Fever," answered Winslow.

"I remember Abel talking about that when I lived in Hollis Village," Prudence said. "Over a hundred people died from that fever. They were afraid that it would spread to Hollis, but the fever stayed mostly in the valley."

Winslow said, "The fever started at the farm of one of the original settlers. He was not hired to help build the mill, so he went upstream and claimed some land on one of the tributaries to the river. The area he chose for his farm was thick with white sumac, and he was allergic to it. To remove the sumac, the settler flooded his farm and let the water kill it off. Once the leaves left the sumac, he hired a couple of shiftless men to help clear the land. Everyone on the farm got sick and died, including the workers."

"It was rumored in Hollis Village that the men he hired had brought back a disease from the French and Indian War," remarked Prudence.

"The people in this valley thought otherwise," said Winslow. "Many of the original settlers died in unusual ways. There is a certain type of insanity which appears to be moving into the valley."

"What happened to your father, Winslow?"

"He was killed one spring in a logging accident."

"Was he one of the original settlers?" asked Prudence.

"Yes, he was."

"What about the widow Adams?"

"She and her husband were two of the original settlers," replied Winslow.

"What about Richard, who disappeared when we came here last fall?" asked Prudence.

"Richard was not one of the original settlers. He came here after the mill was already built. It is thought that he suffered the same fate as William, but nobody saw it happen."

"Winslow, I am frightened. Why did you bring me here?"

"Oh, Prudence, don't be foolish. I do not believe in such idle nonsense. People die tragic deaths all over the country. Life is dangerous, and a workman must keep his head about him. Look at my job. I run the saw, which is very dangerous, but I temper the danger with proper care. Don't worry. Nothing will ever happen."

"Why don't we leave this valley, and you can look for work somewhere else?"

"Aaron pays more for workmen here than we could make somewhere else. His pay keeps all but the very superstitious here and working."

"Winslow, please be careful at the mill. I am beginning to fear this curse on the valley. What I saw, the night the widow Adams died, was not of this world."

"Prudence, I do not believe in such nonsense. Your eyes were playing tricks on you. We will be all right. Trust me."

"I will, but just be careful anyway." Prudence paused and then asked, "Can I have some of the spring water?"

When Prudence moved to North Village she did not like the taste of the water from the wells near the river. She was used to the clean, sweet water that was in the well at Abel's house. She discovered a spring on the side one of the hills, and she went there daily to get drinking water. For the past few months, Winslow had been getting the water after work. Winslow had to agree that the spring water tasted better than the water from North Village, which had a bitter aftertaste.

"Of course. Let me pour you a glass. Sit back and rest while you sip the water."

Prudence took a sip, lay back, and fell asleep. She napped for a few hours and awoke with a start. "Winslow, run and get the midwife! I think it is time for the baby to come."

Winslow opened the door and ran out. He darted away to a nearby house and summoned the midwife to come at once. "Margaret, come quick! Prudence has started her labor."

"Winslow, take these two, large pots back and put them on the stove. Fill the pots with water, and stoke the stove. I will be along in just a few minutes. This is her first baby, and it will take her awhile."

Grabbing the two large pots he rushed back to Prudence. "The midwife will be along shortly. I will have to use water from the well." They did not drink the well water, but they did use it to bathe and to wash their clothes.

Across the river, Sarah was watching from inside John's empty house. She had arrived in North Village during the night. The spirits had guided her to the tumbledown cabin on the north side of the river. Since the death of John, the house had remained empty. People in the village believed the place was cursed, after finding John's body in the mud. They stayed away following the death of William, which preceded the bizarre death of John. Even the children, who ran around wildly, playing in North Village, would not go near the house.

Sarah knew that Prudence could not give birth until she released the soul of Ebb. She realized that since Prudence was having her first baby, she would likely begin her labor in few hours and would stay in labor for at least a few more. Sarah spread her bedroll and napped while the first day of May passed by. She wondered what would happen to her when she no longer carried the soul of Ebb. Darkness approached, and the conditions were right for a heavy mist in the valley. Sarah awoke just before sunset and started to prepare for it. She put on her flowing silk robes and stood regally as she patiently waited for the arrival of the mist.

CHAPTER FOURTEEN

Word spread about the impending mist. The villagers anticipated it to be heavy. The midwife and her assistants made sure their chores were done before dark. They had fed their families and dressed the children in their nightgowns. They had put out snacks for the children and their husbands. The clean chamber pots had been placed inside the doors of the houses in the village. No one had any reason to venture out into the mist.

The midwife was making preparations for the birth of Prudence's child. She brought supplies of clean cloths to cleanse Prudence, along with the few rudimentary implements for birth. The midwife had set a smaller pan on the stove for the sharp, little nippers to cut the cord, along with a few strips of cotton twine for tying it. She had placed everything in the pan, so that they could receive the benefits of the boiling water.

The midwife had a fourteen-year-old daughter who would take care of the two younger children. That way, her husband could be in attendance and help Winslow. Before dusk, Winslow and the midwife's husband created a fire pit outside and gathered a large supply of firewood beside the door. The two men went inside to finish preparing the house. The bedroom was situated at the side of the kitchen and did not have a door. They hung a blanket to provide Prudence with a little privacy. Then, they placed a large pot of water on a space remaining on the stove, and tealeaves were set to steep.

The two men worked feverishly as the shadows of late afternoon lengthened. They lit the fire pit outside and loaded it with wood. Everything was ready. The heat of the fire would keep the mist away from the door, allowing the men to periodically go outside and throw armloads of wood into the fire pit. Shortly before sunset, Margaret, the midwife, arrived, along with her two assistants, and they hustled her inside.

The house was warm and steamy from the pots of boiling water, and Prudence was resting quietly. The men sat at the table and sipped tea while the women attended to Prudence. Every few minutes, Winslow would get up to check on the progress. Several hours went by, and it appeared that the baby would not be born on May Day.

Across the river, Sarah was busy with preparations of her own. As the darkness deepened, she sat on the far side of the cabin, unseen by the inhabitants of the village. The mist was exceptionally heavy, and Sarah could barely see the roaring fire. A bright halo gleamed around the fire, similar to the moon's halo when a storm was pending.

Sarah did not have to wait long. The strong mist soon surrounded her. Thousands of spirits had gathered, awaiting the chief. The Chief and his horse rose from the area where the settlers had watched them disappear, after being fatally wounded many years ago. The Chief stepped off of his horse and walked up to Sarah.

"Sarah, you have traveled many miles and learned a great deal. You have become Sarah the Wise. You have done everything possible to study The White Way, and we are grateful. There is no hope of stopping them. Our way of life is gone forever. The child being born across the river will be the last of the sons from the original settlers. The spirits have determined that he will help our spirits free themselves from the mist. The spirits have not yet told me how. They know more than I. I have been engaged in this valley all these years because of the curse I uttered. I have been dwelling here, in the cusp between two worlds, ever since that fateful day. My spirit has grown tired of being there, at the death of those I cursed. There have been so many, and there are so many more to go. It is time to let go of Ebb's spirit."

Sarah took out the clay pipe and filled it with the concoction from the small clay jar. She took a few shallow puffs. When the pipe was well lit, she deeply inhaled the smoke and then exhaled. The spirit of Ebb drifted out with the smoke and was situated beside the Chief.

"Hey, I can speak now. I am free once again." Ebb was relieved. He had been locked inside Sarah for quite awhile. "Sarah, thank you for taking such good care of my soul all these years and delivering me to this place at the proper time. I have learned a great deal from being part of you. You are a remarkable woman and have learned a lot in your lifetime. When we were with Moses and Anna, I watched you educate their children. You did something wonderful with them. Maybe they can grow up and help change things. Maybe, in the future, they can help restore the valley and save it from doom. It is too late to show the adults the error of their ways, but, by educating the children before their minds are too set, maybe there is hope for them."

Sarah could see the spirit of Ebb. She looked up and down at him. "Ebb, you sure grew up to be an ornery looking cuss. I can tell by the lines on your face and the curve to your body, that you are uh… have ah… lived a long time. You have been no effort to carry, and I also am in debt to you. You were the reason I kept going. Without you, my despair of not being able to stop The White Way would have been too much. It would have overcome me."

"Your job is not yet done," said the Chief to Sarah. "You must stay here, near Prudence, and when the boy reaches the age of five, you must encourage his mother to remove him from this valley. We must insure that Ebb lives a long life. Much time has been put into his preparation. No one, but he, can put an end to this."

Sarah seemed disappointed. "Five more years? My life is going to be occupied for five more years?"

"I am sorry, Sarah, but the rest of your life will be centered on young Ebb. Neither you nor his mother will be allowed to leave this valley alive. It just is not to happen."

Sarah took another deep puff of the clay pipe and held onto the smoke. As she exhaled, she said, "I am sorry for my moment of weakness. It is not everyday that a person finds out the details of their demise. Will I finally succumb to my intermittent despair and take my own life?"

"No. That would lock you in the cusp forever. Unfortunately, you will die at the hands of three, misguided men, but only after you have saved young Ebb. The spirits have already charted the future of us all."

A faint, but soothing, voice came from the mist. "Ebb, come with us. It is time. Chief, we need you, also, to come with us. Sarah, say goodbye to both of the spirits of these men. You will not see either of them again in this lifetime."

The farewell was not a sad one. If they could carry out the wishes of the spirits, all three knew they would forever be together in the Place of Happiness. Did it matter what happened during their short mortal lives, if it would get them to an eternity of joy? That thought was in their minds.

The mist whisked away the spirits of Ebb and the Chief. Sarah was sitting quietly when another comforting voice came from the mist. "Sarah, although the Chief and Ebb cannot visit with you, *we* will be there for you. Whenever you are feeling low because your duty is difficult, we will be there to comfort your soul. Over time, all will be well. Do not fear. We all had mortal bodies once. The journey over is easy after the pain of life leaves your soul."

Sarah responded, "I have done all you wanted of me. I am weary, and my body is growing older faster and faster as the river gets worse from The White Way. Five more years is more than I thought I would have. All is well; I will do my appointed rounds."

The spirits spoke to Sarah again. "The Chief saved your life, and he is responsible for you and your actions. You will save Ebb, which makes you responsible for him and his actions. In return, it has been deemed that Ebb will save the soul of the Chief. Then, Ebb will be responsible for the Chief's soul, and the actions will have come full circle. The tapestry we are weaving is very complex. The threads of life are thin and need to be woven tightly, so that they cannot fray."

The mist took the Chief and Ebb to the window of Prudence's bedroom on the other side of the river. Through the curtains, they could see Prudence on the bed and the flurry of activity between the midwife and her friends. The sheer curtains gave the scene a pure white aura.

"Go to the kitchen, and get the snips and the twine off the stove. Prudence is in the final stage. I can see the head, and it is time," Margaret told one of her assistants.

The assistant scurried into the kitchen. "Hold tight, Winslow, the time of birth is at hand. In the next few minutes, you will become a father."

Winslow turned white. "Take care of them. They are the light of my life."

"Rest easy, Winslow. Neither you nor she is the first to go through this. It is the way of life." The assistant returned to the room, just as young Ebb emerged. She shouted out to Winslow, "You're a father! It is a boy."

"Oh, thank Providence, a son!" Winslow broke down and cried for a moment.

Ebb could not believe his eyes. His spirit as an old man was witnessing his own birth. "This is all so strange. I am here, yet, I am also there."

"Tie the cord here and here," commanded Margaret, "and give me the snips." The spirit of Ebb watched with fascination as an assistant tied the cord in two places and cut it. Ebb's spirit winced with the snip, and the infant let out his first cry.

"That will be the first of many," mumbled the old spirit.

"Come, Ebb," said the Chief. The spirits of the mist have decided that your old spirit will remain with me until your death. Then I do not know what will happen. I have not been allowed to see what happens after your death. I hope that we do not repeat this cycle with the two of us trapped in the cusp forever. You will get to witness what leaving the valley spared you. You will help me complete the rest of my gruesome obligation by joining my sagging spirit. Being the last one, perhaps you will have something to do with bringing all of this to an end. We must leave now; the sun will rise soon. You will now experience what it is like to be a spirit of the mist."

The mist retreated back to the river, and the spirits of the Chief and Ebb faded away and descended into the river. On the opposite side, Sarah could see the sunrise, and she watched Winslow stoking the fire. Then she saw what she was looking for. Winslow came out with the bloody sheets. The afterbirth had been wrapped inside. Winslow tossed the messy pile on top of the roaring fire. Sarah breathed a sigh of relief. She knew the birth had gone well. The fact that the sheets were burned meant that the birth was a success. If it had gone wrong, the bodies of Prudence and Ebb would have been wrapped in the sheets to await burial.

Sarah packed her bags and set off, through the woods, to North Street. She wanted to make her entrance into town from the road, rather than be seen coming from the river. The sun was shining brightly as she entered town. Ebb had been born on May 2, 1812, and the process had begun. The birth of Ebb, however, was not the only notable event on that day.

Rebecca was in the parlor when the maid brought her a letter. "This came for you this morning, madam."

"Thank you," Rebecca said, taking the letter. Her hand quivered as she looked at the envelope. Her address appeared on the front of the envelope, and the return address read: "Daughters of the American Revolution" with no street or city. Rebecca was a member of the organization. She had never received a letter that looked like that before. Usually, the return address was embossed on the front and sealed with wax on the back. This letter looked crude, in comparison. She opened the envelope.

Dear R,

I hope you and the boy are well. I think of you often. You may write me, if you want, at PO Box 406, Newburyport, Massachusetts. All is well with me.

R

CHAPTER FIFTEEN

Sarah strolled down North Street, which reached North Village between the school and the river. The village was bustling with activity since the news of the new baby. The midwife and her assistants were leaving Prudence when they came upon Sarah walking by.

"Where do you come from, old woman?"

"I have been living with my relatives in West Hollis. My name is Sarah."

"Who might they be?" inquired the assistant as she stopped to chat.

"I was staying with Moses and Anna." Meanwhile, Margaret and the other woman hustled home to feed their children.

"Oh, that Quaker couple with the farm. I am acquainted with them. They come to town to sell their oats and other grains. Are you a Quaker also?"

Sarah lied. "No, I am not. They are distant relatives, and their beliefs are different than mine. I could not agree with their faith, so I have left them. I believe in the Puritan way, just like all of you. I have come to this fine village to seek employment and no longer wish to associate with Moses and Anna. I do not agree with their ways."

"That is wise," responded the assistant. "Their ways are evil and the work of the Devil. Quaker women are witches. They can see into the future and alter the ways of what is right. You would not be welcome in this village if you were a Quaker. Moses is allowed to trade his goods here, and that is all. How is it that you come to town on this day? Moses and Anna sold the farm two weeks ago to a God-fearing Puritan family, and we are rid of their Quaker nonsense."

"I left at the beginning of April, when Moses and Anna received notice that an uncle in Boston had willed them a large inheritance." Inside, Sarah was joyous. She knew that they had taken her advice and moved to Boston to educate the children. The decision was best for all. The valley was no longer a place to raise children. "I had gone up to the village at Potanopa looking for work, but no one was hiring. I was hoping I might find a job here. Do you know of anything in the village?"

"Well, yes I do," replied the assistant. They are looking for a rag picker in the shoddy shack. It does not pay much, but, at least, it is something. Go over to the mill and inquire about it. I have to go home now and tend to my family. I have been here with Margaret all night, attending to Prudence and her new son who was born just before dawn."

"There was a baby born here this morning?" asked Sarah.

"Yes, right in there." The assistant pointed toward the home of Winslow and Prudence.

"Does she need anymore assistance?" asked Sarah. "I am well-versed at being a midwife."

"Prudence and the newborn are resting, but it might be nice if you went in and sat with her, in case she needs anything. Margaret and I will be back in a little while to check on her. The baby is all washed. If he wakes up, tell Prudence to nurse him again. He did not nurse for very long, after being born. Prudence was in labor for almost a day, and she and the baby were both exhausted."

Sarah smiled. "I can do that. After you and Margaret come back, I will go over to the mill and ask about employment."

Sarah went up to the house, knocked lightly, and went inside. Prudence was in bed, with the infant lying beside her, asleep. She looked up at Sarah. "Who are you?"

"I am Sarah. I just came to North Village this day. I saw one of the midwives outside, and she asked if I would tend to you for a short while. Where is your husband?"

"He had to go to work at the mill," replied Prudence. "He runs the big saw. If he does not cut the logs into boards, all of the production at the mill suffers. That saw mill drives the commerce of this entire village."

"Well, you just rest easy. The lady outside said your name was Prudence."

"Yes. I am Prudence. This is Ebb, and my husband is Winslow. He will be home after he does his work."

"Well, my dear, just ask me if you need anything. I am here to make sure everything goes well."

"I could use a sip of water."

"Prudence, where did that water come from?"

"It is spring water from the side of the hill below the mill. I do not like the taste of the water from the wells here in the village."

"That is good. Sarah leaned down, close to Prudence. "Do not ever drink the water from the wellsss."

Prudence was a little startled by the voice she heard. It sounded as if it were more than one voice, but she was exhausted and imagined that she had not heard Sarah correctly. Prudence napped for a while. When she awakened, Sarah was still sitting in attendance and began humming gently. Prudence listened to the unfamiliar tunes and fell back to sleep. Sarah looked outside, through the window, and stopped humming when she noticed two of the village women heading their way.

Sarah leaned down to Prudence. "Take care of Ebb. Take care of him, for he is destined to be lassst."

Prudence was half asleep and began to stir. She gave Sarah a slight affirmative nod, and she was back asleep. The two village women entered the home. The scene was tranquil. Sarah was sitting in a chair near the bed, and Prudence and Ebb were napping.

"You must be Sarah. I am Margaret, the midwife. Thank you for staying with Prudence, so we could attend to our family needs. I heard you were looking for work. My husband works at the mill. When he came home for lunch, I told him to put in a good word with Aaron. When you leave here, go directly to the mill. I am sure they can start you out tomorrow."

"Thank you, Margaret. That was nice of you. Now, all I need is to find a place to stay. What is that old, tumbled-down place across the river? Would anyone mind if I cleaned the place up and lived there?" (19)

"Sakes alive, woman! There is not a person in this village that will go near there," Margaret blurted out.

Sarah acted ignorant. "Why is that?"

"Well, it is believed that the place is possessed with evil spirits."

"Oh Margaret, I don't believe in such things. I have no fear of that place. As long as no one will mind, I will go over there this afternoon after I go to the mill."

Margaret said, "If you can stand the place, there is no one here who will complain. It might actually be better if someone cleaned the place up, instead of it being cluttered and scary-looking. At one time, when John was young, people came from all over to visit him and nothing bad ever happened. I must warn you, though. People fear the mist from the river. They say something evil hides within it. I am not trying to scare you away. I just want to be honest with you."

"I am not afraid of such things, and I will never fear the mist. It is just moisture from the river water."

The assistant added, "Well, we will see what you think after you stay there for a while."

"Thank you, ladies, for the advice and the help," said Sarah. "I am going to the mill to see about work." Sarah rose from the chair and went outside, closing the door. As she walked, she peeked into a few doorways until she found the shoddy mill, adjacent to the new velvet shop. Sarah did not want to go into the velvet shop. The royal colors of the velvet, used in the bright greens, reds and blues, were made from dyes containing arsenic and heavy metals. She was relieved that the shoddy mill was a drafty, old shack. She could see that the poisons in the velvet shop were separated from the shoddy mill by a closed door.

The worst part of the velvet shop was the steam closet. Velvet cannot be ironed because the fabric pile would be crushed and damaged. The women needed to hang and steam it, in order to remove any wrinkles that occurred during the sewing process. A fireplace with a grate was outside. A huge kettle of water sat on the grate. The kettle, with a cap on top, contained about twenty-five gallons of water. A spout that was similar to a teakettle pointed towards the velvet shop. The kettle had round, metal ductwork that traveled from the side of the velvet shop into the steam closet. A heavy bead of lead solder had sealed all the seams in the ductwork.

Each morning, one of the women would fill the kettle with well water and light a fire underneath it with scrap wood from the mill. The kettle took at least an hour, during the summer, to boil. In the winter, they waited even longer. The steam would enter through the ductwork, fill the closet, and remove any of the wrinkles. The closet had room to hang several garments. Periodically, one of the women would open the steam closet and remove the garments. Then, steam would waft out into the woman's face and fill the room with an evil, garlic-like smell. The smell developed from the combination of copper arsenate from the green colors, lead vapors from the soldered joints in the ductwork, mercury vapors from the felts used in the collars, and vermilion, which was used for the brilliant reds. The air in the velvet shop was becoming deadly.

Sarah stood there, watching the toxic procedure when the woman in the shop noticed her and opened the door. "Can I help you, old woman?"

"Yes, I heard that I might find employment in the shoddy mill."

"Well, you heard right. The woman who had that job had been sick for quite a while. She finally died last week. Damn workers, there is always something with them. She was almost mad before she died - some type of insanity would be my guess. There is a huge pile of rags against the wall, and there are many more bundles outside under some oilcloths." She stood by Sarah and looked her over. "You look pretty old. Are you well enough to work?"

"Madam, I may look old, but I am still in excellent health. I know how a shoddy mill works, and I can do the job. My name is Sarah, and I know I can do what is expected of me."

"Well, Sarah, my name is Helen, and I run the velvet shop. My office is that little room on the opposite side of the shop. This shoddy mill is different than any you might be used to. The rags are not torn by hand here. We have a wonderful, new contraption that Richard invented before he disa… I mean, before he left. Come over here, and I will show you."

Sarah walked with the woman, across the shop, to a metal hopper. Two metal shafts were inside with long spikes sticking out of them.

The metal shafts continued outside the hopper, surrounded by a leather strap, and they looped around a drive shaft from the mill. At that time, they had disengaged the clutch lever, so neither the leather drive belt nor the shafts in the hopper were turning.

"Now, Sarah, your job is to sort the rags by color first and make separate piles. The white rags go into one pile, and all the other colors go into another pile. The whites, when turned to shoddy, can be bleached clean, and then can be used for linens and such. The colored shoddy gets dyed dark blue or black and is used to make coats and outerwear for work clothes. Do you understand, so far?"

Sarah nodded. "Yes, ma'am. I understand everything, so far."

"Very well, then. Take that pile of white rags over there and put them into the hopper." Sarah was glad she had not been asked to pick from the colored pile of rags, or she probably would not have gotten the job. She threw the rags into the bin. "Good. Now pull down on that lever."

Sarah pulled the lever down, which put pressure on the drive belt. The tension in the belt pulled it tightly against the mill shaft. The belt started turning, which made the drive shafts turn in the rag hopper. The shafts turned in opposite directions, causing the spikes to shred the rags.

"As you pull on the lever, keep your eyes on the rags. We want to shred the rags, but leave the threads as long as possible, so they can be easily spun into new yarn. If you over shred the rags, what is left is only good for making paper and won't be worth as much as what can be made into yarn. See how the rags look now? Lift the lever and stop the mill. See how you can still see the individual threads? That is when you know it is done right. Take those shredded rags, and put them into that other bin over there. That bin is lined with a burlap bag. We keep putting the shoddy into that bin and compressing it.

When the bin is full, the burlap is pulled up and tied. Then, using that wheelbarrow, the bundle is wheeled out to the shipment shed. When we have a wagonload, there is an old man who hauls the bales to East Pepperell where they are sold. The white shoddy goes to the Pepperell weave shop, which makes sheets, pillowcases and towels. The colored shoddy is shipped by flat bottom boat to the new larger mills that are being built downstream in Lowell and Lawrence. They make the shoddy work clothes there."

Sarah smiled. "I know I can do all of that."

"Good. When can you start?

"I can be here in the morning," Sarah replied. "I need to make some arrangements for living quarters. Thank you for the work, Helen. I only have one question. What is my pay?"

"Thirty-five cents a day. If you can produce enough shoddy in a day, then I will raise your pay to forty cents a day."

Sarah did not care what the pay was. She still had many gold coins from Samuel stashed in the bottom of her tote bag. "I'll take the job. What time do I need to be here tomorrow?"

"Work is from seven a.m. until five p.m., and you get half an hour for lunch. Please be punctual, or you will not keep the job."

"Thank you. I will see you at quarter to seven tomorrow."

Sarah headed back to Prudence to pick up the parcels she had left there earlier. She crossed over the bridge and walked along the narrow, overgrown path to John's house. Sarah went back inside to where she had been the night before. She found a dirty mess; dust and mouse droppings covered most of the interior. Because of the darkness at the time she hid out, she had not seen how unkempt the place was. She found a broom and began sweeping the floors. She felt grateful that she was able to find what was needed to make a home. Pots and pans were in abundance, and two lamps had plenty of oil. A pile of firewood was even beside the fireplace. Sarah put some wood in the fireplace and saw a flint kit on the crude mantle. She bent down. With a few strikes of the flint, she sparked the tinder, and the fire began crackling. Instantly, the place felt more like a home. Sarah spent the rest of the day cleaning the inside. She wore a damp cloth over her mouth and nose to protect her from the dust. Just before sunset, Sarah walked to the store to buy some tea.

"How much for a pound of tea?" she inquired to the storeowner, who was standing outside. She noticed that the owner was different than the one a few years ago.

"Seven cents," he replied.

She used a few pennies from her purse. She did not want anyone in the village to know that she had a stash of gold twenty-dollar coins. Having to explain how she had gotten them would be too difficult. She looked like a pauper, and she wanted people to think she was poor. That would be easier. No one, especially those with money, ever noticed a poor old pauper.

Sarah counted out seven pennies. "Here you go, my good man. I will wait here for the tea."

The storeowner returned few moments later. "Here you are, Madam. I see that you are new to our village. I have put some crackers in the bag for you. It is a welcoming gift from me. I hope to see you often."

"Thank you, kind sir. I start work in the shoddy mill tomorrow, and after I receive my pay I will be back for more supplies. Do you have any dried cod?"

"I do not have any right now, Madam. When it is spring, the locals eat the fish from the river. Dried cod is a winter staple, but I will have the supply wagon bring in a couple of boxes. By the time you get your pay, I will have the cod for you."

"Thank you, sir. You are too kind. May I ask if you can get hardtack bread?"

"I can, indeed. I can order it from Boston, from the same place that has the dried cod. I never have had a request for it. Are you from Newfoundland? I know that hardtack is a favorite of the Newfies."

"No, kind sir. I spent some time in Boston many years ago, and an old, retired ship captain showed me how to fix a dish called 'Fish and Brewis.' When you get the supplies in, I will make some and bring you a bowlful, in return for being so kind and giving me the crackers."

"You don't have to do that, Madam."

"It is no effort, sir. I will make myself a batch, and there will be plenty to share. May I ask one more question?"

"Certainly, Madam."

"If I leave a list of supplies with you, on my way to work, can you fill the order, so that when I get out of work I can pick it up on the porch, here? Although you have a wonderful looking store, I find that some of the odors of paint and other supplies make my nose twitch. Oh, and, by the way, my name is Sarah."

"I am pleased to have made your acquaintance. I know what you mean about the smells. Sometimes I get tired of them, myself. That should not be a problem. I will leave your order on the porch."

Sarah then returned to her new home. She felt that, overall, the first day in North Village went well.

CHAPTER SIXTEEN

The summer was passing quickly. Sarah worked diligently in the shoddy mill, and her pay increased to forty cents a day. She was quite a sight to see. She had found a couple of stout sticks and a few long nails, lying about the mill. Winslow helped her by pounding nails through the sticks. She then used the sticks in the shoddy mill to move around the colored rags. She wore a damp cloth over her mouth and nose to avoid inhaling the shoddy dust. At first, people thought it was strange, but Sarah told them her lungs were weak from working in the shops in Boston and she needed to avoid the dust.

At that time, the villagers accepted her ways. The first year was going well, and Sarah felt comfortable. She carefully communed with the mist, making sure she was out of sight. She befriended several people in the village but did not get too close to anyone. Not wanting her secrets revealed, she hid her knowledge from them. Each day, she played the part of a poor pauper and performed her simple tasks in the shoddy mill. While at work, she made sure the door to the velvet shop stayed closed at all times.

Winter came early that year, and the river was frozen in late December, halting production at the mill. One Saturday, Sarah dressed and made the short walk to the general store. The storeowner was sweeping out front. "I need some fishing line and a perch-jerking lure," said Sarah.

The storeowner laughed. "A perch-jerking lure?"

"That is just a silly term I use. I want a small silver lure, so that I can go up to Heald Pond and jig a few perch for food."

"I will be right back." The shopkeeper went in and came back with several, small, handmade lures.

Sarah looked them over. "I'll take this one."

She paid the storekeeper and then walked home. Earlier in the week, Winslow had grounded an edge onto an old piece of broken mill shaft that she intended to use as an ice chopper. The next morning, she left the village. The walk to Heald Pond was a long one, and it took several hours to get there.

When she arrived, Sarah walked around the pond on the ice. She saw that the pond had no major inlet. A small, seasonal brook ran on the south side, down a narrow ravine. The flow was too weak for industrial use. A small, open spot existed, where the brook entered the pond. Sarah took off her canvas mitts and reached into the water, picking up some sand and mud. She rubbed it on the back of her hand. The cold hurt her hand, but she did not feel any toxins.

"Perfect. The fish here should be safe to eat," she said out loud to herself.

She walked a few feet towards the middle of the pond and chipped a hole through the ice. She took her homemade pole and dropped the line with the lure into the water. "Excellent. The water is about six feet deep." The older Sarah got, the more she talked to herself. She lowered the pole, so the lure hit the bottom. Then, she lifted and dropped the pole and began jigging the lure. "Here, fish, fish. Here… fish, fish." The line twitched, and, with a jerk, she pulled out a nice, yellow perch. "Ah, my little fish, you will make a fine chowder. Let's see if we can get your brother."

Sarah caught three perch from that hole. She chipped another hole and captured three more. "Well, thank you, pond. That will be enough for this fine day. You have met my needs nicely."

Sarah hid the ice pick in some heavy mountain laurel and walked back to North Village. On the way, she passed a small farm with a welcoming appearance. A sign on the gate read, "Milk-Butter-Eggs." Nestled away from the industry of the area, the farm had its own spring, from which the animals were watered. The farm also had its own hay and grain fields. It appeared to be safe from toxins, so Sarah opened the gate and knocked at the front door.

The door swung open, and the farmer's wife greeted Sarah. Her cheeks were red from the heat of the cook stove. "Yes, madam, can I help you?"

"I would like to purchase some milk. I saw your sign, but I do not have a vessel."

"That is no worry. For an extra penny, I can sell you one of my canning jars."

"Give me a quart of milk. I have six, fine, yellow perch, which I am going to use to make chowder." Sarah opened her small canvas bag and showed her the fish.

"Our milk will make rich chowder. The milk is from this morning. When you get home, let it sit for a spell, and use the cream off the top. You will love the flavor it will give your chowder. We also have potatoes, onions, and bacon for sale. Would you care for some?"

Sarah gave into temptation. "Certainly. Give me three potatoes and an onion. How do you cure your bacon?"

"We soak it in salt only, and Frederick, my husband, smokes it over hickory wood. We raise our pigs only on grains we grow. We keep all our food as pure as possible. We are not Quakers, but we believe in their ways when it comes to food."

"Well, madam, I certainly will come back for more supplies when I need them. Also, give me just a small piece of bacon." Sarah was glad she had found a better source of food than the store in town. She did not trust the quality of food that was commercially prepared in the city.

Sarah paid the woman with the small amount of change she had brought with her and walked back to North Village. Once inside the house, she lit the fireplace and hung a pot on a hook over the fire. She cleaned the fish while the potatoes and onion were cooking. When the potatoes were soft, she added the whole fish. Then, she tossed the fish skins into the fireplace. Soon, her place was warm, and she could smell the chowder in the air.

"Ah, this is very good," she said to herself as she ate a big bowlful. Sarah had made enough chowder to last for days. She looked out the window and noticed Prudence across the river, bringing in wood for her stove. "I shall bring them some chowder tomorrow, in payment for Winslow making my ice pick."

Sarah got up the next morning, filled the quart Mason jar with chowder, and set off to see Prudence.

"Hello, Prudence. I brought you some chowder for today's lunch. I wanted to give Winslow something for all the work he did in making my ice pick. I got six, yellow perch yesterday."

"You did not have to do that. Winslow expected nothing in return for his efforts."

"I know, but there is more chowder than I can eat in three days. Tell him thank you."

"Come in. There is tea on the stove. Warm yourself before your walk back home. It is very cold outside."

"Thank you. I will stay and have a bit of tea."

All had been quiet in the mist. The spirits of the Chief and Ebb remained inside the river. However, since they were in the cusp, they could not communicate with the spirits in the mist around them. On a cold, winter day, the Chief and Ebb suddenly rose out of the river, unseen to the villagers.

"Chief, what is happening?"

"I have to go to a house not too far away. One of the original settlers is about to die, and I have to be there. You have been commanded by the spirits to accompany me from now on."

The spirits of Ebb and the Chief made their way through the woods and, then, to North Street. They were making their way along the road when they saw a sleigh coming their way.

"Chief, there is someone coming. What should we do?"

"Nothing. The driver cannot see us. Keep going along, and they will pass."

As the horse nearby was pulling the owner's sleigh, Ebb could hear its bells jingling when it approached them. Before the sleigh passed them, the horse became spooked. It started rearing up and braying. The driver was yelling at the horse and snapping at the reins.

"Easy boy, easy! What's wrong with you? Giddy up! Get moving. Giddy up!" The driver kept shouting at the horse, but the horse was terrified of something.

Ebb stopped moving. The Chief turned to him. "Keep moving!" exclaimed the Chief.

"I thought you said they could not hear us," remarked Ebb.

"They cannot *see* us. But animals and certain people are more sensitive and, somehow, can sense our presence. Just keep moving."

Ebb and the Chief were right next to the horse. Ebb could see terror in the eyes of the animal as it neighed and reared back. While they floated next to the sleigh, the driver looked in their direction, trying to see what was spooking the horse.

The driver felt a sudden chill and shivered involuntarily. He turned up the collar on his coat and snapped the reins against the flank of the horse. "Giddy up! Go."

Ebb and the Chief had passed by the horse. This time, the horse took command and raced forward at a gallop. "Whoa boy, slow down. Whoa." After a few hundred feet, the horse slowed to a fast walk. As the sleigh moved away from them, the horse kept turning its head and looking back. "What is it, boy?" He turned and looked behind him. "There is nothing there. What has you so spooked?'

Ebb could hear the driver comforting his horse as they disappeared from sight. He and the Chief continued on. They soon came to a disheveled house with overgrown shrubs and peeling paint. No one had done any major work on the house for quite a few years.

"Here we are, Ebb."

They approached the front door. Ebb was about to witness the first death since being commanded to accompany the Chief. The Chief started to pass through the door and stopped short. "Remember, we have no flesh and blood. Pass through the wood as I do."

Ebb followed the Chief and the horse, finding himself on the other side of the wooden door. They drifted up the stairs, and, at the top, they passed through a door into a bedroom. The house was dirty and dark. An old lady was lying in bed under a stack of comforters. She was near death when she stirred. She raised herself up a little and looked at the Chief and the horse. "I knew you would come. The rumors and whispers were true. It is the death horse, just like they said." (11) As she lay back down, she released one last, raspy breath and died. Ebb could see her spirit rise up out of her body and disappear.

"Chief, where did her spirit go?"

"To her Place of Happiness. Her body was dead when she left, so she is not condemned to the cusp. With many of the first settlers' deaths, I was still full of anger. I would try to scare them just before they died to try and feed my revenge. I am weary of this curse. Now, I just go and quietly watch them die."

"Who was she?"

"That was Winslow's mother."

"If that was Winslow's mother, then that makes her my gr...."

"Yes, I am sorry. That was your grandmother."

Sadness washed over Ebb. "I never met her."

"Do not be sad about her crossing over. She had a long life. It was her time. It is simply the nature of things. Let us leave here."

They passed through the bedroom door and were outside in the hall when the front door opened. The neighbor from across the road stood there. She had not seen any smoke from the chimney that morning and had come over to check on the old woman. "Hello? Hello?

There was no answer, and the woman went upstairs. She walked right through the Chief, Ebb, and the horse and paused for a moment.

"Good God, it is as cold as death in this hall," she said as she opened the door. "Oh, no!" she cried out when she saw the old woman. She ran out and passed through the Chief and the horse one more time as she headed across the road.

"Come, Ebb, we must leave." The Chief, the horse, and Ebb floated out of the house and back to the river.

"What now?" asked Ebb.

"We return to the river to await the next one. That is our curse, yours and mine. It is my curse for what I have said, and it is your curse for being the last." The Chief, the horse, and Ebb disappeared back into the river.

CHAPTER SEVENTEEN

Baby Ebb was two years old. Since Ebb's grandmother died, no more deaths had occurred in the village. The early winter day was cold, and snow was blowing around when the Chief, the horse, and Ebb ascended from the water.

"Come along. We have to go to the next death."

Ebb did not like the first one. He did not want to attend anymore, but he had to because he had become part of the curse. The Chief led Ebb towards the mill, and before long, they were standing there, watching Winslow run the saw.

"No! Not my father!" cried Ebb.

Winslow thought he had heard something and looked away from his work. "Oh, my God. It is the death horse!" he cried out.

Several of the workers had heard his cry. They looked up, just in time to see Winslow lose his balance and fall, tragically trapped by the teeth of the saw. The scene was horrible. Winslow was instantly decapitated, with blood and gore flying all around. The workers who had heard him cry out were terrified.

Although he had no physical body, Ebb felt sick. "Why, Chief? Why did you do it this way?"

"It is not my choice. I do not choose who. I do not choose when. I do not choose how. My curse requires that I just be there. Other than that, I have no control over the events. Do not blame me. He would have died that moment, whether I was there or not. It is the curse I uttered as I fought while my family died. I had the horror of watching my whole tribe slaughtered. I did not ask for that either. The curse was uttered, and the spell was set. It is now out of my control. I must be there when they die."

Ebb was sobbing. "This is all so horrific and sad."

"If we could have shared the valley in peace and the settlers had respected the mist, this would not have happened. My people had lived peacefully in this valley forever and did not deserve to perish. That sin, which the settlers committed, cannot go unpunished. We were all innocent when the tribe perished." The Chief was genuinely sad as he led the horse and Ebb back to the river.

The bell was clanging at the mill. Prudence felt apprehensive. She knew that it signaled an accident at the mill. Moments later, a mill worker ran towards her house, half-covered in blood. He was crying, and Winslow's blood was nearly everywhere, even smeared on his face.

"Prudence, Winslow has been killed at the mill." Prudence collapsed on the floor. Winslow was gone, and her world changed forever.

Sarah heard the bell and saw the commotion across the river. She walked down her narrow path and went to join Prudence. Sarah had a dream the night before and had seen the dreadful accident. She had stayed home because she did not want to be there when it happened. She knew she was powerless to change the outcome. Young Ebb had to leave the valley at five years of age, and Winslow had to die in the process. Sarah was incapable of saving either herself or Winslow. She knew she had to save Ebb. Since she had known the spirit of old Ebb, she knew she would be successful. Other than knowing she had at least three more years before dying at the hands of three men, she did not know anything else that would happen. The spirits were deliberately silent about the events that were going to take place. After all, sometimes ignorance is bliss.

By the time Sarah got across the river, a few of the village women had laid Prudence on her bed. Young Ebb was only two, but he knew something was wrong, and he was crying in his crib. Sarah entered the house. Some of the women were crying while others hovered around silently, muddled and stunned beyond words.

"I will take care of Prudence and Ebb if someone here will make arrangements for the body of dear Winslow," Sarah said sadly.

One of the women asked, "How did you know Winslow was dead? You just got here."

Sarah thought quickly. "I passed one of the mill workers on my way here."

She did not dare mention her dream. The valley was already beginning to be filled with fear and mistrust.

Sarah's answer apparently sufficed the woman's curiosity. "Oh, I'm sorry, Sarah. I am just not myself today. There seems to be an unexplainable string of tragedies in this place. I am beginning to feel that we are cursed. Stay and care for Prudence. I will come back later. Trouble not with fixing any food. The other ladies and I will cook some meals and bring them by later today and during the next few days. Just try and console Prudence; the next few days will be very hard on her."

One by one, the ladies left and Sarah remained inside. The instant she picked up Ebb, the child stopped crying. Sarah began to quietly hum the strange, yet soothing, melodies she had hummed at Ebb's birth. "Why did you stop fussing? Does your soul somehow recognize me? I carried your spirit before you were born, but that was the spirit of old Ebb. I should be a stranger to you," she said. The toddler reached out towards Sarah, transfixed by the soothing music. "Rest quiet, Ebb.

You are assured a long life. The grief of the moment will pass. In time, all will be well. You have been chosen. You are special, and you will be the last; you will be the one who saves us all. That much, the spirits have let me know."

"Winslow, Winslow?" Prudence cried out as she gained consciousness. "Oh, my poor Winslow." Mercifully, Prudence blacked out again while Sarah tended to Ebb, quietly singing songs from faraway places.

Later in the day, three local women came with food for Prudence and the child. Ebb eagerly ate his meal, but Sarah could not revive Prudence, so she let her rest. The afternoon slowly drifted into night. Sarah tended to Ebb who seemed happy since he was too young to understand what had happened.

Prudence had a fitful night, tossing and turning. She was crying out for Winslow, only to start sobbing again, and then, cried herself unconscious. Sarah held her hand and tried to comfort her by singing quietly, but Prudence's grief was overpowering. In the morning, Prudence was laying in bed, dazed. Sarah took a small amount of food to her in a bowl and tried to feed her. Prudence took one spoonful and vomited in the bowl, gagging in sorrow. "Dear God, why did you take Winslow from me?" She began sobbing and cried herself back to sleep.

In the morning, the women returned to check on them. Ebb was well fed and playing happily in his crib. Prudence was comatose on the bed, exhausted with heartache.

"How is she, Sarah?" asked one of the women.

"She is sick with grief and has not spoken."

Another woman added, "Winslow's remains have been taken to Hollis Village and will be buried in the family plot, alongside his mother and father. The service will be tomorrow. We will bring Prudence there and back. Can you stay with Ebb?"

"Of course," replied Sarah. "I knew Winslow quite well and enjoyed him when he was alive. I do not need to see his closed casket or watch the continued suffering of Prudence."

"Thank you. We will come for her at ten. The service is at eleven. We will have Prudence back here just after noon. We will spell you for a time, so you can have a break and tend to some of your needs. The woman at the shoddy mill was asking where you were. We told her about you being with Prudence. She would like to talk to you."

Sarah stayed and tended to Ebb while looking after Prudence. She brought her the chamber pot late that night, when Prudence weakly told Sarah that she needed to relieve herself. Afterwards, she fell back into an exhausted sleep. Sarah went outside and emptied the chamber pot into the outhouse. The night was calm and dry. No mist could be seen, only a small amount of snow from the day before, glistening in the moonlight. "How could such a pretty place have so much misery?" Sarah asked herself as she turned to go back inside.

The next morning, Sarah gently woke up Prudence. "Prudence, you must get dressed. The service for Winslow is in a couple of hours." Prudence fell back into another fit of tears. Her body was limp as Sarah dressed her for the service. At 10 a.m., three of the village women arrived, as scheduled, with one of their husbands and a wagon. The gentleman lifted Prudence and placed her on the seat in back, between two of the women. The women held Prudence on each side and kept her upright as the wagon drove off.

The mill had closed down for the funeral. Half of the townspeople sadly walked up the hill towards Hollis Village. Shortly after noontime, the procession softly made its way back into the village, and the woman's husband helped Prudence into her bed. One of the women stayed behind. She repeated, "Sarah, the woman at the velvet shop would like to talk to you." Then she added, "She is back at the mill now."

Sarah arrived at the shop and found Helen. "Hello, Helen. I am sorry to have missed work. I felt ill and stayed at home the day Winslow died, and I have been tending to Prudence's needs since then."

"That is fine. You are caught up on the shoddy. Come back next week or when you are able. That is not why I have sent for you. My business is doing well, and I am shipping my garments all over New England. One of my seamstresses is becoming quite ill. Prudence is an accomplished seamstress, and I would like to offer her a job when she feels up to it."

"I will tell her as soon as she begins to recover from her grief. At this time, she is beyond consoling. Soon, though, her motherly instinct for Ebb will outweigh her grief, and she will begin to heal. That is the nature of such things. Good day."

Sarah slowly walked back towards Prudence's place and was thinking out loud. "I don't want her working there with all those poisons, but I do not see any other option. It is not my choice anyway. Prudence has to decide what she will do."

Aaron seemed almost happy about Winslow's death. One less heir remained from the original settlers whom he had to give a share of the mill. All of the original settlers had died. Only half of them had heirs, so Aaron was receiving seventy-five percent of the profits, instead of fifty percent.

He was beginning to suffer from toxic exposure at the mill. He could no longer be intimate with Rebecca. He was becoming more abusive and would often lose his temper. Aaron was slowly going insane, and his actions became stranger and stranger.

Rebecca was miserable. When Richard had sent her the cryptic message a year earlier, she was afraid and had burned it in the fire. She was beginning to regret her actions. A week after the death of Winslow, Richard received a letter from North Village. Before he left town, he had formed a close friendship with Ronald, one of the mill workers. He had written a letter to Ronald a few months after he left the village. In the letter, Richard had confided to him the details about Rebecca and fathering Aaron Junior. Ronald had kept his allegiance to Richard and never told anyone. Everyone else in the village thought Richard had perished. Periodically, Richard would write to his friend and Ronald would reply. He mentioned how Rebecca was doing and how much Aaron Junior had grown.

When Richard opened the most recent letter from Ronald, he became concerned as he read it.

Dear Richard,

Things continue to go badly here in North Village. Death seems ever present at every turn. Young Winslow, one of the heirs of the settlers, was killed yesterday in a horrible accident at the mill. One of the ladies in the velvet shop is very ill, and I fear she will be the next fatality.

Aaron is gradually going mad, and Rebecca and your son are suffering from his abuse. She always looks so forlorn. Aaron Junior is becoming a recluse. The children in North Village do not accept him because of his elite status. He takes his lessons at home and spends the rest of his time wandering the woods and trails. They were once close, but Aaron's growing insanity has driven them apart.

You should try writing Rebecca a second time, and find out if you can save them from his madness. I see no hope for them here in North Village.

Faithfully Yours,

Ronald

Richard felt troubled and immediately penned a letter to Rebecca. Compared to his previous letter, he was even bolder in his writing.

Dear R,

Lately I have been thinking about you and the boy. After I left North Village, I patented the device I made for the shoddy mill. I have had a great deal of success selling and installing it in the larger mills in Lowell, Lawrence and Haverhill. I have a nice place on Plum Island, right on the ocean. There is plenty of room for you and our son.

I feel that we should tell Aaron Junior and beg his forgiveness. I have wealth enough for all of us to live on, and I can send the boy to a proper school for matriculation. You will need nothing from Aaron. Take what you need for the journey, and I will meet you at the train station.

I love you and our son and regret that I ever left you there alone. Please come to me; life is too short, and you need someone who will give you the love and respect that a wonderful woman like you deserves. Come at once; save yourself and our son from that evil man and his village. Nothing good will ever come of the place. I truly believe the place was cursed. It was taken by bloodshed. It was built with the blood of many. The village will never be right. Please heed my advice. I ache for you and our son. You may write me if you want at PO Box 406 Newburyport, Massachusetts. All is well with me.

Love,

R.

Rebecca was stunned. Recently, she had been thinking about Richard and wished he had been determined enough to write a second time. Her wish had come true. Aaron was not at home, so she decided to be daring and respond. Aaron was hardly ever at home anymore. He was always at the mill, pushing the men to increase production and profits. He made the decision to request more workers from Lowell. After Winslow's death, several of the mill workers had decided that North Village was cursed. Upon hearing Winslow's cry about the death horse, they packed up and left town. Aaron forbade any discussion about it at the mill, but that did not stop them from talking over ale at the tavern.

Rebecca knew she would not see Aaron until after dark when he returned from the mill. She sat at her desk and tried to compose a letter but could not find the right words to begin. She put away the writing utensils and went downstairs. When Aaron came home, he started screaming at the servants for his supper, and Rebecca ran upstairs to her room. Aaron was mad, and she could no longer share a bedroom with him. She sat at her desk with a pen and some writing paper. The madness had to end.

Dear Richard,

The timing of your letter is curious. My life is deteriorating into hell. Aaron is completely insane and is impossible to live with. Aaron Junior suffers because of the madness.

The village is cursed and death is becoming common. Two weeks ago, a nice, young man named Winslow was killed in a horrible accident, leaving a widow and son behind. This week, one of the women from the velvet shop died a horrible death. She was totally insane and died screaming in the night.

I have made arrangements for Aaron Junior to attend a new boarding school in the next town. In two months, he will begin classes at the Groton School. I will keep your offer in mind and let you know my decision.

Please do not write again. I will write you again when Aaron Junior is in school. Aaron is completely insane, and I fear for our safety in the village. All the old growth trees have been cut down, and the profits of the mill are suffering because the wood to cut gets smaller and smaller.

Something has to change soon. I love you and miss you. Every time I look at our son, I think of you. Life here is intolerable. I wish to come to you, but I need time in order to make it work.

I love you and adore you. I will be yours soon. Please be patient.

Lovingly Yours,

Rebecca

The following morning, she brought the letter to the Paugus post office. Her hand was shaking as she handed it over to the postmaster. "Aaron asked if I would post this for him. Can you send it special delivery?"

"Most certainly, Rebecca. It will go out with tomorrow's mail. It may take about a week to get to Newburyport."

Rebecca smiled coyly. "That's fine, sir. I am sure Aaron will not mind. Please do not remind him that I posted this for him. His mind is not quite right, and he will not remember writing it anyway. So, if you speak to him about it, he will only get upset. He has been quite difficult lately."

"Very well. He is a bit too ill tempered for me to converse with anyway. He brings his letters, mumbles and only talks to himself."

Rebecca left the post office, and, for the first time in many years, she had hope - for her son and herself. She had never been a part of this valley. Aaron Junior's bloodline was not from this valley. She was determined that she and her son would not be casualties of the growing madness around them.

Rebecca took the long way home. She walked up Prescott Street towards Pepperell Center and followed the back road used for deliveries to the house. She did not want to run into Aaron and have to make up an excuse. She detested the sight of him. Rebecca was glad that Aaron Junior did not have any of Aaron's blood. She hoped that someday he might be able to satisfy a woman better than Aaron.

Rebecca was frustrated and lonely. More and more, she found herself longing for Richard. She was glad he had written her again. Before the letter had arrived, she thought that Richard was lost forever.

CHAPTER EIGHTEEN

Aaron Junior was all packed and ready for the wagon ride to the Groton School. "Goodbye, Mother. Sorry Father isn't here to see me off. Tell him that I said goodbye."

"Well, your father is becoming so mentally infirm that he does not even remember his name, at times. I will tell him when I see him. Lately, he spends every waking moment at the mill. We have plenty of money for our needs, but he is always fixated on the money from the mill and what the profit margin is."

"Yes, I know. He is sick. He is gripped by the madness, which is filtering through the valley. Don't be too hard on him. It is not his fault."

"Take care of yourself, A. J., and write often. We will see you on Thanksgiving."

"Goodbye, Mother. Take good care of yourself and stay healthy. Stay away from the mill. I think the different chemicals used there are bad for the workers. If I owned that foolish mill, I would either shut it down or sell it. Something does not seem right there. I intend to study hard and learn much. I don't want to be a mill worker, as Father would like me to be. He was very angry when you told him I was going to boarding school. He treats the workers so badly that I hate to be around him."

"I understand, A.J. Stay well. The school in Groton will be good for you. Things will not be bad here forever. Goodbye." Rebecca leaned forward and kissed A. J. on the forehead.

A full year had passed since the death of Winslow. Aaron was having a difficult time finding a workman with Winslow's skill for running the saw. During the past year, he had already fired two men because they were not aggressive enough with the saw. They feared for their lives and operated the saw slowly and cautiously, which made production at the mill even slower.

Rebecca had written Richard several times that year. His letters kept her going. She had wanted to leave Aaron when she heard from Richard again, but at that time, she wasn't able to do it. She felt guilty, and the guilt had kept her there, long after her love for Aaron was gone. She was determined that this would be the year she would do it.

Sarah had helped Prudence by giving her some of her hidden money when she needed it. When Prudence went to the store she would tell the storekeeper that the twenty-dollar gold pieces were from savings that Winslow and his mother had left her. The villagers had begun gossiping about the money Prudence was spending. Sarah heard the women at the velvet shop talking about it. At that point, Sarah decided she would walk to Hollis Village to buy supplies and to cash the gold pieces. She returned with smaller coins to spend in North Village. Almost a year later, Sarah's method was working. People in North Village no longer noticed Prudence with any large coins.

Ebb was almost five years old when Sarah took half of the remaining coins to Hollis Village. She had learned from Prudence where her Uncle Abel had his farm. On her way back to North Village, she stopped at the gate to the farm. One of Abel's daughters summoned him to the front door.

"Father, there is an old woman by the gate. She has been there for a while; she gives me the jitters. Go out and make her move along."

Abel walked out to the gate. "What is the nature of your business, old woman?"

"I need to talk to you, Abel."

"How do you know my name? I have not met you, old woman."

"I have come to you to talk about Prudence."

"I will not talk to you about her. She is dead to me."

"She soon will be dead to all of us."

"What is this talk?"

"She works in the velvet shop, and the toxins in the fabric are in her body. She will be dead in less than two years."

"That is her fault for marrying that man. He can take care of her."

"Winslow died three years ago in a horrible accident. Prudence is a widow and has a five-year-old son. She is sick. I am getting old and infirm and cannot raise him."

"That is not my issue."

"You would condemn your nephew to the poor farm?"

"Prudence made her choice many years ago. She can live by her choice." Abel turned to walk away.

Sarah was furious. She thought, "How stupid these people are with their foolish pride." She said aloud, "I will pay you five hundred dollars if you will raise Ebb until he is old enough to care for himself. He is strong and will be of help on your farm."

Abel stopped walking. He had wanted to buy some new farm equipment and the money was tempting. "I will take the boy, and only the boy, because we have a business arrangement. Have Prudence write me." Abel took the twenty-five gold coins and returned to his home.

"Hypocrite," Sarah mumbled under her breath as she walked away.

Sarah returned to North Village and went to Prudence's house. She found Prudence resting in a comfortable chair. "Prudence, I'd like to discuss something with you. You are sick, and I fear for Ebb. I am getting old and will not be able to take care of him."

"That I know. You are right. I feel that I have been cursed, and this valley is killing me. It is too late for me to leave. I have no place to go. I also fear for Ebb - that he will end up alone, and the valley will consume him too."

"What about your uncle in Hollis Village?"

"He will not help me," replied Prudence.

"Maybe he will help Ebb. Write him and ask. Maybe he has changed his mind," Sarah said.

"All right. I will write him, but I hold no hope."

Prudence brought her letter for Abel to the post office. A week later, she received a reply to bring Ebb to Hollis Village. Prudence began preparing for her journey.

Ebb had turned five. Sarah was walking past the millhouse where Ebb and his mother had been playing near the road during one of her few days off. Sarah said to Prudence, "If you love the boy, you will get him out of here. If you get him out of here, he will still be the lassst."

Prudence did not want to give up custody of Ebb, but she was becoming increasingly ill. Her nails were white, and they had become thick and brittle from the poisons in the felt. She looked about sixty years old, yet she was only thirty. She had once been young and beautiful, but, in five years, she appeared to have aged forty. "I will do it this Sunday when I have the day off. Starting next week, I will be running the steam closet at the velvet shop."

Sarah sighed as she departed. She knew that working the steam closet would mean certain death. Since the velvet shop had opened, the closet had already killed three women. Even with her knowledge,

Sarah remained powerless to stop what the spirits had set in motion. Sarah wondered when she would see the three men who would cause her demise. Now that Ebb was leaving, her mission was over. She knew that soon her life would be over also.

The woman who had been running the steam closet was extremely sick at home. The toxins had poisoned her and driven her insane. She was a descendant of the original settlers, and her time had come. One misty night, the Chief, the horse and Ebb rose from the river.

"Come along, Ebb. We need to go to another death."

"There have been so many, Chief, that I am tiring of it."

"So have I, but the spirits have set our paths together for this."

"The three spirits glided over to the house of the dying seamstress and passed through the front door. The woman had gone completely insane and was having convulsions. She was screaming, twitching, and throwing herself around the bed. Ebb stood by watching, looking horrified.

The tortured spirit of the woman soared from her body, which was still alive. She was in the cusp and could see her visitors. Her spirit plummeted into the faces of Ebb and the Chief.

"Get out! Get out. Get out. You cannot have me." The Chief was startled, and even the great horse was afraid. The woman's spirit sped around the room, then went to a different part of the house and started throwing things.

"What was that?" Ebb asked.

"Her spirit left her body too early. She is trapped in the cusp, like us. Her spirit will haunt this place forever," answered the Chief.

"Let's get out of here."

"In a moment. We must wait until her body dies," said the Chief.

They stood and watched the final twitches of her body. They could hear her spirit in another part of the house, still tossing things around.

When her body took one last, rattled breath, the Chief, the horse and Ebb departed from the house, which was then haunted by her spirit.

"How often does that happen?" asked Ebb.

"With the growing insanity, it is happening all too often. You and I only see the deaths of the original settlers. There are many innocents who die with the guilty. Troubled spirits will roam this valley forever."

"Chief, I am beginning to get a heavy heart with all this death. I feel guilty that I was allowed to leave this valley and that my mother stayed and died."

"The spirits have something special in store for you. Come, we will wander the mist this evening, and, tomorrow at dawn, something unusual will happen. It will help to calm your troubled soul."

"What is it? Please. Tell me," begged Ebb.

"Be patient. You will see."

They continued wandering in the mist until the sun was about to rise. The Chief brought Ebb to the house where Prudence and young Ebb lived. Through the window, they could see that Prudence was packing Ebb's belongings for the trip to Abel's farm in Hollis. The mist was clearing. Ebb's mother clasped his hand and opened the front door. Even though a bit of the mist still lingered in the air, they left the house and walked outside into the swirling mist.

The Chief looked at the spirit of old Ebb and could feel his heartache. Ebb was consumed with grief and regretted hating his mother for all those years. He had always thought her actions had been selfish. He could now see she had performed an act of unimaginable love. Ebb was moved to learn she relinquished the son she had loved, so that he could survive. He now realized, because of her love, he had lived a long life. He understood that she had lifted him out of the mist with her last bit of strength, so that he could continue to live.

"Speak to her," urged the Chief. "Make it right, and sooth both your soul and hers. Fix it, so that your souls can be at peace. It is her noble act that has made you the last. Tell her, before it is too late."

"Mother, this is Ebb. The spirits of the mist have allowed me this precious moment to come back from the future and speak to you. I lived to a ripe, old age because of what you are about to do. I love you deeply for the sacrifice you are about to make."

It was just before the mist evaporated when Ebb's mother stopped short. Young Ebb looked up impatiently at his mother. She looked as if she had been listening to something. Then she nodded and smiled before continuing.

"What is it, Mother?"

"Nothing, Ebb. Someday you will understand."

Young Ebb continued bouncing and hopping down the road with his mother.

The spirit of old Ebb finally gained the purity required to proceed to the Land of Happiness and felt a great release. Sarah was ready, and now Ebb was ready; his soul was clean. The last soul that needed to be saved belonged to the Chief, and it would require another eighty-eight years.

The Chief, the horse, and Ebb returned to the river for a few months. Later that year, they were called upon for another death. The three spirits rose from the river and traveled towards the mill.

Aaron was screaming insanely at the saw operator. "You run that saw like an old lady! You are too slow and wary! The mill suffers because of your ineptness."

"But, sir, the saw has killed before and deserves respect."

"You will respect my authority and run the saw the way I want, or you will find another job."

At that moment the Chief spoke. "Aaron, it is your time."

Aaron looked up and saw the Chief and the horse. "It is the death horse! You will not take me!" Aaron was totally insane and was screaming uncontrollably. All of the mill workers had heard him, and they stopped working to watch what was happening.

"Leave here, you horse of death and misery! I will not let you take me!"

Some of the workers' faces turned white. They could not see what Aaron was shouting at. Aaron screamed one more time as he was backing away from the trio. "I said, you will..." Aaron let out a blood-curdling scream as he lost his balance and fell into the saw -- suffering the same fate as Winslow.

Many of the frightened mill workers ran home and packed their belongings. The unmarried men moved out first, followed by the men with families. They fled as quickly as they could from the escalating pestilence of the valley.

Rebecca closed the mill and made arrangements to bury Aaron. She was determined that this would be the last death caused and paid for by the sawmill. She did not care if it ever reopened. She hated the mill; she hated the valley she once loved; she hated Aaron and was glad he was gone. She sent notes to three places on that fateful day.

First, she sent word to A. J. to come home at once because of the death of his father. After that, she penned a letter to Richard. Her heart fluttered as she sealed the envelope. Then, finally, she sent a note to three men in East Pepperell who had approached Aaron about selling the mill, only to be chased away by Aaron's madness. The three men were surprised at the inappropriate timing of Rebecca's letter, but they cast aside propriety because they strongly desired the mill site. They went to see Rebecca the next day. While Aaron's body was being prepared for burial, Rebecca struck a handsome deal with the three men. Aaron's precious mill had been sold before Aaron's body was in his grave.

The day Aaron died, Richard's friend, Ronald, had had enough of the cursed valley. He went to Hollis Village and got on the train to Boston. The following day, he boarded a different train and arrived in Newburyport. There he used the last of his money to take a coach to Plum Island where Richard lived. Ronald knew he needed to act quickly if Richard's dream would come to fruition.

Richard answered the door and was instantly filled with fear. "Oh, my God, is Rebecca all right? Has something happened to A. J.?"

"No, no. They are well, Richard. Yesterday Aaron was killed in a horrible accident. He will be buried tomorrow. You must go to Rebecca and remove her from that cursed valley."

Richard was stunned. "My goodness! Thank you, my friend. You have been loyal, and when I return I will reward you generously. You can stay here until I get back. It is too late to make the train to Boston, so I will leave tomorrow." He grabbed a train schedule from his desk. "There is only one train to and from Boston; it arrives from Boston at eleven. That was the train you just arrived on. The train has a three-hour layover, to be unloaded and then loaded with the morning's catch of fish, and then leaves for Boston at 2 p.m. I need to get my bags together and go to the bank. I would like to make the trip to the village today, but there is no time."

Ronald accompanied Richard to the bank that afternoon. "Here, this is just part of what I will give you. I will have more when I return. This should keep you in good supply for however long it takes me to get back."

"But, Richard, this is one hundred dollars. How long will you be gone? I can live on this for a year."

"My friend, I will be gone for as long as it takes for me to return with Rebecca. I will not return without her."

The two men returned to Richard's house and got Richard's bag ready for traveling. The next morning, Richard was anxiously pacing the floor waiting for the coach to arrive. He had made the arrangements the day before and told the coachman to be prompt. Meanwhile, in Newburyport his coach had been ready to leave when the driver saw a scruffy-looking passenger get off the train, which had just arrived. The passenger waved to the driver who then went over to him.

"I need a coach to Plum Island, right away."

"Sir, you are indeed lucky, for I am going to Plum Island at this very moment. Please step into my coach."

The driver was delighted, as he now would have paying customers both ways. "Where are you going?"

The customer gave the driver the address. "What is this, a trick? I am on my way out to pick Richard up right now."

"Well, then make speed, my good man. I must see Richard immediately."

The coach lurched ahead and soon arrived at Richard's house in Plum Island. "Well, it's about time," Richard said as he saw the coach coming toward his house. "Who is that?" he asked, watching someone get out of the coach.

"One of the mill workers," answered Ronald.

Richard was terrified. "Oh, my God. Something else is wrong."

The mill worker walked up to Richard and looked puzzled. "How can this be? You are the same Richard who perished many years ago."

"I didn't perish. I simply ran away."

"Rebecca sends this letter to you, sir." They all waited as Richard opened the envelope.

Dear Richard,

Yesterday Aaron was killed at the mill. I am leaving this cursed place. If your love is still strong, I still want to come to you. Please send this messenger back with your reply. Do not come in person. The valley is unsafe.

Rebecca

Richard laughed so loudly that the men thought he had lost his mind. He reached into his pocket, took out fifty dollars, and gave it to the mill worker. "Go back with the coach and make haste. Tell Rebecca to come a week from today."

"Sir, Rebecca has paid me already."

"Then, this is your lucky day, sir. Take the money, and return with this coach." Richard turned to the driver. "I was about to scold you for your tardiness. But Providence is at work by retarding your journey. Here is a fifty for you also. Take this man to the station immediately."

The mill worker jumped in, next to the driver. "It is such a fine day. May I ride up front with you?"

"Why, of course."

Richard could hear the men laughing as the coach raced away in the sunlight to the station in Newburyport.

CHAPTER NINETEEN

Richard felt as if he were a giddy schoolboy while he waited for Rebecca. He had been in town several times during the week, making arrangements. Finally, Wednesday arrived, and Richard was pacing up and down the passenger platform at the station.

"I hope she arrives, after all the work you have done. If she is not there, you will look like a fool," said Ronald.

"Do not fret, my friend. She will be here. Besides, I would play the part of a fool a thousand times if it gained me her love. " At that moment, the train whistle signaled in the distance. The day was calm and clear, and the sound carried from miles away. Ronald noticed his friend's mounting nervousness as Richard began to pace the platform, even more vigorously.

"Do you think she will like it?" asked Richard. The women I hired put quite an effort into her reception."

Ronald gazed over to the area where they would wed. The women had formed an archway of dried grapevines. Then, they scoured the local farms and gathered all the flowers in bloom and had placed them into the vines, forming a beautiful canopy. A mixed bouquet of flowers sat on a small table to the side of the canopy. Two golden rings were beside the flowers.

The smoke from the approaching train filled the air above as the whistle blew one more time. The minister excused himself from a conversation and moved to the front of the crowd. All was ready. Richard had even arranged for extra ice to be available with the daily shipment of fish. He was a prominent citizen, and a good showing from the town had turned out for the grand celebration.

A day earlier, the women had spoken to the engineer, regarding the position of the canopy. At that time, they made arrangements with the conductor to allow Rebecca off the train before the other passengers. The train finally pulled into the station.

Rebecca stepped from the coach into Richard's waiting arms, and the two of them embraced inside the canopy. Half of the townspeople surrounded them. After Richard raised his arms to silence the crowd, Ronald handed him the bouquet. Richard bent on one knee and proposed to Rebecca while the crowd quietly murmured waiting for her answer. She paused for a moment, and the crowd grew silent again. "Yes, Richard, yes!" A cheer burst out from the crowd.

Then Richard asked, "When can we wed?"

"Right now!" exclaimed the minister. He stepped forward with the rings in one hand and the Bible in the other.

Once more Rebecca said, "Yes." Again the crowd screamed with jubilation.

In the warmth of the late fall sun, Richard and Rebecca wed before the elated crowd. The fishermen scurried to load the daily catch onto the train, eager to join in the celebration. Even the trainman attended the joyous occasion, and for the first time ever, the train returned to Boston several hours late. Luckily, rails were able to guide the train to Boston, or the fish would not have made it to market that day.

The same coach, which had brought Richard the good news a week earlier, transported the couple, back to Plum Island. As they approached

Richard's house, Rebecca could hear the waves. The sound rekindled distant memories of pleasant, summer outings with her parents when she was a child. She nuzzled up against Richard.

Richard turned to her. "Hear the rhythm of the waves?"

"Yes."

"You will learn to live your life to the rhythm of the waves. Soon, the sound will be as natural as breathing."

Richard led Rebecca into the house. In the upstairs bedroom - with a gentle sea breeze coming through the window - Richard and Rebecca made shameless love to the rhythmic sound of the waves as the bright sails of the ships caught the last rays of the setting sun.

Even North Village seemed to be a happier place for a while. The three new mill owners had surveyed their property and retained all of the workers who had stayed in town. The village could have perished, and, for the sake of humanity, should have perished, but instead, it was reborn.

Workers had begun to remodel the old sawmill and were converting it into a paper mill. Change was in progress. The village had to persevere until the curse on the remaining heirs of the original settlers was complete. No reprieve would exist for those who remained. The timing was too late for them - and those who were yet to be born.

The mill was renamed Moore, Knowles and Appleton Company. The three men brought dryers, rollers, and other equipment for making paper, which had been replaced by larger and faster machines installed in the mills of East Pepperell. However, the equipment could still be used efficiently in the smaller mill in North Pepperell. Soon, the mill began production. The paper mill was better suited for using the smaller, younger trees. Most of the same businesses continued operating. The owners decided to keep the shoddy mill and the velvet shop, but they dismantled the sawmill. After cleaning off the blood from the saw blade, they sold it to a mill on Beaver Brook in Littleton.

With the Industrial Revolution underway throughout the country, the area mills underwent changes. The brook in Littleton was too small to generate power, so the newly renovated mill was going to be equipped with a steam engine instead. Water rights and waterpower were becoming antiquated. Steam provided a continuous source of power, and the mills did not need to be shut down when the rivers froze.

North Village was thriving, once again. The new paper mill was a success. One of the owners had developed a method for making waterproof paper. This product alone was generating much income. Most of the charts and maps used on the boats at sea were made of this paper. The maps would no longer rot and decay from the constant moisture on the sailing ships.

Meanwhile, the ghostly trio had been busy haunting the surroundings where the heirs of the settlers were dying. By this time, all of the original settlers had died. Many of those who had lived on the side hill had died of old age. The toxins in the river had not worked their way out of the valley, but soon, change would occur. The second and third generations of the hill's inhabitants would not be that lucky.

Those who lived by the river were dying the fastest. Illness and insanity were becoming common. No one wanted to talk about the insanity. They often said the individual died in an unusual way. Anyone who lived in or near North Pepperell knew exactly what that meant. People endured fits of hallucinations and frantically went mad. The ghostly trio visited many heirs who lived nearest to the river. Ebb was still upset about having to be there with the Chief. He did not like witnessing the deaths and was frightened by those souls who left their bodies too early. The unhappy ghosts trapped in the cusp were beginning to haunt many more of the old houses near the river.

Prudence was becoming quite sick from running the steam closet at the velvet shop. After a year and a half, she had to quit her position. Sarah had become her caretaker and no longer had time to walk to Hollis Village and cash the gold coins. Reluctantly, she started spending them in the store in North Pepperell. Then Prudence got so sick that Sarah quit her job in the shoddy shack and took care of her full-time.

Sarah employed some of the Indian ways to help Prudence. The village people could hear her chanting late at night. At other times, they saw her quietly singing strange songs to Prudence. They concluded that the twenty-dollar gold pieces Prudence had been spending several years ago were from Sarah. They believed the only way Sarah could have furnished those coins was through the Devil. They were backwards and fearful people. Once again, they suspected Sarah of being a Quaker witch.

During this time period, the ministers had become demigods. Parishioners would hire them to receive heavenly guidance. In reality, ministers were just men, subject to temptation and the abuse of their power. If people outwardly opposed the minister's ideas or beliefs, the minister would claim they were the "Devil's children" and that "Satan's hand was ruling them."

Either you believed everything the minister said and did, or you were seen as a Devil worshipper. The opportunity for free thinking did not exist in their world. In the best interest of the ministers, they included the Devil in their conversations, leaving people in constant fear. By doing so, the ministers had more power over the people.

They could not explain simple acts of fate or chance occurrences. If a violent storm arose, they believed it was not a random weather event simply created by natural developments. Instead, they preached that God, himself, sent the storm to punish the sinners. They were told the whole town would suffer because of the unfaithfulness of a few nonbelievers. If you dared to disagree, then you were a heretic. You would be cast out of the parish and those who saw themselves as the faithful would sneer at you.

Because Sarah was seen as a witch, children would run in horror when they saw her coming their way. By this time, she was very old looking and walked hunched over. She hobbled along as she entered the store for supplies and walked to the spring for water. She had once been accepted in North Pepperell, but now she was hated and feared, simply because the source of her money was unexplained. In that fearful environment of persecution that the ministers cultivated to retain their power, anyone seen as slightly different was either a witch or an agent of the Devil. Many innocent people died because of the shortsightedness of the greedy and powerful ministers.

The ministers studied their Bibles, embellishing the scriptures, so their unforgiving and unholy ways could continue to control the masses. Although Jesus had thrown out the moneychangers from the temple, somehow these ministers found ways of corrupting the message of Jesus. They continued to collect money from the parishioners. The ministers did not care if the people donating the money had obtained it in unholy ways. The success of a minister did not depend on how happy or healthy their parishioners were. They measured it by how large the church was and how lavishly the church was decorated with gold and stained glass. The ministers in the great cities were not renowned for what they said but for how extravagant their churches were.

The fact that people in their church were dying of hunger or disease did not matter to the ministers. Their pay and the size of their flocks mattered to them. People died of neglect, so the parish could buy a solid, gold chalice or fine stained glass windows. Parishioners would donate large sums of money for the church to obtain these items. The stories from the scriptures never mention Jesus having money, yet these ministers felt that God was rewarding them with the donations of their flocks. They believed that money, which is truly the source of all evil, was their just reward. Whenever large sums of money were donated, they never asked how the money was acquired. It did not matter. They failed to see that this money actually brought the Devil to them. The ministers believed they were agents of God and they were above the temptations of greed and of the flesh. Nevertheless, they were men, and no matter how pious they thought they were, the lust for cash could entice and distort them.

People who donated generous sums of money to the church would feel they had purchased a seat in Heaven. The fact that it was blood money they donated did not seem to matter. These same, pious people who would pray to Almighty God on Sunday would pass a suffering or starving person on Monday. They would walk past someone destitute and look the other way, never offering a helping hand. The mill owners would never help their fellow men with any of their money; the wealthy needed that money to buy their way into Heaven. The ministers prevented any interruption to the holy flow of money.

The greed of the church and the ministers was unending. Somehow, the church twisted the idea of money, which Jesus saw as evil, into something holy. People did not donate food for the hungry or clothes for those who died of exposure. Instead, they donated money. Money had perverted the churches, and they were becoming blind to the actual needs of their parishioners.

An atmosphere of hate and mistrust blanketed North Pepperell. Instead of investigating what was really killing the people, the ministers were happy to keep the cycle of ignorance in motion. Rather than acknowledge they were possibly dying from what they did or breathed or drank, the ministers were content to keep telling people that the Devil was at work.

They preached how powerful God was, but their sermons implied God worked only on Sunday and the Devil worked the other six days. If anyone questioned how the Devil was able to exist if God was all-powerful, the church would renounce that person. Ministers would not answer such questions. They would give no explanation and take no action, other than label the person a heretic and isolate the heretic from the flock.

CHAPTER TWENTY

Late one night, the spirits of the mist called for the Chief, the horse, and Ebb. The Chief tried to prepare Ebb for what he was about to see. "This next death will be very difficult for you. We are going to the house of your mother. Her body is spent, and it is her time. She is not from the bloodline of the early settlers, but we will be there to make sure she does not end up in the cusp."

Ebb was afraid to go. He would be seeing how his mother really died and why she had to have a closed coffin. He had seen many of the deaths that were described as happening in "an unusual way." In fact, this manner was actually the usual way, but no one in the valley wanted to admit it. People were ashamed to acknowledge a relative had died a raving lunatic.

The Chief left his horse outside. They had not come to torture the poor, dying soul, so he did not take the horse with him. The two spirits faded into the wall and entered the house. They were surprised to see Sarah sitting with Prudence.

Sarah sensed their presence. "Is that you, Chief?" she asked. "Is Ebb still with you? I cannot believe that you two were called here. She is not one of the settlers. She is just an unfortunate casualty who got involved in this predicament." Sarah pleaded with the spirits within her. "Please, let me see them. There can be no harm. I have done what you have requested. Prudence will be gone at any moment, and I don't have much life left in me either."

As the Chief and Ebb suddenly appeared, Sarah asked, "Where is the stallion?"

"He's outside," said the Chief. "There was no need to bring him in. The spirits have allowed us to be here, so we can make sure she gets out of the cusp. Her spirit is quite tortured, and there is a great danger of her not making it through to the spirit side."

Ebb was horrified. His mother had aged dramatically during the few years she had worked in the steam closet. He watched her as she rested.

"She is quiet right now," said Sarah, "but she went through a bout of insanity just before you got here. The heavy metals, the arsenic and all the other toxins have consumed her body and her mind."

The three of them sat quietly and gazed at poor Prudence's wasted body. Sarah began to sing quietly. Ebb remembered the words and softly sang along. After a while, Prudence began to stir. Then her eyes opened and she began ranting. She was so intoxicated with sickness that her speech was incoherent. Her body began quivering in a fit of spasms.

The Chief cried out, "Ebb, come here to me!" The Chief was leaning over Prudence. "She is too tortured, and her spirit is trying to escape. If you see any part of her spirit start to come out, push it back down inside her. Don't be startled when your hands enter her body. After all, we are spirits. If you see her spirit, push it deep down inside of her."

Prudence then fell into a deep fit of madness. "Get ready, for I fear it will happen any moment," warned the Chief.

Ebb could see part of her spirit trying to emerge. The Chief put his hands on top of the spirit and forced it back down into the body.

"Oh my God!" Ebb gasped as he watched the Chief plunging his hands deep inside Prudence's chest. She shook violently as her spirit tried to flee from her body. Then, the spirit tried to materialize again, and both Ebb and the Chief had to coerce it back inside. Again, her body shook in violent spasms.

"Sarah, you have to help us. Suffocate her with the pillow while Ebb and I hold her spirit within her." Sarah had never killed anybody and was reluctant. "Sarah, you are not killing her," yelled the Chief. "You are saving her soul. She is respected by the spirits for being Ebb's mother, and they have deemed her worthy enough to be with the spirits when they go to the Place of Happiness."

Ebb felt better knowing he would be able to be with her in the afterlife. "Please, Sarah, do it. The Chief and I cannot hold in her spirit much longer. Her torment is great."

Sarah complied, Prudence had to make it out of the cusp, and although it was against her nature to take a life, she killed Prudence out of love and respect. She took the pillow and held it over the dying woman's head. As Prudence died from lack of oxygen, her body shook even more violently. The house was full of commotion. A boy from the village, in his late teens, was passing by and went to the window. He looked inside, and what he saw horrified him. He could not see the Chief or Ebb. He could not see the stallion standing next to him. He only could see Sarah suffocating Prudence with the pillow

He ran away in fear. Before witnessing the tragedy, he had already suspected that Sarah was a witch because of her strange clothes and manners. He would not have entered that house to save even his own life. He went back home and lay in bed all night wondering what to do.

Back in the house, the Chief and Ebb released Prudence's spirit and let it float out of her body. Her spirit floated past them, and to Ebb, it seemed as if she looked down on them and smiled. Her spirit drifted through the door and down to the river where it joined the rest of the spirits of the mist. The madness would not end until more than eighty additional years of suffering had passed.

Ebb and the Chief returned to the river to wait for the next death. The villagers were not about to accept Sarah's act of compassion. They had all come to despise and fear her. Sarah was exhausted and returned to John's old place to lie down and rest.

The following day, the teen was still feeling troubled. He went to Pepperell Center to seek counsel from the minister. He felt he had to report what he had seen. After all, someone had to take action. They could not allow the witch to suffocate people in their sleep.

Upon reaching the parsonage, the youth called out, "Reverend Mather, I need to talk with you."

The Reverend came to the door with a cup of tea in his hand. "Who is that who calls out?"

"It is Robert, sir, from North Village."

The Reverend had a fearful look as he spoke. North Village had been having some odd occurrences for quite a while. "Oh yes, young Robert. What is wrong? You look very upset."

"I saw Sarah, the old Quaker woman, suffocate the widow Prudence last night. I could see her through the window pressing a pillow over Prudence's head. She was possessed and was talking to the air around her."

"Are you sure she killed her?"

"Yes. I waited until I was sure. The old woman went home last night, and this morning she went to Prudence's, and upon opening the door, she acted like she was surprised that Prudence was dead."

"Now, young Robert, are you sure you saw her suffocating Prudence and talking to the air?"

"Yes. I saw her do all of it. After Sarah left to get someone to go to the undertaker, I looked through the same window I was at last night. It was horrible. Prudence was lying there dead. Her face was contorted, and she looked like she died screaming. It was horrible to look at."

"Who is that woman, Sarah? I have not seen her at church before."

"She came to the village sometime in 1812. Everybody thought she was a Quaker, but she never said she was. She has been working in the shoddy shack. She never got paid much, but she always had money. She had been seen up in Hollis Village over the last few years spending twenty-dollar gold pieces. She seems to have an endless supply of them."

Robert captured the interest of the Reverend. The subject of money would always get his attention, especially if it involved someone who had money and did not attend church or make donations. In his mind, people like that were wrong.

"Well, something seems amiss here. How could she have so much money? I have seen her in the village. She looks like a beggar, yet she has so much wealth. Why would a woman who has so much money deliberately make herself look so poor?"

"I don't know."

"Well, I'll tell you. She hides her money because she must not want anyone to know where it came from. If she does not want anyone to know, then she must have gotten it surreptitiously. I think the Devil is at work here. Let me get my carriage, and I will go to the village and do a little investigation. We will get to the bottom of this, young Robert. Go home, and tell no one of this until I have had a chance to look around and ask a few questions."

"Yes, Reverend Mather."

The Reverend hooked up his horse to the carriage and headed for North Village. He never went there much as there was something about the area that scared him. The village had seen many strange deaths and many horrible accidents. North Village was beginning to look as if it were consuming people.

The village looked quiet and peaceful when the reverend arrived. "Why is such a pretty place so evil?" he thought as he looked at the idyllic setting.

"Good morning, Reverend Mather. What brings you to the village?" asked one of the townspeople.

"Well, my good man, God came to me in a dream last night and told me that my presence was needed here in the village."

The villager looked surprised. "Well, you must be in God's favor, for just last night poor Prudence died. Maybe you can say a few words over her. Her house is the one over there. The undertaker just arrived from Hollis Village. You can see his hearse."

"Thank you, sir. Have I seen you in church before?"

"Well, er… no, sir. I have not had the time to go."

The Reverend looked sternly at the man. "You do not have time to save your immortal soul? I might consider my priorities if I were you, good sir. You make sure you come this Sunday, and I might suggest that you make a substantial donation to atone for your truancy."

The Reverend drove his carriage to Prudence's home and parked next to the hearse. He jumped down from the carriage and went into the house. The undertaker was about to move Prudence as the pastor entered the room.

The Reverend took one look at Prudence and was startled. "Good God! What a horrible face. What an unusual look of horror."

The undertaker looked up and saw Reverend Mather. "Well, it is not an unusual look for this area. Over half the people I haul away from this village have the same look on their face. It is bad for my business, as I have to have far too many closed caskets at the services. It makes it look like I don't know my trade. No matter what I do, I cannot take that look of horror off their faces. It is most strange."

"Well, sir, I think we have the Devil at work here," said the Reverend. "It is time that I take a little closer look at this troubled area. Tell me about this Prudence."

"As far as I know, sir, she was the widow of Winslow who was slain by the saw at the mill a few years ago."

The Reverend leaned in toward the undertaker and spoke in a hushed tone. "Tell me, sir, who made these arrangements?"

"This old woman named Sarah. She paid me with a twenty-dollar gold piece and also asked me to find Prudence's brother who lives in Hollis Village and inform him. He is on his way down here and will be here shortly."

"Did the woman tell you where she got all that money?" asked the Reverend.

"No, sir. It is not my business to know where the money comes from, but it did seem strange for someone who looked like a pauper to have such a tidy sum."

"It is strange, indeed. The Devil is at work here," said the minister, giving the undertaker a menacing look.

"Heaven or hell, it makes no difference to me. Help me throw her in the hearse. Take that end of the sheet, and I will take this end. That's it. Lift her up."

By this time, the robust young body of Prudence resembled a skinny, shriveled up old lady. Effortlessly, the two men carried the sheet to the back of the hearse and put the remains inside. A small group of villagers had gathered, hearing that the reverend was there.

As the hearse began to move, the reverend folded his hands. "Dear God, please forgive this woman and take her to your side. Remove any spells and incantations that may have been placed on her by the Evil

One. Forgive Prudence for her association with the Evil One, for she never got over the loss of her Winslow and was in a weakened state."

As the hearse drove off, the Reverend turned to the people. "Pray for this village as there is evil amongst us."

"What evil is amongst us?" asked one of the villagers.

"I suggest you go and speak to young Robert," the Reverend replied as he climbed into his carriage. As he drove away, the reverend thought, "That will put the fear of God into them, and then, when they are all stirred up, they will come to me. All I have to do is simply confirm it. Attendance and donations will both benefit, and I will have more resources to fight the Devil."

Once the minister was gone, the group of villagers went off in search of young Robert. They found him sitting on his porch, looking a little dazed.

"Robert, what is this about evil in the village?" cried one of the villagers.

Robert's voice was full of emotion. "It's that Sarah. She is a witch. I saw her kill Prudence last night by suffocating her with a pillow. Sarah was possessed and was talking to the air around her while she took the life out of Prudence."

"Are you sure about what you saw?" asked a different villager.

"Yes, I am sure of what I saw. I will swear to it on the Bible."

"Let's go tell the rest!" cried one of the villagers, and the group turned and dispersed throughout the village. The news traveled quickly, and before long, chaos erupted throughout the entire village. A group of people had gathered near the mill to decide what to do. The air was chilly, so a few of the locals used some scrap wood to light one of the fire pits.

"I think we should go see Reverend Mather," someone in the group shouted.

"Yeah, yeah," responded several from the group.

They singled out six men who had horses to go to Pepperell Center and ask for the Reverend's advice. They chose horses instead of a wagon for greater speed. The men gathered their belongings, saddled up, and rode away, eager to hear the words of the reverend. From the window of the parsonage, he saw them coming.

The Reverend looked at the clock. "A little over an hour. That didn't take long," he thought as he stepped outside.

"Reverend Mather, we need your help immediately! There is evil in the village, and we need your advice," explained one of the men.

"Yes, I have heard about a certain witch who has managed to infiltrate your village and lives amongst you. She has been in consortium with the Devil. He pays her in gold coins."

"You are right. There have been many rumors in the village of this Sarah going to Hollis Village, changing twenty-dollar gold coins into smaller coins," responded one of the men.

As he had planned, the Reverend took advantage of their vulnerability. "And why would anyone do such a thing?"

"I don't know. Tell us," demanded another man.

"I'll tell you why. She did it to try and conceal the fact that she was getting her gold from the Devil. Why else would an old woman walk almost ten miles in each direction just to get change for her coins?"

"You're right," responded one of the other men. She could not have made that much money sorting shoddy. She never got any mail, and no one ever visited her. She had to be getting those coins from the Devil. Oh, what can we do?"

"Go get the town clerk and bring him to the mill. We'll need him to witness what we have to do. Make sure one of the fire pits is burning. I will be along shortly, and we will drive this demon from your village and pray for salvation."

"Now we will have some good, old-fashioned religion just like in Granddad's time," remarked one of them as the men galloped away.

Salem was not the only place where witches were tortured and killed. The Reverend's grandfather had run a remote parish. When they were alone together, his grandfather would recount stories about witchcraft, dating back to his own father's time. The family had a long lineage of divinity. His grandfather would proudly speak about his father having driven the witches out of the village, branding them with a "W," so the world could see their evilness. His grandfather had always hoped to do the same, but after the Salem witch trials, the public outcry ended such practices. The Reverend's grandfather never had an opportunity to brand any witches. The Reverend's father was a gentler man and did not listen to his father's stories about branding witches. However, the grandfather had found a willing student in his grandson. Through the years, the Reverend listened to his grandfather's tales and became a fire-and-brimstone preacher because of those stories.

"Where is it?" the Reverend mumbled as he searched the attic. "There you are," he said as he found the black cloth.

"Your time has come again. You are needed once more to fight the demons. May the spirit of my great-grandfather guide my hands in your use. Come, we are needed in North Village." The Reverend placed the black shroud on the seat next to him as he drove his carriage towards North Village. When he arrived, nearly all the villagers had gathered at the mill.

"Here comes Reverend Mather!" cried one of the villagers.

The Reverend drove his wagon into the crowd and stood in the carriage. "My people, I have come to save you. I have brought you a tool my great-grandfather used to remove the witches in his parish." The Reverend picked up the black cloth. It wrapped around something long and narrow.

"It's a rifle! He's going to shoot her!" screamed someone from the crowd, before seeing the contents of the cloth.

The Reverend dropped the cloth. "No, it is an iron in the shape of a "W." We are going to heat the brand in that fire. Then, we are going to find this Sarah and brand her forehead. We will then drive her from this valley, and she can wander the world with the brand of a witch, for all to see."

Frenzy erupted among the simple people of the village. One of the men took the brand and placed it in the fire. They stood and watched, as the iron grew red hot. When the iron was sufficiently charged with heat, the Reverend removed it from the fire and headed towards the hovel where Sarah had been living. The Reverend, flanked on one side by young Robert and the other side by the town clerk, set off down the overgrown path, followed by the rest of the frantic villagers.

CHAPTER TWENTY-ONE

The spirits of the mist had called upon Ebb and the Chief to attend another death. It was time for Sarah's suffering to end, and the spirits informed them that she had earned the right to join them in the mist. The two of them silently slipped through the wall and appeared on either side of the bed, looking down at Sarah while she slept. Ebb felt sad while looking at her. He had been part of her since she was a child. She had grown into a spent, old woman, drawing shallow breaths as she slept. The peaceful scene was interrupted, as three men kicked open the door and entered. Sarah awoke with a start and looked at the men. She knew her time had come. The spirits had told her that three men would kill her and they had arrived. She knew the one in the middle was Reverend Mather from Pepperell Center. She also recognized young Robert, but she did not know the third man. Sarah rose from her bed and faced the men. She was trying to be brave; she knew she would not survive what they were about to do.

Sarah spoke to Reverend Mather. "Who are you, the three unwise men?"

The Reverend was not amused. "Sarah, even now at this moment of judgment, you make jest of our lord, Jesus Christ. I accuse you of being an agent of the Devil. We intend to brand you with this hot iron, so all can see that you are a witch." As he spoke, the reverend started to approach Sarah, who was now standing. The other two men moved to opposite sides of Sarah and grabbed her arms. The Chief and Ebb watched in horror. They had no power over these men, especially in the daytime.

"I saw you kill Prudence last night!" shouted young Robert. I saw you press a pillow over her face and hold it there until you stole the life out of her."

"I did not kill Prudence. You all did," stated Sarah. "She is a victim of your precious watershed. Your ancestors killed her. Your poisons killed her, and it was your industry that killed her."

"Silence, woman! I will do the talking here. You were seen killing Prudence last night. Admit your deed, and we will spare your life and save you for the constable," shouted the town clerk.

"She was already dead," Sarah said flatly.

Young Robert was perturbed. "I saw her struggling while you killed her. She was not dead when you put the pillow over her head."

"See how she works for the devil?" interrupted the Reverend. See how you cannot get a straight answer from her? We will put an end to her treachery. Sarah you have poisoned our village and you must go."

"I have not poisoned your village. You and your ancestors have poisoned yourselves. I had nothing to do with it. Your white ways have killed this whole village. In time, the village will die, and those who are left will flee the village as from pestilence. (11) Because you cut down all the trees and over-farmed the land, the river will dry up and seep away. In a few decades, no one will be living in this thriving village. Your poisons are already making their way out of the valley and into the surrounding farms. Your poisons are addling the minds of the villagers and making them careless, which will cause many accidents, and many buildings will be consumed by fire. Many of you have already heard about how the death angel makes his entry in an unusual way, and he will not stop until the bloodlines of the original settlers are gone. There are skeletons in all of the closets here. They are the skeletons of the peaceful Indians who were ruthlessly murdered, so that the precious watershed could be acquired. But, what will be the ultimate irony for all of you is that the very thing you lusted and killed for will be the very same thing that kills you all. You have all killed the river, and now the river will kill you all."

"Be silent!" shouted the Reverend as he approached Sarah with the hot iron.

Ebb was becoming distressed. "Can't we do something?"

"No, we can not change her destiny. We are only here so you can see how the village is dying. We are here so you can see that it was the result of their carelessness about what is around them that killed them all. But it is more than that. You are here to help my people reach the Land of Happiness."

"Hold her, boys, while I place the iron upon her." (17)

Sarah stood there proudly. "You, sir, are the one who is the instrument of the Devil. You and your church do more harm to people than your so-called Devil. You steal people's money for your own glory. Your closed mind hurts many. You will get to meet your Devil when you die."

The Reverend was furious. "How dare you speak that way, you witch! When I die, I will be sitting by the hand of God. I am worthy of a spot in Heaven."

Sarah laughed. "It is only those who don't think themselves worthy of Heaven who get to go through the gates. You are a fool if you think you are going. The very fact that you think you are going makes it certain that you are not. If you think that you are pious enough and your actions worthy enough for Heaven, then you are a fool. You are not the one who decides."

Reverend Mather was so upset that saliva sprayed from his mouth as he screamed. "How dare you talk to me like that, you heretic!"

Sarah stood bravely, even though the two men were still grasping her. "You, sir, are the ultimate heretic. Money is what motivates you, and you control people in the name of God. You use this control to make people do unholy things."

"You witch, shut your mouth!" The parson held the hot iron and pressed on Sarah's forehead, deeply burning a "W" into her weathered skin. (17) The pain was excruciating, but Sarah did not flinch. The iron had severed the vein in her forehead. Blood spurted out, into the face of the Reverend, drenching his eyes and mouth.

Sarah held her composure. While blood streamed down her face, she spoke. "You have now assured yourself a place in hell, for the blood of yet one more innocent is upon you. God will not forgive your arrogance. No one speaks for God. You are no exception."

"Die, witch, die!" Reverend Mather had lost complete control and was screaming from his blood-soaked face.

The men who were holding Sarah released her and backed away. All of the blood terrified them, and the Reverend looked like the embodiment of evil. He was soaked in blood, and all he could do was scream, "Die, witch, die!"

Ebb and the Chief rushed to Sarah's side. Her time had come. They were allowed to come to her aid by helping her glide through the door and towards the river. Sarah appeared in the doorway with blood streaming down her face. The village people gasped and backed away. She was a terrifying specter with dripping blood staining her plain cotton garments. When the Reverend appeared in the doorway, the crowd gasped. Sarah's blood covered his contorted face as he screamed, "Die witch, die!" He looked fanatical as he followed at Sarah's heels.

"Die, witch, die!"

Sarah was nearing death. Ebb and the Chief were fully supporting her as she walked. The village people could not understand how Sarah was able to continue walking, and the ongoing spectacle horrified them.

The Reverend followed directly behind Sarah. "Die, witch, die!" By this time, the reverend looked completely demented. He most certainly was not a loving and caring agent of God as he kept screaming, "Die, witch, die!"

The crowd trailed behind Reverend Mather, and the procession moved along, towards the river. As the line of people approached the river, the mist began to rise outward to meet Sarah. The mist flowed gently around her feet. The village people cried out and ran in horror as ghostly arms reached out from the mist and guided Sarah to the embankment. Sarah fell forward into the river. By the time she had hit the water she was dead. Sarah had collapsed in the exact spot where the Chief had fallen years before. Once again, the river boiled with blood. Reverend Mather had never seen anything like this before and was momentarily horror-struck. The crowd began screaming louder and ran away from the river. The reverend was running alongside them. Even his grandfather's outrageous stories could not compare to this. The Reverend gathered his composure and began urging the crowd to stop running.

"Stop, everyone, stop!" he shouted. "Gather round. We must pray immediately," he added. This turn of events was not what the Reverend had hoped would happen, but he figured it would work, in time, to turn their fears into devotion and donations.

"What you have just witnessed is proof that Sarah was a witch," said the Reverend. Let us fold our hands and pray to God for giving me the strength to face the witch and banish her. I have saved you all from her. Praise God."

"Praise God!" the crowd responded.

It was getting late in the day, so one of the villagers asked, "Sir, will you stay the night and protect us?"

"I cannot stay. I have duties to perform at the parsonage," he replied, knowing he would never spend the night in such a cursed place.

"Please, sir, it is during the night that the spirits of the mist run over our village, and we fear to go out."

"There are no spirits in the mist. What you just saw was the witch using the last of her power to try and continue her reign of fear," preached the Reverend.

"But, sir, the mist contained evil, long before Sarah ever came to the village," responded one of the villagers.

"Do not question me, sir!" shouted the Reverend. "My ancestors and I have been instruments of God for almost two-hundred years. Follow me back to her hovel; we must make sure no more witches can inhabit that evil spot." In reality, the Reverend was afraid to go back alone to get his horse and carriage. The members of the remaining crowd gathered their courage and followed Reverend Mather down the narrow lane to the old cabin.

"Now, let us burn this place and destroy the witch's den," ordered the Reverend. He looked inside and saw a bottle of lamp oil. "Let us take this and pour it on the floor to torch the place. Throw all the dead brush and branches inside."

The villagers quickly filled the interior with dead branches and brush that had been cluttering the site. The steel hit the flint, creating a large white spark. The tinder was lit. While the dry, rotted cabin burned ferociously, the Reverend had the people gather around and pray. "Almighty God, please have compassion for these poor wretches and remove all evil from this place," he prayed. The house was almost totally burned down. "I must go now. Go back to your houses, and pray again before going to bed. You will all be better in the morning."

"But sir, will you not stay with us for just one evening?"

"I told you that I have pressing business back at the parsonage." The Reverend then climbed onto his wagon and headed back to Pepperell Center. The villagers' faith quickly returned to fear as the Reverend rode out of sight. Immediately, they began to walk away from the burning embers.

"The place is consumed and will not flare up. Let us return to our homes and prepare for evening," announced one of the men.

"Yes, the sun is setting and we must get inside," responded another.

A new moon followed the sunset, and the village descended into complete darkness. Meanwhile, the spirits of the mist had welcomed Sarah. The other spirits that had been inside of her were released back into the river. The spirits were saddened and displeased that Sarah, who had always tried to help people and had never hurt anyone, was called an "evil witch" and had died such a terrible death.

Spirits gathered from up and down the river. As nighttime shrouded the village, a mist rose from the river, thicker than ever before. It blended with the smoke from the smoldering cabin and filled the air with choking vapors. Horses and other animals sensed the presence of the spirits. The unusual number of spirits around them caused the animals in the village to panic. Horses brayed and kicked at their stalls, dogs barked to come inside and then paced around, growling at the door. Cats sat on their windowsills with their fur standing on end, mewing into the darkness.

The village was alive with sounds. Skunks, raccoons, and other scavengers rummaged though the trash piles, rustling cans and making noise. The squirrels and the mice feverishly chewed at the houses, making loud scratching sounds as they tore at the wood. Dogs barked and howled, cats cried insensately, and the agitated wildlife thrashed around, causing a huge commotion. This petrified the residents.

A light began to show, across the river where Sarah had lived. The fire had risen from the ashes and filled the village with an eerie, orange glow. Anyone who dared to look outside claimed to see shadows circling the burning cabin. The night was terrifying, and fear gripped all of the villagers. Periodically, the flames would erupt, illuminating the darkness. Then they would subside, and the village would plunge into darkness, making it even scarier.

Just before dawn, the flames at the old cabin site soared high above the trees, creating the sound of rushing air. The villagers were afraid the flames would destroy the village, but no one dared to go out. As the sun began to rise, the flames grew weaker, and the mist subsided. The small scavenger animals crept away, and the village was quiet once again. After the sun rose, everybody stayed inside for a short time. Slowly, people ventured out and began to gather at the mill. They decided to dispatch someone to find the Reverend. They gathered in little groups and spoke in whispers. After awhile, the coach, with the rider and the reverend, arrived at the mill yard. The crowd clustered around the Reverend as everyone tried to speak at once.

"Let us pray for guidance." The Reverend waited a moment, in silence, before he continued. "Dear Lord, remove these evil spirits from this village. Give us the strength to overcome this adversity. Let us go to the cabin of Sarah and extinguish that evil fire, once and for all."

The crowd was silent. Nobody wanted to go. "But, Reverend…" shouted someone in the crowd.

"No 'buts' here. Let us go. It is time for you all to show a little faith. There is nothing there that God cannot help me to eradicate."

With the people of the village following him, the Reverend set off across the bridge and towards the site of John's cabin. He instructed the men to collect washtubs and buckets along the way, so that they could extinguish the last of the fire. They arrived at the site of the cabin, but nothing was left to burn. The shallow cellar was full of white ash with no sign of any heat. The men filled the buckets, and they poured water into the cellar hole and onto the ashes. The slightest sign of heat was not found anywhere.

One of the men reached down and touched the rocks of the crude foundation. "The rocks are stone cold. How can that be? This place was an inferno just before sunrise."

The crowd began to panic, and the Reverend feared he wouldn't succeed. "Praise, be to God! It is a miracle. Our prayers have been answered, and the evil has been repelled. Even the heat of Satan has been removed. The village has been saved. Thank you, Dear Lord." Before the villagers were able to think about what he had said, the Reverend added, "Let's all pray together and thank the good Lord for saving this village through the power of our prayers."

CHAPTER TWENTY-TWO

Reverend Mather prayed for a few moments at the foundation of the burned cabin before addressing the crowd. "Go back to your duties of life. There is paper to be made, children to tend to. I have dispatched the witch, Sarah. We should be more careful and give strangers a more vigilant eye from now on."

After the death of Sarah, the strange incidents diminished. Some of the older residents were still dying in an unusual way, but no one was especially concerned since they had grown accustomed to that kind of death. The villagers accepted that a certain number of people would die after experiencing fits of dementia. Occasionally, they called in medical experts from Boston when one of the wealthier residents exhibited strange symptoms, but none of them could find any direct cause.

Reverend Mather was spending a lot of time in North Village. He visited the sick and was often seen talking to the mill workers and their families. When the woman who ran the velvet shop died, the reverend was by her side. She had outlived many of her coworkers, and even though her office was set off to the side, the poisons eventually made her sick. She died in the same, unusual way with her panic-stricken face frozen in a wild, contorted position that even the most talented undertaker could not remove. After the velvet shop closed, the death rate of the women in the village diminished, and life returned to normal. In 1826, construction of the Erie Canal began. Many of the young families in the village decided to relocate, in search of a better life, since the work crew hired for the canal received good pay.

After witnessing the deaths of his tortured parishioners, Reverend Mather still felt uneasy about North Village. Whenever new individuals came to town, the Reverend would meet and evaluate them. He was in the store, talking to the owner, when a large man filled the doorway.

The gruff Norwegian stepped inside the store. "Is there any work here, ya?"

"Try down at the mill. I know they have been shorthanded for quite awhile since many of the men went to work on the Erie Canal," replied the storekeeper.

"Ya, down at the mill, over there?"

"Yes, sir. I think Mr. Appleton (13), who is one of the new paper mill owners, is there right now. Go and ask for him directly."

"Ya, thank you. I shall go there right now," said the Norwegian with a heavy accent.

Reverend Mather stepped forward. "Pardon me, sir. I am the local Reverend, and I would like to welcome you to town. Might I see you in church this Sunday?"

"No, sir. You will not be seeing Sven. Sven prays at home, by golly."

The Reverend turned to the storeowner. "I have a bad feeling about that man."

The paper mill owner watched the Norwegian walk to the office. He seemed a bit strange, but the mill certainly needed some new, stronger workers since many of the young men had left for New York.

The Norwegian knocked on the door. "Come in," came the call from inside.

The Norwegian entered. "Ya, sir, I am Sven, and I hope to come here for work. You have work, ya?"

The size of the foreigner surprised Mr. Appleton. "You are new to this country, sir?"

"Ya, I come to the country three years ago. Ya, I live in south of country but it too hot for Sven, ya."

"Well, Sven I need a good, strong worker to help move the heavy rolls of paper. Are you interested?"

"Ya, Sven would like job. Ya, Sven be strong and move paper like nobody business, I tell ya."

"You can start tomorrow. Do you have a place to stay?"

"Ya, Sven has no place to stay."

"There are a few empty millhouses in town. Take one as your home."

"Ya, Sven see one already, by golly. Can Sven have house between schoolhouse number four and river, ya?"

"Yes, that house is empty; you can take that one, if you want."

"Ya, Sven like that house. Sven like being next to school number four. Sven like watching little girls…" Sven abruptly added, "and little boys play in schoolyard. Ya, children make Sven happy, ya. Ya, Sven make you a present." He reached into his pocket and took out a handful of peanuts. "These peanuts. I grow them last summer. You try, ya?"

"Well, sir, I have never seen nuts like these before. I don't know."

"Ya, Sven show you all right. Open the shell like this, ya. Then take off the skin and see, there is nut, ya."

Mr. Appleton reluctantly tried the peanuts. "Why, Sven, these nuts are very good."

"Ya, Sven grow last summer, bring with me, and grow here this summer. Ya, by golly, Sven like peanut, also."

"Go home and rest for now. Come back here at four o'clock tomorrow, and you can start your new job."

"Ya, Sven be here bright and early."

"I'm sorry, Sven. I meant 4 p.m. tomorrow. You will be in charge of moving the daily paper production and keeping the paper dryers filled with charcoal, so they do not cool overnight. Also, you will clean up the paper scraps and any spills of paper products."

"Ya, very good. Sven come at 4 p.m., and you see how hard Sven work."

"Kind of an odd fellow," thought Mr. Appleton as Sven left the mill. "But, if he loves children, then that is the right house for him."

Sven returned to the mill at 4 p.m. the next day and met the other two owners, Mr. Moore and Mr. Knowles. His size and strength impressed them. The three owners showed him around the mill personally and explained the operation.

"Here is the loading dock, Sven," said Moore as he pointed to the area with its roof and sides. "Your job is to roll these finished paper rolls up that ramp and onto the freight wagon. When one is full, cover it with these oilcloths, and the teamster will take them to the train in East Pepperell. The freight wagon goes out every other day."

Then Knowles said, "These are the paper dryers, and you need to check them periodically and put charcoal in them. At night, keep these dampers closed to save on fuel. It will help keep the dryers hot for the next day's production of paper."

"Then, when all of that is done," chimed Appleton, "sweep up all the floors, and mop up all the spills and messes from the day. You will work from 4 p.m. until 2 a.m. The last thing you do before going home is to add charcoal to the two dryers, so they are fully charged and hot when the first workers come in at five-thirty in the morning."

"Ya, by golly. Sven going to make this place neat. You just wait and see." He took off his jacket and began with the day's production of paper. The mill made newspaper stock, and the rolls were 3 feet wide.

Sven examined the first roll and was surprised at how heavy it was. He discovered if he put his back to the roll and pushed with his feet while pulling up at the edge of the roll, it would reluctantly move.

As the three owners watched, Sven muscled the roll up the ramp and onto the freight wagon. The owners looked at each other and smiled. "You sure found a good one this time, Appleton," said Knowles.

The three owners were grinning from ear to ear as they left for East Pepperell where they lived. "Sven is so big, he can do the work of two men," Moore commented as they rode away.

Sven loaded the paper, cleaned up all the paper scraps, and discarded them in one of the dryer's fireboxes. Then he mopped all the floors. Just before 2 a.m., he filled the fireboxes on the two dryers and puttered around the mill. He stayed until the first workers arrived at 5 a.m.

"Hello. I am Sven. I do good job, ya?" he said, greeting the first workers.

The work crew looked around and saw the mill was spotless. "Well, Sven, you did a good job at cleaning. I will make mention to the owners when they come in later. Go home now and rest, so you can do it again tonight. My name is Robert."

Robert extended his hand. Sven offered his enormous hand, which enveloped Robert's, and they shook hands. "Ya, Sven be glad meeting you all."

Sven went back to his house and made tea. He was sitting on the front porch of the house when the school bell rang. The children of the village passed by the house, walking in groups of two and three. Sven sat on his porch, transfixed. "Ya, Sven be liking this house already." When the last of the children went by, Sven went inside and slept. Not being accustomed to the heavy millwork, he slept all day.

Just before he had to leave for work, the school bell signaled the end of the school day. Again, Sven sat on the porch watching the parade of children go by. "Ya, by golly, Sven certainly like it here."

Once the children were gone, Sven went to his job at the mill. As the months passed, he structured his life around the parade of schoolchildren. He would come home from the mill, sleep a few hours, and then get up, so he could sit on his front porch and watch the children. He would go back to sleep, so he could be outside at noon when the children had recess. Sven spent his afternoons clearing a spot by the side of the river. He found a nice location, which got flooded in the spring rush and had plenty of rich sediments from the river for the nuts to grow in.

Sven did not have any gardening tools. He only had a piece of metal from the mill to turn the soil. Mostly, he wrenched out the rocks and stones with his bare hands. The sharp points would often cut his fingers. He would rub mud from the river bottom onto his wounds, believing that the sediments had healing properties. He had no well and drank directly from the river.

School ended and Sven was disappointed. He no longer had any daytime entertainment. During the warm weather, he devoted his time to growing peanuts. By the end of the summer, he had a bumper crop of nuts that he harvested and dried in the sun. At the store, Sven traded peanuts for sugar to make peanut brittle and was well stocked for the upcoming school year. (19)

"Ya, I'll be ready for school now, by golly," Sven thought as he stored his cache of peanuts in the house. "Ya, by golly, I'll be ready."

Sven noticed that the school had no well. At noontime recess, two children would pass by his house and cross the river to the closest house that had a well. Two girls would complete the trip, and the next day two boys would go. Sven looked forward to the days when the girls would go by. He would stare at them as they walked by, studying them. He would watch them laugh and noticed how their hair blew around in the breeze.

One bright day, at noon, the girls had their turn. "Ya, good day, girls. I made this for you at school number four. Ya, Sven make all of you peanut brittle. Sven leave it here on corner fence. You get it on way back from well, ya?"

The girls were afraid of Sven. He was a huge man who talked funny and seemed a bit odd. All of the children instinctively knew to stay away from him. Sven was careful. He had waited until the girls were just past his gate when he first spoke. He was several feet from the road. He placed the pan of candy on the fence, after they went by, and then sat in the chair on the porch. From the porch, he saw the two girls coming back, on the opposite side of the road, with the bucket of water. One of the girls ran across the road, snatched the pan of candy, and ran back across the road.

"Ya, I be making that just for you. Is very good, ya."

The girls ran the rest of the way back to the school, giggling and laughing as sparkling water splashed out of the bucket while they ran. The children and the teacher relished the candy. The teacher distributed the broken pieces as evenly as possible. The candy tasted delicious, and the new kind of nut made for lively conversation.

The next day, at noon recess, a couple of boys came by with the bucket and the empty pan. "Hey, mister, here is your pan. Got any more?"

"Sven have nothing for you, ya. You put pan on fence corner and go." Sven's voice sounded angry.

"Geese, mister, you don't have to get all hot about it."

"Ya, you just move along now," replied Sven sternly.

Sven would make peanut brittle every few weeks and put it out for the children, making sure it was when the girls went for water. People thought he was big and dumb, but Sven was really clever. He made candy often enough to keep the interest of the children, who longed for its golden sweetness, but not often enough to attract the attention of the adults. After awhile, the girls were not as afraid of Sven and would walk to the well on his side of the street. The boys still walked on the opposite side of the road. They did not like something about Sven.

"Ya, by golly, girls like Sven," he said to himself as two girls picked up the candy on the way back to the school. "Ya, you take. Sven make for you. There is little bit of extra candy on top for you two, ya. You stop and eat before going back."

The girls quickly ate the additional pieces and scurried off back to school, without telling the teacher about the extra candy. The girls, however, talked amongst their friends. Whenever the time arrived for the girls to get water, an eager showing always appeared. They all wanted to go for water, knowing if there were candy for them, they would each get a secret extra piece.

Although Sven was a good worker, the people in the village did not trust him. People began talking, and some parents were alarmed about his strange behavior concerning the children. He had not done anything wrong, but people worried.

A few years passed, and Sven was becoming more peculiar. He had Saturday nights off from work, and he spent them at the tavern, drinking copious amounts of ale. Sven could out-drink any man and could swallow a pitcher of ale in an instant.

"I don't trust him," Jonathan said to his friend. They sat at a table in the tavern, gazing over at the bar where Sven was alone drinking.

Jonathan continued. "He is always alone. Many have tried to be friendly to him, but he does not seem to like anybody - that is, except the schoolgirls he makes candy for. I tell you, something is not fitting here."

"He seems to get meaner and stranger with time," replied the friend.

They had a few more pints of ale and left the tavern. Sven was still drinking and sitting alone when they left. As they separated to go home, Jonathan said, "I tell you, something is not decent about him. There will be trouble somehow - just mark my words."

Even the teacher was becoming concerned about Sven. She did not want to tell him to stop making candy for the school, since the children liked it. However, she was uncomfortable with him staring at the little girls when they walked by. In addition, she noticed him acting strangely towards the boys.

The teacher visited the school a few days before classes. She prepared her lessons for the upcoming year and cleaned the classroom. Reverend Mather arrived at the schoolhouse, and he and the schoolteacher walked away, towards Sven's house. She wanted to check with the people who owned the nearest well to see if the schoolchildren could continue to draw water from it. More importantly, she wanted the reverend to talk to Sven.

"Hello, Sven," called the teacher as she neared the house.

Sven was in his usual chair on the porch, watching people walk by while waiting to leave for work. "Ya, hello teacher. Hello, Reverend. Is school to be starting soon?"

"Why, yes, Sven. It starts in a couple of days. Why do you ask?"

"Ya, I be asking, so I know when to make peanut candy for the children."

Reverend Mather spoke gruffly. "That is very nice of you to make candy for the children, but may I ask a question?"

"You be asking Sven a question?"

"Yes. Why do you only give the candy to the girls and not the boys?"

"Sven not be liking little boys. Where Sven live before now, little boys make fun of Sven and call names. Sven not be liking little boys. Little boys be too mean to Sven. Little girls be nice to Sven, so Sven make them peanut candy." (19)

The teacher was still concerned, but did not know what to say. "When school begins, try being a little nicer to the boys, and maybe they will like you also."

The Reverend's voice remained stern. "Try a little harder to be nice to the boys, and maybe they will treat you better."

"Ya, Sven try a little harder," he remarked as they walked away. "Thank you for talking at Sven."

Sven was finding it harder to control his temper. The mercury in the soil from tending the peanuts had been entering his body through the cuts in his fingers. He drank the river water and was consuming whatever had been tossed into the water upstream. In addition, he was handling the toxins in the mill. He dealt with a daily triumvirate of poisons that were having an effect on him. The men stayed away from Sven because he was easy to anger and big enough to intimidate them.

The new school year began, and Sven resumed his candy making for the girls. He would leave the treats out on sunny days because he loved to watch the young girls with their straight, shining hair or curls bouncing in the sunlight.

Early one Sunday morning, Sven could not sleep. He sat, wrapped in a blanket, on his front porch drinking tea. Nightmares were constantly waking him up and making sleep difficult.

"Ya. Who is that walking?" Sven asked himself. "I think it is one of the girls from school number four, ya."

Joan had risen early to do some chores at one of the farms in the valley. She carried a bucket in each hand. She would receive two pails of milk to bring home for Sunday breakfast as her pay. Joan had started working at the farm to get cream for butter. The cows in North Village were having trouble producing milk, and the cream from the milk was difficult to churn into butter.

Suddenly, Ebb and the Chief found themselves in Sven's yard, watching the situation develop. "Not the young girl?" asked Ebb. (18) (17)

"Yes, Ebb, there is nothing we can do," replied the Chief. "She is a descendant of one of the original settlers."

"Ya, good morning to you," said Sven as the girl approached.

"Good morning to you, sir," replied Joan.

"Ya, you be going for milk?" asked Sven.

"Yes," replied Joan. She had walked by his home for several years and had brought back numerous pans of candy.

"You like some peanut candy to eat while you walk to work, ya?"

Joan stopped. She had heard people talk about how strange he was, but she had known him for a few years. Hence, the innocence of her youth prevented her from seeing his true evil.

"Why, yes, sir. Some candy might help my journey."

"Ya, well, you come over to door, and Sven will get you some peanut candy."

Joan was a little nervous. No one had dared to enter Sven's yard before. She hesitated for a moment and then went up to the porch. Sven went inside to retrieve a fresh batch of candy. He had prepared it for the girls who would be coming by that week.

"What is your name, young girl?"

"My name is Joan, sir."

"Joan, you just reach in here, and take a little candy for your walk."

Joan was afraid, but the big piece of candy Sven was holding out towards her quickly grabbed her attention. She put the two pails in her left hand. Timidly, she reached into the doorway to get the candy. Sven grabbed her arm and pulled her into the house, slamming the door.

"Aaahhhh!" Joan screamed. The pails clanged as they fell from her hands.

"No, little Joan, not to be making noise." Sven covered her mouth with his massive hand. "I just be wanting to touch your pretty hair, ya. Joan have such pretty hair." Sven stroked her hair as he held her. The harder she struggled, the tighter he held her. His hand was so massive that it covered Joan's mouth and nose. Soon, the struggle ended.

The Chief and Ebb watched Joan's spirit float away. Sven just stood there, stroking her hair. After awhile, Sven noticed how quiet Joan was and let her go. Her limp body slumped to the floor. Sven was filled with fear.

"No, Joan, get up. Sven not mean to do this. No, Joan, you all right. Get up."

The Chief turned to Ebb. "Let us leave this sickness. Our job is done."

As they returned to the river, Ebb said, "Of all the deaths we have gone to, this was the saddest."

Sven was consumed with dread. "Oh, Sven in trouble now. Kill Joan like puppy. Bad Sven."

When Sven was a young boy in Norway, his parents had come home with a puppy for him. Sven loved the puppy dearly and played with it all the time. One time, when the puppy was barking, Sven tried to make it stop. He put his hand over the puppy's mouth, and he accidentally suffocated the pup.

"Oh, Sven, you in trouble now. What to do? I know. Sven hide Joan. Nobody know what Sven do."

The only outside door was the front door, so he carried the dead girl and hurled the body out a back window. The body hit the ground with a thud, breaking a few bones when it hit the ground. Sven went outside to the back of the house with a dirty, old sheet wrapped around the pails and collected the body. A barn stood between Sven's house and schoolhouse number four. When it was first built, it had served as the barn to his house. By this time, moisture from the river mist had it falling down and rotting.

Sven carried the body to the back of the barn. He buried Joan and the pails deeply in the ground. He had excavated the grave during most of the morning, using the simple tool he had for tending peanuts. After burying the body, he carefully scattered junk from the barn onto the new grave to cover any evidence.

When he was done, Sven was proud of how he had camouflaged the grave. "Ya, Sven may be crazy, but Sven not stupid. Sven never tell anyone, and Sven will not get in trouble like with puppy, ya."

Sven returned to the house and cleaned up, just as the villagers began a search for Joan. When Joan had not returned with the milk and cream for Sunday breakfast, her father rode his horse to the farm and discovered that she never arrived. On his way back to the village, he began knocking on doors.

"Have you seen my daughter, Joan, this morning? She is missing." He continued to inquire at each household, only to be told "no."

He stopped at Sven's place. "I always suspected this fellow of being evil," thought Joan's father as he approached the door and knocked loudly.

"Did you see my daughter go by your place this morning, sir?" he asked.

"Er, Sven not see young girl this morning."

"How did you know she was a young girl? I asked if you saw my daughter. I did not say she was young."

"Sven not see your daughter. Sven be inside all day resting for work tonight, ya."

"Well, sir, if I find that you hurt my daughter, I will kill you."

"No. Sven see no young girl."

"I warn you, sir. It will be very bad for you, if you are lying."

"Sven no lie. Sven not see young girl."

Joan's father stopped at the few, remaining houses on the way home. The people on the west side of the river had remembered seeing her go by. No one on the east side of the river had seen her. Sven's house was the first one on the east side. Joan's father rode to Pepperell Center and went to see the constable. He told him about the disappearance of his daughter and the strange behavior that Sven had displayed towards the young girls in the village. He mentioned the peanut brittle and how he only gave it to the girls. He pointed out how Sven would chase the boys away.

"This man sounds a bit queer to me," stated the constable. "Let me get a couple of the deputies, and I will go visit this fellow. Return to your house, and I will stop in afterwards and tell you what I find out."

Joan's father unwillingly went home and watched for the constable. A half-hour later, he and his deputies went by the house. They stopped in front of Sven's house and went to the door. Sven had seen them approaching and opened the door before they could knock.

"Ya, you be wanting something?"

"Yes, sir. We would like to talk to you about the disappearance of young Joan. She went missing this morning," stated the constable.

"Ya, Sven tell father that Sven not be seeing the young girl."

"Tell the truth, sir. Did you have anything to do with the disappearance of that girl?"

Sven remembered the trouble he had gotten into, after telling the truth about the puppy. "Sven no see girl. Sven not know what you talk about. You act like Sven kill somebody."

The constable stiffened. "What was that, sir? We did not accuse you of killing anybody. We simply asked if you saw the girl. Now I ask you, sir. Did you kill the girl?"

"No. Sven not kill young girl."

The deputies and the constable pressed up closely to Sven as a threatening gesture, but Sven was so huge that the small stature of the men made the threat look ridiculous.

Sven looked down at the men. "Ya, I tell ya. Sven not hurt young girl."

The constable and the men backed up a little. "When was the last time you saw young Joan?"

"Sven see her last week when she go to well."

"Did you give her candy then?" asked the constable.

Sven looked visibly nervous. "Ya, Sven give two girls peanut candy to bring to school four. Sven give peanut candy to lots of girls."

The constable leaned forward. "Tell me this, Sven. Why did you only give candy to the girls?"

"Girls say 'thank you' to Sven."

"Do you like young girls, Sven?"

"Ya." Then, Sven changed the focus. "Ya, Sven like all children, by golly. I make candy so they all be happy, ya."

As the constable and his men were walking towards the door, the constable stopped and turned to Sven. "I would not leave town, Sven. We will be back with more questions."

Next, they went to the house where Joan's father lived. "Wait here, men. I want to talk with the father alone."

Joan's father met the constable at the door. "Did he do something to my Joanie?"

"Sir, he claims the last time he saw her was last week."

"Where is my daughter then?"

"I don't know, sir. I will be back tomorrow with more people to help look for her."

"Thank you, sir. I will take the day off from work and search also," said the father, his eyes full of tears as he closed the door.

Reverend Mather heard about the disappearance of the girl, which confirmed his suspicions about Sven. During the Sunday evening service, he called for volunteers to try and find Joan.

On Monday, close to thirty people gathered outside the school to look for the girl, as planned. School had been cancelled, and all the schoolchildren helped in the search. They started searching around the school first and then went off in different directions.

"Joan! Joan!" could be heard from the searchers as they moved away from the school. Jacob and Simon, twin brothers, were two of the schoolchildren searching. They headed to the west side of Paugus Pond and then, along the bank of the Nissitissit. Soon they were far upstream, at the mouth of Sucker Brook.

"Jacob, look at this!" exclaimed Simon. "I found an overgrown entrance to a root cellar. It is small, but there are some clay jugs in there." Simon struggled as he tried to move a jug. "And they are as heavy as sin."

"I fear we should return, lest they go searching for us also," said Jacob. "We can come back this weekend and dig up those jugs. Let us get back to the village." Simon complied and the twins walked back, along the river.

Sven did not join in the search and sat on his porch, watching. When the constable came into Sven's yard, he asked, "Care to tell us where she is, sir?"

"No. Sven not be knowing what you ask."

Although the constable searched the yard for signs of a grave, he found none. He tried searching the old barn, but the structure was too fragile, and he feared it would fall down on him. "This place is so weak that a man his size could not have come in here without it falling down," thought the constable.

They searched all week and could not find young Joan. Everyday, the number of searchers lessened as the village lost hope of finding the girl. On Wednesday, a federal marshal from Boston accompanied the constable. Everyday they searched the village, and every night they grilled Sven for information.

"I don't trust what he says," the marshal told the constable. "I know he is hiding something. And it's strange that the more we question him, the less he is able to speak English."

Sven was clever and created the language issue to hide behind. He found he could dodge a lot of questions by acting as though he did not understand what was said.

"What can we do? He cannot be allowed to get away with this," stated the constable.

"It seems the only thing you can do is drive him from the town," replied the marshal.

"But then he is free to do this somewhere else," responded the constable.

"Then deport him," said the marshal. (18)

"Can we do that?" asked the constable.

"Not legally, without a federal trial, but if we did and acted as if we had a judgment, nobody would question us. Let me contact Boston and see if any vessels are leaving for Norway. I will take the train into the city tonight and will return in the morning," said the marshal as he left.

On Friday, the constable met the marshal at the train station in East Pepperell. "We are in luck," said the marshal as he stepped from the train. "There is a ship leaving for Norway Sunday afternoon. I have talked to the captain, and he will hold the ship until we get there, but he wants to be paid for his effort."

"How much?" asked the constable.

"He wants three twenty-dollar gold pieces."

"That is a lot, but it will be worth it. Let us go find the selectmen and see what they want to do." The constable and the marshal traveled to the homes of the selectmen and found that they were agreeable. They collected the money that was needed before the end of the day.

The constable and the marshal then went to North Village to make the arrangements. "How do we capture him without a lot of injury?" asked the constable.

"We let him capture himself."

"How is that, Marshal?"

The marshal reached into his vest pocket and pulled out a small bottle. "We will knock him out with this potion I got from the doctor. After his first pitcher of ale Saturday night, we will have the barkeep pour this liquid into his next pitcher. There is enough here to keep a man of his size out cold for at least twenty-four hours. Get the carpenters at the mill to put together a makeshift casket, so we can move him without attracting attention."

The whole village knew about the plan. Joan's father was upset. He thought that Sven's punishment was not severe enough, but without any evidence, they could do no more. All was in order, and the village waited for Saturday night. As usual, Sven entered the tavern for his plentiful servings of ale. He sat at the bar by himself and finished drinking his first pitcher. Then, the barkeep inconspicuously poured the clear liquid into the bottom of the second pitcher and filled it with ale.

Sven glanced around the room. One of the men raised his glass. "Here's looking at you."

"Ya, Sven be looking at you." He lifted his pitcher to the man.

Sven gulped down the second pitcher of ale and immediately felt the effects. He fell from the bar onto the floor. The men in the tavern instantly put the plan into motion. The casket and a wagon arrived at the tavern. Six strong men were needed to lift Sven into the casket. They nailed on the lid. A few holes provided air. Then, under the cover of darkness, they shipped off the unconscious Norwegian to East Pepperell. They planned on sending him into Boston in the freight car of the morning train. No one in East Pepperell questioned that yet another body was being shipped out of North Pepperell. Six men in the village offered their money for train fare to make sure the casket got loaded onto the ship for Norway. Two of the men, who had pistols in their coats, rode in the freight car atop the casket, trying to be as inconspicuous as possible. The other four men discreetly entered the passenger coach. When the train arrived in North Station, they arranged for a wagon. The six men headed out to the docks with the casket.

"We were beginning to wonder if you were going to show up," cried the Boston marshal as he saw the wagon. "Where is the constable?"

"The constable stayed behind as his presence would be missed," stated one of the men.

They unloaded the casket and sent off the wagon. "Do you have the money?" asked the marshal.

"Of course."

The marshal pointed to the captain of the boat. "Give it to him, and his crew will load the cargo. It's an American ship. They will work him hard, and they will throw him overboard when they reach the

Norwegian shore."

The deal was done. The crew opened the casket. "Captain, he is indeed a huge man," cried one of the crewmen as they forced him up the ramp.

"Tie him up, and put him below. He might wake with a bad attitude, but it is nothing that a few days without food and water won't cure. I have not seen a man yet who did not eventually yield and willingly work for food." The captain turned to the mate. "Order the crew on deck. Cast off those lines, and prepare to set sails. The tide is in our favor, and we will put out now." The crew set about their tasks, and the tide sailed the boat out of sight.

The marshal turned to the men. "Officially, we never had this meeting."

"What meeting?" asked one of the men.

"Exactly," said the marshal as he walked off.

CHAPTER TWENTY-THREE

Jacob and Simon woke early and planned on returning to Sucker Brook. Joan had been missing for more than two weeks, and people had stopped looking for her. Some people in the village thought Sven had been deported too soon. They wondered if he should have been tortured. Perhaps then, he would have revealed what he had done to the girl. Unfortunately, no evidence linked him to her disappearance.

As an excuse, the twins said they were going fishing for the day. They got their fishing gear and a shovel from the barn to dig worms. As soon as they were out of sight from their house, they hid the fishing gear and ran off towards Sucker Brook.

"Let us go find those jugs."

"I am with you," replied Jacob. The boys reached the side of the hill and began digging out the clay jugs. "Let us dig out one jug to see what they are. They are quite heavy," Jacob said, complaining.

"This one is almost out. We can wrestle it down to the brook."

"I've got one handle. You take the other," said Jacob. The two boys dragged the jug to the edge of the brook. Jacob pried off the cork and looked inside.

"What is it?" asked Simon.

"It looks like liquid silver."

"How can it be liquid silver? That is foolish."

"I have got an idea," said Jacob. "If we pour some of it out onto this flat rock, then we can take a look at it. See how silvery it is? Look how it collects in the hollows of the rock."

The two boys spent a lot of time moving the pools of liquid silver around the rock and then, watching how the liquid would collect in the hollows. Soon, they grew tired of that and were sitting there, staring at the liquid.

"What do we do with it, Jacob?"

"Run home and get a can from the shed. We can bring some home to play with. While you are gone, I will cover the other jugs, so no one can find them."

Jacob worked hard at burying the remaining jugs, while Simon ran home, sneaked into the shed, and grabbed a can. By the time he returned, Jacob had buried the other containers and was playing with the liquid silver. He picked up small amounts from the rock and put it in the palm of his hand where it accumulated in the middle.

"Feel it. It feels slippery," Jacob said as he poured some into the palm of Simon's hand.

"Let us fill the can I got," said Simon. He moved his hand around, watching the liquid silver wiggle and then poured it into the can.

"Do not tell Ma and Pa about this just yet," mumbled Simon. The twins hid the jug, covering it with brush before leaving for home.

They brought home the liquid silver and went upstairs to their bedroom where they played with the shiny liquid. After a few days, they brought a small amount to school. At lunch break, the teacher noticed a group of boys hunched over to the side. "What have you got there, boys?" asked the teacher.

Without having enough time to hide it, Jacob held out his hand. "I have liquid silver."

The teacher looked down at Jacob's hand. "That is mercury. It is commonly called quicksilver. It is nothing for a young boy to be playing with. Where did you get it? The only thing made with that, around here, would be a thermometer."

"I found it," replied Jacob, fumbling for words.

"Where?" demanded the teacher.

"From broken thermometers I found laying in the village," said Jacob, lying.

"Well, run down to the bridge, and pour it into the river. It is believed that mercury is bad to touch."

Jacob raced down to the bridge and poured out a small amount from the glass he had smuggled into school. After school, he joined his brother to walk home. "Simon, what do we do with the rest of the mercury?"

"We will go home and pour the contents of the can into the river. This Saturday, we can go up to Sucker Brook and pour out the jug we have dug up."

"What about the other buried jugs?" asked Jacob.

"We shall leave them where they are."

On Saturday, the boys went to Sucker Brook and dragged the jug to the bank of the brook. They poured the mercury into the water where the brook joined the river.

"Look how it collects in the low spots of the brook," said Jacob.

"What about the jug?" asked Simon.

"Put the cork in it, and throw it into the river. We will throw rocks at it and sink it."

Simon followed his brother's wishes. The boys chased it down the river, throwing rocks as they ran. The flow of the river slowed, just before reaching the village as it reached Paugus Pond. Jacob firmly hit the jug with a rock, creating a hole in the side and sinking it. The mercury settled to the bottom of the deep pools. It continued to slowly make its way downstream, whenever the surging river would scour the river bottom, during the spring floods.

The twins soon forgot about the incident since the mercury that poured into the river caused no immediate reactions. The mercury would be traveling a few years before reaching Paugus Pond. The village had a brief period of peace when nothing tragic happened.

Simon and Jacob had grown and were too old for school. They never learned enough to graduate, and they were needed on the family farm. They were left with twitches and lapses of memory from handling the mercury, years before. They had visited the doctor several years ago but did not realize that it was actually the mercury hurting them. The doctor had been overwhelmed by strange maladies in North Village and could not relate their symptoms to any known disease. He looked upon the situation as simply another unusual occurrence that had taken place in the village.

Excitement began to stir in North Village. A major rail line, which would run up to Lake Potanopa, was replacing the existing, two-footer railroad. The rail would be used to haul ice from Lake Potanopa to ice houses in the cities. The icehouses of urban America would store it for summer use. The builders repositioned the new rail line to run through a collapsed barn. The barn had grown rickety over time and caved in one night during a windstorm. Because of the terrain, the new railroad caused a deep cut in the land as it passed through North Village. By using a wood-spanned bridge, they intended to have Prescott Street extend over the railroad. The excavation was approaching the old barn beside Prescott Street. They dragged away and burnt the remains of the barn. A workman was removing the soil under the barn when his shovel hit something metallic.

"Hey, look. I found a pail," shouted the workman. He kept digging next to it. "I found another old pail. And there's something else. Oh, my God. It is a skeleton!" cried the workman as he jumped out of the trench.

The foreman immediately barked out orders. "All right, you men. Take your picks and shovels, move up the line one hundred feet, and begin anew. We will save this sight for the constable to investigate. You, over there, take a company horse and go get the constable, and make it quick. I cannot have this hold up the progress of the rails."

The constable immediately arrived at the site and went to the foreman. "What have we got?"

The foreman snapped back. "We have two pails and a skeletal hand. I pulled the workers and sent them up the line." The foreman turned to the man who had been sent to get the constable. "You, go up and get two more workers, and come back here and help the constable excavate the site."

They dug and dug, and before sunset, they had completely excavated a skeleton. The constable excused the workers, so they could go eat and rest. The foreman walked over to him. "What have you, sir?"

"I have a small skeleton, probably a child. Help me throw a tarp over it, and I will return in the morning with the doctor," ordered the constable.

The foreman was irritated. "Certainly, but let me inform you, I am on a very tight schedule and need to get this cut done."

"I assure you, after the doctor examines the skeleton, we will remove it. Then, I want the full crew over here, and I will stay while they dig in this area. That way, I am not impeding your progress, and I can see if there is any other evidence."

The foreman smiled. "Thank you, sir. I appreciate your concern for my schedule. I will help you with anything you need."

The next morning, the doctor and Reverend Mather accompanied the constable to the excavation. The constable removed the tarp, and

Reverend Mather said a prayer while the doctor examined the skeleton. "It is the skeleton of a girl about ten to fifteen years of age. She has been here for quite a while," remarked the doctor as he came out of the trench. "Send for me if you find anything else. Send the bones back to my office later. I must get back to my patients," the doctor said as he headed for his horse. "Are you coming, Reverend?"

"Just a moment. I need to talk to the constable."

Reverend Mather moved close to the constable. "I told you, sir, that we let him go too soon and that I should have applied the hot iron to his forehead. I told you that Sven was guilty. I could feel it. I will not hesitate the next time the Devil invades this village."

"Go along. The doctor is becoming impatient," said the constable. He ordered the workers to remove the remains and transfer them onto the wagon he had brought back with him that morning. He remained at the site all day, delivering the bones to the doctor on his way home.

The constable returned the next day, but found nothing else. For a second time, he stopped off at the doctor's office on his way home. "Pardon me, Doc, anything on the girl's body?" asked the constable.

"Well, there were a couple of broken bones that happened at death or just after death. I would say that we have a murder here," answered the doctor. (18)

The constable started shrieking. "I knew it! I knew it! The Reverend was right. It was that bastard we sent back to Norway years ago. Although I could never find the connection, I just knew he did it. Now, so many years later, we find her body in his barn. That would have been enough circumstantial evidence to convict him. I supported deporting him because there was no evidence, and I feared that the villagers would take the law into their own hands."

North Village knew whose skeleton it was, and they were furious that Sven had succeeded with the crime. The railroad continued on, towards Potanopa, unimpeded by the finding. Sven was gone, and they had no way to get him back for a trial. Since the evidence was circumstantial, they needed a confession from him. People began wondering if the Reverend had been right about the hot iron. In the end, justice did not follow the murder of Joan.

The crew completed the new rail line and built station Paugus a few hundred feet north of Prescott Street, near the edge of North Street. A brand new, granite curb ran along the side of the rail. From the view of the train, an outhouse was located upon a little hill, off to the right, and a freight house sat to the left of the station. A well-worn trail started on the west side of the railroad, leading back to the river and the center of North Village. Schoolhouse number four was only a short walk down North Street.

Although icehouses existed around Potanopa, the ice shipped better when the weather was cold and the shrinkage would be minimized. Yet, the railroad ran year-round. New Hampshire was secretly called the *Arsenic State* because it led the country in arsenic production. The public was not aware of that information. Producing arsenic was important. Factories used it with copper as a pigment in paint; they used it in wallpaper, and they were beginning to use it as an insecticide. The railroad passed through only two villages before it got to the main line in East Pepperell. Those of influence in the village knew what the railroad hauled in the summer and said nothing. They realized that without the railroad they would be hauling by wagon, and the small mills had no choice. Because of the erratic flow of the Nissitissit, the small mills were finding it difficult to compete with the newer, more profitable mills on the larger rivers; so another toxin was allowed to enter the valley.

East Pepperell was beginning to outpace North Village in mill productions. The town had built the mills in East Pepperell with large dams at the rapids, which had enough drop that water turbines could be built inside the mill buildings, eliminating freezing. The headwaters of the millpond were huge, allowing useful flow year-round. Even when a drought occurred, the river still flowed. Slowly, the old mills on the smaller rivers began to lose their competitiveness with the ongoing Industrial Revolution.

On one of the upstream tributaries to the Nissitissit, the Berkinshaw Village had become a profitable knife factory. A small, clustered community of workers formed around it on Sucker Brook. The demand for knives, during the developing Industrial Revolution, outstripped the potential of the factory with its small millpond. Eventually, it closed, moving the production and its workers to a larger mill on a powerful river with unlimited power for production and no seasonal slowdowns. The area established huge mills that used the power of the steam turbines. These mills gave birth to large cities around them. They were built on main rail lines to reduce the cost of coke, charcoal and coal from the mines.

Shoes with cut right and left soles were produced in North Pepperell. (18) Soon after, the manufacturer moved to a larger location because the small mill could not produce enough year-round power to compete. Also a Brogan shoe shop opened in 1834 had cut into local sales. (17) Through all of this, North Village survived, adapting to what it offered as times changed.

Mr. and Mrs. Lincoln (18) had taken one of the empty houses just outside of North Village. They were Quakers, and most of the village despised them. Their home had wild, overgrown gardens. They allowed their animals to roam around the property. The Lincolns never mended their broken fences, and their animals would often escape, invading neighbors' gardens and terrorizing children. Mr. Lincoln did odd jobs around the village and fed his family with the animals they raised and the fish from the river. At sunset, he would trek down to the river with a lantern, sit on the bridge and catch hornpout.

Mrs. Lincoln created many recipes for the fish and served hornpout almost everyday. Her husband knew the hornpout routed around the bottom of Paugus Pond to feed, and he was very adept at catching the fish. He had no idea that the hornpout ingested the heavy metals in the river bottom and stored them in their body fat. The couple liked how the belly fat of the fish would crisp up when fried in bacon fat.

The residents allowed their pigs to rut in and around the river during late summer when many of the small springs would dry up. The pigs were also ingesting heavy metals that built up in their fatty tissues. A meal of hornpout fried in bacon grease was a double dose of toxins. Bacon fat was never thrown out; butter was too valuable to use in the fry pan. Besides, the fat from the smoked bacon added flavor to fried food. The residents of the valley were consuming the toxins stored in the fat of the pigs. The insanity and misery of North Village proceeded up the hillsides and into the houses of many innocent villagers. Bizarre accidents continued to happen in and around the village.

On a damp afternoon following a storm, the Chief, Ebb and the horse emerged from the mist of the river. Although many had died in and around the area, most were not descendants of the original settlers, so Ebb and the Chief did not have to be present. However, that day was different. The spirits had foreseen a series of outlandish accidents, and all three men were original descendants.

The Chief, his horse, and Ebb found their way to a road outside of the village. "I have been commanded to start here," said the Chief, pointing toward a house. The three of them went through the wall.

A family was eating their evening meal. "It's the death horse!" cried a man at the head of the table as he began to choke on a piece of meat.

(11) (19)

The family could not see the misty trio. The children ran to their grandfather, trying to save him but were unsuccessful, and he choked to death.

"Come with me, Ebb. Now, we must go to the neighbors' house and stand by the door."

Soon, one of the children came running over from the scene of the choking. He ran right through the misty three and threw open the neighbors' door. "I need help!" cried the child.

The neighbors had just finished their meal, and the head of that household was leaning back in his chair. At first, he had only seen the boy but then saw the horse. "It's the death horse!" screamed the man, falling back in his chair. He succumbed to a broken neck.

"Come with me to yet one more spot," the Chief said to Ebb.

Ebb queried the Chief. "I thought you said spirits in the cusp could not take actions on those who are living."

The Chief responded. "I am not causing any of this. Fate has chosen this moment, but come. We must stand in the road over here."

Another neighbor heard the chaos in the two houses next to him and went to investigate. Seeing the disasters in the two homes, he rushed back, hooked his team to his wagon, and set off determined to return with the doctor.

He snapped the reins. "Giddy up!"

The horses took off with a start and were galloping down the road towards the misty three. The neighbor was not holding on when the horses saw the misty three and halted unexpectedly, tossing the neighbor out of the wagon. He hit his head on a rock in the road and died instantly. His last sight had been of the death horse.

"Let's go, Ebb. This is the beginning of the end of the last lineage," the Chief said as he pointed in the direction of the river.

Ebb was confused. "But all three men had children. Will they not continue the bloodlines?"

"No," the Chief responded. "All of them have been affected by the potions thrown into the river and are barren. None will produce any offspring. With the end of the bloodline assured, we will not have to be present when they die. The spirits are content with letting them be. Besides, some of them will become trapped in the cusp, anyway."

The deaths of the three neighbors recreated a frenzy of superstition and fear in the village. The church in Pepperell Center held funerals for the three men during the week. That Sunday, Reverend Mather devoted his sermon to Satan and his ever-present danger in the village.

More Quakers were moving into North Village. The aging Reverend and the rest of Pepperell saw them as the Devil's children. To Reverend Mather, the Devil was as active as when he had branded the Quaker Witch. The minister remembered the words of the old woman. However, he changed what she had said and, when asked, would quote her as saying that "the river would dry up and run away," and that "the mills and houses would be consumed by fire." He claimed that Sarah predicted "the inhabitants would flee from the village as from the pestilence," and that "in a few decades, no one would be living where once was a thriving village." The Reverend cast Sarah as the cause, saying, "The farms out of the village did not escape her wrath," because Sarah had said, "in every home the Death Angel would make his entry in an unusual manner." (11) The words were powerful, and he used them many times over the years. After the Quaker witch branding, the Reverend had returned the iron back to his attic for the next time it might be needed. The iron had worked for him once, and it could work again.

The Civil War had begun, and the first few men who had enlisted before the war was declared, left home for their assigned training in Lowell. Later, as the war progressed, the draft began with many inducted into the Union armies. The old and the very young were left to run North Village.

Mr. Lincoln had not been inducted and was still living in North Village. He and his family were starting to experience health problems from the heavy metals in their food. They were having visible tremors in their limbs - including the child - and were losing their tempers more frequently. The child was especially difficult to control.

The animals continued running amuck in the neighboring yards. The children in the neighborhood started taunting Mr. and Mrs. Lincoln, who would then shout back at them. Their visible shaking gave the children more to make fun of. A neighbor had become concerned because she had not seen the Lincoln child outside, nor had she heard him yelling inside. The Lincoln household had been quiet for quite a few days.

"Isaac, I have not heard the child next door in a few days, and the house has been strangely silent. What should we do?" asked Lucy.

"You are right. I have also noticed how quiet the house has been. There has been no shouting in days. I have talked to the Reverend about them before. Maybe I will ride up to the parsonage and ask his advice."

Isaac saddled his horse and rode to Pepperell Center. The day was warm, and Reverend Mather was sitting at the table on the porch, working on his sermon for Sunday.

"Reverend Mather, may I have a word with you?" asked Isaac.

"Of course, Isaac. What is on your mind?"

"Do you remember the Lincolns?"

"Oh yes. How could I forget those instruments of the Devil?"

"Well, Reverend, something is wrong. The place has been quiet, and no one has seen the child in awhile."

The Reverend had feared the Lincolns for a while, and attendance from North Village was beginning to lag. Quakers had inhabited many of the vacant farms, and a religious war of sorts was taking place in the area. Some of the churchgoers had successfully petitioned the church, so that traveling ministers of different denominations were being invited to preach the Sunday service. (16) Usually, the ministers appeared for six weeks out of the year, at midsummer when the attendance was lowest. The Reverend had ambiguous feelings. He liked having the time off, but at the same time, he felt as if he were losing control of his church. He had been looking for a way to put fire and brimstone preaching back in his church. He felt that maybe he could benefit from the Lincolns.

"Let me get my coach, and I will accompany you back to North Village." The Reverend put his sermon inside and went to the barn. When the two men arrived in North Village, they went to the Lincolns, and the Reverend knocked loudly on the front door.

"Is there anyone in there?" shouted the reverend, knocking again. He turned the doorknob. "Hello, is there anyone here?" The Reverend opened the door and he and Isaac stood there, horrified by what they saw. The child was obviously dead but had been situated in a chair in the living room. Mrs. Lincoln was knitting, and Mr. Lincoln was reading a book.

"Come in, would you like some tea?" asked Mrs. Lincoln.

Reverend Mather was flabbergasted. "What do you mean, woman? What is wrong with your child? How can you just sit there?"

"Isn't it nice?" replied Mrs. Lincoln. "Mr. Lincoln finally got the child to stop crying."

Mr. Lincoln looked up from his book, grinning sheepishly. "Yes, he has been quiet and well-mannered for a few days now."

The Reverend was overwhelmed. "Isaac, go get the rest of the men in the village. Send someone for the Constable. I will stay here."

Isaac rushed out. Mrs. Lincoln looked up again from her work. "Sure you don't want some tea, Reverend?"

The Reverend remained quiet, fearing the madness might be contagious; he stayed away from the couple and remained near the door.

"Well, suit yourself. Just let me know if you change your mind," said Mrs. Lincoln as she returned to her handiwork and hummed as she knitted.

Moments later, Isaac returned with the men, their wives following along to see what was wrong. The entire crowd stood at the door in disbelief.

The Reverend took command. "Men, seize Mr. Lincoln and bind him up. Get the women to do the same with Mrs. Lincoln. Leave the child alone until the Constable investigates what has happened here."

Mr. Lincoln sat there sullen and quiet, while Mrs. Lincoln kept talking. "I don't know what all this is about, but if you just untie me, I will make us all some tea." Mrs. Lincoln smiled sweetly as she made the outlandish offer.

"She is quite demented," said Isaac.

"No, Isaac, she is possessed. You are seeing the Devil at work here," said Reverend Mather.

"I would not have believed it if I had not seen it. You are right, Reverend Mather. Something is definitely amiss here. It could be nothing else but the Devil," replied Isaac hastily.

Mr. Lincoln was beginning to shake. Moments later, he was having uncontrolled fits of rage. He was screaming at the men and started to foam at the mouth.

Mrs. Lincoln smiled. "Can somebody release me, so I can fix Mr. Lincoln his tea? He is such a bear if he does not get his afternoon tea."

The village people had never seen anything like this. Mr. Lincoln was flopping around on the floor screaming and cursing, while Mrs. Lincoln sat there demurely waiting for someone to untie her, so she could make tea for Mr. Lincoln. Thankfully, the Constable arrived, along with the doctor. The doctor immediately went to the body of the son.

"He has been dead for several days now," said the doctor. "It looks like the cause of death was strangulation. The bruises on the neck indicate it was a large hand that did it."

Mr. Lincoln's hands were massive and powerful, while Mrs. Lincoln's hands were tiny and delicate. "I would say the husband did it," said the doctor, looking at Mr. Lincoln's hands.

The doctor walked over to Mrs. Lincoln. "Madam, what happened to your son?"

"Why, nothing, sir. He is over there in his chair," replied Mrs. Lincoln, smiling.

"He is dead," the doctor announced.

"Don't be silly, sir. Mr. Lincoln has merely taught him to be quiet; that's all. Please, sir, untie me. I will make us tea, and all will be fine." Mrs. Lincoln grinned. "The boy has learned to be quiet. All will be just fine now."

The constable was disgusted with the whole scene. "You men, take that raving lunatic, and put him on a wagon. Take him to the new, brick jail in East Pepperell - the one by the rail line to Nashua."

"What about her?" asked one of the men.

"Untie her. The poor woman has no idea what is going on," replied the constable. "Hurry up, Doc. Let's get out of here."

The two men departed, and the villagers untied Mrs. Lincoln. "Thank you," she said. "Now, let me make some tea. My granny said that a good cup of tea could improve even the worst day." She wandered off to the kitchen, and the villagers left quickly, before she could come back.

A day later, Mr. Lincoln appeared in Lowell for trial. During the arraignment, the constable and his wife had taken Mrs. Lincoln to the courtroom, and the prosecutor could see that she was completely witless. The judge determined that Mrs. Lincoln was not a threat to society and that she possessed sufficient property and wealth to meet her needs. In his ruling, he took into account that the prisons were already overloaded. He concluded that Mrs. Lincoln would never understand any form of punishment. No matter how many times she had been told the boy was dead, she did not believe it. She kept saying she had to have tea ready when Mr. Lincoln and the boy came home. She was released that day.

The trial was quick, and Mr. Lincoln was sentenced for life. The Sunday following the sentencing, Reverend Mather gave a stirring sermon about the Devil's children who had been invading the area, especially in North Village. The growing Quaker population alarmed the Reverend, and he believed that the Lincolns were appropriate recipients for his fire and brimstone. After the service, one of the old men spoke to the reverend. "Reverend Mather, could you come by later with the iron, so we can brand the woman?"

"Yes. I will come by just before dark."

The elderly reverend thought if he could repeat the performance that he had with Sarah, he could increase church attendance. Late that afternoon, he arrived with the iron and met up with some men behind the mill. The Civil War had left behind only young boys and old men. With the folly of feeble old minds added to the volatility of youth, they fired up the iron.

"It is ready. Let us go, men!" cried the Reverend.

They left the mill and headed towards Mrs. Lincoln's house. The house was located on the outskirts of town. It took a few minutes for them to get there, so the iron was not as hot as when they had used it on Sarah. Upon hearing the knock, Mrs. Lincoln opened the door. "Oh, company. Come in, and I will make a fresh pot of tea."

The group rushed forward and forced the iron onto Mrs. Lincoln's head. She screamed and pulled away. A few gasped at what they saw. They had inadvertently turned the iron upside down, so instead of bearing a "W," her forehead showed an "M."

"That will serve just as well," remarked the Reverend. "The "M" can stand for murder." (11)

The Reverend did not get the response he had wanted. Mrs. Lincoln was lying on the floor, sobbing. "All I asked was if you wanted tea." She had no idea why this was happening to her.

The band of boys and men lingered for a short time. They began to wonder if their actions had been wrong. They dispersed and went home. Reverend Mather had left the black cloth for the iron at the mill and returned to get it. He had overstayed his welcome in North Village. As he prepared to leave, the mist rose heavily from the river. The Reverend did not believe in the power of the mist. He left the mill, taking the lower road that brought him out to Prescott Street near the bridge. The thickening mist was rolling out of the river and moving towards him. The Reverend turned up his collar and headed towards the center of town. At the next curve, the river was close to the road, and the mist was billowing out across the road. Fearlessly, he drove his horse into the colossal mist when the horse suddenly stopped. "Giddy up," ordered the Reverend, snapping the reins.

The air was still and Reverend Mather sat for a moment. Then it started. The Reverend could hear the murmuring of thousands of voices in the mist.

"Who is it?" he cried in fear.

No one answered. The murmuring became louder and louder.

"I command you to tell me who you are," demanded the Reverend.

The loud noise in his ears was overwhelming. "Stop!" he screamed. The murmuring persisted and proceeded to infiltrate into the reverend's head. The sound became unbearable and finally corrupted his mind. The coach sat in the mist all night long with the Reverend inside. Then he began mumbling incoherently. Suddenly, he stood up and threw the iron, which had grown cold, into the river. Just before sunrise, the horse headed off towards home, looking for its daily feeding of grain. Reverend Mather awoke and found himself in his own barn, still in the coach with the horse pawing at the floorboards for attention.

"What a strange dream," he thought, until he started looking for his iron. Somehow, he remembered throwing it into the river. Then he recalled the murmuring voices in the mist, and his whole body shivered.

Luckily, the following Sunday began the six-week period for the visiting ministers. The parishioners thought the Reverend's suffering was caused by his advanced age, and they had made arrangements for a new minister. Reverend Mather spent the last few years of his life at the home of one of the parishioners, murmuring over cups of tea.

After the branding of Mrs. Lincoln, the people of the valley felt ashamed. She had given birth to a child who was sickly and never stopped crying. Many of the woman sympathized with her. Some had felt that their own misbehaving children had nearly driven them insane at times. The lunacy of the Lincolns was soon forgotten and replaced with good news. The War Between the States was over, and the men were starting to come home. The soldiers had suffered both mentally and physically. Few of the men returned home the same as when they had left.

CHAPTER TWENTY-FOUR

Jacob and Simon had survived the war. Although they never suffered any battle wounds, they had endured difficulties. They even made it through Baltimore unscathed, after leaving with Ebb and the others who had enlisted early. The twins arrived in North Village to a jubilant crowd. Both of them cast an evil look at the shoddy shack as they entered the village.

They had fingers and toes cut off because of frostbite. Their uniforms had been produced in Lowell, Massachusetts by mills that had government contracts to make winter clothes for the Union Army. In their greed to make huge profits, the mills had compromised on the construction. The chemicals needed to make the shoddy clothes were in short supply. Instead of limiting their production of quality clothes, the mill owners cut down on the chemicals used. The finished shoddy clothes passed the inspections, but when subjected to the effects of adverse weather, they deteriorated on the backs of the soldiers. Mittens made from the shoddy basically fell apart.

Many men had died because of the greed of the mill owners, and the shoddy industry suffered. Shoddy workmanship came to be known as poor workmanship. The city that supplied some of the first soldiers had provided its enlisted men with inferior goods, causing injury to many. Instead of being tried for treason, the Lowell mill owners became the leaders of the new Industrial Revolution. Their huge mills and large bank accounts resulted from the frozen limbs and deaths of soldiers faraway. The mill owners made large donations at their churches to settle their minds.

The twins returned in worse condition than when they left. They were strong men when they went to war, but they came back gaunt from lack of food. They had more shakes and tremors than before. Their loss of weight had caused their bodies to release some of the mercury stored in their bones and fatty tissue, which adversely affected them. In addition, they had been assigned to a demolition team and experienced much exposure to black powder. The twins loved the assignments that involved explosions. They worked with men who had gone to California for the gold rush, as well. The forty-niners explained how they had used quicksilver to extract the gold from the ore. The twins listened carefully, knowing they had a hidden supply of quicksilver back home waiting for them.

Soon after they returned home, they went to Sucker Brook to dig up the remaining jugs of mercury. They brought them back and concealed them in their barn.

"That's the first step in our plan," remarked Jacob as they finished hiding the jugs.

"The next step is to acquire a lease on the mine," replied Simon.

Mrs. Lincoln roamed around the village and she kept to herself, always covering her head with a scarf. Word arrived that Mr. Lincoln had died in prison. The villagers decided they would not tell Mrs. Lincoln. The village had come to believe they had been wrong in their actions and that the Reverend had lost his mind as punishment for his dastardly deed. The people of the village never mentioned it, preferring to hide the incident.

The storeowner noticed Mrs. Lincoln entering the store. "Yes, ma'am," said the owner.

"Sir, I need some fresh tea. Mr. Lincoln and the boy will be home this evening, and I must make sure that I have fresh tea."

The storeowner was a little surprised. "How do you know that, ma'am?"

"Why, last night I saw Mr. Lincoln in the mist of the river. He said he and the boy would be home this evening. I must have fresh tea for him."

The storekeeper felt unsettled from the conversation and sold Mrs. Lincoln her tea. He thought about what she said and trembled, for he feared the mist. The mist was heavy that night, and in the morning the village people noticed Mrs. Lincoln's door was open. One of the villagers went to the door and knocked. "Mrs. Lincoln?" There was no response. He knocked again. "Mrs. Lincoln?"

Then he peered inside. The table had been set for three with a basket of fresh muffins and a pot of tea that had turned cold, but Mrs. Lincoln was not to be found. The news spread throughout the village, and soon the storekeeper was telling his strange tale from the day before. They never found Mrs. Lincoln and assumed that she had become more disoriented and wandered off. They dared not say what they actually thought.

Jacob and Simon were able to obtain a lease on the existing mine below Heald Pond for three years with options. Previous attempts at getting the mine to produce convinced them that amateurs had been responsible. Under the tutelage of the forty-niners, the twins knew they could make the mine finally pay off. Before signing the lease, they toured the mine. They could see the veins of crystals the other miners had been following and knew they matched the descriptions of the forty-niners. The twins believed that their knowledge of quicksilver would make all the difference. Being masters of explosives, they knew they could blast deeper than others before them.

"Get that last jug of quicksilver in here before someone sees it," commanded Jacob.

"Oh, hush. I am going as fast as I can," Simon responded as he dragged the last jug into the mine. They had been quarreling a lot lately, and their limbs were trembling more.

"Let us begin drilling," said Jacob.

The two men worked diligently through the summer of 1866 and had quite a large spoil pile for the sluice run they were planning in the fall. During the heat of summer, they spent their time drilling, blasting, and removing what would hopefully be ore-bearing rock. They found a lot of fool's gold and cast the ore aside, but they had another stockpile they hoped would contain some real gold. They set a goal to mine all the ore they could during the summer, run the sluice in the fall, collect their gold, and live gainfully over the winter.

"What are you going to do with your gold?" Simon asked as they used the wheelbarrow to move ore out of the mine.

"Well, I am going to the hotel in East Pepperell and get a good, hot meal. Then, I am getting a room there and spending the winter at the tavern."

"That sounds good, Jacob. Maybe I will do the same," Simon said as they went back to hauling heavy loads out of the mine.

Fall arrived and the twins built their sluice according to the instructions of the forty-niners. It took about one quarter of the mercury to power up, and they started the process. They put crushed ore in the top of the sluice and ran water through it. Periodically, they would scoop out the slurry from behind the stops, put it in a pile, and then add more mercury to the top. They repeated this practice until all of the mercury and ore had been used. They ended up with a great pile of silvery slurry composed of ore particles that were suspended in the mercury.

The twins had built a huge tripod out of three logs with a chain hanging down. "Let us fill the fire pit and get the great kettle on the chain," said Jacob. They had constructed it over the fire pit, which had a crudely built bellows made of boards and leather. It looked primitive, but, in fact, was quite functional as a smelter.

"Well, we are all set. The sun is going down, and I think we should go to the tavern and have us some ale," suggested Simon.

"I agree. First thing tomorrow, we will fire the pit and smelt our gold," answered Jacob.

The next morning, the twins arrived at the mine, nursing hangovers. "Let us get that fire going," said Simon.

The large dose of alcohol the night before had aggravated the existing tremors of the twins. "I am on it. I cannot stop shaking enough to light a match." Finally, he struck a match and the fire lit.

"Let us spell each other on the bellows," Simon said as he started pumping the bellows.

"Get that kettle good and hot before we add the slurry," said Jacob. A few hours later, the bottom of the kettle was glowing red. "All right. Put a few shovel loads of slurry into the kettle," added Jacob.

Simon threw in a shovel full of slurry, which hissed as it hit the bottom of the hot kettle. It immediately released an evil smoke as it vaporized the elemental mercury and wafted out of the kettle.

"I cannot avoid the smoke. Spell me on the bellows for a while. I need to step back and catch my breath," said Simon.

Jacob took the handles of the bellows and did his share of pumping while trying to avoid the smoke. Periodically, they added more slurry to the kettle and more wood to the fire.

"The kettle is almost full," said Jacob, a few hours later. Take this chain, and pull the kettle from the fire. Between last night's ale and the smoke today, my head is pounding. We can take a nap in the afternoon sun while the kettle cools."

"I agree. A nap in the sun would be nice."

The twins lay down in the warm afternoon sun and slept. Dreams of the Civil War troubled them. Soon, the sun went down and the fall air brought a chill. Jacob awoke trembling. "Simon, wake up before you freeze." Jacob's shaky hands grabbed Simon's shirt and shook him. "Wake up, Simon."

Finally, the violent shaking woke Simon who continued to quiver, even after Jacob released him. "What, Jacob? Brrrr, I am freezing. I need to get by the fire pit. Brrr… brrr… Quick, throw some wood in. Pump the bellows a couple of times, and it will fire the wood."

Jacob threw an armload of wood into the pit, and the bellows ignited it. The twins stood together and shook by the pit. Their last, heavy exposure to the mercury vapors was poisoning them. Their thoughts were becoming scattered.

"Let us check the kettle, now that we are warm," said Jacob.

"Yes, we need to get our g… gold. Put one of those wide boards down by the fire pit, so we can stay warm," ordered Simon as he got a shovel and headed to the kettle. He brought back a full shovel and spread the contents on the board near the fire pit.

Jacob lit a lantern, looked at the ore, and said, "I do not see any gold. It is all just stone."

"Dispose of the kettle, and take some from the bottom. Simons's voice revealed early signs of desperation. Gold is heavy, and it must be on the bottom."

Jacob emptied the kettle and Simon removed a shovelful from the pile. They rushed back, cleaned the board, and spread around the new sample. "There is no gold," wailed Jacob.

"All that time," wailed Simon.

"What do we do, now? That was our only plan. I guess we will have to clean up the old farm and work it, like Pa," said Jacob as he began shaking uncontrollably.

The stress of the moment, intensified by the mercury they had just ingested, drove the two into a fit of madness. They both shook and sputtered words at each other. Finally, Simon was able to speak. "There is one thing that we planned."

"What was that?" asked Jacob as he tried to control his shaking.

Simon looked down at his hands. "Remember we were going to burn the shoddy shacks because they made inferior cloths, and we both got frostbite?"

In his state of madness, Jacob had something to focus on. "Yes, I remember that. I remember our chant. "Shoddy, shoddy, not even good for potty." We used to chant that over and over. The shoddy was so bad, you could not even use it to clean yourself after toileting as it would just come apart and stick to you."

"Well, remember how we swore we would burn down every shoddy shack we saw? Well, let us begin in North Village," said Simon, with crazed eyes. (19)

Jacob's madness was fueled by the idea of having someone pay for the suffering they endured from shoddy workmanship. "Let us get the horses and get to the village."

Darkness fell as the twins headed toward North Village. The mist was thick around the river. The spirits had grown agitated. The final deathblow stemmed from all of the mercury induced into the watershed by the twins. The heavy metals would poison the valley for generations.

The horse, the Chief, and Ebb rose from the mist and headed towards the mill. "We are going for the last two, and after that, you are the last," the Chief said to Ebb.

"Who are they?" asked Ebb.

"It is time for the twins," responded the Chief.

The misty trio went to the mill and waited. A few moments later, the twins rode into the mill. It was Saturday night, and the mill was completely shut down and empty. The twins went to the shoddy shack and started throwing rags and shoddy onto the floors and walls. Then, the two of them went into the paper mill and began to uncork jugs of chemicals. Jacob sniffed an open container. "This smells flammable," shouted Jacob.

"That will do. Spread it around the shoddy shack," said Simon.

Jacob splashed the liquid onto the cloths and the shoddy he had thrown everywhere.

"Fire it up," Jacob demanded.

Simon was trying to light a match, but his tremors were too strong. Jacob went over to him, and the two of them were anxiously trying to light a match.

"Let us now go," said the Chief. The three of them drifted through the wall and into the shoddy shack.

Finally, Jacob fired a match. As it flared, he looked up and saw the misty trio. "Simon, look."

Simon looked and saw the trio as Jacob's unsteady hand dropped the match. The brothers had not realized how flammable the liquid was that they had distributed. The shack erupted in a rush of flames, consuming the twins and then spread to the mill.

"That makes you the last, Ebb," said the Chief.

"But I don't die for another twenty-nine years," responded Ebb.

"Yes, I know. It will take the spirits that much time to cleanse your mind of the war. Let us go back to the river and await that time."

"But, Chief, I do not have the answer."

"What answer is that?" asked the Chief.

"The answer to how to save your soul," replied Ebb.

"Be patient. You have twenty-nine years to make sense of it."

The fire was so hot that it entirely cremated the twins, leaving no trace. A new eradication of fish in the river occurred the next day, and the mill was completely burned down. Those in the valley thought it was another stage of the curse they believed existed. Many more families moved out of the valley during the next few months. The village was slowly dying.

The owners sold the mill. The new owner was going to install another paper mill, powered by a recently improved steam power plant. The new mill would need fewer workers because of the latest developments in making paper. The Nissitissitt River would only be needed to wash away the waste from the paper process. The power of the water would no longer be used to run the mill.

After the mill was rebuilt in 1867, strange occurrences happened at night during the end of October. They continued for a few years. A white horse with someone wearing the garb of an Indian Chief would gallop down a lane on the west side of the river. They would hear him whooping all the way down the lane, through the village and up North Street. It became the topic of conversation at the tavern and reinforced the fear behind the legend of the white death horse.

A few years after the new mill opened, Ebb and the others rose from the mist of the river. They floated a mile upstream, where an old cart road forded the river at a shallow spot.

"I thought the twins were the last two," Ebb said to the Chief.

"They were, but you must witness this, as you, in your living life, were partly responsible."

Ebb knew why they were there. "It was just as much their fault as mine."

"That I know, but to purify your soul, you must witness what happens at the spot," commanded the Chief.

"I know what happened. Amos's youngest son fell from his horse and hit his head. We would get together at Amos's farm when the first of the hard cider was ready, and we would celebrate the end of October by having the youngest dress as an Indian chief and go whooping through North Village. There was a spot at the bottom of the orchard where a cart road crosses North Street and goes down to this ford where we are standing. We found his body right next to where we are standing."

A white horse and rider came down the cart road. The new moon made it hard to see. The horse and the rider appeared at the edge of the river.

"I think this is not a very good idea," muttered the rider. As they were crossing the river, the horse stumbled, tossing the rider off. The rider hit his head on a rock and died instantly.

Ebb stood there, crying. He knew that the death of his youngest son had driven Amos crazy. Amos had bad head wounds crossing Baltimore, and the army sent him home. After the death of his son, Amos experienced more problems from the old wounds and spent his time tending the orchards.

"Can we go now?" asked Ebb sadly.

"Yes. We can go. The next time we meet will be when your living self returns to the river to die."

CHAPTER TWENTY-FIVE

As other parts of Pepperell were growing, North Village was diminishing. The town no longer used the river for power. When houses and businesses burned, no one rebuilt them. The coveted watershed had been used up. As the dumping area for unwanted paper dyes and chemicals, that was its only use. Because of the large number of paper mills located on the Nashua River, upstream from the Nissitissit, the color of the Nashua River changed daily. The various hues of the river depended on the color of dyes used for paper and cloth at the mills. The Nissitissit deposited its own load of chemicals into the Nashua River, and the toxins flowed downstream, awaiting the waste from the next town. Throughout history, the rivers in New England had never seen pollution to this extent.

Salmon no longer swam upstream in either river. The White Way had killed all life in the rivers. The spirits had to wait for Ebb to come to the river and die. The spirits knew Ebb could take them from the polluted river into the Land of Happiness.

The last mill in North Village, which was built after the fire of 1866, continued to exist for one more generation. In 1884, that mill burned, and thus began the downfall of North Village. All industry in the village had ceased.

The spirits waited quietly, and, in time, the pollution in the river started to decline. The Industrial Revolution had caused most of the industry to move out of the Nissitissit River Valley. Industrial expansion and the growing population overloaded the larger rivers, and they continued to suffer as businesses relocated.

The day they had all waited for finally came. The time had arrived for the last to visit the village and complete the circle. Ebb knew that this was the day. He rose from bed early and put on his best clothes. His dreams of the mist during the night signaled that today would be his last. The tumor lodged in his stomach had just about drawn the life out of him. He knew what he had to do and where he had to go. As the sun was rising, Ebb set off down the road, fueled by the last bit of his strength.

The spirits had waited patiently for this. The sound of shuffling, old feet could be heard on Prescott Street. The elderly man who was the last, hobbled slowly past the old school, which remained the last building. No one was there to witness the poignant moment in history.

The old man staggered over to the river and lay down against a tree. The mist had become heavy and drifted towards Ebb. He eased back further against the tree. He could see it coming and he was ready. He relaxed as the mist enveloped his body. His tumor no longer hurt, and the old war wounds stopped aching. Ebb was at peace and he let go. He was the last, and he had made it to a ripe old age.

The Indian reign of North Village existed for thousands of years and the white reign spanned hundreds of years. All of the struggles, all of the living, all of the dying, and all of the noise and pollution of industry did not end in epic tragedy. It ended with the last, rattled breath of an old man.

The spirits of the mist watched, in anticipation as the standing spirit of the old man conversed with the spirit of the Chief. While the spirits watched, the Chief had taken the spirit of Ebb on the journey back in time and then placed his spirit within Sarah. The time his spirit had spent with Sarah and the Chief lasted for an instant. In the spirit world, an eternity can be lived in one moment of time.

"Well, Ebb, you have closed the loop and are as wise as the ages. Do you have the answer?" asked the Chief.

"Let's just talk for a moment. Right now, I don't have an answer. Let us think for a moment. After all, from what I understand, we can spend all the time we want and still not lose this moment. When we have the answer, we can be right back at this moment, and we can continue."

The Chief smiled. "You have, in fact, become wise."

Ebb looked at the Chief. "Just what am I supposed to be able to do?"

"You are supposed to find a way to remove the stain on my spirit, which was caused when I uttered the curse. You are supposed to cleanse my spirit, so I can join you all in the Place of Happiness."

Ebb thought for a moment. "But is your soul stained? I think not."

The Chief snapped back. "Of course it is stained. Look at all the deaths - the settlers and the heirs of the settlers. I was there when they all died."

"Yes, you were there when they died, but did you cause their deaths?" asked Ebb.

"I cursed them, and they all died," stated the Chief.

"Do you feel responsible for the death of the others who were not related to the settlers but died in the village, none the less?"

"No. They died because of their white ways."

Ebb continued. "Well, don't you think the others died because of the same thing and not because of your curse?"

The Chief was getting angry and was not used to being told he was wrong. "I cursed them and they died," he said sternly. "Is this my fate to argue with you for all eternity?"

"Chief, let me call Sarah. She and I will show you how you are not to blame for their deaths."

"All right, Ebb. Let us both focus on calling her from the mist."

Sarah swiftly appeared out of the mist. She was young and beautiful. She had chosen her body form to appear as she looked when she lived with her uncle in Boston. She wore the white flowing silk robes and looked like a priestess.

"Ebb, we finally get to talk with each other," said Sarah. "It was an honor to have carried you. You saved me from despair several times during my life. Knowing that you were there made me more responsible. If I had ended my life, I would have ended yours, and it was not in my constitution to take another's life."

"Well, Sarah, I owe you also, as the education you gave me was the equivalent of having two lifetimes," Ebb responded. "I had the life I lived and another life, which I got to experience, by being part of you. When I first traveled with the Chief, we went back into time to see how it once was, but the time I spent with you was in real time, just as if I had lived it. I got to exist as a spirit, yet live one more life, and by having so much time, I know my spirit has it right. I have asked for you to be here, so you and I can show the Chief that his spirit is still pure. He has been delivering the settlers' spirits and has not seen the devastation of all of the rivers and streams. He needs to see what has happened outside of this one valley."

"Leave the stallion here, and the three of us will travel the watershed of the Merrimack," Sarah replied. "Using the way of the spirits, you can come with us, and we will return back to this very moment. I think the Chief should see what has happened to all of the Indians in the river valley."

The three of them began traveling down the river. Wherever they went, the Indians were gone. They would stop at many places, travel back to a time when Indians inhabited each location, and then go forward in time to see what had happened.

New England was made up of roughly twelve Indian Nations. Many sub-tribes were within these nations. North Village was at the edge of the Pennacook Indian Nation. As they continued downstream, they came to the Nipmuc Indian Nation. The eastern Nipmuc and the Wampanoag initially suffered from the white settlers. Sarah brought the Chief back to the period when the Nipmuc and the Wampanoag had first met the white settlers. Then, they went forward in time, so the Chief could see what had taken place. In some villages, the Indians had a ninety-percent mortality rate when they came in contact with the white men and their urban diseases.

Next, Sarah took them up a tributary into Littleton. "What I want to show you, Chief, is that even if you had tried to live peacefully with the white men, you still would not have survived."

Sarah led the Chief to the village of praying Indians. (20) "These are the Indians who tried to live in harmony with the white men. At the time, there were many tribes of praying Indians that lived north and south of the area, also. The Indians had turned Christian and swore their alliance to the white men. As a result, the Indians who still lived in the wild hated these praying Indians. Sarah paused for a moment. "Chief, remember the King Phillip's War?"

"Yes," replied the Chief. "I remember. My tribe survived because the great Chief Wanalancet was still trying to befriend the white men, so they never crossed the Nashua River and left our village alone."

Sarah continued. "Well, these Indians were not so lucky. All of the praying Indian tribes were taken hostage and moved to Deer Island in Boston Harbor. (20) More than half died, during the first winter, from lack of food, clothing, and proper shelter. The white men just rounded them up, put them on a bleak island, and proceeded to starve them to death. After the first winter, many of the Indians were sold as slaves to Europeans and shipped overseas. It was fashionable for a nobleman to have slaves from all over the world."

"Sarah, why do you show this to me?" asked the Chief.

"So you will understand there was no way that your village could have lived in peace with the white men. Your refusal to share your land with the white men was not what caused the end of your village. Your standing proud and refusing to share your land did not doom your village. Your village would have died, no matter what you did."

"Thank you," responded the Chief. "You have removed some of the heaviness of my heart. I always wondered if my actions were justified, but there remains a concern. There is the matter of the curse I uttered."

Ebb interrupted. "Chief, the spirits of the mist had me accompany you on all the death calls for a reason. What I learned from having been part of Sarah was that your curse meant nothing."

"But I cursed them and they died," said the Chief.

"Yes, you cursed them, and, yes they all died, but they did not die as a result of your curse," said Ebb.

"How then, did they die?" asked the Chief.

"They died at their own hands," replied Ebb.

"What do you mean?"

"They died because of all the poisons, heavy metals, and the potions that they threw into the river. Not a single settler died because of your curse."

"What about John?" asked the Chief.

Ebb replied, "John was going to die that night, anyway. The spirits of the mist allowed you and the stallion to think that you slew John.

By allowing you to think you killed him, they hoped the grief in your heart might lessen. The very moment the stallion reared up and kicked John in the head was the very moment he was going to die anyway, from the foulness that the white men had cast into the river. There is no dark stain on your soul. You only think your soul was too stained to go to the Land of Happiness. The truth is, your soul is quite pure and will be able to make the journey."

Sarah joined in. "Let us return to North Village. They returned to the same moment they had left. Ebb's dead body was still lying by the bank of the river as if he had never left.

"The spirits were wise. They knew if the settlers were given enough time, they would end up taking their own lives," said Ebb. "That way, it seemed as if it was your curse that killed them. The spirits wanted you to feel as though you were getting revenge, but they orchestrated it, so you were free from guilt. In reality, your spirit is pure, and all the suffering you saw was a result of their own poisons."

The Chief was astounded. "That is not the way that I saw it; I was too close to the suffering and could not lift my head enough to see the whole perception. Now all the circles of life are complete. I cannot wait to see my family again."

"Do you want to go to our Place of Happiness or do you want to go to your own place?" the Chief asked Ebb.

Ebb was visibly confused. "I don't understand. I thought Heaven was Heaven, and we all went there."

"That is the way of your religion - one God, one Heaven. Your religion can never work. How can one Heaven be right for everyone? Suppose there was a brave warrior who never bowed to anyone in his life. Do you think that his idea of Heaven would be to spend eternity sitting at the feet of your God? What you are in life, you bring with you to the other side."

"What you say, Chief, makes sense to me. I always had concerns with all of that. Like the warrior you were talking about, I have never served anyone in my life. The thought of spending eternity serving someone else just doesn't appeal to me. I never believed in the church, so I just thought I was going the other way."

"Ebb, the church is the source of evil for the white men. How can one religion be the only religion? What about us? Do you think that because we are not Christians, we are not entitled to have a Heaven? Do you think that those of us who lived true and just lives have lived them in vain?"

"He is right, Ebb," answered Sarah. You learned from the studies I did, while your soul was within me, that the world is full of many different religions, all of which have churches and all of which claim they are the true religion. They are either all right or they are all wrong, and I can tell you, from what I have learned, they are all wrong."

"That makes sense," said Ebb. "A person's soul cannot spend eternity in rapture. It would rot and die. The Devil is supposedly an angel that was unhappy with God and fell out of rapture. If God was all-powerful, then how could that happen? Also, if there is only one God who started everything, then where did the angels, like the Devil, come from? Did God create them also? How could a God that is perfect create something imperfect? The whole idea always seemed odd to me. Plus, if an angel can fall from grace and leave Heaven, then in time, anyone in Heaven can fall from grace. So to me, Heaven seemed like some prisoner-of-war camp. You worship and stay in constant rapture or you fall from Heaven. If that's the case, then I know where I'll eventually end up, so I might as well start off there."

The Chief laughed. "We all know you will not end up there. In our Place of Happiness there is a spot for you, either with all of us or a place of your own."

"What do you mean when you say 'with us or a place of my own'?"

"Eternal happiness is something very personal. An eternity spent somewhere that brings one soul happiness might be an eternity of hell for another."

"I'm a little confused," said Ebb.

"For example, that warrior I spoke about. For him, Heaven would mean never-ending game to hunt and worthy adversaries to fight. But, a squaw in the camp might want nuts and berries to gather, handiwork to do, and to give care as she did in life. The happiness for the warrior would not be the same happiness for the squaw."

Ebb was confused. "So, does that mean that you have many heavens?"

"Yes. We can have one Heaven or many heavens. It does not matter. We do not have the concept of one Heaven that fits all souls, and we do not believe that a vengeful God who constantly needs servitude runs Heaven. Why would an all-knowing God want an eternity of praise? Is the need for praise not a human quality? Why would free and proud people want to spend an eternity in servitude? In my tribe, my race served no one. We are free and, Heaven, for us, is to remain free. My tribe - the ones contained in the mist of the river - has sworn an allegiance that we would all go to the same Place of Happiness."

"And where is that?" asked Ebb.

"We do not know yet," answered the Chief.

Ebb staggered back. "How can you not know?"

"When we are ready we will all leave the mist and travel back in time until we find the happiest moment, and then we will spend eternity there."

"What is this personal Place of Happiness you said I could have if I wanted?" asked Ebb.

"You can travel back in your life or your ancestors' lives to a Place of Happiness and spend your eternity there."

"Alone?" asked Ebb.

"No. You would be amongst those you chose to be with, and you would have the memories of people you wanted around you. Then, you would spend eternity in that happy moment."

Ebb was still confused. "How can you spend an eternity in a moment?"

The Chief was amused. "You saw how it worked. You spent a lifetime with Sarah, yet you were back at the same instant you left. There is no such feature as time in the land of spirits. There is no progression of time. Time is an aspect of man, not spirits. By finding a time in the past which truly makes you happy, you can spend eternity in that moment and always be happy."

"But, what if, in time, I get unhappy there? What if I end up picking the wrong moment?"

"There is that word again. There is no time from now on. You would not become unhappy. If you chose a moment in which you were happy, you would stay in that moment, forever happy."

"What if you chose an unhappy moment? Is that the equivalent of hell?"

"If a spirit is pure, it would not choose an unhappy moment. A tainted spirit would be sent back to the earth to be born and live again until the spirit became pure. Spirits are destined to be pure. For some, it takes longer to get there. If a child is born into an evil environment and becomes evil himself, it is not the fault of the child's spirit. It is the fault of the environment. That spirit keeps being born until it lives in the right environment to become pure. It is not the nature of a spirit to be impure. Evil and impurities come from life, not the spirit world. Every spirit born is pure. How could an unborn infant be anything other than pure?"

"I think I understand. I did not like the world in which I lived and do not want to spend an eternity in any of the moments there, so I think I will swear allegiance with your tribe and spend eternity with you."

The Chief smiled. "Then it is done. Let us summon the spirits from the mist and we will go."

Where will we go?" asked Ebb.

"We will visit happy times until we choose the same one."

"How long will it take to find a place?" asked Ebb.

"It does not matter how long it takes. As I said before, time is only a concern on the earth. Whether it is an eternity filled with happy moments or an eternity spent in one moment, it is all the same. There is one last thing for you to do, Ebb."

"What's that, Chief?"

"You have to choose your body. You can decide on anytime in your life, and that will be your form. So, if you were a warrior wounded in battle or a squaw mauled by a bear, you would not have to spend eternity in a mangled condition."

"I think that I would like to be thirty again."

Ebb looked at his arms and legs and was instantly pleased. He had transformed into the body he had at thirty. The Chief turned and faced the river, holding his arms above his head. He was the last chief of the tribe, and it was his duty to call the rest of the spirits. His voice echoed, "It is time for all spirits to come out of the mist."

After the command, thousands of spirits began to emerge. While in the mist, the spirits kept the same form they had at the time of their death. At first, Ebb found it gruesome to watch as some manifested without scalps, some were missing arms, and many were old and withered. However, as soon as they completely separated from the mist, they assumed whatever appearance they wanted. Ebb was amused by all of the changes. Suddenly, old women became young maidens again; old men turned into younger men, and some even chose to have the form of a child, once more. More Indians appeared than Ebb was able to count. The tremendous crowd enchanted Ebb, and Sarah looked on with a smile. They prepared to travel in unison to find that special moment at a place where they would live in eternal happiness. The spirits of the mist departed, and the once thriving valley became silent.

"So to us who walk in summer 'mid the ruins old and gray,
Comes the thought that through the ages it is ever nature's way
With forgiving hand to cover human creature's sad mistakes
And in time turn to beauty all the failures that man makes."(1)

Epilogue

I have estimated that the Nissitissit River Valley drains thirty to forty thousand acres. It is not a huge watershed and never contained the potential flow of the larger rivers of the area. The six villages that used this watershed threw everything unwanted into the river. Many businesses and hundreds of farms were located along the river.

As industry grew, more and more toxic substances were used. Many were poured onto the ground or dumped into the river for disposal. In 1976, when I moved to Groton, next to Pepperell, the town dump was located at the bank of the Nashua River. Much debris settled into the river, after the spring flood washed away the previous year's trash. All of the rivers in this area had suffered the abuse for hundreds of years.

In the nineteenth century, the toxins thrown into the river were funneled down into North Village, which is located on a gravel aquifer. Those who lived in North Village were clustered around the river. They owned shallow, hand-dug wells near the river, which were recharged by the water of the Nissitissit.

When canoeing on the Nissitissit, one can see that the river is not large. Summer droughts would lessen the flow, and the toxins were then concentrated in the quiet pools along the river. The prediction of the legendary curse, claiming that the river would dry up and go away, never happened. The flow did diminish over time, but it resulted from the abandonment of mills along the entire river.

The old mills had millponds with dams and would hold backwater from the spring rush. As spring storms ended and summer arrived, these mills could then use the impounded water for power. By drawing water from the ponds, water was returned to the river for other mills downstream to catch and use.

North Village was one of the lowest villages on the river and benefited from the water releases of the other mills. The millponds upstream would supply more water for North Village to use during the dry summer months. In addition, thunderstorms would recharge these millponds in the summertime. The sudden run-off, from a two or three-inch rainfall after a summer storm, filled the millponds, which could then be held and used for power.

A small village known as East Pepperell was located where the Nissitissit crosses Hollis Street. The dam and one of the grand old houses still remain. This village eventually disappeared, and the business area on the east side of the Nashua River is now considered to be East Pepperell. The disappearance of North Village was not unique. Little villages disappeared all over New England.

As the smaller mills closed along the river, the abandoned millponds were eventually washed out during the spring floods. With fewer millponds impounding and holding water for use during dry times, the summertime flow was lower and gave the impression that the overall summer flow of the river had lessened. Additionally, the spring floods became higher, as fewer dams were left to intercept and impound the floodwater. It appeared that the destructiveness of the river was increasing, but it was actually the management of the watershed that had changed. As more forests were cut down and turned into farmland, the ecology of the river changed. Less water from the spring storms infiltrated the ground. This increased the spring runoff and also decreased the summer flow.

I have located the original dam in North Village, which is roughly six-feet tall. The dam itself proves that the Nissitissit was never much larger than it is right now; if the river had been larger, the dam would have been larger and more extensive. The dam is an earthen berm with a stone core. Large rocks placed at the base across the river were built upon with smaller stones. As the dam gets higher, the stones get smaller. Eventually, the whole stone structure was covered in fractured stones. Then, the upstream side of the dam was covered in clay to make it impervious. The downstream side was loamed and seeded to prevent erosion and to slow any infiltration through the core.

The site of the mill has some vertical walls along the river made from boulders and cut stone. The mill site is small, and the stone foundation is still there. Even for the times, the mill was not of standard size. East Pepperell soon outpaced North Village and grew much larger and became more profitable. The newer mills in East Pepperell were located on the Nashua River. Both the river and the drop in elevation, through the rapids in East Pepperell, were much more conducive to development. At first, the drop was enough that overshot waterwheels could be used, which were the most efficient. This immediately gave East Pepperell an advantage. The first mills could use smaller channels off of the river. They did not have to rely on the entire flow of the river, as North Village did. This provided the mills with a buffer. They situated the mills off to the side of the river, which reduced the amount of damage from the spring floods. After the first dam was built in East Pepperell on the Nashua River, it allowed the use of newly developed water turbines, which supplied even more power than the waterwheels. The millpond, above the dam in East Pepperell, was huge for this area. When flooded, the area – with over one thousand acres of pond - provided a huge amount of water to power the mills. North Village would only have had, roughly, a ten-acre millpond to rely upon. Nearly all the mills in New England that were located along the rivers were shaft-driven, relying on the power of falling water to drive them.

The fate of North Village and the Nissitissit was the same as other areas with small mills. Many industrial mills were located on rivers in the area. In West Groton, mills were seen along the Squannacook River. This river was similar to the Nissitissit but was slightly larger in size and flow. The locals always called a place, now known as the Bertozzi Conservation area, Silky T's. This spot had a large mill and many millhouses. This mill also disappeared in the eighteen hundreds, and industry moved elsewhere. I happened to come across a plan of the mill and surrounding lots in the Registry of Deeds office while doing research.

Continuing upstream, Townsend Harbor has another milldam, which still stands in testimony of the industry located there, but there are no mill buildings left. Downstream from Silky T's, on the Squannacook, some of the industry survived. The H & V Mill managed to make it into the age of electricity and, as a result, has survived to this day. Further downstream was a very large mill for this area. When I moved to West Groton, the mill was known as the Leatherboard. The last product the mill produced was plate with type used in printing. This mill operated until about 1960 when the printing industry changed. The Carver's Guild, which makes custom mirrors, is another mill still in operation. Mills that survived were the rarity, not the norm. Practically all of the old mills are completely gone. North Village was the most profitable area of industry in Pepperell for only a short time. Because of the water advantage, East Pepperell soon outpaced North Village.

Pollution of the waters in the area led to many deaths. Workers in the mills were exposed to various deadly materials. Often, these materials were inadvertently brought home on clothing or shoes and contaminated the home of the worker. Even now, we see the same occurrence. A few years ago I was told one of the local mills was making paper for oil filters and air cleaners in automobiles that contained asbestos. Not only did the workers exposed to the paper die of lung cancer, but some of the wives also died from handling their soiled clothes.

The mills of New England brutally polluted the rivers with every form of toxin imaginable. The paper mill in East Pepperell closed in the late nineteen hundreds. Many years ago, in the Registry of Deeds office, I found plans on file for what was called an infuser, which the mill in East Pepperell had built. This sounds innocent enough but was a diabolical solution to people's concerns about the growing pollution. Conservationists were concerned, after seeing the pollution from the various outfalls of the mill. In an effort to stop this concern, the mill took measures to hide it from public detection but did not end the pollution. The plans showed that a cistern would be used to collect the spent dyes and pollutants and hold them until it was full. Then the pollution would be pumped out to the diffuser. The diffuser was a perforated pipe that ran down the center of the Nashua River in a deep spot where the current is strong. The pollutants are quickly shot out and mix into the river water.

In the early nineties, I was canoeing past this mill when the diffuser came on. Some nasty, black liquid gushed up to the surface and quickly mixed with the water. The only way you could witness the pollution was from a canoe in the river. Someone on the shore would never see it. This method of waste disposal was used until the mill closed. New regulations, as well as the condition of the worn-out, old paper machines, made the mill too costly to run.

Before it closed, I was hired to do a complete land survey of the mill. The area of the mill was huge with many buildings, and there was tumbledown buildings and junk everywhere. Waste paper was strewn over acres of ground. Recently, I did a re-survey of part of the mill site. An energetic, father-and-daughter team bought the hydroelectric plant that used to produce power for the mill. The push for green energy made operation of the power plant viable, once more. The genius and hard work of this father-daughter combo has restored the operation of the plant. These two individuals are experts in hydropower and fix hydro plants throughout New England. They restore and rebuild old parts, and even manufacture what they need, since the plants are old, and new parts are not available.

With new regulations for pollution, the rivers in New England are slowly cleaning themselves. People quickly forget how bad these rivers were. When I was new to West Groton, the Nashua River would change color daily because of the upstream mill pollution. Also the river stunk from all the sewerage dumped into it. Sometimes, the local television and radio station reporters would jokingly broadcast what color the river was that day. As late as the nineteen-seventies, mills were still releasing toxins into the river, which killed wildlife, fish, and even people whose wells were too close. Life abruptly ended from these toxins as some mill owner upstream smiled on his way to the bank to deposit money he had made from dumping toxic waste into the river, instead of dealing with it responsibly.

The city of Fitchburg, also upstream from West Groton, had built a waste treatment plant with the bright idea of running the sewer line inside the same pipe as the storm water. The pipe was divided in half by a row of bricks, approximately a foot high. The sewerage ran on one side, and the storm water ran on the other side. In times of high storm water runoff, the water would overflow its channel and run into the sewerage. This vast infiltration of storm water would overload the treatment plant, and all they could do was chlorinate the water and release it into the Nashua River. Human waste, garbage, and industrial chemicals were all dumped into the river. Fitchburg has been fixing these pipes and replacing the dual line with separate lines for sewer and storm water, but it is a massive task. Some areas of the city continue to have the old, dual line in place and still being used.

The Nashua River dumps into the Merrimack River, which suffered even more because it was much larger and had more nearby industry and housing. Many houses simply had a sewer line that dumped directly into the river. The larger cities along the river collected the raw sewage in pipes and dumped it, untreated, into the river.

In 1971, I was employed as a rod man in a survey crew. The city of Lowell was forced to build a treatment plant and run sewer lines, closing off the numerous sewer outfalls and sending waste to the treatment plant. My job was to hold the survey rod, so the transit man could take a reading. For two years, I went down either side of the river with the crew locating all of the outfalls and conducting a topographical survey of the banks. I saw it all. The branches of the trees along the river, which were underwater during the spring floods, were covered with pieces of toilet paper. Prophylactics and tampons hung from the branches, like some sort of demented Christmas trees. At the sewer outfalls, schools of giant carp would eat the food particles in the sewage before it flowed into the river. They reminded me of sea serpents as their round mouths skimmed the surface.

Looking down in the water, I could see tampons float by, looking like perverted sperms swimming downstream to the river. The Merrimack had been reduced to a large, open sewer. At the time, I was twenty and had never seen such pollution. However, even the small town of Littleton where I had grown, was not exempt. In the 1960's, Mill Pond was a clear water pond loaded with fish. I remember catching crawfish in the outlet stream below a lumber company. By 1970, the Mill Pond died and turned eutrophic from pollution sources. Even today, in the summertime, the choking weeds are so thick that it looks as if you could walk across the water.

I grew up near Long Lake, and as more summer cottages were turned into year-round houses, the quality of water got worse. The Board of Health started testing septic systems around the lake and owners began fixing failed systems. As a result, the water quality has improved. When I was surveying the Merrimack in 1971, a commercial advertisement from conservationists, who were trying to stop the pollution of the rivers, appeared on television and in print. It featured an Indian, looking at a polluted river as a tear ran down his cheek. For two years, I surveyed the Merrimack, and a tear constantly ran down my own cheek. Now matter how disgusting an area was that we finished, the next bend in the river would have a new spot equally as bad or worse. Those two years were traumatic. It was not only here, but it was all over New England.

During that time, I was sent to Rumford, Maine to do the same work at a paper mill site. The water was dank and polluted, and the air was foul. Smoke spewed from stacks and filled the valley there. The people would joke about the white curtains they hung in their houses and how they would turn yellow from the smoke. The whole time there, my stomach was upset. I was sent there for a week at a time and hated the town. We were surveying in the center of town one day, and the smoke and the stench from the stacks was blowing in the air. People were walking down the street, laughing and talking. I wanted to run up to them, grab them by the collar, and scream, "Can't you smell that? What is wrong with you?" I did complain about the smell to one, local businessman and was told, "It was the smell of money."

I did not know what to say. I tried to swallow down my lunch, which attempted to come back up everyday, from the effects of the putrid smell. While doing my job, I saw the worst areas of pollution there. Surveyors are unsung heroes of sort, as they are thrown into the midst of everything. Places that are deemed too dangerous for people, because of pollution or other hazards, still need to be located by a surveyor- in order to make plans for changing the area. We, as surveyors have worked in some of the most disgusting places on earth.

North Village suffered from pollution that caused a variety of ailments. People want to overlook this and blame the demise of the village on a hypothetical curse uttered by whom, some believe was, a witch. The more I researched this area, the more I found the curse of the witch to be local folklore. Several different women are listed as being the witch, along with several different situations she supposedly caused.

Most agree, after the War of 1812, a woman who appeared in the village was believed to be a witch. They claim, in 1820, she was branded as a witch and cursed the village. The subsequent fires, during the next sixty years, were considered to be part of the curse, yet mills and houses all over New England burnt at the same rate. Heat came from stoves and fireplaces; light was available from candles and lanterns. An open flame was always somewhere in the buildings. Chimney fires in the winter caused many buildings throughout New England to burn.

What self-respecting witch would proclaim a curse that would take over sixty years to complete? If she were angry enough to curse the place, the curse would be sudden and complete. The longer time has passed, the more the legend of the curse has grown. As I conducted more research, I discovered what was earlier seen as the gospel truth is, in fact, still being questioned. For example, John Chamberlain from Groton is credited with killing Chief Paugus at Lovell's Pond.

Sometimes, it is referred to as Lovewell's Pond, which is just outside Fryeburg Village in Maine. In Groton, local historians consider this to be undisputable fact. However, while doing research, I came across a poem entitled, "Ballad of Lovewell's Fight," which was written soon after the Chief was killed, in 1725. The last few lines of the ballad are quoted below: (15)

> *Young Fullem too I'll mention, because he fought well,*
> *Endeavoring to save a man, a sacrifice he fell:*
> *But yet our valiant Englishmen in fight were never dismayed,*
> *But still they kept their motion, and Wyman's captain made,*
> *Who shot the old chief Paugus, which did the foe defeat,*
> *Then set his men in order, and brought off the retreat;*
> *And braving many dangers and hardships in the way,*
> *They safe arrived at Dunstable, the thirteenth day of May.*

Relatives of Wyman are alive today. They vehemently swear their ancestor actually killed Paugus. They allege that the heirs of John Chamberlain waited until everyone at the battle passed away and then proceeded to change the history of the battle. Even the story of how Chamberlain killed Paugus is suspect. (14) The following details go along with the tale. Supposedly, Chamberlain's gun fouled, and he went to the edge of the pond to clean it. At the same time, Chief Paugus had gone to the water to clean his musket. They saw each other, and both rushed to finish cleaning and loading. Chamberlain allegedly had a gun that could be primed at the touchhole for the flint spark. Hitting the stock of the gun on the ground, once the powder and ball was loaded, accomplished it. He was able to avoid the step of pouring powder from the powder horn into the flash pan for the flint to strike. Because of that advantage, Chamberlain had time to aim carefully and kill the Chief, who fired quickly with poor aim and missed Chamberlain.

That story is preposterous for several reasons. It implies they were

Nissitissit Witch

at the water to clean their guns. No one would have simply walked off during the heat of battle. There was no reason to go to the pond, away from the safety of the group, to clean their guns. If they were indeed using the water, they could not simply hurry the process. The guns would have to be thoroughly dried before black powder could be poured down the barrel, in order for the powder to fire. The coincidence involving the men seeing each other, after beginning to clean their guns, seems unbelievable. They would have to be there for a while without seeing each other and, by sheer circumstance, be at the same point, cleaning their guns when they sighted each other. The same spot at the same time doing the same thing at the exact same point in the cleaning process is too farfetched to believe. The tale speaks of them exchanging words as they cleaned and filed their guns. Scientifically, it seems improbable that all those coincidences could happen at once. The heirs of Captain Wyman claim Paugus shot and killed Lovewell and that Wyman returned the fire, killing Paugus. This version of the battle is simpler and more believable and does not rely on a chain of unlikely events.

They named the post office in North Village "Paugus" when Chamberlain's heirs were trying to change the story of the battle. Another story, about a grandson of Paugus, is as ridiculous as the original story of Chamberlain killing Paugus. The tale depicts the (14) grandson arriving from Canada, stopping to drink in a local tavern, and asking where Chamberlain lived. After getting the directions, the grandson waited long enough for someone to run and warn Chamberlain. This story also surfaced at the time Chamberlain's heirs were altering the tales of the fight.

In closing, I feel that many of the details pertaining to early Groton and Pepperell are debatable, and it is uncertain how much they have been stretched over time. I do not deny that women, who are now described as witches, may have existed. Many people in the area claim to own haunted houses. I believe in things that "go bump in the night" and don't want to be visited by an angry spirit some night because I discredited the spirit world. I will conclude, however, that much of the history of North Village has been the subject of fireside tales and, through the generations, some facts have been inflated to make the story more tantalizing.

References

1) Sybil Ramsey, "Deserted Village," written in 1923 as graduation essay

2) MASSMOMENTS, www.braceface.com/medical

3) Report of Col. Edward F. Jones, Sixth Massachusetts Militia, www.//civilwarhome.com

4) *First Blood in Baltimore* by Gary Baker, www.factasy.com/civil_war/book

5) Scheele's Green, Wikipedia, $CuHAsO_3$ cupric hydrogen arsenate, also called copper arsenate, www.//en.wikopedia.org/wiki/Scheele%27s_Green

6) Lead arsenic spray, www.pesticide.org/hhg/arsenicinpesticides.html

7) *Civil War-The Rising of the North*, www.braceface.com/medical/book%20images/Books/Rhodes

8) *History-Massachusetts Infantry (Part 1)*, www.civilwararchive.com

9) *First Blood In The Streets of Baltimore* by Gary Baker, www.civilwarinteractive.com

10) *Summer Dreams* by Rose Chaulk, AG Press

11) *The Witch's Prophecy* by Florence G. Sibley-1910

12) The Mad Hatter, www.hgtech.com/Information/

Mad%20Hatter.htm

13) Historic Map of Pepperell, scale 200 rods to the inch

14) *History of Groton, Including Pepperell and Shirley, 1848* by Caleb Butler

15) Lovewell's Fight, www.hawthorneinsalem.org

16) *Times Free Press,* January 28, 1987

17) *Times Free Press,* January 21, 1987

18) *The Lowell Sun*, May 11, 1972

19) *No One Shall Live in This Town* by Mabel Willard

20) Praying Indians, www.bio.umass.edu

21) *Killer Wallpaper* by Andy Meharg www.spectroscopyeurope.com

Printed in the United States
125396LV00006B/154-168/P